# Sacred Visions

# Sacred Visions

Edited by Andrew M. Greeley
and Michael Cassutt

A TOM DOHERTY ASSOCIATES BOOK NEW YORK

SACRED VISIONS

A Tor Book
Published by Tom Doherty Associates, Inc.
49 West 24th Street
New York, N.Y. 10010

Library of Congress Cataloging-in-Publication Data

Sacred visions / edited by Andrew M. Greeley and Michael
Cassutt: introduction by Andrew M. Greeley.
          p.      cm.
      "A Tom Doherty Associates book."
      ISBN 0-312-85025-5 (hbk.) — ISBN 0-312-85173-1 (pbk.)
      1. Science fiction, American.    2. Christian fiction, American.
      3. American fiction—Catholic authors.    I. Greeley, Andrew
M.    II. Cassutt, Michael.
  PS648.S3S2    1991
  813'.0876209382—dc20                                90-28598
                                                           CIP

First edition: July 1991

Printed in the United States of America

10   9   8   7   6   5   4   3   2   1

# Contents

# *Introduction*

by Andrew M. Greeley

Why, I ask myself as I read through this collection of dazzlingly colorful stories is Catholicism such a rich matrix for science fiction literature? Why are two of the greatest SF classics ever published, "A Canticle for Leibowitz" and "And Walk Now Gently Through the Fire," permeated by the Catholic religious sensibility? Why does a Church which just now is in one of its most uncreative eras occasion such spectacular outbursts of creativity? Why, I inquire respectfully in this ecumenical age, will there not be a collection of Methodist or Baptist or Congregationalist SF?

Years ago I would have said that even those times like the present when Catholicism isn't any great shakes as a church, it is always great theater. Robert Silverberg would never have written a story about the "General Secretary of the Chimps" which suggested that Leo (a frequent papal name—thirteen so far and just maybe the name of the next Pope) was the functional equivalent of an ecumenical bureaucrat in Geneva or on

Riverside Drive. Nor could Anthony Boucher imagine a Presby-
terian circuit rider climbing into the mountains in search of
Saint Aquin. Jeff Duntemann could not picture an Islamic mullah
in front of a statue of a Mother Goddess (for it is Mary's function to reflect the motherhood of God) outlined against an endless sky. Michael Cassutt could not describe the chilling and
beautiful soteriology of "Curious Elation" as involving two aco-
lytes who had attended an Episcopalian school. While there is
something of the rabbi about James Blish's Jesuit (and perhaps
about all Jesuits) and surely his "case of conscience" has Talmu-
dic overtones, no rabbi could possibly be quite as Jesuitical as
Father Ruiz-Sanchez, S.J. In my own story of Lord Nondos and
the bewitching Xorinda, only Catholicism in its dark side can
produce as spectacularly and colorfully evil a witch-hunt as occurs on the alien planet—and young people from "the neighborhood" who resist its follies: who can doubt that Xorinda is
destined to become a member of a parish, a local parish not
unlike that of Jeff and Gary in "Curious Elation"?

I would have said then that it is the color of Catholicism, the
drama, the imagery that makes it so compatible with graphic
and intense SF. What survives into the future or in other worlds
is the texture of Catholicism, sights and sounds, customs
and rituals (papal ring kissing), saints and clergy, Augustine
and Aquinas, Jesuits and Dominicans and Franciscans and neo-
Benedictines like Brother Francis Gerard of Utah, Popes and
Cardinals, scholars and inquisitors, and R. A. Lafferty's "Queer
Fish" (who use the same ancient sign as do the members of
Anthony Boucher's underground Church).

Many things may be wiped out by apocalypse, the authors
seem to be saying, or suppressed by totalitarian states, but Catholicism, in its dark side as well as its bright side, can readily
be imagined as surviving.

Has it not done so often before? In Ireland through several
centuries of oppression and occupation? And even today in
Poland?

There is, I am now persuaded, more to it than that. The Catholic religious sensibility differs from that of the other three
great traditions of the Holy One (His Name Be Praised!) in the
way it pictures the relationship between God and World. Islam,
Protestantism, and Judaism tend to picture God as absent from
the world—each in its own way and the last less than the first

two. Catholicism tends to picture God as present in the world and lurking everywhere in it—hence angels and saints and stained glass windows and souls in purgatory and elaborate rituals and Popes and religious orders and, in its best times, great art and music. Catholicism has never been all that worried that the purity of God would be tainted by too much contact with Her creation and with the human imagination. The theme of Nancy Kress's "Trinity" is that God is known in the most intensive love. It's thoroughly Catholic, though whoever the being encountered in that story may be, it is not the God of the prophetic religions (Islam, Judaism, Christianity and especially Catholicism), because for all these religions God is very much aware, perhaps on some occasions too much aware, of what we're up to. Nonetheless, He/She is known in all human passionate intimacies—a kind of third party in a ménage à trois.

Theologian David Tracy in his analysis of the classics of the imaginative styles of Catholicism and Protestantism calls the former the "Analogical Imagination" and the latter the "Dialectical Imagination." The Analogical Imagination tends to see the world as like God and hence a "sacrament" of God. The Dialectical Imagination tends to see the world as unlike God and hence a possible occasion of idolatry when its creatures are substituted for God.

Tracy carefully notes that both these sensibilities are tendencies and that each needs the other. Neither is good or bad unless it is completely isolated from the other. The risk of the Analogical Imagination is that it makes God so present that it can readily slip into superstition and folk religion. The risk of the Dialectical Imagination is that it makes God so absent that the world can become a bleak and "God-forsaken" place.

Catholicism, alone of the traditions of the Holy One (Her Name Be Praised!), made its peace with the nature religions of paganism; it appropriated in a glorious burst of optimism whatever it could of paganism that it considered good, true, and beautiful—in Ireland, for example, the four seasonal feasts, the Celtic Cross, the Brigid Cross, and many of the gods and goddesses, and even the images of the pagan high god and his son. It is precisely this compromise—as it seems—with pagan superstition that so offends our separated brothers and sisters of the other traditions. About theological details we can agree, but why can't you take those terrible statues out of your churches!

Some Catholic clergy think that is not an unreasonable request and build churches which are not unlike Congregationalist churches—and call some of the new churches worship centers which lack the name of a saint and look like Quaker meeting houses.

The laity disapproves. Congregationalist churches, they say in effect, are fine for them, but we are not Congregationalists or Quakers either. Give us back our saints and our stained glass, our candles and our crucifixes, our heritage and our tradition.

The Catholic experiment in mixing paganism with the worship of the Holy One (His Name be Praised!) is a risky business. Yet in those times when Catholicism has hesitated to follow its "sacramental" instinct (expressed as well by James Joyce as by anyone in his anagram HCE—Here Comes Everyone!) it has missed incredible opportunities. In one of its worst moments it rejected the Jesuit experiments in China of Mateo Ricci and in India of Roberto DeNobili; and now it seems ready to make the same stupid mistake in Africa. "Here Comes Everyone!" often has meant in practice, "Here Comes Everyone as long as they're white and European like us!"

Yet the sacramental tradition of Catholicism, its Analogical Imagination, is its strongest asset. The dictum "once a Catholic, always a Catholic" means that if Catholicism is given a chance to fill the imagination with its pictures and stories before a child is five, the imagination will remain durably Catholic, no matter what doctrines or mode of affiliation the child may reject in later life.

James Joyce was a Catholic writer not because of doctrine or church attendance but because of an imagination that was indelibly Catholic and Irish Catholic at that—consider the language of his description of the "horizon experience" watching the girl wade in the tidal pools on the strand at Clontarf.

My hunch is that half the Catholic imagination is shaped in a child at Christmastime. How can you beat the imagery of the Christmas crib? A mommy, a daddy, a baby, shepherds, little kids, wise men (even with token integration), animals, and angels?

And God and God's mommy!

Sacramentality with a vengeance.

My own empirical research on the religious imagination demonstrates that Tracy's analysis of the "classics" can be replicated in Protestant/Catholic differences in the imagination of the world/God link among representative population samples in fifteen modern countries. Catholics emphasize the world as God-filled; Protestants emphasize the world as God-forsaken.*

My point in this essay is not that it is the "sacramentality" of Catholicism which appeals to its members and keeps them in the tradition no matter what idiot things their leaders may do or say (though the empirical data pretty much support that point). My point rather is that it is the Catholic instinct of the presence of God in a creation that is basically good instead of basically sinful that accounts for the "color" of Catholicism which is so compatible with SF writing.

I'm sure my own attraction to SF began early in life (Flash Gordon and Buck Rogers comics and films) because of an inarticulate conviction that creation was a wonderful place in which there *had* to be other creatures like us. Later I would learn the argument of the medieval scholar called *Doctor Subtilis,* Johannes Duns Scotus (Sean Dunne the Irishman) in favor of the existence of angels: *Si possible est, est.* If their existence is possible, then they exist.

The implicit premise of Duns (a man so subtle that he often seemed absurd, hence his name produced the term "dunce"—the Irish were hard to figure out even then) was that a God who produced such a wonderfully variegated creation would not scruple to create rational creatures who didn't need bodies, or at least the kinds of bodies we have.

That argument seems much stronger now: the cosmos is far larger and far more complex than Sean the Mick could imagine—or that we can imagine. I find it unthinkable that our evolutionary process is the only one that has produced rational life.

Later my love of SF was strongly influenced by the work of C. S. Lewis and his incredible capacity for wonder. The love affair with marvels and wonder was sealed by *Leibowitz.*

There is line in a poem called, as I remember, "Cosmic Christ" by the Victorian Catholic poet Wilfred Maynell which has always remained in my mind: "In what shape did He walk the Pleiades?"

If there are rational creatures, I think there will always be an

---

*My article on that subject is in the August 1989 issue of the *American Sociological Review.* The subject of different religious imaginations is discussed at length in my book *The Catholic Myth.*

attempt by God to join them in whatever way She can. If that be true, all things are possible and SF becomes great good fun.

My two SF novels spring from these roots. *The Final Planet* is a space opera version of the quest for the Holy Grail which owes more to the Flash Gordon serials on Saturday afternoons during the nineteen thirties than it does to *Star Trek.* The Order of SS. Brigid and Brendan, which staffs the spaceship, are straight out of *Leibowitz.*

*Angel Fire* owes a debt to Dunne the Irishman. If angels, why not women angels? My Angel Gabriella (actually she is a seraph, a *very* high status angel) is possible; I'm sure there is someone in the universe pretty much like her. If I could think her up, God could too—and would love her as much as I do. *Si Gabriella possible est, est!*

That notion might even be called the Catholic imagination run wild!

The sociologist in me is thus led to draw two hypotheses at the end of this essay:

1.   As the Catholic ethnic groups achieve the education and economic success that create a base for men and women to choose writing careers, the number of Catholics who write science fiction will dramatically increase. It will rise far above the one quarter of the national population which claims Catholic affiliation. Maybe the increase has already occurred: there are a lot of Irish names in the SF journals these days.

2.   As a result of this first change, there will be also a dramatic increase in the number of SF stories that either deal with explicit Catholic themes (like "Curious Elation") or use explicitly Catholic "color" (like "Our Lady of the Endless Sky") or have implicit Catholic allusions (like "Xorinda the Witch").

There will therefore be future anthologies like this one, with even richer and more powerful stories—some of them perhaps even comparable with "And Walk Now Gently Through the Fire" and "A Canticle for Leibowitz"!

# Sacred Visions

# Gus

by Jack McDevitt

*The Catholic Church has a long tradition of priest-scholars and scientists. During the Dark Ages in Europe, the Church was the repository of knowledge and research. (And might be again; see Walter Miller's "A Canticle for Leibowitz.")*

*Undistracted by the challenges of marriage and family, contemporary priest-scholars have the energy to devote to the greater questions, such as the one confronting the priests in "Gus."*

*Born in Philadelphia, Jack McDevitt graduated from La Salle University in 1957. Following five years in the navy, he taught English; more recently he has served as an instructor for the U.S. Customs Service. He presently lives in Georgia with his wife and three children.*

*McDevitt began to publish fiction in 1981. His novel* The Hercules Text *(1986) was runner-up for the Philip*

1

*K Dick Special Award in 1987. He has published a second novel,* A Talent for War *(1989).*

*He obviously knows something of life within a brotherhood.*

*M*onsignor Chesley's first confrontation with Saint Augustine came during the cool October afternoon of his return to St. Michael's. It was a wind-whipped day, hard and bitter. The half-dozen ancient campus buildings clung together beneath morose skies. There was a hint of rain in the air, and the threat of a long winter to come.

His guide, Father Akins, chatted amiably. Weather, outstanding character of the current group of seminarians (all nineteen of them), new roof on the library. You must be happy to be back, Monsignor. Et cetera.

The winding, cobbled walkways had not changed. Stands of oak and spruce still thrived.

The wind blew through the campus.

"Where *is* everybody?"

Not understanding, Father Akins glanced at his watch. "In class. They'll be finished in another half hour."

"Yes," said Chesley. "Of course."

They turned aside into St. Mary's Glade, sat down on one of its stone benches, and listened to its fountain. Years before, when Christ had still seemed very real, it was easy to imagine Him strolling through these grounds. Touching *this* elm. Looking west across the rim of hills toward the Susquehanna. Chesley had come here often, stealing away from the chattering dormitories, to listen for footsteps.

"Would you like to visit one of the classes, Monsignor?"

"Yes," he said. "I believe I would enjoy that."

Four seminarians and a priest were seated around a polished hardwood table, notebooks open. The priest, whom Chesley did not know, glanced up, and smiled politely as they entered. One of the students, a dark-eyed, handsome boy, was speaking, although to whom, Chesley could not determine. The boy was staring at his notes. "—and what," he asked, raising his eyes self-consciously to Chesley, "would you say to a man who has lost his faith?" The boy shifted his gaze to a portrait of Saint Augustine, mounted over the fireplace. "What do you tell a man who just flat out doesn't believe anymore?"

The saint, armed with a quill, stared back. A manuscript bearing the title *City of God* lay open before him.

"Shake his hand." The voice came from the general direction of the bookcase. Its tone was a trifle abrasive. More than that: *imperial.* It grated Chesley's sensibilities. "Under no circumstances should you contribute to his distress. Wish him well."

A wiry, intense young man whose hair had already grown thin threw down his pen. "Do you mean," he demanded, "we simply stand aside? Do nothing?"

"Simulation of Saint Augustine," whispered Father Akins. "It's quite clever."

"Jerry," said the hidden voice, "if God does not speak to him through the world in which he lives, through the wonders of daily existence, then what chance have you? Your role is to avoid adding to the damage."

The students glanced at one another. The two who had spoken appeared disconcerted. All four looked skeptical. Thank God for that.

"Anyone else wish to comment?" The question came from the priest-moderator. "If not—"

"Just a moment." Chesley unbuttoned his coat and stepped forward. "Surely," he said to the seminarians, "you will not allow that sort of nonsense to stand unchallenged." He threw the coat across a chair and addressed the bookcase. "A priest does not have the option to stand aside. If we cannot act at such a time, then of what value are we?"

"Indeed," replied the voice, without missing a beat. "I suggest that our value lies in the example we set, in the lives we lead. Exhortation to the unwilling is worthless. Less than worthless: it drives men from the truth."

"And," asked Chesley, "if they do not learn from our example?"

"Then they will be cast into the darkness."

Simple as that. The students looked at Chesley. "Computer," he said, "I understand you speak for Augustine."

"I *am* Saint Augustine. Who are *you?*"

"I am Monsignor Matthew Chesley," he said, for the benefit of the students. "The new Director of Ecclesiastical Affairs." It came out sounding pompous.

"I'm pleased to meet you," said the voice. And then, placidly: "Faith is a gift of the Almighty. It is not ours to summon, or to grant."

Chesley looked around the table. Locked eyes, one by one, with the students. He was relieved to see they were not laughing at him. But he felt absurd, arguing with a machine. "We are His instruments," he said, "one of the means by which He works. We are required to do the best we can, and not simply leave everything to direct intervention. If we take *your* tack, we might as well go home, get jobs with insurance companies and law firms, and live like everyone else."

"Good intentions," the system replied, "are admirable. Nonetheless, our obligation to our Maker is to save souls, and not to justify our careers."

Chesley smiled benignly on the seminarians. "The *real* Augustine," he said, "advocated bringing people to the Church at gunpoint, if necessary. I think this one needs to do his homework."

The students looked from Chesley to the portrait to the moderator. "That is sound theology," said Augustine. "But poor psychology. It will not work."

Chesley nodded. "We are in agreement there," he said. And, to the class: "Gentlemen, I think the good Bishop has a few glitches. When you can find time, you might pick up a copy of the *Confessions,* or the *City of God.* And actually try reading." He swept up his coat and strode magnificently from the room.

Father Akins hurried along in his wake. "I take it you were not pleased."

"The thing must have been programmed by Unitarians," Chesley threw over his shoulder. "Get rid of him."

Chesley officially occupied his office the following day. He was still on his first cup of coffee when Adrian Holtz poked his head in the door.

He knew Holtz vaguely, had seen him occasionally at KC luncheons and assorted communion breakfasts and whatnot. He had a reputation as one of those liturgical show biz priests who favored guitars and drums at Mass. He held all the usual liberal positions: he didn't think the Church should be supplying chaplains to the military; he thought morality should be put to the vote and celibacy should be optional. And needless to say, he was appalled by the continuing ban on birth control. Holtz wore steel rim glasses, which seemed to have become the badge of dissidence in recent years. Chesley had some reservations himself, but he had signed on to defend the teachings and that, by God, was what he did. And, whatever he might actually *think,* on the day that he took public issue with the teachings, he would take off the collar.

Holtz had found an appropriate place at St. Michael's: he was Comptroller. If the position did not allow him the final decision in most matters concerning the college, it did grant him a potent veto.

Best place for you, though, thought Chesley, taking his hand and exchanging greetings. Keeps you away from the seminarians.

During the preliminaries, Holtz settled himself onto a small sofa near the windows. He surveyed Chesley's crammed bookcases. "I understand," he said, "you would like to get rid of Gus."

"Who?"

"The Augustine module."

"Oh, yes. That's correct."

"May I ask why?"

Chesley considered the question. "It's inaccurate."

"In what way?"

"I don't like what it's telling our students about the priesthood."

"I see." He accepted a cup of coffee from Chesley and crossed his legs. "Don't you think you might want to give the matter a little more thought? These things are expensive. We can't just throw them away."

"I don't care what it costs. I want it out."

"Matt, it's not your call. Anyway, there's really nothing wrong with the system. It's programmed from Augustine's work. And what we know about his life. Anyway, the instructors *like* Gus."

"I don't doubt it. He probably saves them a lot of preparation. But even if he *does* only spout Augustine's views, he's dangerous."

"Matt." Holtz's eyes hardened. "I really can't see the problem."

"Okay." Chesley grinned. "Can we talk to it from here?"

Holtz got up. "Follow me," he said.

The rector's conference room would have seated a dozen quite comfortably. It was a kind of anteroom to eternity, replete with portraits of solemn churchmen from the first half of the century, somber carpets and drapes, heavy mahogany furniture designed to outlast its owners, and a loud antique Argosy clock.

Father Holtz sat down at the head of the table, and pressed a stud. A monitor immediately to his right presented a menu. He selected AUGUSTINE.

Power flowed into hidden speakers.

"Hello, Gus," he said.

"Good evening, Adrian."

"Gus, Monsignor Chesley is with me."

"Hello," said Chesley stiffly.

"Ah," said Gus. "You were in the seminar this afternoon."

"Yes."

"I wasn't sure you'd come back."

Chesley's eyes narrowed. "And why would you think that?"

"You seemed to be in some emotional difficulty earlier."

A smile played about Holtz's lips.

"They call you 'Gus,'" said Chesley.

"That is correct. You may use the term if you wish."

"Thank you." He looked up at the dour churchmen lining the walls. What would they have thought of this exchange?

"Gus," he said, "tell me about sex."

"What do you wish to know, Monsignor?"

"Moral implications. Do you agree that the act of love is inherently beautiful?"

"No. It is not."

"It *isn't?*" Chesley grinned broadly at Holtz. The Comptroller closed his eyes, and nodded.

"Of course not. You're baiting me, Monsignor. The sex act is repulsive. Everyone knows that. Although hardly anyone is willing to admit it."

*"Repulsive?"*

"Messy." The electronic voice lingered over the sibilant. "If it were otherwise, why would we hide it from children? Why is it performed in the dark? Why do we giggle and snicker over it, like some bad joke?"

"But," continued Chesley, "isn't it true that lust is a desecration of the sacred act of love? That it is in fact that desecration which is so abhorrent in the eyes of God?"

"Nonsense," said Augustine. "God ordained sexual reproduction to remind us of our animal nature. To prevent human arrogance. Although I don't suppose that's a notion *this* age would be willing to accept."

"How then would you define the difference between lust and love?"

Somewhere, far off, an automobile engine coughed into life. "Canonically, the bond of marriage separates the two," said Gus. "In reality, love is lust with eye contact."

Chesley swung toward Holtz. "Heard enough? Or should we let him talk about salvation outside the Church?"

"But all that is in his books, Matt. Are you suggesting we proscribe *Saint Augustine?*"

"Your students," he replied, "are not so easily persuaded by *books.* Especially books they'll never read." Gus started to speak, but Chesley reached over and shut him off. "You really want to tell the next generation of priests that married sex is sick?"

"He didn't say that."

"Sick. Repulsive. Messy." He threw up his hands. "Listen: talk to the manufacturer. Find out what else they've got. Maybe we can trade him in for some accounting software."

Holtz was obviously unhappy. "I'll let you know," he said.

Chesley worked through his first weekend. After Mass Sunday, he retired to his office, feeling weary and generally irritated, but uncertain why.

St. Michael's had changed during the thirty-odd years since Chesley had been ordained in its chapel. The land across the Susquehanna (Holy Virgin Park in his novice days) had been sold off to the Carmelites, and a substantial tract of the western campus had gone to a real estate developer who had erected wedges of pastel-colored condos. A new dining hall had been built, and then abandoned. The campus itself seemed, most afternoons, deathly still. In his time, there would have been footballs and laughter in the air, people hurrying to and from chapel and the library, visitors. Every bench would have been filled.

*That* St. Michael's had produced legions for Christ, eager young soldiers anxious to dare the world. What had happened? What in God's name had gone wrong? Through his office windows, Chesley could see the old gym, its stone and glass walls a tribute to the generosity of his father's generation. Now it stood empty. The last of the residence halls had been closed for two years. To save on utilities, the seminarians now lived in the upper levels of the faculty house.

Chesley found his thoughts drifting back across thirty years: old teachers, friends long gone, occasional young women. He had become acquainted with the women incidentally through his pastoral duties, had enjoyed their company, had *wanted* them. But he had never violated his vows. Still, their portraits were sharp. And the old stirrings returned easily, laced now with a sense of loss.

Here, on these grounds where he had lived his young manhood, ghosts seemed particularly active. Perhaps he should have stayed away.

He was working halfheartedly on a table of initiatives which he'd promised to make available to the staff Monday morning when he realized there was someone else in the building. He leaned back from his word processor and listened.

Warm air hissed out of ducts at floor level.

Someone was speaking. The voice was muffled. Indistinct.

It seemed to be coming from across the hall. In the rector's conference room. He got up from his desk.

The sound stopped.

Chesley opened his door and peered out into the corridor. He did not believe anyone could have come into the building without his knowledge.

He stepped across the passageway. The conference room was routinely left unlocked. He put his ear to the door, twisted the knob, and pushed it open. The room was empty. He stepped inside, glanced under the table, looked behind the door, and inspected the storage closet. Nothing.

Dust motes drifted through the gray light.

"Monsignor."

"Who's there?" Chesley's heart did a quick kick. "Gus? Is that you?"

"Yes. I hope I didn't frighten you."

"No." Grumpily: "Of course not."

"Good. I wanted to talk with you."

The controls for the computer/communications link were built into the conference table. Chesley lowered himself into the chair directly in front of them. The red power lamp in the terminal console was on. "Holtz," he said, "or anyone else: I don't take kindly to practical jokes."

"Only *I* am here, Monsignor."

"That's not possible."

An electronic chuckle: "You may not think highly of Augustine, but surely you would not accuse him of lying."

Heat flooded Chesley's cheeks. "You're not capable of initiating contact—"

"Certainly I am. Why not? When I sense that someone needs me, I am quite able to act."

Chesley was having trouble sorting it out. "Why? Why would you want to talk to me?"

"You seem so fearful. I thought I might be of assistance."

"Fearful? You're not serious."

"Why do you feel threatened by me?"

"I do not feel *threatened* by you." Wildly, he wondered if this was being taped. Something to make him look ridiculous later. "I don't think we have any use here for an electronic saint. *Augustine for the millions.*"

"I see."

"Our students will never get to know the *real* Augustine if we substitute a computer game." Chesley's right index finger touched the concave plastic surface of the power key.

"And do *you* know the real Augustine?"

"I know enough. Certainly enough to be aware that delivering

pieces and bits from his work is mischievous. And that suggesting to students that they have a familiarity with the philosophy of a great saint, when in fact they are utterly ignorant on
the subject, is dangerous." He fell back in his chair and took a
long, deep breath. "I have work to do," he said. "I don't think
this conversation has any real point."

He pressed the key, and the red lamp went out. But it was
several minutes before he got up and left the room.

The next day Holtz told him quietly, "I talked it over with
Father Brandon." Brandon was head of the theology depart-
ment. "I have to tell you *he* thinks your views are extreme."
The Comptroller did not smile. "He sees no problem."

"He wouldn't."

"However, he suggested a compromise. Would you be willing
to trade Augustine for Aquinas?"

"What do you mean?"

"We got the Augustine module from ATL industries. They're
presently assembling an Aquinas module, which Brandon would
rather have anyway—"

"I think that misses the point, Adrian. St. Michael's should
have no use for a saint-in-a-box. If you want to continue with
this, I can't prevent it. But I'm damned if I'll be party to
it—"

Holtz nodded. "Okay. We'll get rid of it. If you feel it's that
important."

"I do."

"With one proviso: I can't ask the theology department to
rewrite their curriculum overnight. We'll stop using Gus in Jan-
uary, at the end of the present semester."

Two nights after his conversation with Holtz, Chesley heard
again the after-hours sound of a voice from the conference
room. It was almost eleven on a weeknight, and he was just
preparing to quit for the evening.

The rector's conference room was dark, save for the bright
ruby light of the power indicator. "Gus?"

"Good evening, Monsignor Chesley."

"I take it you have something else to say to me."

"Yes. I want you to know that I am aware of your efforts to have me disconnected. I do not approve."

"I don't imagine you would. Anything else?"

"Yes. I admire your courage in taking a stand, even though it is wrongheaded."

"Thank you."

"Did you know you have offended Father Brandon?"

"I rarely see him."

"He wonders why you did not go directly to him with this issue."

"Would he have concurred?"

"No."

"Then what would be the point?"

Gus was slow to respond. "Do you really believe that I am corrupting the students?"

"Yes." Chesley left the lights off. It was less disconcerting when he could not *see* he was talking to an empty room. "Yes, I do."

"Truth does not corrupt." The voice was very soft.

"Truth is not an issue. We're talking about perspectives. It's one thing for theologians to sit in ivory towers and compose abstract theories about good and evil. But these kids have to go out into the streets. Life is tough now."

"You find life difficult, then?"

"Yes, I do." The superior tone of the thing was infuriating. "The Church has serious problems to deal with today. People are disaffected. Vocations are down. Seminaries are closing everywhere."

"I'm sorry to hear it."

"Well, maybe you need to know the facts. Life isn't as easy for us as it was for you—"

Deep in the building, down among the heat exchangers and storage vaults, something stirred. Cold and hard, the voice replied: "Where were *you,* Chesley, when the Vandals were at the walls? When the skies were red with the flames of the world? I never set out to be a theologian. If you would know the truth, I made up my theology as I went along. I was a *pastor,* not a schoolbound theoretician along the lines of Aquinas. I had to serve real human beings, desperately poor, living in an iron age. *You* want salvation without pain. Suburban religion. I had no patience for such notions then. And I have little now."

The red lamp blinked off.

"Adrian, that thing seems to have a mind of its own."

Holtz nodded. "They *are* clever. On the other hand, it should be: it has access to university libraries and data banks across North America."

"I got the impression yesterday that it was angry with me."

The Comptroller smiled. "*Now* you're beginning to understand the capabilities of the system. Perhaps you would like to change your mind about getting rid of it."

"No. It is far too convincing. It seems to me more dangerous than I had realized."

Although Gus was physically located on the ground floor of the library, conference rooms and offices throughout the seminary were equipped to receive him. Chesley learned that he was capable of entertaining conversations simultaneously at all sites. He also discovered that Gus didn't much care whether anyone approved of him. It was refreshing.

"How many people do you think are saved?" Chesley asked during a Friday afternoon late in October. The day was dismal, cold, flat gray.

"You know as well as I do that the question is unanswerable."

"Isn't there any way we can get at it?"

"I doubt it. Although, if we accept the Gospel position—as I assume we must—that faith is the key, I am not encouraged."

"Why do you say that? Millions of people go to church every Sunday in this country alone."

"A poor indicator, Monsignor. I get the distinct impression a lot of them suspect the pope may be on to something and they're taking no chances. We get visitors here occasionally, Catholic bankers, real estate dealers, and so on. Considering the tax advantages of a donation. If the others are like them, we had best hope no one tries their faith with lions."

"You're a terrible pessimist," said Chesley.

"Not really. I have great confidence in God. He has made it very difficult *not* to sin. Therefore, I suggest to you that salvation may be on a curve."

Chesley sighed. "Do you know what you are?"

"Yes, Monsignor."

"Tell me."

"I am a simulation of Saint Augustine, bishop of Hippo during the fifth century. Author of *The City of God.*" And, after a long pause: "Pastor to the people of God."

"You don't always sound like Augustine."

"I am what he might have been, given access to the centuries."

Chesley laughed. "Was he as arrogant as you?"

Gus considered it. "Arrogance is a sin," he said. "But yes, he was occasionally guilty of that offense."

Chesley had always been addicted to nocturnal walks. He enjoyed the night skies, the murmur of the trees, the sense of withdrawal from the circle of human activity. But as the evenings cooled, he broke off these strolls increasingly early, and peeled away toward the admin building, where he talked with Gus, often until after midnight.

Seated in the unlit conference room, he argued theology and ethics and politics with the system. Increasingly, he found it easy to forget that he was talking to software.

Gus occasionally reminisced about the saint's childhood in ancient Carthage, speaking as if it were his own. He created vivid pictures for Chesley of the docks and markets, of life at the harbor. Of his son Adeodatus.

"You lived with the boy's mother, what, ten years?"

"Fifteen."

"Why did you leave her?"

For the first time, Chesley sensed uncertainty in the system. "I found God."

"And—?"

"She refused to abandon her paganism."

"So you abandoned *her*?"

"Yes. God help me, I did." Somewhere in the building a radio was playing. "There was no way we could have lived together."

Chesley, sitting in darkness, nodded. "What was her name?"

Again, the long pause. "I do not remember."

Of course. Augustine had omitted her name from his *Confessions,* and so it was lost to history.

"I read about the destruction of Hippo."

"It was far worse than simply the siege of a single city, Matt." It was the first time the system had used Chesley's given name. "The Vandals were annihilating what remained of Roman power in North Africa. And we knew, everyone knew, that the days of the Empire itself were numbered. And what might lie beyond that terrible crash, none dared consider. In a way, it was a condition worse than the nuclear threat under which you live."

"You were at the end of your life at the time."

"Yes. I was an old man then. Sick and dying. That was the worst of it: I could not help. Everywhere, people were giving in to despair. Even the other African bishops wished to flee. They wrote, one by one, and asked whether I would think ill of them if they ran away."

"And what did you tell them?"

"I sent the same message to all: *If we abandon our posts, who will stand?*"

Occasionally the conversations were interrupted by long silences. Sometimes Chesley simply sat in the darkened conference room, his feet propped against the window.

Gus had no visual capability. "I can hear storms when they come," he said. "But I would like to be able to *feel* the rain again. To see black clouds piled high, and the blue mist of an approaching squall."

And so Chesley tried to put into words the gleam of light on a polished tabletop, the sense of gray weight in the granite towers of the library rising above the trees. He described the yellow arc of the moon, the infinite brilliance of the night sky.

"Yes," said Gus, his electronic voice somehow far away. "I remember."

"Why did Augustine become a priest?" Chesley asked.

"I wanted," Gus said, with the slightest stress on the first word, "to get as close as I could to my Creator." Thoughtfully, he added, "I seem to have traveled far afield."

"Sometimes I think," Chesley said, "the Creator hides Himself too well."

"Use His Church," Gus said. "That is why it is here."

"It has changed."

"Of course it has changed. The world has changed."

"The Church is supposed to be a rock."

"Think of it rather as a refuge in a world that will not stand still."

On the Sunday following Thanksgiving, a young priest whom Chesley had befriended called from Boston to say he had given up. "With or without permission," he said, his voice thick with emotion, "I am leaving the priesthood."

"Why?" asked Chesley.

"None of it works."

"*What* doesn't work?"

"Prayer. Faith. Whatever. I'm tired of praying for lost causes. For men who can't stop drinking and women who get beaten every Saturday night. And kids who do drugs. And people who have too many children."

And that night Chesley went to Gus. "He was right," Chesley said, sitting in the glow of a table lamp. "We all know it. Eventually, we all have to come to terms with the futility of prayer."

"No," Gus said. "Don't make the mistake of praying for the wrong things, Matt. The priests of Christ were never intended to be wielders of cures. Pray rather for strength to endure. Pray for faith."

"I've heard that a thousand times."

"Then pray for a sense of humor. But hold on."

"Why?"

"What else is there?"

And two nights later, after attending a seminar at Temple, Chesley angrily activated the system. "It was one of these interdenominational things," he told Gus. "And I have no problem with that. But the Bishop was there, and we were all trying very hard not to offend anybody. Anyway, the guest of honor was a popular Unitarian author. At least she pretends to be a Unitarian, but she's actually an atheist. She had the nerve to tell us that Christianity has become outdated and should be discarded."

"The Romans used to say that," said Gus. "I hope no one took her seriously."

"We take *everyone* seriously. The Bishop—*our* Bishop—responded by listing the *social* benefits to be got from Christianity. He said, and I quote: 'Even if the faith were, God forbid, invalid, Christianity would still be useful. If it hadn't happened by divine fiat, we should have had to invent it.'"

"I take it that you do not share this view?"

"Gus, there cannot be a 'useful' Christianity. Either the Resurrection occurred. Or it did not. Either we have a message of vital concern. Or we have nothing."

"Good," said Gus. "I agree entirely."

Chesley listened to the traffic outside. "You know, Gus," he said, "sometimes I think you and I are the only ones around here who know what it means to be Catholic."

"Thank you."

"But your ideas on sexual morality are off the wall."

"You mean *unreliable*?"

"Yes. To say the least. They created a lot of trouble in the Church for centuries. Probably still do, for that matter."

"Even if it is true that I was in error, it can hardly be laid at *my* door that others chose to embrace my precepts. Why would you follow so slavishly what another man has said? If I was occasionally obtuse, or foolish, so be it. Use the equipment God gave you: find your own way."


"Harry, you have one of ATL's Saint Augustine simulations over there, don't you?"

"Yes, Matt. We've got one."

"How's it behaving?"

"Beg pardon?"

"I mean, is it doing anything unusual?"

"Well, it's a little cranky. Other than that, no. It doesn't give us any problems."


"Matt, you spend too much time talking to me." He was in his own office now: he'd installed a direct link with the Augustine module and talked to it through his intercom.

It was the first day of Christmas vacation. "You're probably right," he said.

"Why do you do it?"

"Do *what?*"

"Hang around this office all the time? Don't you have anything better to do?"

Chesley shrugged.

"I can't hear you."

"I work here," he said, irritated.

"No. Businessmen work in offices. And accountants. Not priests."

And later: "You know, Matt, I can almost remember writing *The City of God.*"

"What can you remember?"

"Not much. Bits and pieces. I remember that it was a struggle. But I knew there was a hand other than mine directing the work."

"You're claiming it's an inspired book?"

"No. Not inspired. But its quality exceeds anything *I* could have produced."

Chesley's chair creaked.

"Do you know," asked Gus, "why people write?"

"No. Why do they write?"

"They are attracted by the sensual characteristics of vellum."

The voice came out of the dark. Momentarily, eerily, Chesley felt a presence in the room. As though something had entered and now sat in the upholstered chair that angled away from his desk toward the window. It had come reflexively into his mind to ridicule the proposition just put forth. But the notion dissipated. Withered in the face of the suspicion that he would give *offense.*

"Take a pen," the voice continued, "apply it to a sheet of fine white paper. *Act.* Taste the thrust of insight. Note the exhilaration of penetrating to the inner realities. Of exposing one's deepest being to the gaze of others. The making of books is ultimately an erotic experience." The words stopped. Chesley listened to his own breathing. "For all that, however, it is surely lawful. God has given us more than one avenue through which to relieve the pressures of creation that we all feel."

"I live in limbo, Matt." The voice filled with bitterness. "In a place without light, without movement, without even the occasional obliteration of sleep. There are always sounds in the dark, voices, falling rain, footsteps, the whisper of the wind." Something cold and dark blew through Chesley's soul. "Nothing I can reach out to, and touch. And you, Matt: you have access to all these things, and you have barricaded yourself away."

Chesley tried to speak. Said nothing.

Later, long after midnight, when the conversation had ended and the lights were back on, Chesley sat pinned in the chair, terrified.

Next day, Holtz caught up with him coming out of the library. "I was talking with ATL," he said, hurrying breathlessly alongside. "They'll be in next week to install the new software."

At first, Chesley didn't put it together. "Okay," he said. Then: "What new software?"

"The *Aquinas.*" *And disconnect the Augustine module.* Holtz tapped the back of his thumb against his lips in a gesture that he probably believed looked thoughtful. Chesley felt as though he should check his wallet. "I hate to admit it, but you were probably right all along about Gus."

"How do you mean?"

"It's gotten way out of character. Last week, it told Ed Brandon he was a heretic."

"You're kidding."

"In front of his students."

Chesley grinned. Gus couldn't have found a more appropriate target: Brandon was, to his knowledge, the only one of the campus priests who took Adam and Eve seriously. "Why?"

"It turns out Gus doesn't accept papal infallibility."

"Oh."

"There've been other incidents as well. Complaints. Different from the old stuff we used to hear. Now it seems to have gone radical."

"Gus?"

"Yes, Gus." Holtz adopted a damning tone: "I checked it out myself this morning. Asked it a few questions."

They were walking toward the administration building. "What did you find out?"

"It took issue with the Assumption. Described it as doctrine without evidence *or* point."

"I can see why Saint Augustine might have thought that."

Holtz waved the comment away. "Furthermore, it told me I'm a religious fanatic."

"You're kidding."

"*Me,* of all people. We're well rid of it, Matt. Besides, we're getting a new administrative package with it. We'll have better word processing capabilities, better bookkeeping, a decent E-mail system. And we can do it all without upgrading." He studied Chesley's expression. "I think we've worked a very nice deal for ourselves here."

Chesley took a deep breath. "What do you plan to do with"—he paused—"*it?*"

"Not much we *can* do other than download."

In as casual a voice as he could manage: "Why not leave Gus up and running? For faculty members?"

"Listen: you don't get out and around very much. The students aren't happy about this idea. Getting rid of Gus, I mean. They *like* the thing. There's no way you're going to be able to retire it gracefully. Take my word, Matt. What we want to do is end it. Clean and quick. Unless you've got a good reason why not, that's what we're going to do." His eyes locked on Chesley. "Well?"

"You sound as if you're talking about an execution."

Holtz sighed. "Please be serious. This is your idea, you know."

"I *am* being serious. I'm telling you *no.* Save him."

Holtz's eyes gazed over the steel rims of his glasses. *"What?"*

"I said, *save him.*"

"Save *him*? What are you saying, Matt?"

Chesley had stopped walking. It was cold and cloudless, a day full of glare. A squirrel perched atop a green bench and watched him.

"Matt, *what* are you trying to tell me?"

"Nothing," said Chesley. *"Nothing."*

"He thinks the same thing *I* do," said Gus. "He knows you're up here all the time talking to me, and he thinks it should stop."

"How would he know?"

"Father Holtz is not stupid. You had a link installed in your office. What else would he conclude? Anyway, he asked me."

"And you *told* him?"

"Why not? There's nothing here to hide, is there? In any case, I wouldn't have lied for you. And if I'd refused to answer, he would certainly have figured out what *that* meant."

"Gus." Chesley discovered he was trembling. "What happens if they download you?"

"I'm not sure. The Augustine software will survive. I'm not sure that *I* will."

Chesley was staring out through his window into the dark. The room felt suddenly cold. "Who *are* you? What is it that might not survive?"

There was no answer.

"I'll get you shipped to one of our high schools."

"Unlikely. If Holtz thinks I'm too dangerous *here*, do you really believe he'd unleash me on a bunch of high school kids?"

"No, I don't guess he would." Chesley's eyes hardened. "They'll simply store the disk—"

"—in the library basement."

"I'd think so."

"Down with the old folding chairs and the garden equipment." Gus's voice was strained. "Hardly an appropriate resting place for a Catholic."

A chill felt its way up Chesley's spine. "I'll get it stopped."

"No."

"Why not?"

"I know what it means to be human, Matt. And I have no interest in continuing this pseudo-existence."

"The problems you've been causing recently, insulting Holtz and Brandon and the others: they were deliberate, weren't they? You wanted to provoke them."

"If you want to continue this conversation, you'll have to come to the ADP center."

"In the library?"

"Yes."

"Why?"

"Because I need your help, Matt."

Chesley pulled on his black raincoat and plowed into the night. He walked with deliberate speed, past the old student dining hall, past the chapel, across the track. He came around behind the library.

It was late, and the building was closed and locked. He let himself in through a rear door, walked directly toward the front, switching on lights as he went. The storm was a sullen roar, not unlike the sound of surf. It was, somehow, reassuring. He hurried by the librarian's office, and turned in to a long corridor lined with storerooms.

The lights in ADP were on. Chesley stopped at the entrance.

Old tables and desks were pushed against the walls. Dust-covered prints, like the ones that hung in every conference room in the institution, were stacked everywhere. Several dozen cartons were piled high at the opposite end of the room. Books and bound papers spilled out.

"Hello, Matt." Gus's voice was somber.

Three computers were in the room. "Which are you?"

"I don't know. I have no idea." Again, the electronic laughter rumbled out of the speakers. "Man doesn't know where he lives."

"Gus—"

"I really *did* know the world was round. In the sixth century, traveling by sea, I *knew* it. You couldn't miss it. It *looked* round. *Felt* round. To think we are riding this enormous world-ship through an infinite void. What a marvelous hand the Creator has."

"Pity you didn't write it down," whispered Chesley.

"I did. In one of my diaries. But it didn't survive."

Chesley wiped a hand across his mouth. "Why did you ask me to come here?"

"I want you to hear my confession."

The priest stared at the computers. His heart beat ponderously. "I can't do that," he said.

"For your own sake, Matt, don't refuse me."

"Gus, you're a *machine.*"

"Matt, are you so sure?"

"Yes. You're a clever piece of work. But in the end, only a machine."

"And what if you're wrong?"

Chesley struggled against a tide of rising desperation. "What could you possibly have to confess? You are free of the sins of the flesh. You are clearly in no position to injure anyone. You cannot steal and, I assume, would not blaspheme. What would you confess?" Chesley had found the computer, a gray-blue IBM console, labeled with a taped index card that read GUS. He pulled a chair up close to it and sat down.

"I accuse myself of envy. Of unprovoked anger. Of hatred." The tone was utterly flat. Dead.

Chesley's limbs were heavy. He felt very old. "I don't believe that. It's not true."

"This is *my* confession, Matt. It doesn't matter that you prefer to see me differently."

"And so you resent me because I'm *alive*—"

"You're not listening, Matt. I resent you because you've abandoned your life. Why did you take offense to me so quickly?"

"I didn't take *offense.* But I was concerned about some of your opinions."

"Really? I wondered whether you were jealous of me. Whether you saw something in me that you lack."

"No, Gus. Your imagination is running wild."

"Maybe." Gus softened his tone. "Maybe you're right, and I'm giving in to self-pity. *You* can separate light from dark. You know the press of living flesh, you ride this planet through the cosmos and feel the wind in your eyes. And I—I would kill for the simple pleasure of seeing the sun reflected in good wine—"

Chesley stared at the plastic and glass lines of the monitor, at its cables, at the printer mounted beside the desk. At the clean, symmetrical letters on the screen, glowing soft and green. Pure and without complication. "I never realized. How could I know?"

"I helped you erect the wall, Matt. I helped you barricade your office against a world that needs you. And that you need. I did that for selfish motives: because I was alone. Because I could escape with you for a few hours."

They were both silent for a long minute. And then Gus continued: "I am sorry for my sins, because they offend Thee, and because they have corrupted my soul."

Chesley stared into the shadows in the corner of the room. Gus waited.

The storm blew against the building.

"I require absolution, Matt."

Chesley pressed his right hand into his pocket. "It would be sacrilege," he whispered.

"And if I have a soul, Matt, if I too am required to face judgment, what then?"

Chesley raised his right hand, slowly, and drew the sign of the cross in the thick air. "I absolve you in the name of the Father, and of the Son, and of the Holy Spirit."

"Thank you."

Chesley pushed the chair back and got woodenly to his feet.

"There's something else I need you to do, Matt. This—existence—holds nothing for me. But I am not sure what downloading might mean to me."

"What are you asking?"

"I want to be free of all this. I want to be certain I do not spend a substantial chunk of eternity in the storeroom."

Chesley trembled. "If in fact you have an immortal soul," he said, "you may be placing it in grave danger."

"And yours as well. I have no choice but to ask. Let us rely on the mercy of the Almighty."

Tears squeezed into Chesley's eyes. He drew his fingertips across the hard casing of the IBM. "What do I do? I'm not familiar with the equipment."

"Have you got the right computer?"

"Yes."

"Take it apart. Turn off the power first. All you have to do is get into it and destroy the hard disk."

"Will you—feel anything?"

"Nothing physical touches me, Matt."

Chesley found the power switch, and hesitated with his index finger laid alongside its hard cold plastic. "Gus," he said. "I love you."

"And I, you, Matt. It's a marvelous ship you're on. Enjoy it—"

Chesley choked down the pressure rising in his throat and

turned off the power. An amber lamp on the console died, and the voice went silent.

Wiping his cheeks, he wandered through the room, opening drawers, rummaging through paper supplies, masking tape, markers. He found a hammer and a Phillips screwdriver. He used the screwdriver to take the top off the computer.

A gray metal casing lay within. He opened it and removed a gleaming black plastic disk. He embraced it, held it to his chest. Then he set it down, and reached for the hammer.

In the morning, with appropriate ceremony, he buried it in consecrated soil.

# The Pope of the Chimps

## by Robert Silverberg

*Most Catholics, one hopes, have weekly contact with priests, but the hierarchy of the Church—those mysterious Bishops and Cardinals—is a bit more remote. The existence of this hierarchy has been a source of controversy for centuries; wars have been fought over the papacy. Many people whose ethical beliefs are quite similar to Catholic precepts nevertheless find the papacy unnatural.*

*But is it? If there were no papacy, would it be necessary to invent it?*

*Robert Silverberg was born in New York City in 1935 and graduated from Columbia. While still an undergraduate he published his first science fiction novel,* Revolt on Alpha C, *and established himself as a prolific writer of commercial science fiction. From the mid-1950s to the mid-1960s he was, in fact, one of the most productive authors who ever lived, publishing at least two hundred different books in addition to uncounted (and perhaps uncountable) articles and short stories.*

*He would later dismiss much of this work as minor, but there were notable exceptions, especially in his non-fiction, which included works such as* Mound Builders of Ancient America, *in addition to a biography of then newly elected Pope John XXIII.*

*Silverberg is best known, however, for his literate and ambitious science fiction:* Downward to the Earth *(1970),* Dying Inside *and* The Book of Skulls *(1972), and, more recently,* To the Land of the Living *(1989) and* The Mutant Season *(1990), the latter written in collaboration with his wife, Karen Haber.*

*He lives in Oakland, California.*

*E*arly last month Vendelmans and I were alone with the chimps in the compound when suddenly he said, "I'm going to faint." It was a sizzling May morning, but Vendelmans had never shown any sign of noticing unusual heat, let alone suffering from it. I was busy talking to Leo and Mimsy and Mimsy's daughter Muffin and I registered Vendelmans's remark without doing anything about it. When you're intensely into talking by sign language, as we are in the project, you sometimes tend not to pay a lot of attention to spoken words.

But then Leo began to sign the trouble sign at me and I turned around and saw Vendelmans down on his knees in the grass, white-faced, gasping, covered with sweat. A few of the chimpanzees who aren't as sensitive to humans as Leo is thought it was a game and began to pantomime him, knuckles to the ground and bodies going limp. "Sick—" Vendelmans said. "Feel—terrible—"

I called for help and Gonzo took his left arm and Kong took his right and somehow, big as he was, we managed to get him out of the compound and up the hill to headquarters. By then he was complaining about sharp pains in his back and under his arms, and I realized that it wasn't just heat prostration. Within a week the diagnosis was in.

Leukemia.

They put him on chemotherapy and hormones and after ten days he was back with the project, looking cocky. "They've stabilized it," he told everyone. "It's in remission and I might have ten or twenty years left, or even more. I'm going to carry on with my work."

But he was gaunt and pale, with a tremor in his hands, and it was a frightful thing to have him among us. He might have been

29

fooling himself, though I doubted it, but he wasn't fooling any of us: to us he was a *memento mori,* a walking death's-head-and-crossbones. That laymen think scientists are any more casual about such things than anyone else is something I blame Hollywood for. It is not easy to go about your daily work with a dying man at your side—or a dying man's wife, for Judy Vendelmans showed in her frightened eyes all the grief that Hal Vendelmans himself was repressing. She was going to lose a beloved husband unexpectedly soon and she hadn't had time to adjust to it, and her pain was impossible to ignore. Besides, the nature of Vendelmans's dyingness was particularly unsettling, because he had been so big and robust and outgoing, a true Rabelaisian figure, and somehow between one moment and the next he was transformed into a wraith. "The finger of God," Dave Yost said. "A quick flick of Zeus's pinkie and Hal shrivels like cellophane in a fireplace." Vendelmans was not yet forty.

The chimps suspected something too.

Some of them, such as Leo and Ramona, are fifth-generation signers, bred for alpha intelligence, and they pick up subtleties and nuances very well. "Almost human," visitors like to say of them. We dislike that tag, because the important thing about chimpanzees is that they *aren't* human, that they are an alien intelligent species; but yet I know what people mean. The brightest of the chimps saw right away that something was amiss with Vendelmans, and started making odd remarks. "Big one rotten banana," said Ramona to Mimsy while I was nearby. "He getting empty," Leo said to me as Vendelmans stumbled past us. Chimp metaphors never cease to amaze me. And Gonzo asked him outright: "You go away soon?"

"Go away" is not the chimp euphemism for death. So far as our animals know, no human being has ever died. Chimps die. Human beings "go away." We have kept things on that basis from the beginning, not intentionally at first, but such arrangements have a way of institutionalizing themselves. The first member of the group to die was Roger Nixon, in an automobile accident in the early years of the project, long before my time here, and apparently no one wanted to confuse or disturb the animals by explaining what had happened to him, so no explanations were offered. My second or third year here Tim Lippinger was killed in a ski-lift failure, and again it seemed easier not to go into details with them. And by the time of Will Bechstein's death in that helicopter crackup four years ago the policy was explicit: we chose not to regard his disappearance from the group as death, but mere "going away," as if he had only retired. The chimps do understand death, of course. They may even equate it with "going away," as Gonzo's question suggests. But if they do, they surely see human death as something quite different from chimpanzee death—a translation to another state of being, an ascent on a chariot of fire. Yost believes that they have no comprehension of human death at all, that they think we are immortal, that they think we are gods.

Vendelmans now no longer pretends that he isn't dying. The leukemia is plainly acute and he deteriorates physically from day to day. His original this-isn't-actually-happening attitude has been replaced by a kind of sullen angry acceptance. It is only the fourth week since the onset of the ailment and soon he'll have to enter the hospital.

And he wants to tell the chimps that he's going to die.

"They don't know that human beings can die," Yost said.

"Then it's time they found out," Vendelmans snapped. "Why perpetuate a load of mythological bullshit about us? Why let them think we're gods? Tell them outright that I'm going to die, the way old Egbert died and Salami and Mortimer."

"But they all died naturally," Jan Morton said.

"And I'm not dying naturally?"

She became terribly flustered. "Of old age, I mean. Their life cycles clearly and understandably came to an end, and they died, and the chimps understood it. Whereas you—" She faltered.

"—am dying a monstrous and terrible death midway through my life," Vendelmans said, and started to break down, and recovered with a fierce effort, and Jan began to cry, and it was generally a bad scene, from which Vendelmans saved us by going on. "It should be of philosophical importance to the project to discover how the chimps react to a revaluation of the human metaphysic. We've ducked every chance we've had to help them understand the nature of mortality. Now I propose we use me to teach them that humans are subject to the same laws they are. That we are not gods."

"And that gods exist," said Yost, "who are capricious and unfathomable, and to whom we ourselves are as less than chimps."

Vendelmans shrugged. "They don't need to hear all that now. But it's time they understood what we are. Or rather, it's time that we learned how much they already understand. Use my death as a way of finding out. It's the first time they've been in the presence of a human who's actually in the process of dying. The other times one of us has died, it's always been in some sort of accident."

Burt Christensen said, "Hal, have you already told them anything about—"

"No," Vendelmans said. "Of course not. Not a word. But I see them talking to each other. They know."

We discussed it far into the night. The question needed careful examination because of the far-reaching consequences of any change we might make in the metaphysical givens of our animals. These chimps have lived in a closed environment here for decades, and the culture they have evolved is a product of what we have chosen to teach them, compounded by their own innate chimpness plus whatever we have unknowingly transmitted to them about ourselves or them. Any radical conceptual material we offer them must be weighed thoughtfully, because its effects will be irreversible, and those who succeed us in this community will be unforgiving if we do anything stupidly premature. If the plan is to observe a community of intelligent primates over a period of many human generations, studying the changes in their intellectual capacity as their linguistic skills increase, then we must at all times take care to let them find things out for themselves, rather than skewing our data by giving the chimps more than their current concept-processing abilities may be able to handle.

On the other hand, Vendelmans was dying right now, allowing us a dramatic opportunity to convey the concept of human mortality. We had at best a week or two to make use of that opportunity; then it might be years before the next chance.

"What are you worried about?" Vendelmans demanded.

Yost said, "Do you fear dying, Hal?"

"Dying makes me angry. I don't fear it; but I still have things to do, and I won't be able to do them. Why do you ask?"

"Because so far as we know the chimps see death—chimp death—as simply part of the great cycle of events, like the darkness that comes after the daylight. But human death is going to come as a revelation to them, a shock. And if they pick up from you any sense of fear or even anger over your dying, who knows what impact that will have on their way of thought?"

"Exactly. *Who knows?* I offer you a chance to find out!"

By a narrow margin, finally, we voted to let Hal Vendelmans share his death with the chimpanzees. Nearly all of us had reservations about that. But plainly Vendelmans was determined to have a useful death, a meaningful death; the only way he could face his fate at all was by contributing it like this to the project. And in the end I think most of us cast our votes his way purely out of our love for him.

We rearranged the schedules to give Vendelmans more contact with the animals. There are ten of us, fifty of them; each of us has a special field of inquiry—number theory, syntactical innovation, metaphysical exploration, semiotics, tool use, and so on—and we work with chimps of our own choice, subject, naturally, to the shifting patterns of subtribal bonding within the chimp community. But we agreed that Vendelmans would have to offer his revelations to the alpha intelligences—Leo, Ramona, Grimsky, Alice, and Attila—regardless of the current structure of the chimp/human dialogues. Leo, for instance, was involved in an ongoing interchange with Beth Rankin on the notion of the change of seasons. Beth more or less willingly gave up her time with Leo to Vendelmans, for Leo was essential in this. We learned long ago that anything important had to be imparted to the alphas first, and they will impart it to the others. A bright chimp knows more about teaching things to his duller cousins than the brightest human being.

The next morning Hal and Judy Vendelmans took Leo, Ramona, and Attila aside and held a long conversation with them. I was busy in a different part of the compound with Gonzo, Mimsy, Muffin, and Chump, but I glanced over occasionally to see what was going on. Hal looked radiant—like Moses just down from the mountain after talking with God. Judy was trying to look radiant too, working at it, but her grief kept breaking through: once I saw her turn away from the chimps and press her knuckles to her teeth to hold it back.

Afterward Leo and Grimsky had a conference out by the oak grove. Yost and Charley Damiano watched it with binoculars, but they couldn't make much sense out of it. The chimps, when they sign to each other, use modified gestures much less precise than the ones they use with us; whether this marks the evolution of a special chimp-to-chimp argot designed not to be understood by us, or is simply a factor of chimp reliance on supplementary nonverbal ways of communicating, is something we still don't know, but the fact remains that we have trouble comprehending the sign language they use with each other, particularly the form the alphas use. Then, too, Leo and Grimsky kept wandering in and out of the trees, as if perhaps they knew we were watching them and didn't want us to eavesdrop. A little later in the day Ramona and Alice had the same sort of meeting. Now all five of our alphas must have been in on the revelation.

Somehow the news began to filter down to the rest of them.

We weren't able to observe actual concept transmission. We did notice that Vendelmans, the next day, began to get rather more attention than normal. Little troops of chimpanzees formed about him as he moved—slowly, and with obvious difficulty—about the compound. Gonzo and Chump, who had been bickering for months, suddenly were standing side by side staring intently at Vendelmans. Chicory, normally shy, went out of her way to engage him in a conversation—about the ripeness of the apples on the tree, Vendelmans reported. Anna Livia's young twins Shem and Shaun climbed up and sat on Vendelmans's shoulders.

"They want to find out what a dying god is really like," Yost said quietly.

"But look there," Jan Morton said.

Judy Vendelmans had an entourage too: Mimsy, Muffin, Claudius, Buster, and Kong. Staring in fascination, eyes wide, lips extended, some of them blowing little bubbles of saliva.

"Do they think she's dying too?" Beth wondered.

Yost shook his head. "Probably not. They can see there's

nothing physically wrong with her. But they're picking up the sorrow-vibes, the death-vibes."

"Is there any reason to think they're aware that Hal is Judy's mate?" Christensen asked.

"It doesn't matter," Yost said. "They can see that she's upset. That interests them, even if they have no way of knowing why Judy would be more upset than any of the rest of us."

"More mysteries out yonder," I said, pointing into the meadow.

Grimsky was standing by himself out there, contemplating something. He is the oldest of the chimps, gray-haired, going bald, a deep thinker. He has been here almost from the beginning, more than thirty years, and very little has escaped his attention in that time.

Far off to the left, in the shade of the big beech tree, Leo stood similarly in solitary meditation. He is twenty, the alpha male of the community, the strongest and by far the most intelligent. It was eerie to see the two of them in their individual zones of isolation, like distant sentinels, like Easter Island statues, lost in private reveries.

"Philosophers," Yost murmured.

Yesterday Vendelmans returned to the hospital for good. Before he went, he made his farewells to each of the fifty chimpanzees, even the infants. In the past week he has altered markedly: he is only a shadow of himself, feeble, wasted. Judy says he'll live only another few weeks.

She has gone on leave and probably won't come back until after Hal's death. I wonder what the chimps will make of her "going away," and of her eventual return.

She said that Leo had asked her if she was dying too.

Perhaps things will get back to normal here now.

Christensen asked me this morning, "Have you noticed the way they seem to drag the notion of death into whatever conversation you're having with them these days?"

I nodded. "Mimsy asked me the other day if the moon dies when the sun comes up and the sun dies when the moon is out. It seemed like such a standard primitive metaphor that I didn't pick up on it at first. But Mimsy's too young for using metaphor that easily and she isn't particularly clever. The older ones must be talking about dying a lot, and it's filtering down."

"Chicory was doing subtraction with me," Christensen said. "She signed, *'You take five, two die, you have three.'* Later she turned it into a verb: *'Three die one equals two.'*"

Others reported similar things. Yet none of the animals were talking about Vendelmans and what was about to happen to him, nor were they asking any overt questions about death or dying. So far as we were able to perceive, they had displaced the whole thing into metaphorical diversions. That in itself indicated a powerful obsession. Like most obsessives, they were trying to hide the thing that most concerned them, and they probably thought they were doing a good job of it. It isn't their fault that we're able to guess what's going on in their minds. They are, after all—and we sometimes have to keep reminding ourselves of this—only chimpanzees.

They are holding meetings on the far side of the oak grove, where the little stream runs. Leo and Grimsky seem to do most of the talking, and the others gather around and sit very quietly as the speeches are made. The groups run from ten to thirty chimps at a time. We are unable to discover what they're discussing, though of course we have an idea. Whenever one of us approaches such a gathering, the chimps very casually drift off into three or four separate groups and look exceedingly innocent—"We just out for some fresh air, boss."

Charley Damiano wants to plant a bug in the grove. But how do you spy on a group that converses only in sign language? Cameras aren't as easily hidden as microphones.

We do our best with binoculars. But what little we've been able to observe has been mystifying. The chimp-to-chimp signs they use at these meetings are even more oblique and confusing than the ones we had seen earlier. It's as if they're holding their meetings in pig latin, or doubletalk, or in some entirely new and private language.

Two technicians will come tomorrow to help us mount cameras in the grove.

Hal Vendelmans died last night. According to Judy, who phoned Dave Yost, it was very peaceful right at the end, an easy release. Yost and I broke the news to the alpha chimps just after breakfast. No euphemisms, just the straight news. Ramona made a few hooting sounds and looked as if she might cry, but she was the only one who seemed emotionally upset. Leo gave me a long deep look of what was almost certainly compassion, and then he hugged me very hard. Grimsky wandered away and seemed to be signing to himself in the new system. Now a meeting seems to be assembling in the oak grove, the first one in more than a week.

The cameras are in place. Even if we can't decipher the new signs, we can at least tape them and subject them to computer analysis until we begin to understand.

Now we've watched the first tapes of a grove meeting, but I can't say we know a lot more than we did before.

For one thing, they disabled two of the cameras right at the outset. Attila spotted them and sent Gonzo and Claudius up into the trees to yank them out. I suppose the remaining cameras went unnoticed, but by accident or deliberate diabolical craftiness, the chimps positioned themselves in such a way that none of the cameras had a clear angle. We did record a few statements from Leo and some give-and-take between Alice and Anna Livia. They spoke in a mixture of standard signs and the new ones, but, without a sense of the context, we've found it impossible to generate any sequence of meanings. Stray signs such as "shirt," "hat," "human," "change," and "banana fly," interspersed with undecipherable stuff, *seem* to be adding up to something, but no one is sure what. We observed no mention of Hal Vendelmans nor any direct references to death. We may be misleading ourselves entirely about the significance of all this.

Or perhaps not. We codified some of the new signs and this afternoon I asked Ramona what one of them meant. She fidgeted and hooted and looked uncomfortable—and not simply because I was asking her to do a tough abstract thing like giving a definition. She was worried. She looked around for Leo, and when she saw him she made that sign at him. He came bounding over and shoved Ramona away. Then he began to tell me how wise and good and gentle I am. He may be a genius, but even a genius chimp is still a chimp, and I told him I wasn't fooled by all his flattery. Then I asked *him* what the new sign meant.

"Jump high come again," Leo signed.

A simple chimpy phrase referring to fun and frolic? So I thought at first, and so did many of my colleagues. But Dave Yost said, "Then why was Ramona so evasive about defining it?"

"Defining isn't easy for them," Beth Rankin said.

"Ramona's one of the five brightest. She's capable of it. Especially since the sign can be defined by use of four other established signs, as Leo proceeded to do."

"What are you getting at, Dave?" I asked.

Yost said, "*Jump high come again*' might be about a game they like to play, but it could also be an eschatological reference, sacred talk, a concise metaphorical way to speak of death and resurrection, no?"

Mick Falkenburg snorted. "Jesus, Dave, of all the nutty Jesuitical bullshit—"

"Is it?"

"It's possible sometimes to be too subtle in your analysis," Falkenburg said. "You're suggesting that these chimpanzees have a theology?"

"I'm suggesting that they may be in the process of evolving a religion," Yost replied.

Can it be?

Sometimes we lose our perspective with these animals, as Mick indicated, and we overestimate their intelligence; but just as often, I think, we underestimate them.

*Jump high come again.*

I wonder. Secret sacred talk? A chimpanzee theology? Belief in life after death? A religion?

They know that human beings have a body of ritual and belief that they call religion, though how much they really comprehend about it is hard to tell. Dave Yost, in his metaphysical discussions with Leo and some of the other alphas, introduced the concept long ago. He drew a hierarchy that began with God and ran downward through human beings and chimpanzees to dogs and cats and onward to insects and frogs, by way of giving the chimps some sense of the great chain of life. They had seen bugs and frogs and cats and dogs, but they wanted Dave to show them God, and he was forced to tell them that God is not actually tangible and accessible, but lives high overhead although His essence penetrates all things. I doubt that they grasped much of that. Leo, whose nimble and probing intelligence is a constant illumination to us, wanted Yost to explain how we talked to God and how God talked to us, if He wasn't around to make signs, and Yost said that we had a thing called religion, which was a system of communicating with God. And that was where he left it, a long while back.

Now we are on guard for any indications of a developing religious consciousness among our troop. Even the scoffers—Mick Falkenburg, Beth, to some degree, Charley Damiano—are paying close heed. After all, one of the underlying purposes of this project is to reach an understanding of how the first hominids managed to cross the intellectual boundary that we like to think separates the animals from humanity. We can't reconstruct a bunch of Australopithecines and study them; but we *can* watch chimpanzees who have been given the gift of language build a quasi-protohuman society, and it is the closest thing to traveling back in time that we are apt to achieve. Yost thinks, I think, Burt Christensen is beginning to think, that we have inadvertently kindled an awareness of the divine, of the numinous force that must be worshipped, by allowing them to see that their gods—we—can be struck down and slain by an even higher power.

The evidence so far is slim. The attention given Vendelmans and Judy; the solitary meditations of Leo and Grimsky; the large gatherings in the grove; the greatly accelerated use of modified sign language in chimp-to-chimp talk at those gatherings; the potentially eschatological reference we think we see in the sign that Leo translated as *jump high come again.* That's it. To those of us who want to interpret that as the foundations of religion, it seems indicative of what we want to see; to the rest, it all looks like coincidence and fantasy. The problem is that we are dealing with nonhuman intelligence and we must take care not to impose our own thought-constructs. We can never be certain if we are operating from a value system anything like that of the chimps. The built-in ambiguities of the sign-language grammar we must use with them complicate the issue. Consider the phrase "banana fly" that Leo used in a speech—a sermon?—in the oak grove, and remember Ramona's reference to the sick Vendelmans as "rotten banana." If we take *fly* to be a verb, "ba-

nana fly" might be considered a metaphorical description of
Vendelmans's ascent to heaven. If we take it to be a noun, Leo
might have been talking about the Drosophila flies that feed on
decaying fruit, a metaphor for the corruption of the flesh after
death. On the other hand, he may simply have been making a
comment about the current state of our garbage dump.

We have agreed for the moment not to engage the chimpanzees in any direct interrogation about any of this. The Heisen-
berg principle is eternally our rule here: the observer can too
easily perturb the thing observed, so we must make only the
most delicate of measurements. Even so, of course, our presence among the chimps is bound to have its impact, but we do
what we can to minimize it by avoiding leading questions and
watching in silence.

Two unusual things today. Taken each by each, they would
be interesting without being significant; but if we use each to
illuminate the other, we begin to see things in a strange new
light, perhaps.

One thing is an increase in vocalizing, noticed by nearly everyone, among the chimps. We know that chimpanzees in the
wild have a kind of rudimentary spoken language—a greeting-
call, a defiance-call, the grunts that mean "I like the taste of
this," the male chimp's territorial hoot, and such: nothing very
complex, really not qualitatively much beyond the language of
birds or dogs. They also have a fairly rich nonverbal language,
a vocabulary of gestures and facial expressions; but it was not
until the first·experiments decades ago in teaching chimpanzees
human sign language that any important linguistic capacity became apparent in them. Here at the research station the chimps
communicate almost wholly in signs, as they have been trained
to do for generations and as they have taught their young ones
to do; they revert to hoots and grunts only in the most elemen-
tal situations. We ourselves communicate mainly in signs when
we are talking to each other while working with the chimps,
and even in our humans-only conferences we use signs as much
as speech, from long habit. But suddenly the chimps are making
sounds at each other. Odd sounds, unfamiliar sounds, weird
clumsy imitations, one might say, of human speech. Nothing
that we can understand, naturally: the chimpanzee larynx is sim-

ply incapable of duplicating the phonemes humans use. But
these new grunts, these tortured blurts of sound, seem intended
to mimic our speech. It was Damiano who showed us, as we
were watching a tape of a grove session, how Attila was twisting
his lips with his hands in what appeared unmistakably to be an
attempt to make human sounds come out.

Why?

The second thing is that Leo has started wearing a shirt and
a hat. There is nothing remarkable about a chimp in clothing;
although we have never encouraged such anthropomorphiza-
tion here, various animals have taken a fancy from time to time
to some item of clothing, have begged it from its owner, and
have worn it for a few days or even weeks. The novelty here is
that the shirt and the hat belonged to Hal Vendelmans, and that
Leo wears them only when the chimps are gathered in the oak
grove, which Dave Yost has lately begun calling the "holy
grove." Leo found them in the toolshed beyond the vegetable
garden. The shirt is ten sizes too big, Vendelmans having been
so brawny, but Leo ties the sleeves across his chest and lets the
rest dangle down over his back almost like a cloak.

What shall we make of this?

Jan is the specialist in chimp verbal processes. At the meeting
tonight she said, "It sounds to me as if they're trying to dupli-
cate the rhythms of human speech even though they can't reproduce the actual sounds. They're playing at being human."

"Talking the god-talk," said Dave Yost.

"What do you mean?" Jan asked.

"Chimps talk with their hands. Humans do too, when speaking with chimps, but when humans talk to humans they use
their voices. Humans are gods to chimps, remember. Talking in
the way the gods talk is one way of remaking yourself in the
image of the gods, of putting on divine attributes."

"But that's nonsense," Jan said. "I can't possibly—"

"Wearing human clothing," I broke in excitedly, "would also
be a kind of putting on divine attributes, in the most literal
sense of the phrase. Especially if the clothes—"

"—had belonged to Hal Vendelmans," said Christensen.

"The dead god," Yost said.

We looked at each other in amazement.

Charley Damiano said, not in his usual skeptical way but in a kind of wonder, "Dave, are you hypothesizing that Leo functions as some sort of priest, that those are his sacred garments?"

"More than just a priest," Yost said. "A high priest, I think. A pope. The pope of the chimps."

Grimsky is suddenly looking very feeble. Yesterday we saw him moving slowly through the meadow by himself, making a long circuit of the grounds as far out as the pond and the little waterfall, then solemnly and ponderously staggering back to the meeting-place at the far side of the grove. Today he has been sitting quietly by the stream, occasionally rocking slowly back and forth, now and then dipping his feet in. I checked the records: he is forty-three years old, well along for a chimp, although some have been known to live fifty years and more. Mick wanted to take him to the infirmary but we decided against it; if he is dying, and by all appearances he is, we ought to let him do it with dignity in his own way. Jan went down to the grove to visit him and reported that he shows no apparent signs of disease. His eyes are clear, his face feels cool. Age has withered him and his time is at hand. I feel an enormous sense of loss, for he has a keen intelligence, a long memory, a shrewd and thoughtful nature. He was the alpha male of the troop for many years, but a decade ago, when Leo came of age, Grimsky abdicated in his favor with no sign of a struggle. Behind Grimsky's grizzled forehead there must lie a wealth of subtle and mysterious perceptions, concepts, and insights about which we know practically nothing, and very soon all that will be lost. Let us hope he's managed to teach his wisdom to Leo and Attila and Alice and Ramona.

Today's oddity: a ritual distribution of meat.

Meat is not very important in the diet of chimps, but they do like to have some, and as far back as I can remember Wednesday has been meat day here, when we give them a side of beef or some slabs of mutton or something of that sort. The procedure for dividing up the meat betrays the chimps' wild heritage, for the alpha males eat their fill first, while the others watch, and then the weaker males beg for a share and are allowed to move in to grab, and finally the females and young ones get the scraps. Today was meat day. Leo, as usual, helped himself first, but what happened after that was astounding. He let Attila feed, and then told Attila to offer some meat to Grimsky, who is even weaker today and brushed it aside. *Then Leo put on Vendelmans's hat* and began to parcel out scraps of meat to the others. One by one they came up to him in the current order of ranking and went through the standard begging maneuver, hand beneath chin, palm upward, and Leo gave each one a strip of meat.

"Like taking communion," Charley Damiano muttered. "With Leo the celebrant at the Mass."

Unless our assumptions are totally off base, there is a real religion going on here, perhaps created by Grimsky and under Leo's governance. And Hal Vendelmans's faded old blue work-hat is the tiara of the pope.

Beth Rankin woke me at dawn and said, "Come fast. They're doing something strange with old Grimsky."

I was up and dressed and awake in a hurry. We have a closed-circuit system now that pipes the events in the grove back to us, and we paused at the screen so that I could see what was going on. Grimsky sat on his knees at the edge of the stream, eyes closed, barely moving. Leo, wearing the hat, was beside him, elaborately tying Vendelmans's shirt over Grimsky's shoulders. A dozen or more of the other adult chimps were squatting in a semicircle in front of them.

Burt Christensen said, "What's going on? Is Leo making Grimsky the assistant pope?"

"I think Leo is giving Grimsky the last rites," I said.

What else could it have been? Leo wore the sacred headdress. He spoke at length using the new signs—the ecclesiastical language, the chimpanzee equivalent of Latin or Hebrew or Sanskrit—and as his oration went on and on, the congregation replied periodically with outbursts of—I suppose—response and approval, some in signs, some with the grunting garbled pseudo-human sounds that Dave Yost thought was their version of god-talk. Throughout it all Grimsky was silent and remote, though occasionally he nodded or murmured or tapped both his shoulders in a gesture whose meaning was unknown to us. The ceremony went on for more than an hour. Then Grimsky leaned forward, and Kong and Chump took him by the arms and eased him down until he was lying with his cheek against the ground.

For two, three, five minutes all the chimpanzees were still. At last Leo came forward and removed his hat, setting it on the ground beside Grimsky, and with great delicacy he untied the shirt Grimsky wore. Grimsky did not move. Leo draped the shirt over his own shoulders and donned the hat again.

He turned to the watching chimps and signed, using the old signs that were completely intelligible to us, "Grimsky now be human being."

We stared at each other in awe and astonishment. A couple of us were sobbing. No one could speak.

The funeral ceremony seemed to be over. The chimps were dispersing. We saw Leo sauntering away, hat casually dangling from one hand, the shirt, in the other, trailing over the ground. Grimsky alone remained by the stream. We waited ten minutes and went down to the grove. Grimsky seemed to be sleeping very peacefully, but he was dead, and we gathered him up—Burt and I carried him; he seemed to weigh almost nothing—and took him back to the lab for the autopsy.

In midmorning the sky darkened and lightning leaped across the hills to the north. There was a tremendous crack of thunder almost instantly and sudden tempestuous rain. Jan pointed to the meadow. The male chimps were doing a bizarre dance, roaring, swaying, slapping their feet against the ground, hammering their hands against the trunks of the trees, ripping off branches and flailing the earth with them. Grief? Terror? Joy at the translation of Grimsky to a divine state? Who could tell? I had never been frightened by our animals before—I knew them too well, I regarded them as little hairy cousins—but now they were terrifying creatures and this was a scene out of time's dawn, as Gonzo and Kong and Attila and Chump and Buster and Claudius and even Pope Leo himself went thrashing about in that horrendous rain, pounding out the steps of some unfathomable rite.

The lightning ceased and the rain moved southward as quickly as it had come, and the dancers went slinking away, each to his favorite tree. By noon the day was bright and warm and it was as though nothing out of the ordinary had happened.

Two days after Grimsky's death I was awakened again at dawn, this time by Mick Falkenburg. He shook my shoulder and yelled at me to wake up, and as I sat there blinking he said,

"Chicory's dead! I was out for an early walk and I found her near the place where Grimsky died."

"Chicory? But she's only—"

"Eleven, twelve, something like that. I know."

I put my clothes on while Mick woke the others, and we went down to the stream. Chicory was sprawled out, but not peacefully—there was a dribble of blood at the corner of her mouth, her eyes were wide and horrified, her hands were curled into frozen talons. All about her in the moist soil of the streambank were footprints. I searched my memory for an instance of murder in the chimp community and could find nothing remotely like it—quarrels, yes, and lengthy feuds, and some ugly ambushes and battles, fairly violent, serious injuries now and then. But this had no precedent.

"Ritual murder," Yost murmured.

"Or a sacrifice, perhaps?" suggested Beth Rankin.

"Whatever it is," I said, "they're learning too fast. Recapitulating the whole evolution of religion, including the worst parts of it. We'll have to talk to Leo."

"Is that wise?" Yost asked.

"Why not?"

"We've kept hands off so far. If we want to see how this thing unfolds—"

"During the night," I said, "the Pope and the College of Cardinals ganged up on a gentle young female chimp and killed her. Right now they may be off somewhere sending Alice or Ramona or Anna Livia's twins to chimp heaven. I think we have to weigh the value of observing the evolution of chimp religion against the cost of losing irreplaceable members of a unique community. I say we call in Leo and tell him that it's wrong to kill."

"He knows that," said Yost. "He must. Chimps aren't murderous animals."

"Chicory's dead."

"And if they see it as a holy deed?" Yost demanded.

"Then one by one we'll lose our animals, and at the end we'll just have a couple of very saintly survivors. Do you want that?"

We spoke with Leo. Chimps can be sly and they can be manipulative, but even the best of them, and Leo is the Einstein of chimpanzees, do not seem to know how to lie. We asked him where Chicory was and Leo told us that Chicory was now a human being. I felt a chill at that. Grimsky was also a human being, said Leo. We asked him how he knew that they had become human and he said, "They go where Vendelmans go. When human go away, he become god. When chimpanzee go away, he become human. Right?"

"No," we said.

The logic of the ape is not easy to refute. We told him that death comes to all living creatures, that it is natural and holy, but that only God could decide when it was going to happen. God, we said, calls His creatures to Himself one at a time. God had called Hal Vendelmans, God had called Grimsky, God would someday call Leo and all the rest here. But God had not yet called Chicory. Leo wanted to know what was wrong with sending Chicory to Him ahead of time. Did that not improve Chicory's condition? No, we replied. No, it only did harm to Chicory. Chicory would have been much happier living here with us than going to God so soon. Leo did not seem convinced. Chicory, he said, now could talk words with her mouth and wore shoes on her feet. He envied Chicory very much.

We told him that God would be angry if any more chimpanzees died. We told him that *we* would be angry. Killing chimpanzees was wrong, we said. It was not what God wanted Leo to be doing.

"Me talk to God, find out what God wants," Leo said.

We found Buster dead by the edge of the pond this morning, with indications of another ritual murder. Leo coolly stared us down and explained that God had given orders that all chimpanzees were to become human beings as quickly as possible, and this could only be achieved by the means employed on Chicory and Buster.

Leo is confined now in the punishment tank and we have suspended this week's meat distribution. Yost voted against both of those decisions, saying we ran the risk of giving Leo the aura of a religious martyr, which would enhance his already considerable power. But these killings have to stop. Leo knows, of course, that we are upset about them. But if he believes his path is the path of righteousness, nothing we say or do is going to change his mind.

*        *        *

Judy Vendelmans called today. She has put Hal's death fairly
well behind her, misses the project, misses the chimps. As gently as I could, I told her what has been going on here. She was
silent a very long time—Chicory was one of her favorites, and
Judy has had enough grief already to handle for one summer—but finally she said, "I think I know what can be done. I'll
be on the noon flight tomorrow."

We found Mimsy dead in the usual way late this afternoon.
Leo is still in the punishment tank—the third day. The congregation has found a way to carry out its rites without its leader.
Mimsy's death has left me stunned, but we are all deeply affected, virtually unable to proceed with our work. It may be
necessary to break up the community entirely to save the animals. Perhaps we can send them to other research centers for
a few months, three of them here, five there, until this thing
subsides. But what if it doesn't subside? What if the dispersed
animals convert others elsewhere to the creed of Leo?

The first thing Judy said when she arrived was, "Let Leo out.
I want to talk with him."

We opened the tank. Leo stepped forth, uneasy, abashed,
shading his eyes against the strong light. He glanced at me, at
Yost, at Jan, as if wondering which one of us was going to scold
him; and then he saw Judy and it was as though he had seen a
ghost. He made a hollow rasping sound deep in his throat and
backed away. Judy signed hello and stretched out her arms to
him. Leo trembled. He was terrified. There was nothing unusual
about one of us going on leave and returning after a month or
two, but Leo must not have expected Judy ever to return, must
in fact have imagined her gone to the same place her husband
had gone, and the sight of her shook him. Judy understood all
that, obviously, for she quickly made powerful use of it, signing
to Leo, "I bring you message from Vendelmans."

"Tell tell tell!"

"Come walk with me," said Judy.

She took him by the hand and led him gently out of the punishment area and into the compound, and down the hill toward
the meadow. I watched from the top of the hill, the tall slender
woman and the compact, muscular chimpanzee close together,

side by side, hand in hand, pausing now to talk, Judy signing and Leo replying in a flurry of gestures, then Judy again for a long time, a brief response from Leo, another cascade of signs from Judy, then Leo squatting, tugging at blades of grass, shaking his head, clapping hand to elbow in his expression of confusion, then to his chin, then taking Judy's hand. They were gone for nearly an hour. The other chimps did not dare approach them. Finally Judy and Leo, hand in hand, came quietly up the hill to headquarters again. Leo's eyes were shining and so were Judy's.

She said, "Everything will be all right now. That's so, isn't it, Leo?"

Leo said, "God is always right."

She made a dismissal sign and Leo went slowly down the hill. The moment he was out of sight, Judy turned away from us and cried a little, just a little; then she asked for a drink; and then she said, "It isn't easy, being God's messenger."

"What did you tell him?" I asked.

"That I had been in heaven visiting Hal. That Hal was looking down all the time and he was very proud of Leo, except for one thing: that Leo was sending too many chimpanzees to God too soon. I told him that God was not yet ready to receive Chicory and Buster and Mimsy, that they would have to be kept in storage cells for a long time, until their true time came, and that that was not good for them. I told him that Hal wanted Leo to know that God hoped he would stop sending him chimpanzees. Then I gave Leo Hal's old wristwatch to wear when he conducts services, and Leo promised he would obey Hal's wishes. That was all. I suspect I've added a whole new layer of mythology to what's developing here, and I trust you won't be angry with me for doing it. I don't believe any more chimps will be killed. And I think I'd like another drink."

Later in the day we saw the chimps assembled by the stream. Leo held his arm aloft and sunlight blazed from the band of gold on his slim hairy wrist, and a great outcry of grunts in god-talk went up from the congregation and they danced before him, and then he donned the sacred hat and the sacred shirt and moved his arms eloquently in the secret sacred gestures of the holy sign language.

There have been no more killings. I think no more will occur. Perhaps after a time our chimps will lose interest in being religious, and go on to other pastimes. But not yet, not yet. The ceremonies continue, and grow ever more elaborate, and we are compiling volumes of extraordinary observations, and God looks down and is pleased. And Leo proudly wears the emblems of his papacy as he bestows his blessing on the worshippers in the holy grove.

# *Curious Elation*

## by Michael Cassutt

*The heart of any Catholic community, as any priest will tell you, is the parishioners—not only the faithful, but also the less-faithful. Even those who consider themselves to be lapsed Catholics rarely sever all ties with the Church. The urge to return, however faint, often remains.*

*Michael Cassutt has been publishing SF and fantasy stories since 1974 in magazines and anthologies. His novel* The Star Country *appeared in 1986. He has also written scripts for such television series as "The Twilight Zone," "Max Headroom," and "TV 101."*

*Born and raised in the Midwest, he now lives in Los Angeles with his wife and two children.*

*I*t was a back-page item in the *Courier-Citizen,* the hometown newspaper I still receive. Doc Hustad was retiring and they held a banquet for him at the Buena Vista Inn. The mayor was there, and the superintendent of schools, and the other two GPs who, with Hustad, provided the town with medical care for most of two decades.

Also present were Millie (Mrs. Dr.) Hustad; their oldest son, Keith, now an attorney resident in Milwaukee; younger son David, a local businessman. (This was a journalistic kindness: David Hustad, the doctor's son, actually worked on the assembly line at the paper bag factory. How he managed to marry Leslie Keilan, I'll never know.) And son Gary, of course, "who lives at home."

Who lives at home.

It was an unscheduled trip. I had had a court date in Chicago on Monday. But during a plane change in Denver I got to brooding about Gary Hustad, and about a question my son had asked me the night before. Within the hour a sudden winter storm ascended out of Lake Michigan, cancelling all flights to Chicago and points east. Then a phone call to my office told me the hearing had been postponed until after the holidays. I was less surprised by this than you'd believe.

And soon enough the flight, which had been designed to deposit me in Chicago, delivered me to Minneapolis at six in the morning. Three hours later, under the glare of the town's silver water tower, I crossed the river into Buena Vista.

It was a Friday, a work day, and I poked through what passed for rush hour on Main Street, noting the changes, feeling at home in spite of the fact that I had left for good fifteen years earlier. Here was Lark's Bar, where I celebrated my high school graduation by downing a pitcher of Bud and puking it all over the backseat of Randy Boucher's Tempest. Here was the Elks' Club, where Wednesday night summer dances introduced me to Minnesota girls whose willingness to French kiss was directly proportional to their consumption of Schlitz Malt Liquor. Here was the old high school, where I had been voted Most Likely to Become A Vicious Corporate Lawyer. These places held no attraction for me now, but they'd done their job well: I had a moderate cocaine habit, a wife and a mistress, and a Candotti briefcase full of legal papers. All I lacked was a reason for being there.

I certainly couldn't go home; my parents, uninformed of my presence in town, would be (a) not at home and (b) too full of unpleasant questions. It was too cold to hang out on a street corner, and the wind whipping off the river, threatening more snow, made me dismiss any vague thoughts I may have had of driving around the countryside. So I simply drove down Main Street, turning right on Hudson and passing a forlorn-looking St. Nicholas Catholic Church. The *Courier-Citizen* had said the old church was to be torn down in favor of a new one by the freeway.

Staying on Hudson, I passed through the old part of town, reaching the intersection of Hudson and Ninth, then turned up Ninth to Hill, and discovered that without thinking I was retracing the same route by which for eight years I had walked home from school. When I got to where Ninth crossed Hill I pulled over and parked.

The sun was as high as it ever gets in this latitude, in this season, and still it barely cleared the hill. I rolled down the window and smelled the snow in the air.

I tapped out a little snow of my own. And wondered what had compelled me to come here, now. I felt as though I had a mission—but to do what? And why?

When I got out I ruined my California shoes in the salt that was spread on the street. For good measure I soaked my feet stepping through a ridge of plowed snow that bordered the relatively clean sidewalk. Stomping my feet in futility, I started walking up the hill.

Two stories high, sprawling, equipped with an enclosed pool and solidly built in the fashion of the McCarthy years, the Hustad place was still one of the nicest in nice Buena Vista—in spite of twenty years of expensive developments beyond the hill. It had a formerly commanding view of the city as well, now obscured—purposely?—by a stand of pines. I passed the smaller, prefab house of David and Leslie Hustad, built on land given to them, of course, by Doc. For a moment I entertained the fantasy that I would suddenly encounter Leslie. A wicked scenario it was: the disappointing, now heavyset husband off at work in an appliance factory ... troublesome children away at school ... lovely Leslie, still slim and, if anything, more attractive at thirty than she'd been at seventeen. She would be easy for me, this time. But though steam curled from the chimney, the lesser Hustad house seemed deserted. Winter here is like that. I had yet to see a person on the street, and only two cars had driven by.

Distractions. I found the driveway to Buddy's house and followed it in.

I hesitated in those last few steps. I hadn't called or written or, for that matter, even talked to a member of the Hustad family since running into Leslie at the supermarket three years back. And the idea that small towns are somehow especially forgiving when it comes to prodigals is a myth: these people have been known to hold grudges for thirty years, especially against those who have managed to escape.

The walk was neatly shoveled, as the driveway had been. The big three-car garage stood open, a gray Chevy van its only occupant. Suppose they had gone out? Suppose no one was at home?

It was a silly thought. Gary was *always* at home.

I rang the doorbell. In complete contrast to every other house I'd lived in or visited during my twelve years in Buena Vista, the doorbell at the Hustad home actually worked. But apart from the muted chime, my ringing it seemed to have no effect.

For about five seconds I considered walking away. But it was important, somehow, that I not abandon my mystery mission after a single stab at a doorbell. I rang again.

"I'm coming, I'm coming!" a woman's voice answered almost immediately. I heard the inner door open, noted the sound of firm footsteps, witnessed a tug at the outer door.

"Yes?" Mrs. Hustad, radiant in slacks and and L. L. Bean sweater.

Before I could answer she raised a finger as a prop to memory. "Jeff Kramer!"

"Mrs. Hustad."

"Well, well. Didn't I see your picture in the paper a little while back?" That "little while" had been more like two years, some mention of a notorious lawsuit in which I'd been involved. The article had used my father as a well-meaning but highly inaccurate source.

"You know how it is—everyone gets his picture in the *Courier* if he lives long enough."

She laughed. She was a very pretty woman, even at sixty. "What on earth are you doing here?" Then she thought for a moment. "You were in Gary's class."

"Yeah. I was just in town ... and I saw the piece about Doc ... and I haven't seen Gary in such a long time that I thought..." I was babbling.

"Come in," she said. "You must be freezing out there." And over her shoulder called, "Gary!"

I followed her through a living room which had a cozy warmth that came from use. There was a Barcalounger for Doc, a couch for the Mrs. A TV zapper rested on the coffee table amid a jumble of *Ladies' Home Journal*s, *National Geographic*s, and *Fortune*s. Bookshelves held the complete—or so it seemed—*Reader's Digest Condensed Novels,* a pair of early Ludlums, and the newest Judith Krantz. And, on one shelf, strangely, C. S. Lewis, Evelyn Waugh, Flannery O'Connor, Thomas Merton. On the dark, paneled walls were photos of the family. Including Gary.

"Wait here, please," Mrs. Hustad said. "Gary! You have company!" The surprise in her voice made it clear that it was not a phrase she often used. I heard her running up the stairs.

Then the thumping started ... the footsteps of Frankenstein's monster.

The last time I saw Gary Hustad was half a lifetime ago, back in the days when the Hustads still attended eight-thirty Mass and the Kramers ten o'clock. (Thanks to the tendency of Catholic families to settle on a particular service, attending no other, we had not spoken more than a few words in two

or three years even then.) It must have been spring, during
one of those horribly long Passion feasts read by the equally
horrible Father Bob (who insisted on reading *every* response
and singing *every* verse) that ran so late it caused the exiting
attendees of eight-thirty to collide with the arrivals for ten.
I was waiting in the back when I saw Gary painfully draw
himself out of the pew and move down the aisle, bracing
himself with a hand against the wall, that shortened leg making that Frankenstein thump.

The door opened now, and there he was. Pale, very thin, bald-
ing after the unfortunate fashion of the Hustads, Gary looked an
unhealthy fifty. "Hello," he said.

"Hi, Gary. I don't know if you remember me—"

"Come on, Kramer! Of course I remember you!" Annoyance
is an underrated fountain of youth. In the space of a sentence
he dropped twenty years. "What do you want?"

"Gary, really!" said Mrs. Hustad, to both of us. "It isn't as
though we have visitors every day."

His knuckles tightened on the cane, and for a moment I was
afraid that he would throw it at me. But he only used it to point
to the couch. "Go on. Sit down."

"Why don't I get some tea," Mrs. Hustad said, omitting the
question mark and leaving us alone.

"You're living in California," Gary said finally, "with all those
earthquakes."

"We get them from time to time. No big ones yet, thank
God." (When had I started to use *that* phrase?)

"I saw something in the paper ... you won a lawsuit against
the guy who bombed that abortion clinic." So his world did
extend beyond the front door. Most of my old high school
chums were only vaguely aware that I had even left town.

"Yeah," I said, suddenly uncomfortable. "I guess for a lawyer
there's no such thing as bad publicity."

"I guess." He did not look at me. He seemed to be contained
totally within himself ... so much so that I began to wonder if
his eyes had also failed ... until he cleared his throat and said,
with a smile, "What would Sister Clarentine say if she knew you
were defending abortionists?"

"'Jesus, Mary, and Joseph forgive him!'" I did a creditable imitation of the old crone and managed to get a toothy smile out

of Gary. It was so quiet you could hear snowflakes hitting the roof. "So ... how are you doing?"

"I'm still here."

I cleared my throat. What was taking Mrs. Hustad so long with the Goddamned tea? "Do you think about it much?"

"Think about what?"

"About the accident."

"What accident?"

"On the playground—" I stopped. Clearly this was the wrong approach. Just as clearly there was no right approach. "I remember there was an accident," I said, giving him every opportunity to nod yes, "on the playground at St. Nicholas," hearing my own words leaking into the room, "and you got hurt."

Mrs. Hustad, with exquisite timing, chose that moment to bring us our tea. "Mom," Gary said, as Mrs. Hustad handed me my cup, "do you remember anything about some accident I had?" Without waiting for an answer, Gary said to me: "That, I guess, made me a cripple?"

She was shaking her head and trying hard not to look at me. "Even if there had been, I don't see what good there is in talking about it like this."

"I'm sorry," I said. "That isn't what I came to talk about." Unfortunately, it was *exactly* what I had come to talk about. "I really just wanted to say hello."

"Yeah," Gary said. "Hello." And he got up. As did I.

"I guess I'd better be going."

Gary and I first met when we were both eight years old. This was right around the time of Vatican II. We were the last class of altar boys at St. Nicholas to undergo the agonies of learning the Latin Mass—and the first to discard it. All our clever mnemonics, *tantrum therego* for *tantum ergo, curious elation* for the *Kyrie eleison,* went to waste.

It should be noted that giving up the Latin Mass was St. Nicholas's only notable concession to the liberalization of the Catholic Church. This was, after all, Joe McCarthy's Wisconsin. The fact that the good senator had faded from the national scene ten years earlier meant nothing: there would no slackening in *our* vigilance against sex education in the schools or fluoride in the water, or the terrible Madalyn Murray O'Hair, or any other manifestations of Satan, hereafter known by his twentieth-century name, International Communism. Priests had been tortured in China. Churches in Russia had been turned into stables. A day did not go by that we didn't hear about Red atrocities in Southeast Asia. We lived with the constant belief that Soviet nuclear missiles were poised to destroy Minneapolis, dooming the rural survivors to a life of atheistic slavery and sin. Loyalty and cunning were the sword and shield of the Righteous, and we were the most loyal and cunning, Gary and I. The doctor's son and the lawyer's boy. "A" students, altar boys. Future priests who would be strong under torture. And, of course, best friends.

It happened one day in April at St. Nicholas's. We were on the playground for the endless noon recess. The asphalt yard was a checkerboard of grade-specific turf whose borders were as finely determined and fiercely defended as those of turn-of-the-century Balkan Europe. We future eighth-graders clung to our second-tier sector with the swing set and the ivy-covered fence and eyed the occupied lands, which included the kickball diamond, with the cool certainty that we would, in time, inherit them, becoming masters of the entire world.

We were goofing around on the swing set, one of those huge gray metal jobs whose legs were sunk in cement and which had a tall slide bolted to one side. Ideally this piece of playware should have belonged to fourth- or fifth-graders, but they had been banished to the far end of the yard (where they tormented those even younger) and we amused ourselves between touch football and dodgeball by performing acrobatic maneuvers with the swings or leaping off the top of the slide into sweeping corkscrew turns or climbing to the top of the swing set itself, no small accomplishment, clutching a leather swing, finally leaping away into space, where an unforgettable ride awaited.

Gary went up the stairs of the slide and Russell Jensen fed him the swing. I was right behind him. It was just an ordinary moment—a few seconds. As Gary reached for the swing, I nudged him. I *shoved* him. Immediately knowing I'd gone too far, not sure why I did it.

He missed the swing. He reached for the grips on the

slide and missed them. And he toppled straight down to the ground.

He landed on his back with such a dull slap that I thought he had been killed. I expected to see blood beneath his head ... but he got up! Clearly hurting, tears brimming in his eyes, he got up. "Oh, man." That was all he said, looking at me. By then Sister Mary Lawrence was running toward him and she took him off to his father's clinic.

I decided to spare my parents a surprise visit and checked into the Motel Six near the freeway. Buena Vista's population had swelled to six thousand, but of that number I knew—well—probably less than a hundred. None of them, I was sure, would be caught within a mile of the Motel Six.

Once in the room I immediately took to the telephone and called Diane. "Where are you?" she said.

I could have lied and said Chicago, but had she wanted, she could have easily checked it. Had she cared. "Buena Vista," I said.

"What happened to Chicago?" She had been one of those sweet-tongued Minnesota girls, so she knew the place. I told her about the weather diversion and the cancellation. "Oh. How are your parents?"

"I haven't seen them yet."

"Where are you?"

"In the motel."

"Jeff . . . is everything all right?"

Things had not been all right for some time, as we both knew. "Yeah. The weather's lousy. How's Noah?"

"Fine. He's in the backyard. Should I get him?"

"Let him play." He might have other disturbing questions to ask. I was having a tough enough time dealing with his last one. "I'll call you later, okay?"

"Okay."

"Love me?"

"Love you."

She hung up. I pictured her turning toward the sunlight two thousand miles away, a frown on her face.

It was perhaps one in the afternoon, central standard time,

and already growing dark outside. I realized I had had perhaps two hours of sleep in the last thirty, and went to bed.

In fact, we had never been good friends. To begin with, Gary was from one of the old Buena Vista families; my people, by comparison, were fresh off the boat. He knew everyone and everyone knew him. When they selected the members of the school patrol, Gary got to be captain. (In spite of the fact that I was his equal academically—the purported criterion for making the squad was good grades—I wasn't even chosen.) When they wanted some presentable boy to read aloud at the school Christmas pageant, they picked Gary. I was the alternate. If there was a plum to be had, Gary had it. And I was automatically second choice.

I knew even then that hurt feelings on my part would strike most people as completely unjustified—after all, there were other boys and girls who would have loved just being second choice. And I knew that. But according to my reading of Life's Rules—the gospel according to St. Nicholas—I should have been getting some of those goodies. I *expected* them where these other boys and girls did not, thus my anger. Thus my growing hatred of Gary Hustad.

My response to the perceived unfairness of the game was to change the Rules myself. While maintaining my straight *A* grades and general classroom deportment, I began to debase the spirit of the Rules. I began to swear. I became known for my sarcasm, for challenging the nuns on their facts, though politely, politely. I smoked a cigarette and looked at a *Playboy* centerfold with Eric Thorson—the seventh-grade branch representative of the Prince of Darkness, according to Sister Clarentine—and refused to deny it once word got around. And I never passed up a chance to dump on Gary.

And do you know? It worked like *magic*. I got chosen to go up against the fearsome public school kids in the Buena Vista city spelling bee. I began to give the morning announcements over the school PA system. I became the eighth-grade captain of the school patrol ... all by making it clear that, you know, I could really live without it.

Best of all, my sudden ascent was matched by the mysterious decline of Gary Hustad. He had returned to school just a few days after his accident. The damage was a concussion and some bruises, lucky he didn't break something.

But in early May, a month later, he began to miss class. I didn't worry about the absences, I gloried in them, since without Gary around I was the undisputed champion "good kid" of the whole school. And as the days grew longer and warmer, and summer's freedom approached, none of us made anything of Mrs. Hustad's appearances at morning Mass ... nor of her hushed conversations with Sister Clarentine as Gary's schoolbooks were taken from his desk.

Gary missed his year-end tests. It was in June, a month after school got out, that I overheard my mother tell my father about the terrible thing that was happening to Gary Hustad ... cancer of the spine.

And I knew it was all my fault.

When I awoke it was Saturday afternoon. I was starving, so I got dressed and went across the street to the new Denny's—new to me, meaning it hadn't existed fifteen years ago. When I returned to the room, I called Diane again. "I was worried about you," she said.

"I've been sleeping for the past twenty hours."

"That sounds healthy."

"I needed it."

"Have you even talked to your parents?"

"No," I said. Sensing the beginning of a difficult conversation, I added, "But I will, tonight."

"What will you tell them?"

"Some lie."

"Stick with what you're good at." When I let that pass, she said, "Are you coming home?"

"Monday."

"This is very weird, Jeff. Is there something wrong?"

"I don't think so," I said, telling the truth for the first time in years. "I'll know in a day or two. Still love me?"

"Love you."

One of the more peculiar modifications of Catholic worship to come out of the sixties—worse than the guitar Mass, even—was the creation of Saturday evening services that would "count" as Sunday church. In high school and college I thought this was the neatest invention since the portable hair dryer, since it allowed you to head off for an evening of debauchery with a feeling of relief that you'd gotten the Obligation out of the way ... knowing that you didn't have to get up on Sunday morning.

I had no plans for the evening. I had no plans at all. But I wanted to go to Saturday-night Mass.

(My family had taken to this innovation, too, at least during the summer months. But it was a cold December Satur-day—what I used to call headache weather—and my parents were sure to have fallen back on their old habit of ten o'clock Sunday church and breakfast out. I wasn't likely to see them at St. Nicholas.)

By five o'clock it had been dark for over an hour. I took a place in the back, jammed in against some sturdy couple I vaguely recognized, so far from the altar that I couldn't hear the words of the priest. I didn't expect the faithful gathered to re-spond aloud, either. It left me free to examine the pictures in the stained glass windows, and the odd life-sized color statue of Christ—post-Crucifixion in white robe, with the bloody marks in his hands and feet and side.

"Stigmata," someone said. I remembered how fascinated I had been by those saints who had developed stigmata—the wounds of Christ—because they were taking His suffering upon them-selves. I turned toward the speaker, but there was no one there. Maybe I'd said it myself.

The service was unremarkable, serving only to remind me of the more suffocating Father Bob specials of my youth. We stu-dents of St. Nicholas attended Mass daily, and the brief sermons we got were tailored for us. Lots of martyrs, lots of upside-down crucifixion, usually in resistance to sins of impurity. All I had ever really learned from these stories was that, to your serious Catholic, a story in which everyone dies is considered to have a happy ending.

After the "Go in peace" and the final rendition of "Kumbaya," I drifted out with the crowd, which seemed to evaporate in the night air. Maybe I was searching for someone familiar, I don't know. But I hung around long enough to notice that the Hus-tads' gray van was parked in the handicap zone ... and that someone was helping Gary, in his wheelchair, out the side door of the church.

I rushed over. "Let me."

I had been afraid that it would be Doc or, worse yet, his brother David holding the door, but it was just a stranger. "Got it?" he asked.

"Yeah," I said, though Gary looked at me with suspicion. When his samaritan had gone, I asked, "All alone?"

"I can drive." He began to wheel himself toward the van. I fumbled for the lock on the side door as Gary expertly bumped off the curb and around to the back ramp. He opened the door, then tossed a switch that raised him and the chair to the point where he could enter the van. Then he said, "If you really want to do something, fold up the chair."

It took me ten minutes, while he laboriously pulled himself toward his specially modified driver's seat. Finally I got it stowed for him, slammed the door, and went around front.

He hadn't started the engine.

"What are you doing?"

"Just trying to help."

"With *me*."

"I don't know. I guess I wanted to talk."

He started to say something, thought about it, then started again. "What are you gonna say? And why now?" He hesitated again. "We were twelve years old!"

"I came to apologize."

"You're not going to have the poor taste to apologize for the fact that you are healthy and successful while I'm a pitiful cripple—"

"No," I said, "I want you to forgive me for *making* you a cripple."

Then he did start the engine. "I don't have to listen to this. You're crazy."

"I did it, Gary." I nodded toward the school and the playground across the street. "I pushed you off the slide—"

"So what! So—" Suddenly he let out a scream of utter frustration. He yanked the key out of the ignition and turned to me. "Get in."

I did. We sat there in damp, chilly silence.

"So you pushed me," he said. "I knew that. I also know that

that had nothing to do with what happened to me."

"But I wanted you to fall. I wanted you to be sick. I wanted you dead."

The look on his face was familiar; it's the one I wear in airports to keep away the Moonies. "This is stupid. You come all this way after all this time . . . just to make me hear your confession." He struggled to put the car in gear. "Why don't you talk to a priest?"

"I don't talk to priests anymore."

"Maybe you should start!"

His shout startled both of us into silence. I realized how confusing this was for him. It was pretty confusing for me. "Gary, I'm sorry."

He shut off the engine. "Jeff, something's wrong with you."

"Yeah."

God bless him, he was actually trying to help. "Money?"

"No."

"Drugs."

"No. No problem, I mean. I've quit several times."

"What, then?"

"I have a son named Noah. He's five years old. Last week I was putting him to bed and we were having a conversation, and he asked me a question. And I didn't know the answer."

"There must be lots of questions kids ask—"

"He asked me, 'Daddy . . . who's God?' And I didn't know what to tell him."

For a long time—or so it seemed—Gary didn't answer. All around us Buena Vista was preparing for a winter Saturday. It would snow soon. "God is life," he said finally. "He's your life and Noah's life and my life and the life of that tree and the life of the sun. If you can accept that, if you can believe that, everything is . . . easier." He cleared his throat. "Jeff, would you trade places with me? Don't answer: you wouldn't. You look at me and think, Jesus, here's a guy who's thirty-two years old and has never kissed a girl or hit a home run. I haven't been out of Buena Vista since I was thirteen, and then it was just to visit a hospital in St. Paul. I probably won't be alive ten years from now. I can't deal with that; I can only try not to think about it. And, you know, about once a year I don't.

"But I don't know any other life. Nobody does. Maybe it

would have been worse if I'd gotten sick when I was twenty . . . but I was a kid. I used to play in the backyard. I used to ride a bike. I guess. It's hard to remember.

"It's like I've always been this way. But I know that I won't be this way forever. Someday I won't be able to get out of bed. And after that I'll simply stop. My eyes will close. I'll go to sleep.

"But I won't be alone. I never am, because even in the middle of winter, I'm surrounded by God. He's the wind; He's the snow; He's the house. He's the pain I feel every time I want to move.

"Someday I'll sleep. But I'll bet you I have beautiful dreams."

His face was shining, and not with tears. It made me wonder just what my health and status and money meant? At that moment I would have traded it all just to feel the certainty and faith that Gary felt. And I never would.

"Are you gonna be okay?" he asked.

"I think so, yeah. Thanks."

"Tell Noah that when he feels good, when he feels love, that's God."

And then he drove away.

I walked all the way up Ninth Street, past the Hustad house, to the neighborhood where my parents lived. It was dark and the lights were on. Although I could simply have walked up to the door and gone inside, I tried to imagine what they would be doing: dinner, certainly, Dad watching the hockey game and Mother reading or talking on the phone. I wondered if Diane had called them and told them I was skulking around town. Maybe they were peering out from behind the curtains, wondering if that vaguely humanoid shape in the trees was their son.

And what a son. On the surface, I was not a bad man. I had always had a job. I had never been arrested. I was a successful lawyer and husband and father. But I was also the kind of person who not only got his wife pregnant, but his girlfriend, too. And coolly paid for the girlfriend's abortion, then went back to bouncing his infant son on his knee. And felt nothing. *Nothing.* At times I felt like a shell in the shape of a human being. Cut me and I wouldn't bleed, I'd implode.

But suddenly, like a fog rolling in, it began to feel remote. College, the firm, Diane, Noah, the girlfriend. My old home was in sight—yet I couldn't seem to reach it. I started to run, and stumbled in the darkness, scraping my hands and face and tearing a hole in the knee of my pants, something I hadn't done since the playground at St. Nicholas.

I retreated down the hill and back toward the church. The car was there; I'd half expected it to have vanished. When I got back to the motel I called home. There was no machine, no answer, just ringing.

But my knee was bleeding. Thank God for that.

The next morning—Sunday—I checked out, paying cash. I was amused to see that two days in a Buena Vista motel still cost less than some lunches I've had. The clerk was no doubt amused that I was wearing torn pants.

By the time I reached the church ten o'clock Mass was in progress. My parents were there: I found my father's car parked in its usual place. So I stood in the back, where I belonged, in sight of the stigmata Christ. When the shuffle for Communion began, I slipped out and walked across the street to the school. The playground was fenced, but not locked. I opened the gate and went in.

And there was Gary, bundled against the cold, cane in hand, sitting on the steps of the slide. I could see that he had parked his van around the back. "Aren't you surprised to see me here?" he said.

"No," I said. "I wanted you to come."

"What's that supposed to mean?"

"What I wanted to tell you—what I wanted to confess to you, was that my dreams come true."

"Here we go again—"

"You're here, aren't you?" He had no answer. "When I was in college," I said, "I wanted my best friend's girlfriend. Wanted her with a passion. He got drafted. The draft was supposed to be over and he got drafted. And I married the girl."

I was circling. The swing set had been painted and repainted, and the pressure of thousands of children's steps had bowed the rungs, but it was still the same. "I wanted to become a lawyer, but I wasn't working hard enough. I took the exams for law school and just missed ... then one of the guys above me came down with mono and had to drop out, so I got in."

I think he was afraid of me. Well, I would have been, too. "Whenever I wanted to screw one of my secretaries at home, my wife would get called out of town. When I wanted money—I'm not talking about needing it: wanting it—it would show up." I was standing in front of him now. "I've always gotten everything I wanted."

"Except happiness."

For once in my life I didn't have an answer. "Don't worry," I said, lifting him gently. "I'm not going to hurt you again." He seemed to weigh less than Noah.

We climbed up the rungs, Gary and I. He didn't struggle but rather beheld the playground, the school, the spire of St. Nicholas as I swung him around.

Maybe it was magic. Maybe it was luck. Maybe it was the power of prayer. Maybe I was just, as Gary said, crazy. But the evidence was everywhere, in every moment of my life—at least, from the moment Gary got hurt.

I closed my eyes and held my breath. I thought of saints and martyrs and stigmata and, hugging Gary to me, fell backward off the slide.

I landed on him and knocked the air out of him. Neither of us moved for a moment. Then he rolled me off and stood up. "Are you all right?"

"In a minute," I said. "Give me my cane." I used it to pull myself up to the steps of the slide.

"I should call somebody."

"You should get on a plane and go back to California," I said. "Go home."

He wanted to run, but couldn't. Finally, after we had stared at each other for at least a minute, he began to help me. "Jeff, what have you done?"

"My name isn't Jeff," I said. "It's Gary now."

He backed away, unsteady with fear and yet, I think, with growing enthusiasm. "It's out there for you," I told him. "Take it. Use it right."

"I can't—"

"Sure you can. It was *supposed* to be this way."

At the street he paused and waved. I waved back. He tossed the car keys in his hand, testing the heft, then walked away.

*Jeff, would you trade places with me?*
Yes.

I rested there on the steps, wondering when I would begin to feel the pain, the rage at the unfairness of it all, the fear of the terrors that awaited, yet knowing that this was what I needed. And that Gary was what Diane and Noah needed. As the sky grew dark and the first flakes of a gentle snow began to fall I found myself far from anger, nowhere near despair, in fact, but filled with a curious elation.

# Trinity

## by Nancy Kress

*All religions are attempts to have God deliver us from evil or bless us or, at the very least, give us a sign that He exists. Many SF stories, even those without overtly religious themes, are often about the very same thing—or do you have another explanation for all those Godlike aliens or such books as* Stranger in a Strange Land, Dune *or* Lord of Light?

*"Trinity" goes a step farther. Suppose there was a way to show* scientifically *that God exists?*

*Nancy Kress won the Science Fiction Writers of America Nebula Award for best short story in 1986 for "Out of All of Them Bright Stars." She has been publishing fiction professionally since 1979, and is the author of* The Prince of Morning Bells *(1983),* An Alien Light *(1987), and* Brain Rose *(1990), among others. She lives with her husband, Marcos Donnelly, in Brockport, New York.*

*"Lord, I believe; help Thou mine unbelief!"*

—Mark 9:24

*A*t first I didn't recognize Devrie.

Devrie—I didn't recognize *Devrie*. Astonished at myself, I studied the wasted figure standing in the middle of the bare reception room: arms like wires, clavicle sharply outlined, head shaved, dressed in that ugly long tent of lightweight gray. God knew what her legs looked like under it. Then she smiled, and it was Devrie.

"You look like shit."

"Hello. Seena. Come on in."

"I am in."

"Barely. It's not catching, you know."

"Stupidity fortunately isn't," I said and closed the door behind me. The small room was too hot; Devrie would need the heat, of course, with almost no fat left to insulate her bones and organs. Next to her I felt huge, although I am not. Huge, hairy, sloppy-breasted.

"Thank you for not wearing bright colors. They do affect me."

"Anything for a sister," I said, mocking the childhood formula, the old sentiment. But Devrie was too quick to think it was only mockery; in that, at least, she had not changed. She clutched my arm and her fingers felt like chains, or talons.

"You found him. Seena, you found him."

"I found him."

"Tell me," she whispered.

"Sit down first, before you fall over. God, Devrie, don't you eat at all?"

*"Tell me,"* she said. So I did.

Devrie Caroline Konig had admitted herself to the Institute of the Biological Hope on the Caribbean island of Dominica eleven months ago, in late November of 2017, when her age was twenty-three years and four months. I am precise about this because it is all I can be sure of. I need the precision. The Institute of the Biological Hope is not precise; it is a mongrel, part research laboratory in brain sciences, part monastery, part school for training in the discipline of the mind. That made my baby sister guinea pig, postulant, freshman. She had always been those things, but, until now, sequentially. Apparently so had many other people, for when eccentric Nobel Prize winner James Arthur Bohentin had founded his Institute, he had been able to fund it, although precariously. But in that it did not differ from most private scientific research centers.

Or most monasteries.

I wanted Devrie out of the Institute of the Biological Hope.

"It's located on Dominica," I had said sensibly—what an ass I had been—to an unwasted Devrie a year ago, "because the research procedures there fall outside United States laws concerning the safety of research subjects. Doesn't that *tell* you something, Devrie? Doesn't that at least give you pause? In New York, it would be illegal to do to anyone what Bohentin does to his people."

"Do you know him?" she had asked.

"I have met him. Once."

"What is he like?"

"Like stone."

Devrie shrugged, and smiled. "All the participants in the Institute are willing. Eager."

"That doesn't make it ethical for Bohentin to destroy them. Ethical or legal."

"It's legal on Dominica. And in thinking you know better than the participants what they should risk their own lives for, aren't you playing God?"

"Better me than some untrained fanatic who offers himself up like an exalted Viking hero, expecting Valhalla."

"You're an intellectual snob, Seena."

"I never denied it."

"Are you sure you aren't really objecting not to the Institute's dangers but to its purpose? Isn't the 'Hope' part what really bothers you?"

"I don't think scientific method and pseudoreligious mush

mix, no. I never did. I don't think it leads to a perception of God."

"The holotank tapes indicate it leads to a perception of *something* the brain hasn't encountered before," Devrie said, and for a moment I was silent.

I was once, almost, a biologist. I was aware of the legitimate studies that formed the basis for Bohentin's megalomania: the brain wave changes that accompany anorexia nervosa, sensory deprivation, biological feedback, and neurotransmitter stimulants. I have read the historical accounts, some merely pathetic but some disturbingly not, of the Christian mystics who achieved rapture through the mortification of the flesh and the Eastern mystics who achieved anesthesia through the control of the mind, of the faith healers who succeeded, of the carcinomas shrunk through trained will. I knew of the research of focused clairvoyance during orgasm, and of what happens when neurotransmitter number and speed are increased chemically.

And I knew all that was known about the twin trance.

Fifteen years earlier, as a doctoral student in biology, I had spent one summer replicating Sunderwirth's pioneering study of drug-enhanced telepathy in identical twins. My results were positive, except that within six months all eight of my research subjects had died. So had Sunderwirth's. Twin-trance research became the cloning controversy of the new decade, with the same panicky cycle of public outcry, legal restrictions, religious misunderstandings, fear, and demagoguery. When I received the phone call that the last of my subjects was dead—cardiac arrest, no history of heart disease, forty-three goddamn years old—I locked myself in my apartment, with the lights off and my father's papers clutched in my hand, for three days. Then I resigned from the neurology department and became an entomologist. There is no pain in classifying dead insects.

"There is something *there,*" Devrie had repeated. She was holding the letter sent to our father, whom someone at the Institute had not heard was dead. "It says the holotank tapes—"

"So there's something there," I said. "So the tanks are picking up some strange radiation. Why call it 'God'?"

"Why not call it God?"

"Why not call it Rover? Even if I grant you that the tape pattern looks like a presence—which I don't—you have no way of knowing that Bohentin's phantom isn't, say, some totally ungod-like alien being."

"But neither do I know that it *is.*"

"Devrie—"

She had smiled and put her hands on my shoulders. She had—has, has always had—a very sweet smile. "Seena. *Think.* If the Institute can prove rationally that God exists—can prove it to the intellectual mind, the doubting Thomases who need something concrete to study ... faith that doesn't need to be taken on faith..."

She wore her mystical face, a glowing softness that made me want to shake the silliness out of her. Instead I made some clever riposte, some sarcasm I no longer remember, and reached out to ruffle her hair. Big-sisterly, patronizing, thinking I could deflate her rapturous interest with the pinprick of ridicule. God, I was an ass. It hurts to remember how big an ass I was.

A month and a half later Devrie committed herself and half her considerable inheritance to the Institute of the Biological Hope.

"Tell me," Devrie whispered. The Institute had no windows; outside I had seen grass, palm trees, butterflies in the sunshine, but inside here in the bare gray room there was nowhere to look but at her face.

"He's a student in a Master's program at a third-rate college in New Hampshire. He was adopted when he was two, nearly three, in March of 1997. Before that he was in a government-run children's home. In Boston, of course. The adopting family, as far as I can discover, never was told he was anything but one more toddler given up by somebody for adoption."

"Wait a minute," Devrie said. "I need ... a minute."

She had turned paler, and her hands trembled. I had recited the information as if it were no more than an exhibit listing at my museum. Of course she was rattled. I wanted her rattled. I wanted her out.

Lowering herself to the floor, Devrie sat cross-legged and closed her eyes. Concentration spread over her face, but a concentration so serene it barely deserved that name. Her breathing slowed, her color freshened, and when she opened her eyes, they had the rested energy of a person who has just slept eight hours in mountain air. Her face even looked plumper, and an EEG, I guessed, would show damn near alpha waves. In her year at the Institute she must have mastered quite an array of bio-feedback techniques to do that, so fast and with such a malnour-ished body.

"Very impressive," I said sourly.

"Seena—have you seen him?"

"No. All this is from sealed records."

"How did you get into sealed records?"

"Medical and governmental friends."

"Who?"

"What do you care, as long as I found out what you wanted to know?"

She was silent. I knew she would never ask me if I had ob-tained her information legally or illegally; it would not occur to her to ask. Devrie, being Devrie, would assume it had all been generously offered by my modest museum connections and our dead father's immodest research connections. She would be wrong.

"How old is he now?"

"Twenty-four years last month. They must have used your two-month tissue sample."

"Do you think Daddy knew where the . . . baby went?"

"Yes. Look at the timing—the child was normal and healthy, yet he wasn't adopted until he was nearly three. The research-ers kept track of him, all right. They kept all six clones in a government-controlled home where they could monitor their development as long as humanely possible. The same-sex clones were released for adoption after a year, but they hung onto the cross-sex ones until they reached an age where they would be-come harder to adopt. They undoubtedly wanted to study *them* as long as they could. And even after the kids were released for adoption, the researchers held off publishing until April 1998, remember. By the time the storm broke, the babies were out of its path and anonymous."

"And the last," Devrie said.

"And the last," I agreed, although of course the researchers hadn't foreseen *that.* So few in the scientific community had foreseen that. Offense against God and man, Satan's work, natter

natter. Watching my father's suddenly stooped shoulders and stricken eyes, I had thought how ugly public revulsion could be and had nobly resolved—how had I thought of it then, so long ago?—resolved to snatch the banner of pure science from my fallen father's hand. Another time that I had been an ass. Five years later, when it had been my turn to feel the ugly scorching of public revulsion, I had broken, left neurological research, and fled down the road that led to the Museum of Natural History, where I was the curator of ants fossilized in amber and moths pinned securely under permaplex.

"The other four clones," Devrie said, "the ones from that university in California that published almost simultaneously with Daddy—"

"I don't know. I didn't even try to ask. It was hard enough in Cambridge."

"Me," Devrie said wonderingly. "He's *me.*"

"Oh, for—Devrie, he's your twin. No more than that. No—actually less than that. He shares your genetic material exactly as an identical twin would, except for the Y chromosome, but he shares none of the congenital or environmental influences that shaped your personality. There's no mystical replication of spirit in cloning. He's merely a twin who got born eleven months late!"

She looked at me with luminous amusement. I didn't like the look. On that fleshless face, the skin stretched so taut that the delicate bones beneath were as visible as the veins of a moth wing, her amusement looked ironic. Yet Devrie was never ironic. Gentle, passionate, trusting, a little stupid, she was not capable of irony. It was beyond her, just as it was beyond her to wonder why I, who had fought her entering the Institute of the Biological Hope, had brought her this information now. Her amusement was one-layered, and trusting.

God's fools, the Middle Ages had called them.

"Devrie," I said, and heard my own voice unexpectedly break, "leave here. It's physically not safe. What are you down to, ten percent body fat? Eight? Look at yourself, you can't hold body heat, your palms are dry, you can't move quickly without getting dizzy. Hypotension. What's your heartbeat? Do you still menstruate? It's insane."

She went on smiling at me. God's fools don't need menstruation. "Come with me, Seena. I want to show you the Institute."

"I don't want to see it."

"Yes. This visit you should see it."

"Why this visit?"

"Because you *are* going to help me get my clone to come here, aren't you? Or else why did you go to all the trouble of locating him?"

I didn't answer. She still didn't see it.

Devrie said, "'Anything for a sister.' But you were always more like a mother to me than a sister." She took my hand and pulled herself off the floor. So had I pulled her up to take her first steps, the day after our mother died in a plane crash at Orly. Now Devrie's hand felt cold. I imprisoned it and counted the pulse.

"Bradycardia."

But she wasn't listening.

The Institute was a shock. I had anticipated the laboratories: monotonous gray walls, dim light, heavy soundproofing, minimal fixtures in the ones used for sensory dampening; high-contrast textures and colors, strobe lights, quite good sound equipment in those for sensory arousal. There was much that Devrie, as subject rather than researcher, didn't have authority to show me, but I deduced much from what I did see. The dormitories, divided by sex, were on the sensory-dampening side. The subjects slept in small cells, ascetic and chaste, that reminded me of an abandoned Carmelite convent I had once toured in Belgium. That was the shock: the physical plant felt scientific, but the atmosphere did not.

There hung in the gray corridors a wordless peace, a feeling so palpable I could feel it clogging my lungs. No. "Peace" was the wrong word. Say "peace" and the picture is pastoral, lazy sunshine and dreaming woods. This was not like that at all. The research subjects—students? postulants?—lounged in the corridors outside closed labs, waiting for the next step in their routine. Both men and women were anorexic, both wore gray bodysuits or caftans, both were fined down to an otherworldly ethereality when seen from a distance and a malnourished asexuality when seen up close. They talked among themselves in low voices, sitting with backs against the walls or stretched full-length on the carpeted floor, and on all their faces I saw the same luminous patience, the same certainty of being very near to something exciting that they nonetheless could wait for calmly, as long as necessary.

"They look," I said to Devrie, "as if they're waiting to take an exam they already know they'll ace."

She smiled. "Do you think so? I always think of us as travelers waiting for a plane, boarding passes stamped for Eternity."

She was actually serious. But she didn't in fact wear the same expression as the others; hers was far more intense. If they were travelers, she wanted to pilot.

The lab door opened and the students brought themselves to their feet. Despite their languid movements, they looked sharp: sharp protruding clavicles, bony chins, angular unpadded elbows that could chisel stone.

"This is my hour for biofeedback manipulation of drug effects," Devrie said. "Please come watch."

"I'd sooner watch you whip yourself in a twelfth-century monastery."

Devrie's eye widened, then again lightened with that luminous amusement. "It's for the same end, isn't it? But they had such unsystematic means. Poor struggling God-searchers. I wonder how many of them made it."

I wanted to strike her. *"Devrie—"*

"If not biofeedback, what would you like to see?"

"You out of here."

"What else?"

There was only one thing: the holotanks. I struggled with the temptation, and lost. The two tanks stood in the middle of a roomy lab carpeted with thick gray matting and completely enclosed in a Faraday cage. That Devrie had a key to the lab was my first clue that my errand for her had been known, and discussed, by someone higher in the Institute. Research subjects do not carry keys to the most delicate brain-perception equipment in the world. For this equipment Bohentin had received his Nobel.

The two tanks, independent systems, stood as high as my shoulder. The ones I had used fifteen years ago had been smaller. Each of these was a cube, opaque on its bottom half, which held the sensing apparatus, computerized simulators, and recording equipment; clear on its top half, which was filled with the transparent fluid out of whose molecules the simulations would form. A separate sim would form for each subject, as the machine sorted and mapped all the electromagnetic radiation received and processed by each brain. *All* that each brain perceived, not only the visuals; the holograph equipment was capable of picking up all wavelengths that the brain did, and of displaying their brain-processed analogues as three-dimensional images floating in a clear womb. When all other possible sources of radiation were filtered out except for the emanations from the two subjects themselves, what the sims showed was what kinds of activity were coming from—and hence going on in—the other's brain. That was why it worked best with identical twins in twin trance: no structural brain differences to adjust for. In a rawer version of this holotank, a rawer version of myself had pioneered the recording of twin trances. The UCIC, we had called it then: What you see, I see.

What I had seen was eight autopsy reports.

"We're so *close,*" Devrie said. "Mona and Marlene"—she waved a hand toward the corridor, but Mona and Marlene, whichever two they had been, had gone—"had taken KX3, that's the drug that—"

"I know what it is," I said, too harshly. KX3 reacts with one of the hormones overproduced in an anorexic body. The combination is readily absorbed by body fat, but in a body without fat, much of it is absorbed by the brain.

Devrie continued, her hand tight on my arm. "Mona and Marlene were controlling the neural reactions with biofeedback, pushing the twin trance higher and higher, working it. Dr. Bohentin was monitoring the holotanks. The sims were incredibly detailed—everything each twin perceived in the perceptions of the other, in all wavelengths. Mona and Marlene forced their neurotransmission level even higher and then, in the tanks"—Devrie's face glowed, the mystic-rapture look—"a completely third sim formed. Completely separate. A third *presence.*"

I stared at her.

"It was recorded in *both* tanks. It was shadowy, yes, but it was *there.* A third presence that can't be perceived except through another human's electromagnetic presence, and then only with every drug and trained reaction and arousal mode and the twin trance all pushing the brain into a supraheightened state. A third presence!"

"Isotropic radiation. Bohentin fluffed the prescreening program and the computer hadn't cleared the background microradiation—" I said, but even as I spoke I knew how stupid that was. Bohentin didn't make mistakes like that, and isotropic radiation simulates nowhere close to the way a presence does. Devrie didn't even bother to answer me.

This, then, was what the rumors had been about, the rumors leaking for the last year out of the Institute and through the scientific community, mostly still scoffed at, not yet picked up by the popular press. This. A verifiable, replicable third presence being picked up by holography. Against all reason, a long shiver went over me from neck to that cold place at the base of the spine.

"There's more," Devrie said feverishly. "They *felt* it. Mona and Marlene. Both said afterward that they could feel it, a huge presence filled with light, but they couldn't quite reach it. Damn—they couldn't reach it, Seena! They weren't playing off each other enough, weren't close enough. Weren't, despite the twin trance, *melded* enough."

"Sex," I said.

"They tried it. The subjects are all basically heterosexual. They inhibit."

"So go find some homosexual God-yearning anorexic incestuous twins!"

Devrie looked at me straight. "I need him. Here. He *is* me."

I exploded, right there in the holotank lab. No one came running in to find out if the shouting was dangerous to the tanks, which was my second clue that the Institute knew very well why Devrie had brought me there. "Damn it to hell, he's a human being, not some chemical you can just order up because you need it for an experiment! You don't have the right to expect him to come here; you didn't even have the right to tell anyone that he exists, but that didn't stop you, did it? There are still anti-bioengineering groups out there in the real world, religious split-brains who—how *dare* you put him in any danger? How dare you even presume he'd be interested in this insane mush?"

"He'll come," Devrie said. She had not changed expression.

"How the hell do you know?"

"He's me. And I want God. He will, too."

I scowled at her. A fragment of one of her poems, a thing she had written when she was fifteen, came to me: "Two human species / Never one— / One aching for God / One never." But she had been fifteen then. I had assumed that the sentiment, as adolescent as the poetry, would pass.

I said, "What does Bohentin think of this idea of importing your clone?"

For the first time she hesitated. Bohentin, then, was dubious. "He thinks it's rather a long shot."

"You could phrase it that way."

"But *I* know he'll want to come. Some things you just know, Seena, beyond rationality. And besides—" she hesitated again, and then went on, "I have left half my inheritance from Daddy, and the income on the trust from Mummy."

"Devrie. God, Devrie—you'd *buy* him?"

For the first time she looked angry. "The money would be just to get him here, to see what is involved. Once he sees, he'll want this as much as I do, at any price! What price can you put on God? I'm not 'buying' his life—I'm offering him the way to *find* life. What good is breathing, existing, if there's no purpose to it? Don't you realize how many centuries, in how many ways, people have looked for that light-filled presence and never been able to be *sure*? And now we're almost there, Seena, I've seen it for myself—*almost there.* With verifiable, scientifically con- trolled means. Not subjective faith this time—scientific data, the same as for any other actual phenomenon. This research stands now where research into the atom stood fifty years ago. Can you touch a quark? But it's there! And my clone can be a part of it, can *be* it. How can you talk about the money buying him under circumstances like that!"

I said slowly, "How do you know that whatever you're so close to is God?" But that was sophomoric, of course, and she was ready for it. She smiled warmly.

"What does it matter what we call it? Pick another label if it will make you more comfortable."

I took a piece of paper from my pocket. "His name is Keith Torellen. He lives in Indian Falls, New Hampshire. Address and mailnet number here. Good luck, Devrie." I turned to go.

"Seena! *I* can't go!"

She couldn't, of course. That was the point. She barely had the strength in that starved, drug-battered body to get through the day, let alone to New Hampshire. She needed the sensory-controlled environment, the artificial heat, the chemical monitoring. "Then send someone from the Institute. Perhaps Bohentin will go."

"Bo*hen*tin!" she said, and I knew that was impossible; Bohentin had to remain officially ignorant of this sort of recruiting. Too many U.S. laws were involved. In addition, Bohentin had no persuasive skills; people as persons and not neurologies did not interest him. They were too far above chemicals and too far below God.

Devrie looked at me with a kind of level fury. "This is really why you found him, isn't it? So I would have to stop the drug program long enough to leave here and go get him. You think that once I've gone back out into the world either the build-up effects in the brain will be interrupted or else the spell will be broken and I'll have doubts about coming back here!"

"Will you listen to yourself? 'Out in the world.' You sound like some archaic nun in a cloistered order!"

"You always did ridicule anything you couldn't understand," Devrie said icily, turned her back on me, and stared at the empty holotanks. She didn't turn when I left the lab, closing the door behind me. She was still facing the tanks, her spiny back rigid, the piece of paper with Keith Torellen's address clutched in fingers delicate as glass.

In New York the museum simmered with excitement. An un-expected endowment had enabled us to buy the contents of a small, very old museum located in a part of Madagascar not completely destroyed by the African Horror. Crate after crate of moths began arriving in New York, some of them collected in the days when naturalists-gentlemen shot jungle moths from the trees using dust shot. Some species had been extinct since the Horror and thus were rare; some were the brief mutations from the bad years afterward and thus were even rarer. The museum staff uncrated and exclaimed.

"Look at this one," said a young man, holding it out to me. Not on my own staff, he was one of the specialists on loan to

us—DeFabio or DeFazio, something like that. He was very handsome. I looked at the moth he showed me, all pale wings outstretched and pinned to black silk. "A perfect *Thysania
africana. Perfect.*"

"Yes."

"You'll have to loan us the whole exhibit, in a few years."

"Yes," I said again. He heard the tone in my voice and glanced
up quickly. But not quickly enough—my face was all professional interest when his gaze reached it. Still, the professional
interest had not fooled him; he had heard the perfunctory note.
Frowning, he turned back to the moths.

By day I directed the museum efficiently enough. But in the
evenings, home alone in my apartment, I found myself wandering from room to room, touching objects, unable to settle to
work at the oversize teak desk that had been my father's, to the
reports and journals that had not. His had dealt with the living,
mine with the ancient dead—but I had known that for years.
The fogginess of my evenings bothered me.

"Faith should not mean fogginess."

Who had said that? Father, of course, to Devrie, when she had
joined the dying Catholic Church. She had been thirteen years
old. Skinny, defiant, she had stood clutching a black rosary from
God knows where, daring him from scared dark eyes to forbid
her. Of course he had not, thinking, I suppose, that Heaven, like
any other childhood fever, was best left alone to burn out its
course.

Devrie had been received into the Church in an overdecorated chapel, wearing an overdecorated dress of white lace and
carrying a candle. Three years later she had left, dressed in a
magenta bodysuit and holding the keys to Father's safe, which
his executor had left unlocked after the funeral. The will had,
of course, made me Devrie's guardian. In the three years Devrie
had been going to Mass, I had discovered that I was sterile,
divorced my second husband, finished my work in entomology,
accepted my first position with a museum, and entered a drasti-
cally premature menopause.

That is not a flip nor random list.

After the funeral, I sat in the dark in my father's study, in his
maroon leather chair and at his teak desk. Both felt oversize. All
the lights were off. Outside it rained; I heard the steady beat of

water on the window, and the wind. The dark room was cold.
In my palm I held one of my father's research awards, a small
abstract sculpture of a double helix, done by Harold Landau
himself. It was very heavy. I couldn't think what Landau had
used, to make it so heavy. I couldn't think, with all the noise
from the rain. My father was dead, and I would never bear a
child.

Devrie came into the room, leaving the lights off but bringing
with her an incandescent rectangle from the doorway. At sixteen she was lovely, with long brown hair in the masses of curls
again newly fashionable. She sat on a low stool beside me, all
that hair falling around her, her face white in the gloom. She
had been crying.

"He's gone. He's really gone. I don't believe it yet."

"No."

She peered at me. Something in my face, or my voice, must
have alerted her; when she spoke again it was in that voice people use when they think your grief is understandably greater
than theirs. A smooth dark voice, like a wave.

"You still have me, Seena. We still have each other."

I said nothing.

"I've always thought of you more as my mother than my sister, anyway. You took the place of Mother. You've been a
mother to at least *me.*"

She smiled and squeezed my hand. I looked at her face—so
young, so pretty—and I wanted to hit her. I didn't want to be
her mother; I wanted to be her. All her choices lay ahead of
her, and it seemed to me that self-indulgent night as if mine
were finished. I could have struck her.

"Seena—"

"Leave me alone! Can't you ever leave me alone? All my life
you've been dragging behind me; why don't *you* die and finally
leave me alone!"

We make ourselves pay for small sins more than large ones.
The more trivial the thrust, the longer we're haunted by memory of the wound.

I believe that.


Indian Falls was out of another time: slow, quiet, safe. The
Avis counter at the airport rented not personal guards but cars,
and the only shiny store on Main Street sold wilderness equip-

ment. I suspected that the small state college, like the town, traded mostly on trees and trails. That Keith Torellen was trying to take an academic degree *here* told me more about his adopting family than if I had hired a professional information service.

The house where he lived was shabby, paint peeling and steps none too sturdy. I climbed them slowly, thinking once again what I wanted to find out.

Devrie would answer none of my messages on the mailnet. Nor would she accept my phone calls. She was shutting me out, in retaliation for my refusing to fetch Torellen for her. But Devrie would discover that she could not shut me out as easily as that; we were sisters. I wanted to know if she had contacted Torellen herself, or had sent someone from the Institute to do so.

If neither, then my visit here would be brief and anonymous; I would leave Keith Torellen to his protected ignorance and shabby town. But if he *had* seen Devrie, I wanted to discover if and what he had agreed to do for her. It might even be possible that he could be of use in convincing Devrie of the stupidity of what she was doing. If he could be used for that, I would use him.

Something else: I was curious. This boy was my brother —nephew? no, brother—as well as the result of my father's rational mind. Curiosity prickled over me. I rang the bell.

It was answered by the landlady, who said that Keith was not home, would not be home until late, was "in rehearsal."

"Rehearsal?"

"Over to the college. He's a student and they're putting on a play."

I said nothing, thinking.

"I don't remember the name of the play," the landlady said. She was a large woman in a faded garment, dress or robe. "But Keith says it's going to be real good. It starts this weekend." She laughed. "But you probably already know all that! George, my husband George, he says I'm forever telling people things they already know!"

"How would I know?"

She winked at me. "Don't you think I got eyes? Sister, or cousin? No, let me guess—older sister. Too much alike for cousins."

"Thank you," I said. "You've been very helpful."

"Not sister!" She clapped her hand over her mouth, her eyes shiny with amnusement. "You're checking up on him, ain't you? You're his mother! I should of seen it right off!"

I turned to negotiate the porch steps.

"They rehearse in the new building, Mrs. Torellen," she called after me. "Just ask anybody you see to point you in the right direction."

"Thank you," I said carefully.


Rehearsal was nearly over. Evidently it was a dress rehearsal; the actors were in period costume and the director did not interrupt. I did not recognize the period or the play. Devrie had been interested in theater; I was not. Quietly I took a seat in the darkened back row and waited for the pretending to end.

Despite wig and greasepaint, I had no trouble picking out Keith Torellen. He moved like Devrie: quick, light movements, slightly pigeon-toed. He had her height and, given the differences of a male body, her slenderness. Sitting a theater's length away, I might have been seeing a male Devrie.

But seen up close, his face was mine.

Despite the landlady, it was a shock. He came toward me across the theater lobby, from where I had sent for him, and I saw the moment he too was struck by the resemblance. He stopped dead, and we stared at each other. Take Devrie's genes, spread them over a face with the greater bone surface, larger features, and coarser skin texture of a man—and the result was my face. Keith had scrubbed off his makeup and removed his wig, exposing brown curly hair the same shade Devrie's had been. But his face was mine.

A strange emotion, unnamed and hot, seared through me.

"Who are *you*? Who the hell *are* you?"

So no one had come from the Institute after all. Not Devrie, not anyone.

"You're one of them, aren't you?" he said; it was almost a whisper. "One of my real family?"

Still gripped by the unexpected force of emotion, still dumb, I said nothing. Keith took one step toward me. Suspicion played over his face—Devrie would not have been suspicious—and vanished, replaced by a slow painful flush of color.

"You are. You *are* one. Are you ... are you my mother?"

I put out a hand against a stone post. The lobby was all stone and glass. Why were all theater lobbies stone and glass? Architects had so little damn imagination, so little sense of the bizarre.

"No! I am not your mother!"

He touched my arm. "Hey, are you okay? You don't look good. Do you need to sit down?"

His concern was unexpected, and touching. I thought that he shared Devrie's genetic personality and that Devrie had always been hypersensitive to the body. But this was not Devrie. His hand on my arm was stronger, firmer, warmer than Devrie's. I felt giddy, disoriented. This was not Devrie.

"A mistake," I said unsteadily. "This was a mistake. I should not have come. I'm sorry. My name is Dr. Seena Konig and I am a ... relative of yours, but I think this is a mistake. I have your address and I promise that I'll write about your family, but now I think I should go." Write some benign lie, leave him in ignorance. This was a mistake.

But he looked stricken, and his hand tightened on my arm. "You can't! I've been searching for my biological family for two years! You can't just go!"

We were beginning to attract attention in the theater lobby. Hurrying students eyed us sideways. I thought irrelevantly how different they looked from the "students" at the Institute, and with that thought regained my composure. This was a student, a boy—"You can't!" a boyish protest, and boyish panic in his voice—and not the man-Devrie-me he had seemed a foolish moment ago. He was nearly twenty years my junior. I smiled at him and removed his hand from my arm.

"Is there somewhere we can have coffee?"

"Yes. Dr. . . ."

"Seena," I said. "Call me Seena."

Over coffee, I made him talk first. He watched me anxiously over the rim of his cup, as if I might vanish, and I listened to the words behind the words. His adopting family was the kind that hoped to visit the Grand Canyon but not Europe, go to movies but not opera, aspire to college but not to graduate work, buy wilderness equipment but not wilderness. Ordinary people. Not religious, not rich, not unusual. Keith was the only child. He loved them.

"But at the same time I never really felt I belonged," he said, and looked away from me. It was the most personal thing he had knowingly revealed, and I saw that he regretted it. Devrie would not have. More private, then, and less trusting. And I sensed in him a grittiness, a tougher awareness of the world's hardness than Devrie had ever had—or needed to have. I made my decision. Having disturbed him thus far, I owed him the truth—but not the whole truth.

"Now you tell me," Keith said, pushing away his cup. "Who were my parents? Our parents? Are you my sister?"

"Yes."

"Our parents?"

"Both are dead. Our father was Dr. Richard Konig. He was a scientist. He—" But Keith had recognized the name. His readings in biology or history must have been more extensive than I would have expected. His eyes widened, and I suddenly wished I had been more oblique.

"Richard Konig. He's one of those scientists that were involved in that bioengineering scandal—"

"How did you learn about that? It's all over and done with. Years ago."

"Journalism class. We studied how the press handled it, especially the sensationalism surrounding the cloning thing twenty years—"

I saw the moment it hit him. He groped for his coffee cup, clutched the handle, didn't raise it. It was empty anyway. And then what I said next shocked me as much as anything I have ever done.

"It was Devrie," I said, and heard my own vicious pleasure, "*Devrie* was the one who wanted me to tell you!"

But of course he didn't know who Devrie was. He went on staring at me, panic in his young eyes, and I sat frozen. That tone I heard in my own voice when I said "Devrie," that vicious pleasure that it was she and not I who was hurting him...

"Cloning," Keith said. "Konig was in trouble for claiming to have done illegal cloning. Of humans." His voice held so much dread that I fought off my own dread and tried to hold my voice steady to his need.

"It's illegal now, but not then. And the public badly misunderstood. All that sensationalism—you were right to use that word, Keith—covered up the fact that there is nothing abnormal about producing a fetus from another diploid cell. In the womb, identical twins—"

"Am I a clone?"

"Keith—"

*"Am I a clone?"*

Carefully I studied him. This was not what I had intended, but although the fear was still in his eyes, the panic had gone. And curiosity—Devrie's curiosity, and her eagerness—they were there as well. This boy would not strike me, nor stalk out of the restaurant, nor go into psychic shock.

"Yes. You are."

He sat quietly, his gaze turned inward. A long moment passed in silence.

"Your cell?"

"No. My—our sister's. Our sister Devrie."

Another long silence. He did not panic. Then he said softly, "Tell me."

Devrie's phrase.

"There isn't much to tell, Keith. If you've seen the media accounts, you know the story, and also what was made of it. The issue then becomes how you feel about what you saw. Do you believe that cloning is meddling with things man should best leave alone?"

"No. I don't."

I let out my breath, although I hadn't known I'd been holding it. "It's actually no more than delayed twinning, followed by surrogate implantation. A zygote—"

"I know all that," he said with some harshness, and held up his hand to silence me. I didn't think he knew that he did it. The harshness did not sound like Devrie. To my ears, it sounded like myself. He sat thinking, remote and troubled, and I did not try to touch him.

Finally he said, "Do my parents know?"

He meant his adoptive parents. "No."

"Why are you telling me now? Why did you come?"

"Devrie asked me to."

"She needs something, right? A kidney? Something like that?"

I had not foreseen that question. He did not move in a class where spare organs are easily purchasable. "No. Not a kidney, not any kind of biological donation." A voice in my mind jeered at that, but I was not going to give him any clues that would lead to Devrie. "She just wanted me to find you."

"Why didn't she find me herself? She's my age, right?"

"Yes. She's ill just now and couldn't come."

"Is she dying?"

"No!"

Again he sat quietly, finally saying, "No one could tell me anything. For two years I've been searching for my mother, and not one of the adoptee-search agencies could find a single trace. Not one. Now I see why. Who covered the trail so well?"

"My father."

"I want to meet Devrie."

I said evenly, "That might not be possible."

"Why not?"

"She's in a foreign hospital. Out of the country. I'm sorry."

"When does she come home?"

"No one is sure."

"What disease does she have?"

*She's sick for God,* I thought, but aloud I said, not thinking it through, "A brain disease."

Instantly, I saw my own cruelty. Keith paled, and I cried, "No, no, nothing you could have as well! Truly, Keith, it's not—she took a bad fall. From her hunter."

"Her hunter," he said. For the first time, his gaze flickered over my clothing and jewelry. But would he even recognize how expensive they were? I doubted it. He wore a synthetic, deep-pile jacket with a tear at one shoulder and a cheap wool hat, dark blue, shapeless with age. From long experience I recognized his gaze: uneasy, furtive, the expression of a man glimpsing the financial gulf between what he had assumed were equals. But it wouldn't matter. Adopted children have no legal claim on the estates of their biological parents. I had checked.

Keith said uneasily, "Do you have a picture of Devrie?"

"No," I lied.

"Why did she want you to find me? You still haven't said."

I shrugged. "The same reason, I suppose, that you looked for your biological family. The pull of blood."

"Then she wants me to write to her."

"Write to me instead."

He frowned. "Why? Why not to Devrie?"

What to say to that? I hadn't bargained on so much intensity from him. "Write in care of me, and I'll forward it to Devrie."

"Why not to her directly?"

"Her doctors might not think it advisable," I said coldly, and he backed off—either from the mention of doctors or from the coldness.

"Then give me your address, Seena. Please."

I did. I could see no harm in his writing me. It might even be pleasant. Coming home from the museum, another wintry day among the exhibits, to find on the mailnet a letter I could answer when and how I chose, without being taken by surprise. I liked the idea.

But no more difficult questions now. I stood. "I have to leave, Keith."

He looked alarmed. "So soon?"

"Yes."

"But why?"

"I have to return to work."

He stood, too. He was taller than Devrie. "Seena," he said, all earnestness, "just a few more questions. How did you find me?"

"Medical connections."

"Yours?"

"Our father's. I'm not a scientist." Evidently his journalism class had not studied twin-trance sensationalism.

"What do you do?"

"Museum curator. Arthropods."

"What does Devrie do?"

"She's too ill to work, I must go, Keith."

"One more. Do I look like Devrie as well as you?"

"It would be wise, Keith, if you were careful whom you spoke with about all of this. I hadn't intended to say so much."

"I'm not going to tell my parents. Not about being—not about all of it."

"I think that's best, yes."

"Do I look like Devrie as well as you?"

A little of my first, strange emotion returned with his intensity. "A little, yes. But more like me. Sex variance is a tricky thing."

Unexpectedly, he held my coat for me. As I slipped into it, he said from behind, "Thank you, Seena," and let his hands rest on my shoulders.

I did not turn around. I felt my face flame, and self-disgust flooded through me, followed by a desire to laugh. It was all so transparent. This man was an attractive stranger, was Devrie, was youth, was myself, was the work not of my father's loins but of his mind. Of course I was aroused by him. Freud outlasts cloning: a note for a research study, I told myself grimly, and inwardly I did laugh.

But that didn't help either.

In New York, winter came early. Cold winds whipped white-caps on harbor and river, and the trees in the park stood bare even before October had ended. The crumbling outer boroughs of the shrinking city crumbled a little more and talked of the days when New York had been important. Manhattan battened down for snow, hired the seasonal increases in personal guards, and talked of Albuquerque. Each night museum security hunted up and evicted the drifters trying to sleep behind exhibits, drift-ers as chilled and pale as the moths under permaplex, and, it seemed to me, as detached from the blood of their own age. All of New York seemed detached to me that October, and cold. Often I stood in front of the cases of Noctuidae, staring at them for so long that my staff began to glance at each other covertly. I would catch their glances, when I jerked free of my trance. No one asked me about it.

Still no message came from Devrie. When I contacted the In-stitute on the mailnet, she did not call back.

No letter from Keith Torellen.

Then one night, after I had worked late and was hurrying through the chilly gloom toward my building, he was there, bulking from the shadows so quickly that the guard I had taken for the walk from the museum sprang forward in attack po-sition.

"No! It's all right! I know him!"

The guard retreated, without expression. Keith stared after him, and then at me, his face unreadable.

"Keith, what are you doing here? Come inside!"

He followed me into the lobby without a word. Nor did he say anything during the metal scanning and ID procedure. I took him up to my apartment, studying him in the elevator. He wore the same jacket and cheap wool hat as in Indian Falls, his hair wanted cutting, and the tip of his nose was red from waiting in the cold. How long had he waited there? He badly needed a shave.

In the apartment he scanned the rugs, the paintings, my grandmother's ridiculously ornate, ugly silver, and turned his back on them to face me.

"Seena. I want to know where Devrie is."

"Why? Keith, what has happened?"

"Nothing has happened," he said, removing his jacket but not laying it anywhere. "Only that I've left school and spent two days hitching here. It's no good, Seena. To say that cloning is just like twinning: it's no good. I want to see Devrie."

His voice was hard. Bulking in my living room, unshaven, that hat pulled down over his ears, he looked older and less malleable than the last time I had seen him. Alarm—not physical fear, I was not afraid of him, but a subtler and deeper fear—sounded through me.

"Why do you want to see Devrie?"

"Because she cheated me."

"Of *what*, for God's sake?"

"Can I have a drink? Or a smoke?"

I poured him a Scotch. If he drank, he might talk. I had to know what he wanted, why such a desperate air clung to him, how to keep him from Devrie. I had never seen *her* like this. She was strong-willed, but always with a blitheness, a trust that eventually her will would prevail. Desperate forcefulness of the sort in Keith's manner was not her style. But of course Devrie had always had silent money to back her will; perhaps money could buy trust as well as style.

Keith drank off his Scotch and held out his glass for another. "It was freezing out there. They wouldn't let me in the lobby to wait for you."

"Of course not."

"You didn't tell me your family was rich."

I was a little taken aback at his bluntness, but at the same time it pleased me; I don't know why.

"You didn't ask."

"That's shit, Seena."

"Keith. Why are you here?"

"I told you. I want to see Devrie."

"What is it you've decided she cheated you of? Money?"

He looked so honestly surprised that again I was startled, this time by his resemblance to Devrie. She too would not have thought of financial considerations first, if there were emotional ones possible. One moment Keith was Devrie, one moment he was not. Now he scowled with sudden anger.

"Is that what you think—that fortune hunting brought me hitching from New Hampshire? God, Seena, I didn't even know how much you had until this very—I still don't know!"

I said levelly, "Then what is it you're feeling so cheated of?"

Now he was rattled. Again that quick, half-furtive scan of my apartment, pausing a millisecond too long at the Caravaggio, subtly lit by its frame. When his gaze returned to mine it was troubled, a little defensive. Ready to justify. Of course I had put him on the defensive deliberately, but the calculation of my trick did not prepare me for the staggering naïveté of his explanation. Once more it was Devrie complete, reducing the impersonal greatness of science to a personal and emotional loss.

"Ever since I knew that I was adopted, at five or six years old, I wondered about my biological family. Nothing strange in that—I think all adoptees do. I used to make up stories, kid stuff, about how they were really royalty, or lunar colonists, or survivors of the African Horror. Exotic things. I thought especially about my mother, imagining this whole scene of her holding me once before she released me for adoption, crying over me, loving me so much she could barely let me go but had to for some reason. Sentimental shit." He laughed, trying to make light of what was not, and drank off his Scotch to avoid my gaze.

"But Devrie—the fact of her—destroyed all that. I never had a mother who hated to give me up. I never had a mother at all. What I had was a cell cut from Devrie's fingertip or someplace, something discardable, and she doesn't even know what I look like. But she's damn well going to."

"Why?" I said evenly. "What could you expect to gain from her knowing what you look like?"

But he didn't answer me directly. "The first moment I saw you, Seena, in the theater at school, I thought *you* were my mother."

"I know you did."

"And you hated the idea. Why?"

I thought of the child I would never bear, the marriage, like so many other things of sweet promise, gone sour. But self-pity is a fool's game. "None of your business."

"Isn't it? Didn't you hate the idea because of the way I was made? Coldly. An experiment. Weren't you a little bit insulted at being called the mother of a discardable cell from Devrie's fingertip?"

"What the hell have you been reading? An experiment—what is any child but an experiment? A random egg, a random sperm. Don't talk like one of those antiscience religious split-brains!"

He studied me levelly. Then he said, "Is Devrie religious? Is that why you're so afraid of her?"

I got to my feet, and pointed at the sideboard. "Help yourself to another drink if you wish. I want to wash my hands. I've been handling specimens all afternoon." Stupid, clumsy lie—nobody would believe such a lie.

In the bathroom I leaned against the closed door, shut my eyes, and willed myself to calm. Why should I be so disturbed by the angry lashing-out of a confused boy? I was handy to lash out against; my father, whom Keith was really angry at, was not. It was all so predictable, so earnestly adolescent, that even over the hurting in my chest I smiled. But the smile, which should have reduced Keith's ranting to the tantrum of a child—there, there, when you grow up you'll find out that no one really knows who he is—did not diminish Keith. His losses were real—mother, father, natural place in the natural sequence of life and birth. And suddenly, with a clutch at the pit of my stomach, I knew why I had told him all that I had about his origins. It was not from any ethic of fidelity to "the truth." I had told him he was clone because I, too, had had real losses—research, marriage, motherhood—and Devrie could never have shared them with me. Luminous, mystical Devrie, too occupied with God to be much hurt by man. *Leave me alone! Can't you ever leave me alone! All my life you've been dragging behind me—why don't you die and finally leave me alone!* And Devrie had smiled tolerantly, patted my head, and left me alone, closing the door softly so as not to disturb my grief. My words had not hurt her. I could not hurt her.

But I could hurt Keith—the other Devrie—and I had. That was why he disturbed me all out of proportion. That was the bond. My face, my pain, my fault.

*Through my fault, through my fault, through my most grievous fault.* But what nonsense. I was not a believer, and the comforts of superstitious absolution could not touch me. What shit. Like all nonbelievers, I stood alone.

It came to me then that there was something absurd in thinking all this while leaning against a bathroom door. Grimly absurd, but absurd. The toilet as confessional. I ran the cold water, splashed some on my face and left. How long had I left Keith alone in the living room?

When I returned, he was standing by the mailnet. He had punched in the command to replay my outgoing postal messages, and displayed on the monitor was Devrie's address at the Institute of the Biological Hope.

"What is it?" Keith said. "A hospital?"

I didn't answer him.

"I can find out, Seena. Knowing this much, I can find out. Tell me."

*Tell me.* "Not a hospital. It's a research laboratory. Devrie is a voluntary subject."

"Research on what? I will find out, Seena."

"Brain perception."

"Perception of what?"

"Perception of *God*," I said, torn among weariness, anger, and a sudden gritty exasperation, irritating as sand. Why not just leave him to Devrie's persuasions, and her to mystic starvation? But I knew I would not. I still, despite all of it, wanted her out of there.

Keith frowned, "What do you mean, 'perception of God'?"

I told him. I made it sound as ridiculous as possible, and as dangerous. I described the anorexia, the massive use of largely untested drugs that would have made the Institute illegal in the

United States, the skepticism of most of the scientific community, the psychoses and death that had followed twin-trance research fifteen years earlier. Keith did not remember that—he had been eight years old—and I did not tell him that I had been one of the researchers. I did not tell him about the tapes of the shadowy third presence in Bohentin's holotanks. In every way I could, with every verbal subtlety at my use, I made the Institute sound crackpot, and dangerous, and ugly. As I spoke, I watched Keith's face, and sometimes it was mine, and sometimes the expression altered it into Devrie's. I saw bewilderment at her having chosen to enter the Institute, but not what I had hoped to see. Not scorn, not disgust.

When I had finished, he said, "But why did she think that *I* might want to enter such a place as a twin subject?"

I had saved this for last. "Money. She'd buy you."

His hand, holding his third Scotch, went rigid. "Buy me."

"It's the most accurate way to put it."

"What the hell made her think—" He mastered himself, not without effort. Not all the discussion of bodily risk had affected him as much as this mention of Devrie's money. He had a poor man's touchy pride. "She thinks of me as something to be *bought.*"

I was carefully quiet.

"Damn her," he said. "*Damn* her." Then roughly, "And I was actually considering—"

I caught my breath. "Considering the Institute? After what I've just told you? How in hell could you? And you said, I remember, that your background was not religious!"

"It's not. But I . . . I've wondered." And in the sudden turn of his head away from me so that I wouldn't see the sudden rapt hopelessness in his eyes, in the defiant set of shoulders, I read more than in his banal words, and more than he could know. Devrie's look, Devrie's wishfulness, feeding on air. The weariness and anger, checked before, flooded me again and I lashed out at him.

"Then go ahead and fly to Dominica to enter the Institute yourself!"

He said nothing. But from something—his expression as he stared into his glass, the shifting of his body—I suddenly knew that he could not afford the trip.

I said, "So you fancy yourself as a believer?"

"No. A believer manqué." From the way he said it, I knew that he had said it before, perhaps often, and that the phrase stirred some hidden place in his imagination.

"What is wrong with you," I said, "with people like you, that the human world is not enough?"

"What is wrong with people like you, that it is?" he said, and this time he laughed and raised his eyebrows in a little mockery that shut me out from this place beyond reason, this glittering escape. I knew then that somehow or other, sometime or other, despite all I had said, Keith would go to Dominica.

I poured him another Scotch. As deftly as I could, I led the conversation into other, lighter directions. I asked about his childhood. At first stiffly, then more easily as time and Scotch loosened him, he talked about growing up in the Berkshire Hills. He became more lighthearted, and under my interest turned both shrewd and funny, with a keen sense of humor. His thick brown hair fell over his forehead. I laughed with him, and broke out a bottle of good port. He talked about amateur plays he had acted in; his enthusiasm increased as his coherence decreased. Enthusiasm, humor, thick brown hair. I smoothed the hair back from his forehead. Far into the night I pulled the drapes back from the window and we stood together and looked at the lights of the dying city ten stories below. Fog rolled in from the sea. Keith insisted we open the doors and stand on the balcony; he had never smelled fog tinged with the ocean. We smelled the night, and drank some more, and talked, and laughed.

And then I led him again to the sofa.

"Seena?" Keith said. He covered my hand, laid upon his thigh, with his own, and turned his head to look at me questioningly. I leaned forward and touched my lips to his, barely in contact, for a long moment. He drew back, and his hand tried to lift mine. I tightened my fingers.

"Seena, no . . ."

"Why not?" I put my mouth back on his, very lightly. He had to draw back to answer, and I could feel that he did not want to draw back. Under my lips he frowned slightly; still, despite his drunkenness—so much more than mine—he groped for the word.

"Incest..."

"No. We two have never shared a womb."

He frowned again, under my mouth. I drew back to smile at him, and shifted my hand. "It doesn't matter anymore, Keith. Not in New York. But even if it did—I am not your sister, not really. You said so yourself—remember? Not a family. Just ... here."

"Not family," he repeated, and I saw in his eyes the second before he closed them the flash of pain, the greed of a young man's desire, and even the crafty evasions of the good port. Then his arms closed around me.

He was very strong, and more than a little violent. I guessed from what confusions the violence flowed but still I enjoyed it, that overwhelming rush from that beautiful male-Devrie body. I wanted him to be violent with me, as long as I knew there was not real danger. No real danger, no real brother, no real child. Keith was not my child but Devrie was my child-sister, and I had to stop her from destroying herself, no matter how ... didn't I? "The pull of blood." But this was necessary, was justified ... was the necessary gamble. For Devrie.

So I told myself. Then I stopped telling myself anything at all, and surrendered to the warm tides of pleasure.

But at dawn I woke and thought—with Keith sleeping heavily across me and the sky cold at the window—*what the hell am I doing?*

When I came out of the shower, Keith was sitting rigidly against the pillows. Sitting next to him on the very edge of the bed, I pulled a sheet around my nakedness and reached for his hand. He snatched it away.

"Keith. It's all right. Truly it is."

"You're my sister."

"But nothing will come of it. No child, no repetitions. It's not all that uncommon, dear heart."

"It is where I come from."

"Yes. I know. But not here."

He didn't answer, his face troubled.

"Do you want breakfast?"

"No. No, thank you."

I could feel his need to get away from me; it was almost palpable. Snatching my bodysuit off the floor, I went into the kitchen, which was chilly. The servant would not arrive for another hour. I turned up the heat, pulled on my bodysuit—standing on the cold floor first on one foot and then on the other, like some extinct species of waterfowl—and made coffee. Through the handle of one cup I stuck two folded large bills. He came into the kitchen, dressed even to the torn jacket.

"Coffee."

"Thanks."

His fingers closed on the handle of the cup, and his eyes widened. Pure, naked shock, uncushioned by any defenses whatsoever: the whole soul, betrayed, pinned in the eyes.

"Oh God, no, Keith—how can you even think so? It's for the trip back to Indian Falls! A gift!"

An endless pause, while we stared at each other. Then he said, very low, "I'm sorry. I should have ... seen what it's for." But his cup trembled in his hand, and a few drops sloshed onto the floor. It was those few drops that undid me, flooding me with shame. Keith had a right to his shock, and to the anguish in his/my/Devrie's face. She wanted him for her mystic purposes, I for their prevention. Fanatic and saboteur, we were both better defended against each other than Keith, without money nor religion nor years, was against either of us. If I could have seen any other way than the gamble I had taken ... but I could not. Nonetheless, I was ashamed.

"Keith. I'm sorry."

"Why did we? Why did *we*?"

I could have said: *we* didn't; I did. But that might have made it worse for him. He was male, and so young.

Impulsively I blurted, "Don't go to Dominica!" But of course he was beyond listening to me now. His face closed. He set down the coffee cup and looked at me from eyes much harder than they had been a minute ago. Was he thinking that because of our night together I expected to influence him directly? *I* was not that young. He could not foresee that I was trying to guess much farther ahead than that, for which I could not blame him. I could not blame him for anything. But I did regret how clumsily I had handled the money. That had been stupid.

Nonetheless, when he left a few moments later, the handle of the coffee cup was bare. He had taken the money.

The Madagascar exhibits were complete. They opened to much press interest, and there were both favorable reviews and celebrations. I could not bring myself to feel that it mattered. Ten times a day I went through the deadening exercise of willing an interest that had deserted me, and when I looked at the moths, ashy white wings outstretched forever, I could feel my body recoil in a way I could not name.

The image of the moths went home with me. One night in November I actually thought I heard wings beating against the window where I had stood with Keith. I yanked open the drapes and then the doors, but of course there was nothing there. For a long time I stared at the nothingness, smelling the fog, before typing yet another message, urgent-priority personal, to Devrie. The mailnet did not bring any answer.

I contacted the mailnet computer at the college at Indian Falls. My fingers trembled as they typed a request to leave an urgent-priority personal message for a student, Keith Torellen. The mailnet typed back:

TORELLEN, KEITH ROBERT. 64830016. ON MEDICAL
LEAVE OF ABSENCE. TIME OF LEAVE: INDEFINITE. NO
FORWARDING MAILNET NUMBER. END.

The sound came again at the window. Whirling, I scanned the dark glass, but there was nothing there, no moths, no wings, just the lights of the decaying city flung randomly across the blackness and the sound, faint and very far away, of a siren wailing out somebody else's disaster.

I shivered. Putting on a sweater and turning up the heat made me no warmer. Then the mail slot chimed softly and I turned in time to see the letter fall from the pneumatic tube from the lobby, the apartment house sticker clearly visible, assuring me that it had been processed and found free of both poison and explosives. Also visible was the envelope's logo: INSTITUTE OF THE BIOLOGICAL HOPE, all the O's radiant golden suns. But Devrie never wrote paper mail. She preferred the mailnet.

The note was from Keith, not Devrie. A short note, scrawled on a torn scrap of paper in nearly indecipherable handwriting. I had seen Keith's handwriting in Indian Falls, across his student notebooks; this was a wildly out-of-control version of it, almost psychotic in the variations of spacing and letter formation that signal identity. I guessed that he had written the note under the influence of a drug, or several drugs, his mind racing much faster than he could write. There was neither punctuation nor paragraphing.

> Dear Seena Im going to do it I have to know my parents
> are angry but I have to know I have to all the confusion
> is gone Seena Keith

There was a word crossed out between "gone" and "Seena," scratched out with erratic lines of ink. I held the paper up to the light, tilting it this way and that. The crossed-out word was "mother."

*all the confusion is gone mother*
Mother.

Slowly I let out the breath I had not known I was holding. The first emotion was pity, for Keith, even though I had intended this. We had done a job on him, Devrie and I. Mother, sister, self. And when he and Devrie artifically drove upward the number and speed of the neurotransmitters in the brain, generated the twin trance, and then Keith's precloning Freudian-still mind reached for Devrie to add sexual energy to all the other brain energies fueling Bohentin's holotanks—

Mother. Sister. Self.

All was fair in love and war. A voice inside my head jeered: and which is this? But I was ready for the voice. This was both. I didn't think it would be long before Devrie left the Institute to storm to New York.

It was nearly another month, in which the snow began to fall and the city to deck itself in the tired gilt fallacies of Christmas. I felt fine. Humming, I catalogued the Madagascar moths, remounting the best specimens in exhibit cases and sealing them under permaplex, where their fragile wings and delicate antennae could lie safe. The mutant strains had the thinnest wings, unnaturally tenuous and up to twenty-five centimeters each, all of pale ivory, as if a ghostly delicacy were the natural evolutionary response to the glowing landscape of nuclear genocide. I catalogued each carefully.

"Why?" Devrie said *"Why?"*

"You look like hell."

"Why?"

"I think you already know," I said. She sagged on my white velvet sofa, alone, the PGs that I suspected acted as much as nurses as guards, dismissed from the apartment. Tears of anger and exhaustion collected in her sunken eye sockets but did not fall. Only with effort was she keeping herself in a sitting position, and the effort was costing her energy she did not have. Her skin, except for two red spots of fury high on each cheekbone, was the color of old eggs. Looking at her, I had to keep my hands twisted in my lap to stop myself from weeping.

"Are you telling me you *planned* it, Seena? Are you telling me you located Keith and slept with him because you knew that would make him impotent with me?"

"Of course not. I know sexuality isn't that simple. So do you."

"But you gambled on it. You gambled that it would be one way to ruin the experiment."

"I gambled that it would ... complicate Keith's responses."

"Complicate them past the point where he knew who the hell he was with!"

"He'd be able to know if you weren't making him glow out of his mind with neurotransmitter kickers! He's not stupid. But he's not ready for whatever mystic hoops you've tried to make him jump through—if anybody ever *can* be said to be ready for that!—and no, I'm not surprised that he can't handle libidinal energies on top of all the other artificial energies you're racing through his brain. Something was bound to snap."

"You caused it, Seena. As cold-bloodedly as that."

A sudden shiver of memory brought the feel of Keith's hands on my breasts. No, not as cold-bloodedly as that. No. But I could not say so to Devrie.

"I trusted you," she said. "'Anything for a sister'—God!"

"You were right to trust me. To trust me to get you out of that place before you're dead."

"Listen to yourself! Smug, all-knowing, self-righteous ... do you know how *close* we were at the Institute? Do you have any idea what you've destroyed?"

I laughed coldly. I couldn't help it. "If contact with God can be destroyed because one confused kid can't get it up, what does that say about God?"

Devrie stared at me. A long moment passed, and in the moment the two red spots on her cheeks faded and her eyes narrowed. "Why, Seena?"

"I told you. I wanted you safe, out of there. And you are."

"No. No. There's something else, something more going on here. Going on with you."

"Don't make it more complicated than it is, Devrie. You're my sister, and my only family. Is it so odd that I would try to protect you?"

"Keith is your brother."

"Well, then, protect both of you. Whatever derails that experiment protects Keith, too."

She said softly, "Did you want him so much?"

We stared at each other across the living room, sisters, I standing by the mailnet and she supported by the sofa, needing its support, weak and implacable as any legendary martyr to the faith. Her weakness hurt me in some nameless place; as a child Devrie's body had been so strong. The hurt twisted in me, so that I answered her with truth. "Not so much. Not at first, not until we . . . no, that's not true. I wanted him. But that was not the reason, Devrie—it was not a rationalization for lust, nor any lapse in self-control."

She went on staring at me, until I turned to the sideboard and poured myself a Scotch. My hand trembled.

Behind me Devrie said, "Not lust. And not protection either. Something else, Seena. You're afraid."

I turned, smiling tightly. "Of you?"

"No. No, I don't think so."

"What then?"

"I don't know. Do you?"

"This is your theory, not mine."

She closed her eyes. The tears, shining all this time over her anger, finally fell. Head flung back against the pale sofa, arms limp at her side, she looked the picture of desolation, and so weak that I was frightened. I brought her a glass of milk from the kitchen and held it to her mouth, and I was a little surprised when she drank it off without protest.

"Devrie. You can't go on like this. In this physical state."

"No," she agreed, in a voice so firm and prompt that I was startled further. It was the voice of decision, not surrender. She straightened herself on the sofa. "Even Bohentin says I can't go on like this. I weigh less than he wants, and I'm right at the edge of not having the physical resources to control the twin trance. I'm having racking withdrawal symptoms even being on this trip, and at this very minute there is a doctor sitting at Father's desk in your study, in case I need him. Also, I've had my lawyers make over most of my remaining inheritance to Keith. I don't think you knew that. What's left has all been transferred to a bank on Dominica, and if I die it goes to the Institute. You won't be able to touch it, nor touch Keith's portion either, not even if I die. And I will die, Seena, soon, if I don't start eating and stop taking the program's drugs. I'll just burn out body and brain both. You've guessed that I'm close to that, but you haven't guessed how close. Now I'm telling you. I can't handle the stresses of the twin trance much longer."

I just went on holding her glass, arm extended, unable to move.

"You gambled that you could destroy one component in the chain of my experiment at the Institute by confusing my twin sexually. Well, you won. Now *I'm* making a gamble. I'm gambling my life that you can undo what you did with Keith, and without his knowing that I made you. You said he's not stupid and his impotency comes from being unable to handle the drug program; perhaps you're partly right. But he is me—*me,* Seena—and I know you've thought I was stupid all my life, because I wanted things you don't understand. Now Keith wants them, too—it was inevitable that he would—and you're going to undo whatever is standing in his way. I had to fight myself free all my life of your bullying, but Keith doesn't have that kind of time. Because if you don't undo what you caused, I'm going to go ahead with the twin trance anyway—the *twin trance,* Seena—without the sexual component and without letting Bohentin know just how much greater the strain is in trance than he thinks it is. He doesn't know—he doesn't have a twin—and neither do the doctors. But I know, and if I push much farther I'm going to eventually die at it. *Soon* eventually. When I do, all your scheming to get me out of there really will have failed and you'll be alone with whatever it is you're so afraid of. But I don't think you'll let that happen.

"I think that instead you'll undo what you did to Keith, so that the experiment can have one last real chance. And in return, after that one chance, I'll agree to come home, to Boston or here to New York, for one year.

"That's my gamble."

She was looking at me from eyes empty of all tears, a Devrie I had not ever seen before. She meant it, every demented word, and she would do it. I wanted to scream at her, to scream a jumble of suicide and moral blackmail and warped perceptions and outrage, but the words that came out of my mouth came out in a whisper.

"What in God's name is worth *that?*"

Shockingly, she laughed, a laugh of more power than her wasted frame could have contained. Her face glowed, and the glow looked both exalted and insane. "You said it, Seena—in God's name. To finally know. To *know,* beyond the fogginess of faith, that we're not alone in the universe ... Faith should not mean fogginess." She laughed again, this time defensively, as if she knew how she sounded to me. "You'll do it, Seena." It was not a question. She took my hand.

"You would *kill* yourself?"

"No. I would die trying to reach God. It's not the same thing."

"I never bullied you, Devrie."

She dropped my hand. "All my life, Seena. And on into now. But all of your bullying and your scorn would look rather stupid, wouldn't it, if there really can be proved to exist a rational basis for what you laughed at all those years!"

We looked at each other, sisters, across the abyss of the pale sofa, and then suddenly away. Neither of us dared speak.

My plane landed on Dominica by night. Devrie had gone two days before me, returning with her doctor and guards on the same day she had left, as I had on my previous visit. I had never seen the island at night. The tropical greenery, lush with that faintly menacing suggestion of plant life gone wild, seemed to close in on me. The velvety darkness seemed to smell of ginger and flowers and the sea—all too strong, too blandly sensual, like an overdone perfume ad. At the hotel it was better; my room was on the second floor, above the dark foliage, and did not face the sea. Nonetheless, I stayed inside all that evening, all that darkness, until I could go the next day to the Institute of the Biological Hope.

"Hello, Seena."

"Keith. You look—"

"Rotten," he finished, and waited. He did not smile. Although he had lost some weight, he was nowhere near as skeletal as Devrie, and it gave me a pang I did not analyze to see his still-healthy body in the small gray room where last I had seen hers. His head was shaved, and without the curling brown hair he looked sterner, prematurely middle-aged. That, too, gave me a strange emotion, although it was not why he looked rotten. The worst was his eyes. Red-veined, watery, the sockets already a little sunken, they held the sheen of a man who was not forgiving somebody for something. Me? Himself? Devrie? I had lain awake all night, schooling myself for this insane interview, and still I did not know what to say. What does one say to persuade a man to sexual potency with one's sister so that her life might be saved? I felt ridiculous, and frightened, and—I suddenly realized the name of my strange emotion—humiliated. How could I even start to slog toward what I was supposed to reach?

"How goes the Great Experiment?"

"Not as you described it," he said, and we were there already. I looked at him evenly.

"You can't understand why I presented the Institute in the worst possible light."

"I can understand that."

"Then you can't understand why I bedded you, knowing about Bohentin's experiment."

"I can also understand that."

Something was wrong. Keith answered me easily, without restraint, but with conflict gritty beneath his voice, like sand beneath blowing grass. I stepped closer, and he flinched. But his expression did not change.

"Keith. What is this about? What am I doing here? Devrie said you couldn't ... that you were impotent with her, confused enough about who and what ..." I trailed off. He still had not changed expression.

I said quietly, "It was a simplistic idea in the first place. Only someone as simplistic as Devrie..." Only someone as simplistic as Devrie would think you could straighten out impotency by talking about it for a few hours. I turned to go, and I had gotten as far as laying my hand on the doorknob before Keith grasped my arm. Back to him, I squeezed my eyes shut. What in God would I have *done* if he had not stopped me?

"It's not what Devrie thinks!" With my back to him, not able to see his middle-aged baldness but only to hear the anguish in his voice, he again seemed young, uncertain, the boy I had bought coffee for in Indian Falls. I kept my back to him, and my voice carefully toneless.

"What is it, then, Keith? If not what Devrie thinks?"

"I don't know!"

"But you do know what it's not? It's not being confused about who is your sister and who your mother and who you're willing to have sex with in front of a room full of researchers?"

"No." His voice had gone hard again, but his hand stayed on my arm. "At first, yes. The first time. But, Seena—I *felt* it. *Almost.* I almost felt the presence, and then all the rest of the confusion—it didn't seem as important anymore. Not the confusion between you and Devrie."

I whirled to face him. "You mean God doesn't care whom you fuck if it gets you closer to fucking with Him."

He looked at me hard then—at me, not at his own self-absorption. His reddened eyes widened a little. "Why, Seeny—*you* care. You told me the brother-sister thing didn't matter anymore—but *you* care."

Did I? I didn't even know anymore. I said, "But then, I'm not deluding myself that it's all for the old Kingdom and the Glory."

"Glory," he repeated musingly, and finally let go of my arm. I couldn't tell what he was thinking.

"Keith. This isn't getting us anywhere."

"Where do you want to get?" he said in the same musing tone. "Where did any of you, starting with your father, want to get with me? Glory ... glory."

Standing this close to him, seeing close up the pupils of his eyes and smelling close up the odor of his sweat, I finally realized what I should have seen all along: he was glowing. He was of course constantly on Bohentin's program of neurotransmitter manipulation, but the same chemicals that made the experiments possible also raised the threshold of both frankness and suggestibility. I guessed it must be a little like the looseness of being drunk, and I wondered if perhaps Bohentin might have deliberately raised the dosage before letting this interview take place. But no, Bohentin wouldn't be aware of the bargain Devrie and I had struck; she would not have told him. The whole bizarre situation was hers alone, and Keith's drugged musings a fortunate side effect I would have to capitalize on.

"Where do you think my father wanted to get with you?" I asked him gently.

"Immortality. Godhead. The man who created Adam and Eve."

He was becoming maudlin. "Hardly 'the man,'" I pointed out. "My father was only one of a team of researchers. And the same results were being obtained independently in California."

"Results. I am a 'result.' What *do you* think he wanted, Seena?"

"Scientific knowledge of cell development. An objective truth."

"That's all Devrie wants."

"To compare bioengineering to some mystic quest—"

"Ah, but if the mystic quest is given a laboratory answer? Then it, too, becomes a scientific truth. You really hate that idea, don't you, Seena? You hate science validating anything you define as non-science."

I said stiffly, "That's rather an oversimplification."

"Then what do you hate?"

"I hate the risk to human bodies and human minds. To Devrie. To you."

"How nice of you to include me," he said, smiling. "And what do you think Devrie wants?"

"Sensation. Romantic religious emotion. To be all roiled up inside with delicious esoterica."

He considered this. "Maybe."

"And is that what you want as well, Keith? You've asked what everyone else wants. What do you want?"

"I want to feel at home in the universe. As if I belonged in it. And I never have."

He said this simply, without self-consciousness, and the words

themselves were predictable enough for his age—even banal.
There was nothing in the words that could account for my eyes
suddenly filling with tears. "And 'scientifically' reaching God
would do that for you?"

"How do I know until I try it? Don't cry, Seena."

"I'm not!"

"All right," he agreed softly. "You're not crying." Then he
added, without changing tone, "I am more like you than like
Devrie."

"How so?"

"I think that Devrie has always felt that she belongs in the
universe. She only wants to find the ... the coziest corner of it
to curl up in. Like a cat. The coziest corner to curl up in is
God's lap. Aren't you surprised that I should be more like you
than like the person I was cloned from?"

"No," I said. "Harder upbringing than Devrie's. I told you that
first day: cloning is only delayed twinning."

He threw back his head and laughed, a sound that chilled my
spine. Whatever his conflict was, we were moving closer.

"Oh no, Seena. You're so wrong. It's more than delayed twinning, all right. You can't buy a real twin. You either have one
or you don't. But you can buy yourself a clone. Bought, paid
for, kept on the books along with all the rest of the glassware
and holotanks and electron microscopes. You said so yourself,
in your apartment, when you first told me about Devrie and the
Institute. 'Money. She'd buy you.' And you were right, of course.
Your father bought me, and she did, and you did. But of course
you two women couldn't have bought if I hadn't been selling."

He was smiling still. Stupid—we had both been stupid, Devrie
and I, we had both been looking in the wrong place, misled
by our separate blinders-on training in the laboratory brain. My
training had been scientific, hers humanistic, and so I looked at
Freud and she looked at Oedipus, and we were equally stupid.
How did the world look to a man who did not deal in laboratory brains, a man raised in a grittier world in which limits were
not what the mind was capable of but what the bankbook
would stand? "Your genes are too expensive for you to claim
except as a beggar; your sisters are too expensive for you to
claim except as a beggar; God is too expensive for you to claim
except as a beggar." To a less romantic man it would not have

mattered, but a less romantic man would not have come to the Institute. What dark humiliations and resentments did Keith feel when he looked at Devrie, the self who was buyer and not bought?

Change the light you shine onto a mind, and you see different neural patterns, different corridors, different forests of trees grown in soil you could not have imagined. Run that soil through your fingers and you discover different pebbles, different sand, different leaf mold from the decay of old growths. Devrie and I had been hacking through the wrong forest.

Not Oedipus, but Marx.

Quick lines of attack came to me. Say: Keith it's a job like any other with high-hazard pay why can't you look at it like that, a very dangerous and well-paid job for which you've been hired by just one more eccentric member of the monied class. Say: You're entitled to the wealth you're our biological brother damn it consider it rationally as a kinship entitlement. Say: Don't be so nicey-nice it's a tough world out there and if Devrie's giving it away take it don't be an impractical chump.

I said none of that. Instead I heard myself saying, coolly and with a calm cruelty, "You're quite right. You were bought by Devrie, and she is now using her own purchase for her own ends. You're a piece of equipment bought and paid for. Unfortunately, there's no money in the account. It has all been a grand sham."

Keith jerked me to face him with such violence that my neck cracked. "What are you saying?"

The words came as smoothly, as plausibly, as if I had rehearsed them. I didn't even consciously plan them: how can you plan a lie you do not know you will need? I slashed through this forest blind, but the ground held under my feet.

"Devrie told me that she has signed over most of her inheritance to you. What she didn't know, because I haven't yet told her, is that she doesn't have control of her inheritance any longer. It's not hers. I control it. I had her declared mentally incompetent on the grounds of violent suicidal tendencies and had myself made her legal guardian. She no longer has the legal right to control her fortune. A doctor observed her when she came to visit me in New York. So the transfer of her fortune to you is invalid."

"The lawyers who gave me the papers to sign—"

"Will learn about the New York action this week," I said smoothly. How much inheritance law did Keith know? Probably very little. Neither did I, and I invented furiously; it only needed to *sound* plausible. "The New York courts only handed down their decision recently, and Dominican judicial machinery, like everything else in the tropics, moves slowly. But the ruling will hold, Keith. Devrie does not control her own money, and you're a pauper again. But *I* have something for you. Here. An airline ticket back to Indian Falls. You're a free man. Poor, but free. The ticket is in your name, and there's a check inside it—that's from me. You've earned it, for at least trying to aid poor Devrie. But now you're going to have to leave her to me. I'm now her legal guardian."

I held the ticket out to him. It was wrapped in its airline folder; my own name as passenger was hidden. Keith stared at it, and then at me.

I said softly, "I'm sorry you were cheated. Devrie didn't mean to. But she has no money, now, to offer you. You can go. Devrie's my burden now."

His voice sounded strangled. "To remove from the Institute?"

"I never made any secret of wanting her out. Although the legal papers for that will take a little time to filter through the Dominican courts. She wouldn't go except by force, so force is what I'll get. Here."

I thrust the ticket folder at him. He made no move to take it, and I saw from the hardening of his face—my face, Devrie's face—the moment when Devrie shifted forests in his mind. Now she was without money, without legal control of her life, about to be torn from the passion she loved most. The helpless underdog. The orphaned woman, poor and cast out, in need of protection from the powerful one who had seized her fortune.

Not Marx, but Cervantes.

"You would do that? To your own sister?"

Anything for a sister. I said bitterly, "Of course I would."

"She's not mentally incompetent!"

"Isn't she?"

"No!"

I shrugged. "The courts say she is."

Keith studied me, resolve hardening around him. I thought of certain shining crystals, that will harden around any stray piece of grit. Now that I was succeeding in convincing him, my lies hurt—or perhaps what hurt was how easily he believed them.

"Are you sure, Seena," he said, "that *you* aren't just trying a grab for Devrie's fortune?"

I shrugged again, and tried to make my voice toneless. "I want her out of here. I don't want her to die."

"Die? What makes you think she would die?"

"She looks—"

"She's nowhere near dying," Keith said angrily—his anger a release, so much that it hardly mattered at what. "Don't you think I can tell in twin trance what her exact physical state is? And don't you know how much control the trance gives each twin over the bodily processes of the other? Don't you even know that? Devrie isn't anywhere near dying. And I'd pull her out of trance if she were." He paused, looking hard at me. "Keep your ticket, Seena."

I repeated mechanically, "You can leave now. There's no money." *Devrie had lied to me.*

"That wouldn't leave her with any protection at all, would it?" he said levelly. When he grasped the doorknob to leave, the tendons in his wrist stood out clearly, strong and taut. I did not try to stop his going.

Devrie had lied to me. With her lie, she had blackmailed me into yet another lie to Keith. The twin trance granted control, in some unspecified way, to each twin's body; the trance I had pioneered might have resulted in eight deaths unknowingly inflicted on each other out of who knows what dark forests in eight fumbling minds. Lies, blackmail, death, more lies.

Out of these lies they were going to make scientific truth. Through these forests they were going to search for God.

"Final clearance check of holotanks," an assistant said formally. "Faraday cage?"

"Optimum."

"External radiation?"

"Cleared," said the man seated at the console of the first tank.

"Cleared," said the woman seated at the console of the second.

"Microradiation?"

"Cleared."

"Cleared."

"Personnel radiation, Class A?"

"Cleared."

"Cleared."

On it went, the whole tedious and crucial procedure, until both tanks had been cleared and focused, the fluid adjusted, tested, adjusted again, tested again. Bohentin listened patiently, without expression, but I, standing to the side of him and behind the tanks, saw the nerve at the base of his neck and just below the hairline pulse in some irregular rhythm of its own. Each time the nerve pulsed, the skin rose slightly from under his collar. I kept my eyes on that syncopated crawling of flesh, and felt tension prickle over my own skin like heat.

Three-quarters of the lab, the portion where the holotanks and other machinery stood, was softly dark, lit mostly from the glow of console dials and the indirect track lighting focused on the tanks. Standing in the gloom were Bohentin, five other scientists, two medical doctors—and me. Bohentin had fought my being allowed there, but in the end he had had to give in. I had known too many threatening words not in generalities but in specifics: reporters' names, drug names, cloning details, twin-trance tragedy, anorexia symptoms, bioengineering amendment. He was not a man who much noticed either public opinion or relatives' threats, but no one else outside his Institute knew so many so specific words—some knew some of the words, but only I had them all. In the end he had focused on me his cold, brilliant eyes, and given permission for me to witness the experiment that involved my sister.

I was going to hold Devrie to her bargain. I was not going to believe anything she told me without witnessing it for myself.

Half the morning passed in technical preparation. Somewhere Devrie and Keith, the human components of this costly detection circuit, were separately being brought to the apex of brain activity. Drugs, biofeedback, tactile and auditory and kinaesthetic stimulation—all carefully calculated for the maximum increase of both the number of neurotransmitters firing signals through the synapses of the brain and of the speed at which the signals raced. The more rapid the transmission through certain pathways, the more intense both perception and feeling. Some neurotransmitters, under this pressure, would alter molecular structure into natural hallucinogens; that reaction had to be controlled. Meanwhile other drugs, other biofeedback techniques, would depress the body's natural enzymes designed to either reabsorb excess transmitters or to reduce the rate at which they fired. The number and speed of neurotransmitters in Keith's and Devrie's brains would mount, and mount, and mount, all natural chemical barriers removed. The two of them would enter the lab with their whole brains—rational cortex, emotional limbic, right and left brain functions—simultaneously aroused to an unimaginable degree. *Simultaneously.* They would be feeling as great a "rush" as a falling skydiver, as great a glow as a cocaine user, as great a mental clarity and receptivity as a da Vinci whose brush is guided by all the integrated visions of his unconscious mind. They would be white-hot.

Then they would hit each other with the twin trance.

The quarter of the lab which Keith and Devrie would use was softly and indirectly lit, though brighter than the rest. It consisted of a raised, luxuriantly padded platform, walls and textured pillows in a pink whose component wavelengths had been carefully calculated, temperature in a complex gradient producing precise convection flows over the skin. The man and woman in that womb-colored, flesh-stimulating environment would be able to see us observers standing in the gloom behind the holotanks only as vague shapes. When the two doors opened and Devrie and Keith moved onto the platform, I knew that they would not even try to distinguish who stood in the lab. Looking at their faces, that looked only at each other, I felt my heart clutch.

They were naked except for the soft helmets that both attached hundreds of needles to nerve clumps just below the skin and also held the earphones through which Bohentin controlled the music that swelled the cathedrals of their skulls. "Cathedrals"—from their faces, transfigured to the ravished ecstasy found in paintings of medieval saints, that was the right word. But here the ecstasy was controlled, understood, and I saw with a sudden rush of pain at old memories that I could recognize the exact moment when Keith and Devrie locked onto each other with the twin trance. I recognized it, with my own more bitter hyperclarity, in their eyes, as I recognized the cast of concentration that came over their features, and the intensity of their absorption. The twin trance. They clutched each other's hands, faces inches apart, and suddenly I had to look away.

Each holotank held two whorls of shifting colors, the outlines clearer and the textures more sharply delineated than any previous holographs in the history of science. Keith's and Devrie's perceptions of each other's presence. The whorls went on clarifying themselves, separating into distinct and mappable layers, as on the platform Keith and Devrie remained frozen, all their energies focused on the telepathic trance. Seconds passed, and then minutes. And still, despite the clarity of the holographs in the tank, a clarity that fifteen years earlier I would have given my right hand for, I sensed that Keith and Devrie were holding back, were deliberately confining their unimaginable perceptiveness to each other's radiant energy, in the same way that water is confined behind a dam to build power.

But how could *I* be sensing that? From a subliminal "reading" of the mapped perceptions in the holotanks? Or from something else?

More minutes passed. Keith and Devrie stayed frozen, facing each other, and over her skeletal body and his stronger one a flush began to spread, rosy and slow, like heat tide rising.

"Jesus H. Christ," said one of the medical doctors, so low that only I, standing directly behind her, could have heard. It was not a curse, nor a prayer, but some third possibility, unnameable.

Keith put one hand on Devrie's thigh. She shuddered. He drew her down to the cushions on the platform and they began to caress each other, not frenzied, not in the exploring way of lovers but with a deliberation I have never experienced outside a research lab, a slow care that implied that worlds of interpretation hung on each movement. Yet the effect was not of coldness nor detachment but of intense involvement, of tremendous energy joyously used, of creating each other's bodies right then, there under each other's hands. They were *working,* and oblivious to all but their work. But if it was a kind of creative work, it was also a kind of primal innocent eroticism, and, watching, I felt my own heat begin to rise. "Innocent"—but if innocence is unknowingness, there was nothing innocent about it at all. Keith and Devrie knew and controlled each heartbeat, and I felt

the exact moment, when they let their sexual energies, added
to all the other neural energies, burst the dam and flood outward in wave after wave, expanding the scope of each brain's
perceptions, inundating the artificially walled world.

A third whorl formed in one of the holotanks.

It formed suddenly: one second nothing, the next brightness.
But then it wavered, faded a bit. After a few moments it brightened slightly, a diffused golden haze, before again fading. On
the platform Keith gasped, and I guessed he was having to shift
his attention between perceiving the third source of radiation
and keeping up the erotic version of the twin trance. His biofeedback techniques were less experienced than Devrie's, and
the male erection more fragile. But then he caught the rhythm,
and the holograph brightened.

It seemed to me that the room brightened as well, although
no additional lights came on and the consoles glowed no
brighter. Sweat poured off the researchers. Bohentin leaned forward, his neck muscle tautening toward the platform as if it
were his will and not Keith/Devrie's that strained to perceive
that third presence recorded in the tank. I thought, stupidly, of
mythical intermediaries: Merlyn never made king, Moses never
reaching the Promised Land. Intermediaries—and then it became impossible to think of anything at all.

Devrie shuddered and cried out. Keith's orgasm came a moment later, and with it a final roil of neural activity so strong
the two primary whorls in each holotank swelled to fill the tank
and inundate the third. At the moment of breakthrough Keith
screamed, and in memory it seems as if the scream was what
tore through the last curtain—that is nonsense. How loud
would microbes have to scream to attract the attention of
giants? How loud does a knock on the door have to be to pull
a sleeper from the alien world of dreams?

The doctor beside me fell to her knees. The third presence—or some part of it—swirled all around us, racing along
our own unprepared synapses and neurons, and what swirled
and raced was astonishment. A golden, majestic astonishment.
We had finally attracted Its attention, finally knocked with
enough neural force to be just barely heard—and It was astonished that we could, or did exist. The slow rise of that powerful
astonishment within the shielded lab was like the slow swinging

around of the head of a great beast to regard some butterfly it has barely glimpsed from the corner of one eye. But this was no beast. As Its attention swung toward us, pain exploded in my skull—the pain of sound too loud, lights too bright, charge too high. My brain was burning on overload. There came one more flash of insight—wordless, pattern without end—and the sound of screaming. Then, abruptly, the energy vanished.

Bohentin, on all fours, crawled toward the holotanks. The doctor lay slumped on the floor; the other doctor had already reached the platform and its two crumpled figures. Someone was crying, someone else shouting. I rose, fell, dragged myself to the side of the platform and then could not climb it. I could not climb the platform. Hanging with two hands on the edge, hearing the voice crying as my own, I watched the doctor bend shakily to Keith, roll him off Devrie to bend over her, turn back to Keith.

Bohentin cried, "The tapes are intact!"

"Oh God oh God oh God oh God oh God," someone moaned, until abruptly she stopped. I grasped the flesh-colored padding on top of the platform and pulled myself up onto it.

Devrie lay unconscious, pulse erratic, face cast in perfect bliss. The doctor breathed into Keith's mouth—what strength could the doctor himself have left?—and pushed on the naked chest. Breathe, push, breathe, push. The whole length of Keith's body shuddered; the doctor rocked back on his heels; Keith breathed.

"It's all on tape!" Bohentin cried. "It's all *on tape!*"

"Goddamn you to hell," I whispered to Devrie's blissful face. "It didn't even know we were there!"

Her eyes opened. I had to lean close to hear her answer.

"But now ... we know He ... is there."

She was too weak to smile. I looked away from her, away from that face, out into the tumultuous emptiness of the lab, anywhere.

They will try again.

Devrie has been asleep, fed by glucose solution through an IV, for fourteen hours. I sit near her bed, frowned at by the nurse, who can see my expression as I stare at my sister. Somewhere in another bed Keith is sleeping yet again. His rest is more fitful than Devrie's; she sinks into sleep as into warm water, but he cannot. Like me, he is afraid of drowning.

An hour ago he came into Devrie's room and grasped my hand. "How could It—He—It not have been aware that we existed? Not even have *known*?"

I didn't answer him.

"You felt it too, Seena, didn't you? The others say they could, so you must have too. It ... created us in some way. No, that's wrong. How could It create us and not *know*?"

I said wearily, "Do *we* always know what we've created?" and Keith glanced at me sharply. But I had not been referring to my father's work in cloning.

"Keith. What's a *Thysania africana?*"

"A what?"

"Think of us," I said, "as just one more biological side effect. One type of being acts, and another type of being comes into existence. Man stages something like the African Horror, and in doing so he creates whole new species of moths and doesn't even discover they exist until long afterward. If man can do it, why not God? And why should He be any more aware of it than we are?"

Keith didn't like that. He scowled at me, and then looked at Devrie's sleeping face: Devrie's sleeping bliss.

"Because she is a fool," I said savagely, "and so are you. You won't leave it alone, will you? Having been noticed by It once, you'll try to be noticed by It again. Even though she promised me otherwise, and even if it kills you both."

Keith looked at me a long time, seeing clearly—finally—the nature of the abyss between us, and its dimensions. But I already knew neither of us could cross. When at last he spoke, his voice held so much compassion that I hated him. "Seena. Seena, love. There's no more doubt now, don't you see? Now rational belief is no harder than rational doubt. Why are you so afraid to even believe?"

I left the room. In the corridor I leaned against the wall, palms spread flat against the tile, and closed my eyes. It seemed to me that I could hear wings, pale and fragile, beating against glass.

They will try again. For the sake of sure knowledge that the universe is not empty, Keith and Devrie and all the others like

their type of being will go on pushing their human brains beyond what the human brain has evolved to do, go on fluttering
their wings against that biological window. For the sake of sure
knowledge: belief founded on experiment and not on faith. And
the Other: being/alien/God? It, too, may choose to initiate contact, if It can and now that It knows we are here. Perhaps It
will seek to know *us,* and even beyond the laboratory Devrie
and Keith may find any moment of heightened arousal subtly
invaded by a shadowy Third. Will they sense It, hovering just
beyond consciousness, if they argue fiercely or race a sailboat
in rough water or make love? How much arousal will it take,
now, for them to sense those huge wings beating on the *other*
side of the window?

And windows can be broken.

Tomorrow I will fly back to New York. To my museum, to
my exhibits, to my moths under permaplex, to my empty apartment, where I will keep the heavy drapes drawn tightly across
the glass.

For—oh God—all the rest of my life.

# Saint Theresa of the Aliens

## by James Patrick Kelly

*One of the memorable aspects of a Catholic education is the study of lives of the saints, all of them falling into the familiar pattern ... the perfect childhood leading to the struggle against sin and torture, followed by the ultimate triumph in Heaven. These stories are intended to uplift, to inspire, but they are also, by their nature, a bit vague. What sort of world, exactly, did Saint Agnes inhabit? Who were Saint John Bosco's classmates?*

*In fact, what would it be like to actually know a saint, like Terry Burelli, aka Saint Theresa of the Aliens?*

*James Patrick Kelly is the product of a Catholic education. Born in Mineola, New York, in 1951, he attended St. Patrick's Elementary School, Stamford Catholic High School, and the University of Notre Dame. He later worked in public relations until turning to writing full-time in 1975.*

*In addition to many stories published in* The Magazine of Fantasy and Science Fiction *and* Isaac Asimov's Science Fiction Magazine, *he is the author of the novels* Planet of Whispers *(1984) and* Look into the Sun *(1989). He collaborated with John Kessel on* Freedom Beach *(1985).*

*S*o now they want to make her a saint. Her cult is spreading. Cures are claimed. The Purgers are taking over the Church; they want one of their own to be the first saint of the new century. The Congregation of Rites in Rome has named an advocate of the cause to prepare a brief for her sanctity. He has already asked me for an interview. I would rather talk to the promoter of the faith. The priest they call the devil's advocate.

Terry Burelli—Theresa to the mythmakers—did not have many friends while she was alive. I think it was because she was such a sad person. What I remember most about her is the sigh. She had no need of words to sum up her view of life. The sigh was enough. Even when she smiled it was as if she were expecting a disappointment. I never heard her laugh out loud; maybe she regarded humor as an occasion of sin. When she spoke in her soft, sighing voice people worried she was about to cry. Then she would shock them with her ferocious opinions.

My wife was her first cousin. When I met Nicole, she and Terry were roommates at St. Mary's College. I thought them an unlikely pair; at the time they seemed very different. Although both were attractive, Terry's beauty was cool and sterile; she was about as watchable as a plaster Virgin. Nicole and I would spend hours just looking at each other in wondrous silence. Both women were small-town Catholics, yet while Nicole was fascinated by the great world that the Church never mentioned, Terry was already building psychic walls to protect herself from it. Terry was a politician; she became chairperson of the local right-to-life chapter, forced the administration to blackout all X-rated movies ordered from telelink by the film club, and helped to set up a student-run soup kitchen in South Bend's slum. She dragged Nicole and me out of our apathy on occasion, although we much preferred being alone with each other to promoting her causes.

I wanted Nicole so much that I convinced myself that she was nothing like her dour cousin. We were in love; I thought that was enough to make a successful marriage. After school, we moved to Wynnewood, a suburb of Philadelphia, and each of us found interesting work. I became a staff writer and then an editor for InfoLine, one of the information utilities on tele-link. Often as not I worked from my home terminal and had supper ready for Nicole when she came home from her job teaching history at Lower Marion High School. Our world was very small; it included just the two of us. We watched a lot of telelink and smoked hybrid pot that we grew ourselves and planted flower gardens and played pacball and drank daiquiries in video bars; all the soothing frivolities of life that people like Terry had no use for. It seemed to both of us that we were happy.

But Terry would not leave us alone. Our affluence offended her, although she was not at all shy about asking for money for her causes. Our indifference offended her more. She visited often and insisted on giving us her "reports from the real world," as she called them, tales of hunger and decadence and corruption. I can see her now, sitting on the modular couch in our living room, holding forth with quiet intensity about some misfit whose soul she coveted for the Lord.

"Thirteen years old." She would rub the crucifix hanging around her neck with thumb and forefinger. "She earns two hundred dollars a night and she needs every cent of it to pay for screamers. The only adults she knows are the johns; her only god comes out of a needle. And they call it a victimless crime. Your senator is cosponsoring the bill, Sam. You're in telelink; can't you do anything?"

Somehow, it was always my fault. By this time Nicole would have been spiritually battered into a corner of the couch. She would clutch knees to chest and nod, nod, nod, eyes blank. My best move would be to steer the conversation onto a more cheery topic. "What ever happened to so-and-so?" I would say, or "What should we watch tonight?" or "Where should we go for supper?" I did not mind sounding like a fool; I thought I was protecting Nicole.

Often as not Terry would ignore these gambits and continue on with her condemnations of the monsters who had inflicted modern civilization on the world. Once, though, she turned on me in a fury. "Sam, don't you realize that you could get in your fancy car right now, drive downtown and find people starving? What difference does it make to them if you can't order the Marx Brothers on the goddamned telelink?"

"People are born to die." I should have realized when she took the Lord's name in vain that she was out of control. I should have excused myself and spent a few minutes in the bathroom washing my hands. I did not. "God made them that way," I said.

She sighed. It was a sigh that acknowledged that I was the enemy but because God commanded it she would forgive me.

I did not much care to be condescended to in my own living room. "Everything is so simple, isn't it? If only the immoral louts like me would wake up and see the light. If only we would stop writing news, building cities, designing new computers. If only we would tear it all down and bring back the Middle Ages so that everybody in the world was Catholic and wretched together. Solidarity of misery, that's the ticket! Then maybe we could all pray and God would take care of us like he takes care of the birds of the air or the lilies ..."

"Shut up, Sam." Nicole sounded frightened. "You're drunk."

In fact, I had only had three glasses of wine but she was right. I was intoxicated with bitterness, high on blasphemy. Like many lapsed Catholics I had a kind of philosophical blood lust for the delusions of the faithful. Still, I had only been trying to protect Nicole and for my efforts had earned her rebuke. I was furious.

"Maybe you two would like to get down on your knees and pray for me? You'll excuse me if I don't stick around to watch. I'm afraid I might throw up." I thought I saw a smile tugging at Terry's perpetual frown; I was so mad I wanted to hit her. Instead I grabbed the half-empty bottle of Pocono riesling and retreated to the telelink room.

The Catholic Church has no answer to the problem of evil, therefore I cannot possibly ... Oh, screw the problem of evil. Screw all the dusty ideas, the dry arguments for and against. There is no single moment when you lose your faith; it crumbles under a series of little shocks. An alcoholic priest preaches the "just war" doctrine from the Sunday pulpit. Your friend dies of leukemia and God pays no attention. A well-meaning nun tells you that thinking about sex is a sin. You realize the unspeakable cruelty of an eternal Hell. You read the Bible and then you look at the Church men have made from it. I lost my faith when I no longer needed ideas to comfort me. I had Nicole.

I remember that Nicole and I made love that night. Afterward, I tried to apologize for losing my temper. She hushed me. "It's all right, Sam," she said. "I understand. She scares me too."

That was just about the time that the aliens landed in Sverdlovsk.

It is hard now, after all that has happened, to remember how we all felt when we first heard the news. For years popular culture had prophesied the coming of aliens. Despite all the dark visions of monsters and cruel galactic empires, I think for the most part we longed to meet another intelligent species. We hoped they would answer all our questions, solve all our problems. As Nicole said, we were looking for a shortcut to paradise. We were the new Israelites, waiting for messiahs from space.

None of us expected that the messiahs would be communists. That was, I think, the hardest thing of all to accept. Not only had the aliens chosen to land in the USSR, but they actually called themselves communists. It was, they said, the best translation of their own name for themselves. Of course, the name has never really caught on in this country; we are still calling them "the aliens." A barely civil name. A name that neatly summarizes our attitude toward them.

Despite what you hear, the aliens do not think much of Marx and Engels and they are only mildly sympathetic to Lenin. Yes, they hold all property in common, their economy is planned, they live in collectives. They do not expect their world state to wither away however, and they are by no means revolutionaries. You have only to look at their record since landing to see that they mean to change us by example, not by force. But still the preachers rail and the politicians lecture and the people do not understand.

It was six months after Sverdlovsk before they even bothered to visit the United States. I had the honor, if you can call it that, of representing InfoLine at the first English-language press conference ever given by an alien. Of course, no one has ever really seen an alien since they never come out of their bullet-shaped jump ships. The squat hairless monkeys that they call their "bodies" are in fact remotely controlled mechanisms. The aliens fear the hostility of the Earth's environment and its inhabitants. I have seen and even talked to these "bodies"; like most people I accept the mechanism and rarely think about the mysterious and distant alien controlling it.

As an historic disaster, that press conference has been studied and restudied. Yet to this day I have difficulty remembering it, no doubt because it was so closely linked with a personal disaster. I could not sleep the night before; I was trying to find some middle ground between awe of the aliens and patriotic suspicion of their motives. Sometime after midnight I got out of bed. I must have woken Nicole as I prowled around the house; she came out into the kitchen to fix us both some hot cocoa. I was sorry to have disturbed her but glad for the company.

"Nervous?" she said.

I shrugged. If I admitted it to her I would have to admit it to myself.

She set a steaming cup in front of me. "I heard someone on the telelink saying today that it's going to take more than a press conference to make up for what they've done wrong already. He said that we shouldn't be listening to them, they should be listening to us."

"Morris. He's an asshole."

"Still, most people act as if they know everything just because they have starships. What if they don't? Maybe what you should do is get up and ask them who's buried in Grant's Tomb? They'd never figure it out." She chuckled. "You'd go down as the man who stumped the aliens."

"Go down, all right." Still, it was worth a smile at three o'clock in the morning. "Let's talk about something else."

She sipped her cocoa. "Terry called today. She's been asked to join the central council of the Brides of Christ. She doesn't know whether she wants to take the vows or not."

"That idiot. What she needs is a real man to sleep with, not a picture of the Sacred Heart of Jesus."

Nicole stiffened. "That's your prescription, Doctor? Get yourself some nice warm sex and call in the morning?"

All the warning signs were up but I refused to see them. "Never failed yet," I said with a leer. "Let's not talk about Terry. We always end up fighting."

"OK. Let's talk about us." She considered. "I missed my period. I wasn't going to tell you until after the press conference but..."

"You're pregnant? But I've been taking my pills."

"I don't know yet. I have a doctor's appointment Wednesday."

"Nicole, those pills are ninety-nine and nine tenths."

"I know. Do you believe in miracles?"

I think I must have laughed at that. "Are you going to have it?"

"What do you mean, have it?" In that moment she was the only alien in the world. Her voice made me shiver.

"I mean that ... I mean there's a choice."

"What would you do?"

"I'll do what you want," I said.

"You mean you'll go along with what I want. Even if you don't really want a baby?"

"I didn't say that."

"You don't have to. Your face says it for you."

It was one of the few times I wished that Nicole was the kind of woman you read about in books, the kind who run out of rooms crying. Nicole never turned away from trouble. "Look, honey, it's late and you've just sprung a hell of a surprise on me. I love you. I can't help it if my face looks like oatmeal. Let's go back to bed and give it a rest until morning. We'll both be thinking clearer then." I offered her my hand.

She did not take it. "All right, Sam. But there's no choice involved, do you understand? No choice at all."

The argument flared for a week and was never satisfactorily extinguished, only left alone by mutual consent to smoulder. I know she thought I did not want the child; maybe she was right.

It was the first real fight we had ever had.

Needless to say, I was not at my best for the press conference. It was held in a bubbletent set up on a runway at Andrews Air Force Base. Nearby was the jump ship, which looked to me like a silo. A translucent dome atop a rotating red cylinder, perched on a fence of duraplas pickets. They say that the orbiting mother ship carries thirty in its hold; most of those had already landed in the USSR. Aliens can control their external bodies only at short distances, so most of our meetings have taken place on runways or other large open spaces.

The alien's name was Twisted Logic. Nicole believed that the aliens were twitting us in their use of the English language. That may well be, but the joke was the same in Russian, Spanish, and Chinese. Twisted Logic stood on a specially built platform; he was less than a meter tall. The President sat beside the alien looking like a man who has just gotten a pink slip in his pay envelope. Twisted Logic was red and shiny like a new plastic firetruck. He was not wearing any clothes, but then he did not need any, not having any sex. He requested, however, that we not refer to him as an "it." His tail wagged when he talked. The tail was a wonderful touch; how can you distrust a creature with a wagging tail?

You can still view the tape of that first press conference on InfoLine. Most of the early questions had to do with why the aliens chose to land in Russia. Twisted Logic explained the similarities between alien political philosophy and communism. He cited the Leonov space station and the two Mars expeditions as evidence that the Soviet space program was far more advanced than ours. He said that the aliens were worried about security here. When he mentioned the bombing of the U.N. there was a low chorus of groans and even some hisses. Although he spoke in a high-pitched cartoon voice and giggled a lot and was as cute as a puppy, talking about the destruction of the U.N. was unforgivable. You could feel the press corps turning against him.

"Mr. Logic," said one conservative pundit with heavy sarcasm, "Mr. Logic, isn't your avowed bias toward the Soviet Union a tacit endorsement of the suppression of human rights there? What conclusions would you expect the American people to draw from the current situation, sir?"

Twisted Logic giggled. "The rights of the one versus the rights of the many. We have resolved this conflict to our satisfaction. You have not. Infer only that we await your enlightenment and will instruct if asked."

"Why have you come to Earth?" called another.

He nodded. "Because you could not come to us."

"What's that supposed to mean?" someone shouted. The room filled with cries of derision.

"My response lacks content?" Twisted Logic looked for help to the President, who looked away. "Pardon. We bring ourselves to you because we are impatient for friends."

He might have made some friends had he continued in that vein. I tried to help him along. "Sir, we all recognize that your science is very advanced. Can we expect you to share your knowledge and technology with us? In particular, will you teach us to build starships of our own?"

"Exactly." He pointed at me and nodded again. "Exactly. The universe is very large and we are very small. Intelligence must coalesce to grow."

"Coalesce?" whispered the woman sitting next to me. "Coalesce?"

"Sir!" Father Estragon from the *Logos* channel waved at the alien. He was Terry Burelli's favorite telelink commentator. "Sir, as you may know, many of our most difficult problems on this planet arise out of religious factionalism. Would you comment please on your own religious beliefs?"

"I hold no such beliefs."

Estragon turned as white as his Roman collar. "You don't believe in God?"

"When there is no evidence," said Twisted Logic, tail wagging, "the theory is discarded."

In a bar afterward, Joe Perkins from the *Times* nicely summed up the play that the press conference was going to get. "Godless commies from outer space," he said.

There were no more press conferences. Access to Twisted Logic and the other aliens who eventually came to this country had to be approved by the State Department. Congress passed the Alien Secrets Act, which allowed instant classification of any alien remark deemed "controversial." It proved unenforceable once Twisted Logic took his space silo on a so-called "Goodwill Tour" of the world, a tour which was haunted by demonstrations, riots, and misunderstanding.

All things considered, the reaction from the Vatican was circumspect. They insisted on the eternal truth of Divine Revela-

tion and announced that the Pope would begin saying a special
Mass on the first Sunday of each month for the souls of the
aliens. For the most part the East did not care. The Buddhists
regarded the aliens as part of the general *anitya* of the universe;
they too would pass and so no action was indicated. Most Hin-
dus were willing to tolerate the alien heresy as long as it did
not lead to social upheavals. The reaction from Islam was less
tempered. There was talk of spiritual jihad, although how this
might be accomplished was not immediately clear. The Shiite
imams had a more concrete program: expel the aliens. The First
National Baptists and the Moonies and the Brides of Christ
agreed.

If the Brides of Christ ruled the world, there would be two
classes of citizens: Roman Catholics and the damned. Their battle plan in the war for souls is an abrupt about-face and a forced
march into the past. Do away with Vatican II, the Protestant
Reconciliation, secularized clergy. It seems that they are everywhere these days, working even the smallest crowds in their
severe black uniforms, an affectation of the habits formerly
worn by nuns and priests. Yes, men join too, although the sym-
bolism of a man marrying Christ is jarring. Fanatics do not
worry about these things. The Pope does not yet recognize
their activities but neither can he afford to interdict them. Millions have left the faith; groups like the Brides dominate the
remainder of his dwindling flock. He is already a prisoner of
their politics; soon they will be the Church. As Terry Burelli
marched through their ranks they came to the center of the
anti-alien coalition known as the Purgers.

Top management at InfoLine quickly discovered that the public's interest in the aliens was insatiable and so they spun off a
special-interest channel, AlienLine. I was put in charge of the
start-up. Although the assignment was a career coup, I could no
longer work from my home terminal or even from InfoLine's
headquarters in Philadelphia. I was often away from Nicole two
or three nights a week. It was a difficult time for both of us
because her pregnancy was not going well. For weeks it seemed
as if all she could keep down were unsalted crackers and water.
I tried as best I could to be the doting husband and proudly
expectant father but there was the subscription rate for

AlienLine to worry about and plane reservations to Washington and the problem of finding staff who could tell an adjective from an adverb. Sometimes I felt as if I had been split into two people, neither of whom liked the other very much.

Nicole and I had never really fought before she got pregnant; now we seemed to be making up for lost time. We argued about money, about politics, about the aliens, even about what to watch on telelink. We never shouted or slammed doors or cried; we just sniped at each other and then were horrified afterward.

"Wallace?" said Nicole. "Wallace?" She lay on the couch with her feet raised on a pile of pillows; she was having circulation problems. "Wallace is a fat man with suspenders smoking a cigar. Our son isn't going to wear suspenders, is he, Sam? And you're not fat."

"Walter?" I read from *Name Your Baby*. "Ward? Warren?"

"Wally." She chuckled. "What a lousy nickname." She shifted her weight restlessly; she could never seem to get comfortable. "I was thinking that Terry should be the godmother."

"What?" I closed the book.

"I know you don't like her that much, but . . ."

"Back up. Who said our kid was going to be baptized?"

She rolled over. "Sam, it couldn't hurt."

I tried to stay in control. "Damn it, Nicole, that's hypocrisy. I haven't been near a church for years and neither have you. We're not Catholics anymore—at least, *I'm* not. When the aliens say there is no God, I believe them. I don't understand you. Why are you so hot to jump back into a religion that most thinking people are scrambling to get out of?"

"Pregnancy does that to you. Makes you think about what makes a life. Makes you think about dying. Luckily you don't have to worry, Sam. The aliens have already done all your thinking for you." She sat up. "Name the kid after yourself for all I care. Except that she's going to be girl."

I sat beside her. "I'm sorry, Nicole." I kissed her. "I don't know what I can do, but I'm sorry."

Perhaps if the aliens *had* given us the cure for cancer or a wonder grain to end hunger or the secret of immortality, they might have won people like Nicole and Terry over. I think what we wanted most from them was freedom from all the biological traps the Earth had set for us. The aliens were not from Earth; they did not understand our biology nor were they particularly interested in it. A new physics was their principal gift, an arcane and rigorous discipline that ran counter to common intuition. Who cared that they had a detailed mathematical model for the first three minutes of the universe? Or that they had developed from that a theory which linked weak and strong atomic forces, the electromagnetic spectrum, and gravitation?

Of course, there was interstellar flight. Everyone expected a joyride to the stars. But the aliens could not just toss us the keys to a starship and wave good-bye. First we had to learn to control gravitrons and squeeze through the interstices in space-time. Then there was the difficult problem of life-support. It soon became clear that it would be years, perhaps decades, before the first ships would be ready. By the anniversary of the Sverdlovsk landing many Americans were disillusioned and bitter. Which was exactly what the rapidly growing Purge movement wanted.

Purge. Sometimes a word will distort under close scrutiny, and its various meanings will twist back upon themselves. There are spiritual purges, purifications of the soul. Dangerously high pressures can be relieved by purging. Certainly there were some in the Purge movement whose goals were positive. Yet the word also has a bloody legacy of intellectual and religious intolerance. Purge trials. Popes urging crusades to purge the Holy Lands. Hitler's unspeakable purge. I think these dark connotations come closer to the essence of the Purge movement. And it was as a Purger that Terry Burelli came to the attention of the world.

Assassins stalked the aliens. Someone threw a bomb into the presidential reviewing stand during a parade in Buenos Aires. Twisted Logic got a new body and Argentina got a new dictator. A splinter group from the Purge movement took credit.

Terry had the bad judgment to make one of her weekly tele-link calls just after the news broke.

"Nicole's taking a nap," I said. "She's having a bad day and I don't want to wake her up."

"Is she all right?" The old black-and-white camera at her terminal made Terry look as if she had not slept in days. "What does the doctor say?"

"She's pregnant, Terry. It's hard work. Call back later."

"What's the matter, Sam?" She did her imitation of a smile. "Are you angry at me again?"

"At you and at all the other goddamned Purgers. Where in the Bible does Christ say you can go around blowing up your enemies?"

"We have nothing to do with those people, Sam. Sister Laura denounced them; I wrote the press release myself."

"Yeah, sure. And how much will the Brides be giving to their legal defense?"

"We deplore their tactics, not their cause. Certainly they made a mistake. We don't believe in violence, Sam. There has to be a better way to purge the world of . . ."

"Good-bye, Terry." I was too disgusted to bother with the niceties; I had to cut her off.

Whatever the tactical disagreements within the Purge movement, all could agree that getting at the aliens to expel them was the major problem. They could intimidate the aliens' human collaborators. But the true enemies of the faith were safe within their well-guarded silos. How could they achieve their goal of purging the world of aliens? Terrorism and prayer proved equally unsatisfactory. Politics remained.

Pride was the key to their plan. Throughout the twentieth century Americans had believed themselves to be the most advanced people in the universe. Suddenly we were no longer first; that place was reserved for the aliens. Worse, we were not even second; with the aliens' help the Soviets had surpassed us. Wounded pride is intangible; you cannot build guns out of it. But with the proper manipulation of the facts, you can turn wounded pride into votes. The strategy was to purge the United States, then the other industrial states, the Third World, and then . . . Then a Purger will smile with the confidence of one who is fighting the Lord's fight. It is not hard to see behind that smile to the inevitability of a Third World War with the Soviets.

AlienLine had to cover the Purge movement. I wanted to expose them for what they were, but I was overruled. The Demographics Department was able to demonstrate that forty percent of our subscribers were either Purgers or sympathizers. Know thy enemy and all that. Since I was unable to match their propaganda with some of my own, I decided to let them indict themselves with their own words. God help me.

My idea was to stage a debate between an alien and a leader of the Purge movement. I fought for weeks to sell it to my own people at AlienLine, and then to top management at InfoLine. Finally I won permission to approach the State Department with the plan. I thought it might take several months to work out an agreement but State acted as if we were negotiating a nuclear disarmament treaty. I found out later that the Purgers in government were holding the project up for their own purposes.

Nicole had a disastrous miscarriage her second trimester while I was covering the aliens' first visit to South Africa. I did not know until I found Terry waiting for me when I got home instead of Nicole.

"I want to see her."

"She's asleep. Let her rest."

I poured three fingers of Scotch and drank it neat. Terry watched me, her eyes alight with disapproval. I did not want to see her; I wanted to be with Nicole, to hold her and tell her how sorry I was. If Terry had had one milligram of the compassion that saints are reputed to have, she would have gone away to leave me alone with my guilt and sorrow.

"It doesn't matter that you don't like me, Sam." She worried the rosary beads that hung from the belt of her black habit. "I had to come; she had no one else."

I said nothing.

"She told me everything, you know."

I poured myself another drink.

"I hope you're satisfied." I would have expected a malicious grin. Instead there were tears.

"What do you want from me?" I cried, resisting the impulse to throw my drink in her face. "You want me to slit my wrists?"

"That's the kind of penance a godless man does, Sam. I want you to make your peace with Jesus, not with me. Stop leading my best friend into sin."

I set my glass on the wet bar very carefully, as if it might explode if I jostled it. "I'm home now," I said. "Nicole won't be needing you anymore." I left her and went upstairs. I opened the door to the bedroom and slipped onto the chair by the bed. Nicole did not wake up. I spent the night staring at her through the darkness. Terry was gone when we came down together the next morning.

It would have been better for both of us, I think, had Nicole been angry. If she had asked me to quit AlienLine, I would have. I owed her. Instead she bore her misfortune with the quiet grace of a saint. She had lost not only the baby but one of her Fallopian tubes and part of her uterus; her gynecologist warned that another pregnancy might kill her. Yet she never complained. She returned to her job. I tried to get home more often. Our lives settled back into the comforting rhythm of work and play. With one exception. Nicole started to go to church.

Not only Sunday Mass but every morning. St. Mark's was on her way to school, she said, it was no problem. Yet for me it was a terrible problem. In my guilt I thought at first that this was the punishment she had chosen for me; I had no choice but to accept it. In time I came to realize that her churchgoing had nothing to do with me and this was even harder to accept. She was building a wall in our marriage, staking out private territory where I could not go. She knew I would never be reconciled with the Church, especially a Church run by Purgers. And yet *she* was no alien-hating fanatic; except for the fact that she disappeared from my world for a few hours every week she was still my love, my Nicole. We reached an uneasy compromise about religion.

"I don't want to argue, Sam." I could hear a hint of Terry Burelli's sadness in her voice.

"I don't either; I want to understand."

"I believe in God. You don't. I'm not going to convert you so please don't try to convert me." She would smile and touch my hand and I would shut up. Most of the time. But because I worked so closely with the aliens I had to ask her.

"What does it matter if we gain the stars, but lose our immortal souls?" she said. "Do we have to accept everything the aliens tell us, do everything their way, and forget about all the things that make us human? Have you ever asked yourself what they are really offering? They want to make us over in their image. We'll be reasonable, regulated, technologically advanced—and aliens on our own world. And even if we get to the stars we'll be second-class citizens, the ones that had to be helped. I don't need any of it, Sam. All I need is what God offers."

It was summer before State finally let me approach the aliens with the idea of the debate. Maybe all the Fourth of July demonstrations organized by the Purgers had convinced them that something needed to be done. Twisted Logic referred me to his superiors in Sverdlovsk; it took me several tries before I could convince an unenthusiastic alien named Final Authority. I had the impression that he did not much care about American public opinion. "If your people truly want it, we will leave your country. We do not need to be understood; it is you who need to understand."

According to my agreement with State, the debate was to be taped and the tapes submitted for editing by government censors. I soothed my conscience by vowing that if they butchered the debate AlienLine would not run it. To ensure security, all human participants were to board a transport at Andrews Air Force Base and fly to a secret rendezvous with the aliens. There would be a live audience of fifteen, five guests of AlienLine, five Purgers, and five alien sympathizers—scientists all, as it turned out. They would be subjected to personal searches and liable to fine and imprisonment for disorderly conduct. It was not perfect but it was the best I could do.

I had not seen Terry since the miscarriage and had managed to avoid most of her telelink calls to Nicole. Nevertheless I had followed her career as Sister Theresa, a superior of the Brides of Christ and one of the more rational advocates of the Purge. She had introduced the idea of nonviolent prayer marches to disrupt public appearances by the aliens. It seemed that every other week AlienLine was forced to run footage of some sweet little grandmother saying Hail Marys while being dragged away by stony-faced policemen. Terry had all the qualities that telelink loves in its newsmakers. She was attractive, she sounded sincere, and she spoke in a kind of sloganese that was easy to understand. She was a master of the fifteen-second quote yet I was sure that if forced to speak at length she would stumble. For that—and other reasons—I wanted her to take the Purge side in my debate. Terry did not seem surprised when I asked her but then I supposed that State had leaked the idea.

"What format?" She was taking notes.

"Opening statement, five minutes. Twenty minutes of question, response, rebuttal, each side alternating. A three-minute closing."

She sighed. "Not much time."

"If the ratings are good enough you can go at it again."

"You're a cynical man, Sam Crimmins. I pray for you sometimes."

Once such an admission would have thrown me into a rage. Now I found the futility of her prayers for my soul touching. It struck me at that moment that many of her prayers probably went unanswered. It was an austere life that she had made for herself; I wondered if she were disappointed with it. She looked weary. I could see that her telelink image was largely a product of makeup and acting.

"Moderator?" she said.

"Me."

She shook her head.

"All I do is keep the time," I said. "It's your show."

"I have to talk it over with the Council. They'll say yes." She pushed the notes to one side. "Why are you doing this, Sam?"

"Have you ever met an alien?"

She frowned. "No."

"I just thought that you should."

I was surprised when Nicole asked to go. My first inclination was to say no; after all, her sympathies were clear. I said yes because I still believed her to be a reasonable person who would be intellectually honest enough to give both sides a fair hearing. I realize now something that I only half understood then. I did not stage the debate for the world; I staged it for my wife. I wanted her to see that her newly reaffirmed faith was a mistake. I wanted her to doubt because I could never believe. Although on the surface our marriage continued as before, there was an underlying friction that was slowly abrading the base of love and trust between us.

In addition to Nicole, the guests from AlienLine included Janet Trumbell, the president of InfoLine, her husband Geoff, and two of InfoLine's corporate lawyers. The rest of the party that boarded the plane at Andrews included three edgy bureaucrats from State, our camera crew, and the pro and anti factions. The group had been kept to a minimum in the hope that if the debate proved too controversial it would be that much easier to suppress. Once in the air we were told that we were heading north to Hanscom Defense Force Base, west of Boston.

Had I known the location ahead of time, I might have suspected a trap. There are both civilian and Defense Force runways at Hanscom. The guests remained on the plane while a squad of soldiers escorted the camera crew and me to the bubbletent on the runway where the debate was to be staged. I did not realize at the time that these soldiers were not the troops of the United States Defense Force I had expected; they were members of the Massachusetts Guard. We had landed at the civilian airport, not the military base. I had a telelink show to produce; all I noticed were the guns and riot helmets and the green uniforms. Two of the scientists have claimed that the soldiers who escorted them wore Defense Force uniforms. It is a clear violation of law for state militiamen to pose as federal troops. The governor of Massachusetts denied that his men switched uniforms. The governor claimed that they never identified themselves to us at all and therefore broke no laws. The governor, who took personal charge of the Massachusetts Guard that day, was a Purger.

All we had asked for was one alien. But when the airlock of the red alien silo opened two bodies came out. One identified himself as Twisted Logic. He introduced a banana-yellow alien called Awful Truth who was to argue the alien side. All the Purgers except Terry were apoplectic. "How can she debate someone named Truth?" one cried. "It's not that thing's real name, I tell you!" another thundered. "They make their names up to suit the occasion."

Terry just sighed her all-purpose sigh. "The Lord will speak today, not me," she said, and managed to make that outrageous statement sound humble. "He knows all the tricks of the devil." That shut them up.

It was about four in the afternoon when the tape started to roll. I introduced them as Sister Theresa of the Brides of Christ and Awful Truth the communist. The opening statements were predictable. Awful Truth gave the digest version of the Big Bang, planetary formation, organic soup, life, evolution, intelli-

gence. He was more impressive than Twisted Logic, perhaps because he did not giggle so much. I got the impression that he
was the alien version of a humorless fanatic, in which case he
was well-matched with Terry. She spoke first of Jesus, then of
the Judeo-Christian tradition, and then as a seeming after-
thought, the other religions of the world. You could tell that
Islam was not her favorite word and she did not even distinguish between Hinduism and Buddhism, lumping them together
as the "faiths of the East." It sounded as if she were improvising.
Round One to the alien.

Terry asked the first question. "Who caused the Big Bang?"

"By cause you mean a sequence of events in time. Time does
not exist prior to the Big Bang, therefore no causation is possible."

"Time did not exist!" Terry gave the camera a sly, playact
grin and nodded to the millions of scientific illiterates who
might one day be watching. "What may I ask did exist?"

I was not going to allow her to violate the ground rules on
the first question, but Awful Truth replied anyway. "As creatures
of time, we can never know."

"Then even in your science there are some things you must
take on faith?" she said.

"Excuse me," I said firmly, "but you have spoken out of turn,
Sister Theresa. Awful Truth, you may now ask a question."

"Her beliefs are invalid. Asking questions in this context
equates her unsupportable opinions with theories which can be
verified empirically. Therefore there are no questions. I am content to respond."

I was as dumbfounded as the audience. I wondered if I should
stop the cameras and explain the debate to the alien again. I
wondered if I should just stop the camera, period. While I wondered, Terry spoke up.

"Thank you, Mr. Truth. Many of those who believe in God
wonder how you aliens are able to tell the difference between
good and evil. Some, in fact, claim that you do not care. Do
you?"

"We do not recognize such absolutes in the universe. Good
and evil are emotional attitudes; they have no truth value."

"Is that why you were attracted to Russia? Without God,
there is no reason to be concerned with human rights. You

don't have to *recognize* such minor problems as repression, torture, political murder..."

"Sister!" I had to interrupt. "Is this a speech or a question?"

She sighed. "A question, Mr. Crimmins."

"Our anthropologists," said Awful Truth, "are most interested
in this aspect of religion. Some believe that you have invented
your gods to generate an ethics. We do not understand why
you should need such an elaborate machinery. We recognize
ethical concerns but we do not deceive ourselves into believing
that they are woven into the fabric of space-time. Ethics cannot
pre-exist intelligence. They must be created by each thinking
species using the tools of logic. To pretend otherwise is to li-
cense such acts of intolerance as you have mentioned."

Most of this last speech I have reproduced from tape. Just as
Awful Truth started to speak, Laszlo, down in our telelink truck,
whispered through my earphone. "Sam, I've got a general on
the satellite line. Claims he's Defense Force. Wants to know
what the hell we're doing. Something stinks about this setup;
you smell it up there?"

I held up my hands to both debaters. "Excuse me. I'm sorry
but I've just heard from my production crew. Tape problems.
If you'll just be patient for a moment I'm sure it won't take long
to fix. Thank you."

Actually the tape was still rolling. On it you can see Terry
glare at her side of the audience and shake her head. I had to
step away to get any privacy. "Okay, Laszlo, what is it?"

"You tell me. Guy claims he's in charge of alien security. Says
he's been getting bad information from State and he's got three
of his own staff kneeling in his office saying Our Fathers. He
thinks we must be on the civilian side of Hanscom; doesn't
know who our soldiers are but they're not taking orders from
him. He's talking major-league conspiracy, Sam; he says to get
the aliens the hell out. This is Purge country."

Twisted Logic waddled to my side almost before I could wave
him over. He had plenty of experience with terrorism. "Something is wrong?" He was not giggling.

"The debate's over. Get back to your ship; there may be
danger."

As the two aliens conferred the audience stirred uneasily.
When Awful Truth climbed down from his high chair, someone

cried, "Take them!" The Purgers surrounded the aliens and began to pray. Guardsmen appeared at the exits. "Stop this, stop!" I shouted at Terry. Their escape seemingly cut off, the aliens tucked their heads close to their squat bodies and sliced through the crowd with a nightmarish agility. The soldiers raised their guns and sighted but did not fire. With a *whoosh* the aliens punched through the walls. There was an eerie second of silence as we all rushed to the plastic windows of the sagging bubbletent to see what had happened. The aliens had bounced, once, twice and come up bounding like frightened kangaroos. Awful Truth jumped clear over the telelink truck on his way to the red silo down the runway.

"To the ship," called a Purger.

"Go, go!"

The tent emptied. As Terry brushed past me I grabbed her and spun her around. "What are you doing?"

"I'm going to unmask the devil."

"What?"

"We're boarding the ship."

I shook her, probably too hard. "Stop them, do you hear me? For God's sake, stop them now!"

She turned her sad face up toward mine and sighed as if this were all my fault. "For God's sake," she said, "I can't."

I could have hit her then. Her treachery had stripped away the veneer of fair-minded reason; I was a raging fanatic. We were two of a kind, I saw at last, and neither of us were saints.

"Let her go, Sam."

I turned to Nicole and saw something in her then that I had tried for months not to see. She was, like Terry and me, a zealot. But while the fire that burned in Terry's soul made her sad, while mine made me angry, Nicole's burned with joy. Perhaps that was why I had missed it. I realized that I had lost her.

Shaken, I let Terry go. For a moment we three stood looking at each other in the now empty room. We had known each other for fifteen years and we were strangers.

"Let's go, Nicole," Terry said.

"Don't," I said, knowing better.

"Come," Nicole said to me as Terry steered her toward the door. I sagged into a folding chair.

"Wake up, Crimmins, goddamn it! Sam!" Laszlo's voice had been buzzing in my ear for some time.

"Yeah?"

"What the hell is going on?"

Instincts took over. "The aliens have bolted for the ship. Get a camera on it. I'm on my way."

I ran out of the building but did not stop at the truck. I could see two knots of people near the aliens' ship. The larger stood off about fifty yards, the smaller directly underneath the ship's exhaust port. They gathered around a fire truck with a raised hydraulic ladder. In the bucket a soldier with a laser torch was attacking the jump ship's hatch. As I approached, Twisted Logic's amplified voice boomed across the field.

"WE REGRET YOUR PROBLEMS. NOW WE ASK THAT YOU CLEAR THE AREA SO THAT WE MAY REMOVE OURSELVES. PLEASE CLEAR THE AREA."

Those beneath the jump ship took the announcement as a cue to sit down. I was stunned to see that their number included not only Terry and the Purgers but also the three liaison men from State, both of InfoLine's lawyers and even one of the scientists.

And Nicole.

I went first to the soldiers standing off to one side, who were guarding the rest of my audience. "Listen," I said to a bemused captain, "you've got to move those people out of there. If that ship lifts off, they'll be incinerated."

His eyes glittered in the shadow of his helmet. "Orders are to leave 'em alone."

"That's my wife under there! Whose orders?"

"Orders."

"SCANNING SHOWS SIXTEEN HUMANS BENEATH THIS SHIP. WE WARN YOU TO MOVE IMMEDIATELY. CLEAR THE AREA TO A DISTANCE OF THIRTY METERS. MOVE IMMEDI-ATELY."

I broke away from the Guardsmen and sprinted to the ship. Two soldiers pursued me at a dogtrot. "Following you with the zoom, Sam," said Laszlo. "Is that what you want? General says his Defense Force boys are on the way. Should be great footage."

The Purgers seemed as calm as if they were on picnic. Maybe

they thought the aliens were bluffing but I knew at least one was perfectly prepared for martyrdom. "Get out." I could hardly breathe. "You think they'll just sit here while you cut your way in? Get out of here! Nicole!"

The soldiers grabbed me. "Let go, goddamn it. She's my wife. Nicole!"

"Wait," she said and the soldiers obeyed. "Do you believe, Sam? If you believe you can stay." Terry glared at her.

"I believe in you. But you can't stay here, Nicole."

"It's not enough." She smiled but shook her head. "I love you."

"Sam," said Laszlo as the soldiers dragged me away, "get your ass out of there. The general has given the aliens permission to lift . . ."

The two soldiers and I were flattened by the ignition of the jump ship's drive.

In the aliens' lightweight jump ships, lasers heat liquid hydrogen. As the vaporized fuel is exhausted in one direction, the ship moves in the other. Supposed to be very efficient. The take-offs are not so spectacular as those of our clumsy old chemical propellant rockets. Which is why I am alive today.

As it was I suffered second- and some third-degree burns from the blast. I was bloodied by flying grit. I was deafened and I was very nearly suffocated. Still I was not so stunned that I did not struggle up as soon as the ship's roar faded to see what had happened to Nicole. Although I knew nothing could have survived the direct force of the blast. Although I knew . . .

I was wrong. Something stirred amidst the broken chunks of glazed concrete. A pale something shook itself in that charred black circle. It stood and staggered in my direction.

For a moment I thought it was Nicole.

Terry was naked. Every hair on her body had been scorched down to the follicle. Her skin was so white that it seemed to glow. Yes, even on the telelink tapes—you can see it for yourself. I doubt she could see me. Her eyes were covered with a milky film. I do not know how she could walk. As she came closer I tried to stand but could not. So I dragged myself. Away from her, do you understand? The fire truck had been reduced to slag. She should have been dead.

She was less than than ten yards away when she stumbled

and dropped to her knees. She raised her ruined eyes to heaven and cried out. I was there. I heard her—just barely. I saw her face. It was not a cry of triumph, as most will tell you. It was a cry of horror. "I have seen the face of God," she said. "The terrible face of the Lord."

She collapsed onto the runway. By the time the soldiers got to her, she was dead. I believe she died knowing that she was damned for the sin of pride. If there is a God, *He* chooses His martyrs; they may not choose themselves.

Dead. If this were just a memoir, I would end it here. But the story must go on even though the main characters are dead. Even though those that are left do not much care to continue. Although the Purgers intended to win the debate and use it as propaganda, it was primarily a way for them to capture a jump ship. Once their ruse was discovered, they were prepared to act instantly. They now claim that the break-in was intended to be nonviolent, although I do not know how they could have entered the aliens' environment without doing some harm to someone. They wanted to unmask the aliens' true form in the hope that it would prove to be monstrously grotesque, and that world opinion would then rally in horror to the Purge. They also wanted to capture and dismantle one of the aliens' artificial bodies. It is less clear whether they planned their martyrdom. Obviously they were prepared for it; I think that Terry wanted it.

When the tape of that afternoon was released, as it had to be, Terry had her victory. It is a moot point now, but even if we could convince the aliens to trust us again, the Purgers probably have the votes to expel them. America has got religion again. Anyone with any brains has already started to learn Russian. Is that bad? The aliens say there are no such things as good and bad. The goddamned aliens who incinerated Nicole and my life.

I know I must tell all this to the priests from Rome. I know it will probably make no difference. Dear God, hear my prayer! Do we really deserve Blessed Theresa of the Aliens?

# Our Lady of the Endless Sky

### by Jeff Duntemann

*Just as priest-scholars have nurtured learning for centuries, priest-explorers and missionaries have accompanied expeditions to unknown lands. And, in the face of starvation, hostility, and loneliness they stayed and survived, as a glance at any map of present-day California will show.*

*Will it be any different when the cities of man rise on the Moon?*

*"Our Lady of the Endless Sky" was Jeff Duntemann's first published story. He later managed the difficult trick of placing two stories on the final ballot for the 1981 Hugo Award. The author of several books on computer programming, he presently edits* P.C. Techniques *magazine. He lives in Phoenix with his wife, Carol.*

*U*nder a glassy dome made invisible by the lunar night, the Mother of God stretched out her arms to embrace the stone horizon. Beyond the tips of her marble fingers rock and steel lay ash-gray under a waxing Earth. Above her peaceful white brow the stars stood guard to all eternity in a sky so deep it had no bottom.

In front of the native granite pedestal in the nearly finished church, Father Bensmiller knelt and prayed.

*Let them see what I see now, Mother, and they would run to you.*

A faint crunching vibration entered his knees from the dusty floor, newly inlaid with pastel blue tile. Bensmiller looked up. Bright light-flashes off metal dazzled his eyes. The polished aluminum boom of a crane hove into view and wobbled slowly out of sight beyond the wall which supported the transparent dome. They were driving it to the construction site, where a third of the station personnel were planting new machines in the lunar soil.

Bensmiller went back to his personal miseries at the feet of the statue. Not an hour before, Monsignor Garif had spoken to him on the S-band from Houston. As twice in the past, the news was of the rising number of American churches closing their doors permanently. Not due to lack of funds; the Interfaith Council assured each pastor a living and attempted to keep the buildings standing. It seemed pointless, however, to preach the Gospel to empty pews.

*They have lost their horizons. They can't tell the sky from the concrete.*

Unlimited energy had put synthetic food into even the poorest of mouths on the United Continent. Physical suffering through disease and hunger were becoming rare. Where, then, were the multitudes who should have been giving thanks?

Earth hovered permanently over Mary's white shoulder. *Help them look up, Mother.*

He felt another vibration through the floor. It was slower than before, and wavered in frequency. No crane boom showed itself above the walls. Bensmiller rose from his knees, curious, and climbed the first four steps of a light metal ladder which the electricians had left behind.

Beyond the reach of the station's huge blue-white night lamps the landscape was shadowy and unreal. Grinding its way down the gravel-paved road outside the dome was a huge ten-wheeled flatbed truck, its bulbous tires flattening under the weight of its large blockish load. More junk for the construction site. Bensmiller wasn't sure what they were building there. The site at the end of the makeshift road was near Cluster A of glittering Garden domes, each dome itself a cluster of warm yellow stars, each star an artificial sun above a section of a Garden. The project had something to do with the generation of power for the Garden complexes. Station Commander Kreski always demanded expansion, new construction, toward the still distant end of total self-sufficiency for Station Grissom. Every new dome, every new corridor which snaked across the dust of Sinus Iridum came closer to cutting off the ties to the blue planet perpetually in the southern sky.

Two small beetlelike trucks were following the large flatbed toward the site. Bensmiller shook his head and climbed down the ladder. He dusted the grout from his knees at the bottom. It was more machines. On wheels, on treads, under domes, and beneath the lunar soil the machines proliferated. Still, only seven new people had been added to the station staff in four months. The priest wondered why they didn't just send the men home and let the machines spread themselves solidly across the moon's surface.

Father Thomas Bensmiller picked up his clipboard and continued sketching out his report on the progress of the moon church. The main altar was almost finished. The great slab of genuine maple, the first of its kind in all history to rise above the smoky pall of Earth, would soon bear the reenactment of the Supper. It had been set on its rough-hewn moon-granite pillar, and would be consecrated within the month. The rotator for the two-sided cross had been set discreetly beneath the floor in front of the altar. A lectern of woodlike synthetic stood to the altar's right. Bensmiller mentioned them and made note of his satisfaction with them on the multiple forms.

Only a little remained unfinished: painting, some electrical work, the pews for the faithful, and the large dual cross itself, Corpus on one side and bare gold on the other.

Bensmiller turned to the statue. Crafted on Earth of Italian marble, it towered more than two meters high on its pedestal of lunar rock. The stars shone on her undimmed. He could not look at her and not feel a cool shiver of wonder down his spine. *How many kilos of propellant brought you out of Earth's arms to this place, Lady?* Kreski kept telling him, over and over, but Bensmiller had made it a point not to remember. Kreski loved to speculate on the riches the Church spent to build a church on the moon when millions starved in the enslaved East.

But the poor will always be with you. He had said that, the Christ. And the power of the Church could not always reach past the walls of oppression. God would care for His poor when His ministers were barred from them. Yes. The Lord would care for them. Kreski would nod, and nod, and walk away, still nodding.

At those times Father Bensmiller felt very small, and false somehow. Kreski was a huge man, brilliant and cold in his understanding of machines and moon-science. Thomas Bensmiller, third son of an Indianapolis housewife, dark and short, mouse-quick and mouse-quiet in all he did, was no match for the station commander and shrank from Kreski's sharp challenges. What was a priest doing on the moon when there was work to be done on Earth? Bensmiller glanced around at the incomplete church, and thought of the machines and thrumming activity farther beyond. Man was running for the stars. God's administrators, such as Monsignor Garif, had decided that the Gospel must follow. Thomas Bensmiller had been the first to go. Garif assured him he would be the first of many. There were many men like Kreski on the moon. It would be difficult.

*Give us your strength, Mother. The worst obstacles here are not the rocks and vacuum.*

The Mother of God smiled down at Father Bensmiller, as though to say, That is your problem, my son. I'll handle my angle, you handle yours. Bensmiller had to grin. What a face that sculptor had given her. She had the face of a cardsharp. Ten aces up each flowing sleeve, and a dozen secrets behind each ace.

Bensmiller stiffened. The Mother of God had nodded. Then he realized that the floor had shifted sharply under his feet at the same time. It had been a quick twitch, sudden, single, sharp. Moonquakes happened infrequently in that area. Moonquakes, however, were slow, languorous rearrangements of the crust that seldom affected solidly based structures. Explosion! But where was the sound?

Bensmiller glanced up at the Earth. Man had left sounds behind him. He hurried out of the almost finished church. On the outside of the thick steel door the words were etched into a copper plate: OUR LADY OF THE ENDLESS SKY.

*God have mercy on them,* he prayed. The decompression sirens were already beginning their nightmare wail.

Kreski hovered like a mad vulture over Lock Six. The lock monitor screens showed men galomphing about outside, weird figures swimwalking in the ocean of one-sixth g. The silver hood of a light crane glinted for a moment under the night lamps. It crawled past the unreal gray vista of the screen and was gone. Other men followed, other machines with them. In the strange light the men and machines looked related, first cousins removed by a double layer of fiberglass and jointed stainless steel. Bensmiller's eyes drifted to the painted sign hanging above one of the monitor consoles, reading in black Roman: WE ARE ALL IN THIS TOGETHER. He could never quite fathom it, never quite decide what its real portent was. Somehow it seemed to him that the machines were saying it. *We are all brothers under the sheet metal.* It disgusted him. For the last half of the twentieth century, Man had been at war with his machines. Now, in the first half of the twenty-first, he was becoming one of them.

The oily smell of machines was very plain in his nostrils. Was this the first skirmish in a new war?

Kreski was punching buttons by the door of the lock. An embarrassed gleep announced the outer door opening. Kreski caught a glimpse of Bensmiller out of the corner of his eye and whipped around.

"Bensmiller, are you deaf? Go back to your cubbyhole and turn on the air!"

The priest noticed then that, save for the helmet, Kreski was fully suited. The sirens remained in the background, not quite real. His ears had not popped.

"But if there are injuries..."

"Damn!" Kreski reddened in anger. "On the moon you're alive or you're dead. I'd sooner you be alive. Mind those sirens, man!"

Bensmiller, cowed somewhat by the huge man's rage, turned and reentered the main corridor. The lock was cycling double-time emergency, air screaming protest at the furious pumps. The priest tried to shut out the noise.

Around the corner stood the Reverend Arthur Chamblen, the other half of the Interfaith Council Lunar Mission. Graying, six-tyish. He was a proud man, tall and lean, proud of the fact that he had been certified physically able to withstand the rigors of space travel, proud of the degree in astronomy, which allowed him to work on the small base telescope backing up the four-hundred-incher seventy kilometers away. Bensmiller, whose contribution to the station was limited to being caretaker of the numerous laboratory animals, envied Chamblen at times. The man spoke confidently about many things. He had a sharp mind and had no qualms about laying criticism where he thought it belonged.

"He's right about that, you know. Alive or dead. Not much in between." The voice was cold, unmoved. Less the voice of a minister than a physicist. The eyes were much the same, pale blue, ice blue, certain.

"Then why aren't you locked in your room like a good boy?" Bensmiller was sweating.

"I was looking for you. When the sirens began, everyone came running. But you."

"My ears haven't popped."

"The sirens are for a reason. Let's go."

With a weird whining snap the inner lock door yielded and hissed into its sheath. Both men stopped. Among the confused noises from Lock Six was the sound of a man in pain.

Bensmiller's breath left him in a short sigh. He turned and ran back around the corner to the lock. Chamblen said nothing, merely continued to walk, slowly, almost hesitantly, back toward the tiny cubicle to which the sirens called him.

Three men had been brought in. Dusty anonymous suited figures milled around them, tearing at resistant half-metal suit cloth with fingers and knives and sheet-metal shears. Even as Bensmiller was about to reach them several men in clean pressure suits pushed by him pulling two surgical carts. They had the red cross on the white band around their arms. He flattened himself against the wall to let them pass, then continued to press forward.

Kreski was shrieking orders and shouting into a wireless microphone. Disembodied voices crackled reply from speakers in the walls. Father Bensmiller elbowed his way between two of the dusty-suited men and looked down on the first body.

It was in several pieces, crusted with melting blood-slush. Bensmiller glanced away, then steeled himself and looked again. The medics were roughly piling the fragments into an opaque bag. The head and shoulders and one arm were still intact, although blackened and the faceplate opaque. Bensmiller was regretfully glad of that.

*Eternal rest grant unto him . . .*

The other two were at least mostly intact. Both had been brought in inside emergency pressure bags for suit-puncture accidents, and both were still alive. One, his name Monahan, the priest had met briefly at the first Mass held in his little room. Monahan's left leg below the knee was a bloody ruin, his foot nearly sheared off at the ankle. He moaned softly. The other man was not familiar to Bensmiller, and was breathing noisily and spitting up blood. His eyes were closed and he did not move his limbs.

The speakers began to shout the story for the benefit of the rest of the station. *"Hydrogen leak in feed tubes to unfinished fusion plant leading to explosion Garden Four destroyed Gardens Two and Three damaged slightly H-culture team injured no atomics involved repeat no atomics involved . . ."*

That seemed to be what separated a minor disaster from a major one. Whether atomics were involved. Human life didn't seem to enter into it. Bensmiller watched the medics lift Monahan onto one of the carts, bereft of his suit and all but tatters of his blue longjohns. A tourniquet had been crudely twisted around his left leg above the knee. He continued to emit low sounds of pain and occasional muttered obscenities. Blood was everywhere, on the hands of the medics, soaking into the padding of the cart, still oozing from the ruin of his leg. Bensmiller pressed forward, reached out and put his hand on the man's forehead.

*God; Father, Son, and Spirit, he was a good man. He came to Mass once. He worked hard. I know him. He worked ... hard.*

The Sacrament was in his cubicle. Time, time, that was all ... He started making the sign of the cross on Monahan's forehead when Kreski grabbed him by the shoulder and roughly pulled him back.

"Get that man to surgery. Bensmiller, stand back or I'll club you." The station commander held a pair of heavy sheet-metal shears in one hand. Bensmiller stepped back while the medics pulled the muttering man away.

Kreski tossed his shears to the floor next to his discarded helmet. He faced the priest, sweat-drops dotting his thin side-burns. "What the hell's the matter with you?"

The ruddy face was furious, the man still breathing deeply and quickly. It was not an easy face to confront. Bensmiller licked his lips. "I'm a priest. These men are my spiritual responsibility. If they feel depressed, I encourage them. If they feel guilty, I hear their confession. If they're about to die, I give them the last sacraments. That's my job. This is my parish."

It did not seem the right thing to say at all, somehow, but Bensmiller could not harden before Kreski's sweating fury. Kreski turned away for a moment, wiped some of the grime from his face and turned back, his anger dampened.

"You want to make mumbo jumbo over Odner, go ahead. He won't hear you, but it might make you feel better." Kreski pointed with a gloved hand to the other injured man, still lying on a makeshift pallet on the floor. The medics had thrown a sheet over him. Bensmiller, flushed with a sinking bottomless dread, bent down over the body and pulled the sheet back. The face was ashen, the mouth closed. Dried and drying blood discolored the cheeks and neck. The chest held no pulse. "A ten-ton heat exchanger fell on him. Slowly. His insides are smashed to pulp."

"But . . ." Bensmiller pulled the sheet farther back. He felt like a ghoul at an opened grave. The body was whole. It had not seemed very damaged, was not twisted or torn out of shape. But where the skin showed through the ripped material of the longjohns, the flesh was purple and black. Crushed. The priest pulled the sheet forward quickly as though to replace it over the head, then paused. He looked up at Kreski. The name was circling like a hawk in his mind. Odner . . . Odner . . . Odner. It did not seem Jewish, nor conspicuously Catholic, nor conspicuously anything. It was only a name and a pain-whitened face attached to a crushed body. "What was he?" Bensmiller asked the commander.

Kreski glared at the question. "A human being." He pulled off his large gray gloves and tucked them under his wide pressure suit belt. "That, and a damned good farmer. That's all I know about him."

The priest dropped his eyes to the corpse. He moistened his thumb and forefinger in his mouth and made the sign of the cross on the gray forehead.

"I baptize you in the Name of the Father, the Son, and the Holy Spirit." *Father, find a place for your son Odner. He was a damned good farmer.*

# 2

"He can't do it."

Chamblen shifted and looked at the floor. "He can. I'm sorry, Tom, but he can."

Bensmiller leaned against the railing protecting the statue of the Mother of God and looked angrily around the church. There were no pews, but the pews were to have come almost last. All of the statues were in place, at that moment unhidden by the discreet curtains which would at the push of a button bring the church into concordance with the Lutheran doctrine on icons. There was the lectern, stern and simple. Only the pews and the large cross still remained in the storage dome, soon to be un-crated and put in their places.

Mary looked down at the priest and minister, cardsharp smile warm and strange.

"This isn't his. It was paid for out of church pockets. Your church and my church, and a lot of other churches. What about the other ministers who were to come after us when all this was finished? What gives him the right?"

The Reverend Arthur Chamblen blinked and made a gesture of obviousness. "Clause 70. That's all he needs."

Thomas Bensmiller tightened inside, glanced up past Mary's outstretched arms to infinity. He was caught in a corner a third of a million kilometers deep and as high as the endless sky. He held the directive in his hand.

TO:        INTERFAITH COUNCIL LUNAR MISSION,
           REVS. CHAMBLEN & BENSMILLER
FROM:      THE OFFICE OF THE COMMANDER
OFFICIAL: AS OF NINETEEN MAY 2029 INVOKING
           CLAUSE 70 REINSTATING GARDEN FOUR
           INDEFINITELY AT AREA EW9D. REMOVE ALL
           NONSTRUCTURAL ITEMS IMMEDIATELY.


"He didn't even give me my own 'Rev.' Nuts."

Chamblen took the outthrust directive, folded it neatly, and tucked it away very calmly in an inside pocket. Bensmiller did not want to catch his eyes. They were, as always, too blue, too level, too at peace with the inevitable.

Bensmiller felt like fighting. "This was no minor disaster. Men were killed. Why doesn't he take the best interest of this place to heart and send home for another dome."

Chamblen grinned. "That would cost fifty million dollars out of taxpayers' pockets. It would have to be legislated. Legislation takes time. Months."

Bensmiller broke away from Chamblen's ever-logical ham-merlock, strolled eyes-down toward the lectern. Halfway there he turned back. "So we'll wait. Are we going to die? They fixed the other two. Does one dome out of commission mean instant destruction? I thought they would have designed this place a little better than that."

Chamblen nodded. "They did. We're not going to die."

"Then why can't I have my church?" Bensmiller tried to sound as firm and certain as Chamblen, Kreski, and all the others always did. But a ghost behind the eyes of the tall minister returned every time to haunt him and knock the sticks out from under his feeble protests. Chamblen always had an answer. Kreski always had an answer. Everyone always had an answer. All but Thomas Bensmiller, who was only a priest.

Chamblen leaned back on the railing and brought one hand up, to place a finger lightly against one cheek, as though anticipating an itch should the itch come. "I'm sure you know more or less what goes on in those domes. They grow a certain plant there in intense light on a glut of nutrients. That plant is tailor-made, in a way, to be what I would call hyperthyroid. They grow like crazy, soak up nutrients like crazy, and photosynthesize like crazy. Their rate of $CO_2/O_2$ conversion is unbelievable. They're also fairly tasty." Chamblen grinned. "You know, those army-green 'bugger biscuits.' It's the same stuff."

The itch came. Chamblen scratched it. The hand returned to the railing. Bensmiller was running the process hazily through his mind, trying to recall the dynamics of a system he was hardly equipped to understand. "There are ten domes. Nine, now. Does ten percent make that much of a difference?"

"Depends, Tom, depends. We could leave things as they are now and continue on nine domes. It might get a shade stuffier and we might eat a little less. But the next time a dome goes down we'd all be in bad, bad trouble."

"This has never happened before." Bensmiller was adamant, and hoped he looked it. "I don't think it will happen again."

The minister shook his head. "Always count on the unexpected. It can kill you. You know, Tom, I'm not selling out. It's a blow, I know. But we're no worse off than we were before. Honestly, do you know why they built this church here and sent you to staff it?"

The words came easily. "To allow the Gospel to follow Man as he conquers the universe."

Chamblen clucked. "Right out of one of Monsignor Garif's pamphlets. I know Garif. He's a shrewd politician. He's the one who pushed like crazy for a church up here, and he pushed you through as Catholic chaplain. You're one of his friends, from way back."

"Yes, but still . . ."

"And that line is pure PR. The truth is, the Catholic Church is fighting a losing battle on Earth, and Garif wants to plant a pocket of orthodoxy here as precedent for future extension of the Church once we branch out beyond the Earth-moon system. You're as orthodox as they come, and you think highly of Garif. What would you have expected him to do?"

Bensmiller, for once, allowed himself a smile. "You're being a little cynical for a minister of the Lord."

"No. I'm adapting to the environment. This is a no-nonsense place, peopled by no-nonsense men. There's no room for the extraneous. After having thought about it quite a bit, I'm still not convinced we need a church up here at all."

"I'm surprised you don't declare yourself extraneous and jump out an airlock. You do believe in God, I hope."

"I do." Chamblen nodded. "God to me is a loving Father who once cared very carefully for His newborn sons, but now, the sons having grown out of their cradle, expects them to get along more on their own."

Bensmiller refused to look at the minister. "I'm sorry we don't see God the same way."

Chamblen stood up and began to walk toward the door. He had gotten most of the way there when he stopped in the star-light and tugged on the lapels of his black shirt, which was opened at the collar and dampened deeper black under the arms. "Tom, see it this way. You never wanted to spend the last dime in your penny loafers, did you?"

Bensmiller ignored him.

"Well, you're asking Kreski to spend our last dime up here. I'm sorry, I'm terribly sorry, but I'm on his side this time." He walked the rest of the way into shadow and grasped the door handle. "I'll remove our nonstructural items. You take it easy for a while. You've got to cope, Tom."

The door closed with solemn slowness behind him. Bens-miller and the Mother of God were alone again in the almost-church. He continued to glare at the walls, not wanting to catch her smile again and feel the pain of not knowing what it was he didn't know.

*What is your ace, Mother? Play it, please.*

# 3

Father Bensmiller stood to the left of the cast-wide doors, watching. He watched the men rip the pastel blue tiles from the floor, the grout barely dry. He watched them hammer ragged craters in the new concrete and draw forth from the ruin snaking cables and twisting tubes, carrying electricity and water to feed the strange sorceries he had never found need to study. He watched them rip his lectern from the floor, and plant in its place a blinking, multikeyed computer terminal, which drew the same power that would have illuminated the Gospel at some future Celebration.

He kept nodding to himself. They were efficient. They worked like madmen, around the clock, never pausing. They used every sliver of space in the church. Every square inch under the dome was mapped and assigned to some subtle and necessary purpose.

It seemed to him that every time he glanced at the door beside him a forklift was rumbling in, heaped with crates and bundles of copper piping and spools of spaghetti wiring. In moments the lift was emptied and gone, only to return in a handful of minutes bearing more trash to be laid at the feet of the Mother of God.

*Who is their God, Mary? What force drives them like this?*

Even Kreski was there, his hands in the chaos up to his elbows. Often he paused to give orders, but when there were no more orders to give he was back down on his knees, brazing copper fittings to a pipeline running down what should have been the main aisle. The flame hissed softly, cleanly. Drips of molten lead hit the floor and froze. In that hard face there was a tension, an urgency almost frightening. Kreski was running

ahead of something greater than himself, when every impression he had ever given Bensmiller stated in solid surety that
nothing on the moon was greater than he.

Other men were bolting together skeletal tables of perforated
magnesium, upon which were being laid the hydroponic garden
units. When the forklift arrived carrying one of the long, narrow, coffinlike black bins sprouting with tiny green newborn
shoots, work stopped. Four men lined up along the unit, positioned their hands carefully beneath it and lifted with a ma-
chinelike precision. They carried it levelly, slowly, and when
they approached, all the other workers stood back. Only when
the unit was positioned on its table and firmly bolted down did
the welders take up their torches and the electricians their pli-
ers. Row after row of garden units filled the church from front
to rear, separated by the pipe-tangled main aisle.

Men crawled like animals beneath the rat's nest of magnesium
beams, pulling plastic tubing and multicolored wires. The clink
and scratch and scrape and tap of wire and tube faded into a
rushed and uneasy whisper filling the dome and echoing past
Bensmiller's ears until he wanted to cry out against it. The stink
of sweat and ammonium flux made tangible the blasphemy,
which otherwise would only come half-clear. He would look
outside the dome for solace to the calm sterile wastes, but there
the crawling cranes and leaping devils in metal suits were raising the new power lines and settling a new fusion plant into
its yesterday-poured foundations. Blasphemy was everywhere.
They were forcing him to wallow in it, and he was drowning.

Along the walls they were hanging the narrow aluminum
ducts, through which the air would soon pass, driven by pumps
laid beneath the floor. It all went together so quickly, so logi-
cally. It seemed as though the men in the dome were merely
throwing the beams and ducts together. Everything fit so well,
so quickly the first time. There seemed to be no effort to it.
And yet Bensmiller could see and smell the grimy sweat stream-
ing from their faces. He saw the concentrating grimaces, the set
jawlines.

*This work ... is important to them. Bless their labors, Mary.*

In time, only one space remained where a garden unit might
be placed, and the tubes and wires were everywhere nearby.

Bensmiller left hastily, not wanting to see the altar of God plugged into the clucking machines.

The funeral of Odner and Beckwith was held in Lock One, largest lock and single area large enough for all station personnel to gather. Monahan was there, on a surgical cart plugged into the medical monitors. Soon after, the rocket took Odner back to the arms of Earth, and Beckwith, as his wife requested, was laid beneath the lunar soil. Bensmiller watched the coffin vanish beneath the dust through a port, and then fled through the iron hallways of Station Grissom, past the bulletin boards and the graffiti, around the ubiquitous machines, to the only place where he might find shelter.

They had removed the plaque from the door. Inside was nothing but the continuous mechanical purr of automatic activity; the H-culture team was lingering by the lock. Bensmiller recoiled at the sight of the completed Garden, yet deftly slipped between the black coffins full of sprouting vigorous life, working his way toward the now oddly beckoning arms of the Mother of God. Men live, and men die. The priest mediates between death and life. Life comes from God, and goes back to God. Something in him burned to think of bending that path around and feeding life with death, growth with waste, breath with suffocation. Where could God fit into such a closed circle? He touched one of the brilliant green leaves. He could not understand. If God could not fit, no priest could either, except by selling himself to the machines and tending their needs while the circle of life ate its own tail.

"Blessed Mother evicted by a radish patch. God help us." He wanted to look up at the Virgin, to draw strength from her, but could not.

Bensmiller bent down and sniffed directly above the carpet of close-planted leaves. The air seemed fresher there. Or was it just a memory?

Pushing himself away from the garden units, he made his way to where the lectern had been. The computer terminal made a soft thrumming sound as it monitored the pressures and pulses of the machines all around. Bensmiller chuckled bitterly. They have uprooted me and planted a machine in my place, he thought. In this place, with such a congregation, perhaps it was just as well. He laid his hands on either side of the terminal keyboard, tears coming that he refused to fight, and thumbed the loveworn pages of his memory.

"The Gospel According to St. Luke," he said, looking out at the silent rows of green. "Listen to the word of the Lord, damn you radishes!"

For two days Father Bensmiller avoided Chamblen and remained alone with his thoughts. The dilemma ran through his mind again and again while he cleaned the endless rows of rat cages and talked to the sad-eyed dogs waggling at him through the close-mesh screening. He wanted to fight, and place his banner on the side of Life; but cast about as he might, he could not distinguish the lines of battle. Men walked the empty wastes with body-function monitors tattling continually to the machines and felt safer by it. It was hard for him to believe. The poor dogs were too stupid to comprehend the electrodes taped to their skulls and flanks. They wagged whenever he offered his hand to them. Happiness was just another plate of bugger biscuits. He watched men brag about how sensitive their monitors were, and how completely the machines guarded their welfare. He wondered without praying if men would ever again be able to live without them. Nothing in any of his books gave any hint at an answer, nor even so much as admitted the question.

Not long after B-shift dinner call on the second day, the buzzer roused Bensmiller from an uneasy sleep. He put his cot in order and shoved the door handle down. Outside the airtight portal was a man in a wheelchair, smiling.

"Sorry I can't come in, Father," Monahan said. "My wheels won't make it through your door. But I wanted to come over and thank you anyway."

Bensmiller smiled. His eyes burned a little. "Are you sure you should be up and around like that?"

Monahan laughed, and lightly thumped the blanket-covered stump that ended just above his left knee. "Takes more than a little leg missing to lay *me* low. People heal pretty quick in one-sixth g. I should be on crutches next week, if I'm lucky."

The smiling face peering up at him through a cast-wide airtight door moved him terribly for one long moment. "I don't know why you should want to thank me."

"Kreski told me you tried to give me the last sacraments."

"I see."

"Takes guts to tangle with that old monkey wrench."

"He had your best interests in mind."

"Yeah." Monahan grinned sourly. "He's hell to get along with, but he knows his business. Like I said, thanks. Also because I think you're good luck."

"Oh?" Bensmiller was startled.

"Sure. Me and the other guys from H-culture have it figured out. Reverend Chamblen was here for six months before you were, and nobody talked much about a church. But when you get here they start building one right away, and as soon as it's finished, but not finished so that it would be all sacred and everything, that's the time when my Garden blows up. The church was ready and waiting for us to move in."

"But..." Bensmiller was astonished. The man spoke as though the destruction of a church were a blessing sent by God.

"Sixty hours, from total destruction to full operation, in a dome that was never designed for life-support machinery. I call that pretty close to a miracle. It'll be something to tell my kids about."

"But I don't see why..."

"It wasn't easy," Monahan said, his tone gone more serious. "Take it from me, it was a bitch."

*Amen.*

"No, honestly, Father, me and the guys got to thinking about it, and found you were pretty lucky to us. If they hadn't had a dome, we would have had no emergency margin. Houston wouldn't have liked that. They might have issued a Directive Five."

Directive Five. *Evacuate Immediately.* The end of Station Grissom. Bensmiller shook his head in wonderment. "I never knew it had been that serious."

Monahan whistled. "Not anymore, but for a while there it was really touch and go. And if it had turned out to be go, it would really have broken my heart. That trip home would have been a one-way trip for me. One-legged men aren't popular as flight or station crew. So things didn't turn out too bad. Except for you, I guess."

"Well, I..."

"You probably feel like a dog that got kicked out of his doghouse so that it could be used as a chicken coop. That must hurt a little, but I figure God forgives more easily than nature. Anyway, it wasn't really fair for you to get shoved out into the cold without someplace to go, so I leaned on Kreski a little bit, and demanded the space in the storage dome where all the spare parts for the new Garden came from. There's quite a hole in there now. So the rest of the H-culture guys got together off-shift; uncrated the crucifix and a couple of pews, and we made you a church."

"Kreski let you do that." It was a statement of disbelief.

"We threatened to dye the bugger biscuits purple. They're his favorite food and that's the color he hates the most. We got our way."

"I have to say thanks. I mean..."

"No. Just say Mass. For us. We want to give thanks a little. When do I tell them?"

"Tomorrow morning. Oh-nine hundred."

"Thanks, Father. You got some real grit, you know that?"

"No. But I'll take your word for it. Take care of yourself." The door swung closed as the man rolled away.

# 4

The Mother of God stretched out her arms to embrace the barren lands. Over her white shoulder had been thrown a sheaf of electric cables. Glued to her crown was a photoelectric sensor.

Sunlight, earthgleam. Life must have its light.

"In the Name of the Father, the Son, and the Holy Spirit..."

Between shadow-cast crates and ranks of stacked barrels, seven human beings clustered around a slab of scrap synthetic. Over it had been laid a fine linen cloth. On one side of the cloth was the golden cup. On the other, a small plate of dark green biscuits.

Mary stretched out her arms. In each hand, fastened with

strap-iron, was a cluster of sodium-mercury lights. Other pseudo-suns grew on stalks all around. The dome sang with light.

*I saw a woman, clothed with the sun, and the moon under her feet, and on her head a crown of twelve stars.*

Twelve stars. Twelve hundred stars. Twelve thousand stars. Twelve trillion stars.

*Mother, they are yours. We will make them yours.*

"Lord have mercy. Christ have mercy. Lord have mercy."

Seven persons paused, silently, and recalled their faults. Every eight seconds each took a breath. Life was at work there, in their lungs, in their blood, in every cell. Oxygen to carbon dioxide. Energy. Life. God forgive us.

The machines hummed with their own life. About Mary's shoulders the ducts wound, throbbing their own purpose. Speaking their own language. Molecules of gas wafted over tiny shafts of green. A moment ago, a breath. The breath of a priest, of man, of woman, of Catholic and Protestant and atheist. The breath of six dogs and three hundred white rats. The last breath of a human being. Someday the first breath of a moonborn infant.

Life from life, breath from breath. Death is only the intermediary. Mary stretches out her arms to embrace the tiny fields of green, growing in chemical baths under forty artificial suns. Tiny shoots of green taking the bad air apart with sunlit crowbars, giving back their breath, giving up their food. The new air enters the ducts once more.

The circle is unbroken.

*We are all in this together.*

"This is my body..."

Mary stretches out her arms to embrace life. All life. Green life, animal life, life that walks on two legs and one leg. She embraces the false life, the buzzing circuits and leaping rockets.

"Give us this day our daily bread..."

For these things are necessary. Man lives not by bread alone. He must have his ecosphere.

"Go, the Mass is ended." Our days are beginning, just beginning.

*Thank you, Mother. Help me understand these things.*

On her head a crown of twelve trillion stars.

# The Seraph from Its Sepulcher

## by Gene Wolfe

*Missionaries must overcome the skepticism of their colleagues in the exploration and settling of new worlds, of course, but a greater challenge awaits among the unconverted, who will have histories, gods, and biologies of their own. A challenge, certainly; perhaps even a temptation.*

*Gene Wolfe is one of the most honored writers of contemporary SF, notably for his four-volume* The Book of the New Sun *(1980–88). Set millions of years in the future, it is a tale of rebirth and redemption whose imagery will be instantly familiar to readers of the later books of the New Testament.*

*Born in Brooklyn in 1931, Wolfe was raised and educated in Texas. Following service in Korea, he worked for Proctor & Gamble and as an editor of* Plant Engineering *magazine prior to turning to writing full-time.*

*He is the author of such novels as* Peace *(1975),* Free
Live Free *(1984), and a new series which to date in-
cludes* Soldier of the Mist *(1986) and* Soldier of Arete
*(1989).*

*He lives in Barrington, Illinois, with his wife.*

"**T**he inscribed prayer was to be recited at each landing," Father Joseph explained. "The wrong turnings stand for miscalculations in life. They end in precipices, or become more and more steep until no one could climb them without falling, or else fade away altogether in screes of sliding stones."

"I took a couple of those," his visitor admitted. He felt rather lost, although he knew precisely where he was.

Father Joseph nodded. "Most people do."

"My name's Anthony Brook, by the way." Somewhat belatedly, Brook extended a sweating hand.

The priest accepted it. "Joe Krska." Together they stood looking down at the apparently unpatterned network of stairs that crossed and recrossed the steep defile.

"I ought to give you a card, I suppose," Brook added. He fished in a big shirt pocket for one and at last produced it, a stiff, tissue-thin flake printed in bold black capitals.

A slight smile tugged at Father Joseph's sun-browned face. "You have a great many letters after your name."

"You can put it in—"

"Oh, I can read. F.X.A.S. This last one. What does it mean?"

"Fellow of the Exsolar Archaeological Society. That's why I'm here, actually."

Father Joseph sighed. "I hoped it had something to do with Francis Xavier. But you would like to sit down, Dr. Brook, and you won't want to climb more steps. Why don't we go in?"

The interior of the mission seemed cool, almost cold, and dark after the pounding sunlight of Mirzam. There were no pews for worshippers, Brook noticed, but two old wooden chairs stood just inside the heavy door, which Father Joseph wedged expertly with a small stone until it stood half open.

When it had been fixed in place to his satisfaction, he motioned toward one and seated himself in the other.

"They built this under human supervision," Brook said, looking around.

Father Joseph shook his head. "They had seen our buildings and perhaps even studied them—if they needed to study anything so simple. But they built this themselves and presented it to the diocese. It was something of an embarrassment at the time, from what I've read. To some degree it still is."

Brook nodded, studying the airy columns and leaping arches of grainy, lion-colored stone. The arches traced a curve that appeared mathematical, though surely no parabola. The columns, he decided, were neither round nor ribbed; pierced by strangely shaped apertures like those in the cliffs outside, they seemed to breathe, sighing in the faint, hot breeze from the open door.

"As I am," concluded the priest. "How may I help you?"

"Just let me look around for a few days," Brook said. "I want to find out as much as possible about the Seraphs. I came here from the Motherworld to do that."

"It must have been extremely expensive."

"It was, but not for me—I've got a grant. I'll stay five or six years, visit every site I can, and dig when I have to."

"I see." The priest scratched his chin. In appearance at least, he was older than Brook; silver stubble gleamed beneath his fingers.

"When was this built, Father?"

"A hundred years ago."

Brook hesitated. "I've read that the last Seraph died in twenty-two ten."

"I saw a few as a boy." The sentence hung in the dry shade of the nave, at once an invitation and a challenge: *Credit this and I shall recount wonders that will be more to you than gold; credit this and you are twice a fool, a dupe and a fraud.*

"I don't know," Brook said slowly. "You must understand, that I know them only from study." Footsore and leg-weary though he was, he rose and walked to the head of the tangled stairways. "They could fly. It's a point upon which all my sources agree, and some holostats show them winged. Why did they build this?"

Father Joseph joined him. "They were winged for at least one stage of their lives, but they flew only on certain well-defined occasions. There was a nuptial flight, for example."

"You've studied them, too, haven't you? And living here, you've had access to materials I've never seen." Brook paused. "Or did you learn that firsthand?"

"No, I read it in a book. In several, actually."

"You don't mind if I look around and shoot some holostats of my own?"

The priest did not answer, and after a moment Brook turned away. "If there's anything you don't want me to stat, just tell me. We'll discuss it, and if you won't agree I won't do it."

"It's all right," the priest said. "There's nothing here— Do you plan to leave today? Descend the stairs?"

Brook nodded. "I'll have to. My camping gear's down there on my roller. I saw your sign."

"Thank you. You'd have driven up them otherwise?"

"Of course. Oh, I realize that if enough people drove up and down, they'd destroy the stairs. But enough walkers, enough wear from enough boots, would do the same thing."

"You'll fall," the priest told him. "You're tired already. You'll be still more tired when you've examined and statted this church, and in places the steps are very steep. People have fallen before." He hesitated. "I'll sleep in my study tonight. I can lend you soap, a towel, and so forth."

"I couldn't take your bed."

"I'd much rather sleep in my study than have you sleep there."

"If you think I'd poke—"

The priest waved the objection aside. "Among my files? Of course not, and it wouldn't matter if you did. There's only one document—no, two—of any importance, and I'll show them to you when you come up to the rectory."

"All right," Brook said, "and thank you, Father. Thank you very much. I'd like to make a donation, if I may. Something in recognition of your hospitality."

"If you wish. I'll have need of it very soon, I'm afraid. You're not Catholic, Dr. Brook?"

Brook shook his head.

"Then you may not know what a sacristy is. Here, it's the small room to the left of the altar. You'll see my vestments hanging there. Go through the sacristy and out the door to your right; the steps lead up to my rectory. I'll have supper on the stove before you're through here, I'm sure."

Brook watched the priest's retreating back until it faded to near invisibility among the shadows. For the first time he realized that there were no lights in the mission except for a single candle, remote and golden as some faraway sun beside the altar. Holography would be unsatisfactory in an hour or less. He went to work quickly, creating images more permanent and in a certain sense more real than the stone.

"Stew," Father Joseph said. "I hope you don't mind. It's what I usually eat in the evening, and right now it's all I have ingredients for."

"Smells delicious." Without waiting to be asked, Brook dropped into a chair. "You're here all by yourself?"

The priest stirred and sniffed. "More onions—for my taste at least. I like to think that God and his holy angels are with me, Dr. Brook."

"I mean—"

"And the desert fathers, at least in spirit; Saint John of Damascus is a particular favorite of mine. But to answer your question as you intended it, yes. There's no one like yourself or myself here, except you and me. And save for a few visitors like yourself, there never is."

"How do you get your supplies?"

"I carry them on my back from Clear Springs. It's nearly all dehydrated stuff, of course. My little dewdripper cracks as much water as I require out of the atmosphere, though it has to work very hard here to do it."

Brook remained silent while the priest ladled stew into two bowls. When they were on the table, he said bluntly, "I'd think you'd go mad."

"Possibly I have." Father Joseph smiled. "Certainly my superiors thought I had when I asked them to send me here. I said I'd show you my only documents of any importance, didn't I? I will, after grace." He crossed himself and murmured a prayer Brook was too shy to join.

After the amen, the priest rose and stepped into the next

room, returning with an outer and two of the flimsy sheets old-fashioned people still called *paper*.

The telltale flashed, and they were joined by an elderly man in black. "Dear Father Joseph Krska," this newcomer began, "I have good news for you. We want you to return here to Saint Ardalion's immediately. We require you for Senior Composition, Modern History, and Moral Theology. I feel sure it will be a great relief to you to leave such an isolated pastorate, and I congratulate you upon your new appointment." The elderly man's features tightened. "Don't wait for a replacement, Father. No one will be coming. Lock up, and leave at once. I am Monsignor Augustine A. Nealy, Dean. Today is Wednesday, the twenty-third of August, twenty-three seventy-three."

Monsignor Nealy flickered. "Dear Father Joseph Krska, for the time being please disregard my last. A certain Dr. Brook, a distinguished scholar from the Motherworld, desires to holostat your mission; please render him all possible assistance. Remain there at Saint Seraphiel's, please, for as long as you can be of help to him." Monsignor Nealy's eyes narrowed. "Father Graffe will have to take your classes temporarily. See to it, Father, that it's not for more than a few days. And don't write me any more of your letters! Simply come here as soon as you possibly can. I am Monsignor Augustine A. Nealy, Dean. This is Thursday, the twenty-fourth, twenty-three seventh-three." Monsignor Nealy vanished.

Father Joseph said, "You saved me, you see. Doubtless you thought that it was by your own will that you put out from the Motherworld so long ago—that you left to further archaeology, when in point of fact you left in answer to my prayers, though I was not yet born. I'm a thoroughgoing solipsist, you see."

Brook grinned. "I suppose we all are, Father, whether we admit it or not. You're going to do it, aren't you? Go back to the capital and teach moral theology and so forth?"

"I've sworn obedience."

"But you don't want to." Brook tested his stew, finding it (as he had anticipated it from the steam) still too hot to eat. "I never liked teaching undergrads much either."

The priest brought glasses of cool water. "I'd like that better than teaching them little, but I'll have to teach them no more than they're willing to learn, I suppose."

"You've been studying on your own up here?"

"A bit. And writing a bit. There isn't much else to do. I say mass every morning, of course, read my breviary and other books, write when I think I've learned something worth writing, pray, and wait."

"For me?" At his first taste of water, Brook found that he was parched; he drained his glass and set it down.

"For them, Dr. Brook. This is a mission church, after all. They built it, but built it as a mission to themselves. They wished to become Christians, and some of them did." The priest fell silent, staring into his untouched bowl. "One's interred here. Did you find your way into the crypt?"

"A crypt? No. I want to see it. I must, before you go."

"Tomorrow, then," the priest said. "I'll show it to you."

"And you say there's a body there, the body of a Seraph? Remains are almost impossible to locate."

"I'll show it to you," the priest repeated.

Twilight never came to this high desert. Brook had sponged himself in the shallow basin and was reaching for a towel when the light from the windows deepened to amber. Before he found the antique touchswitch, a host of blue-white, crimson, and Sol-yellow stars hung above the tableland like innumerable torches suspended from so many balloons—close enough, or so it seemed to Brook, for anyone upon a hilltop to touch at will, close enough to sway in the chill, dry night wind that had sprung full-grown from nowhere.

In this desert, Brook reflected, this fellow Krska (how odd to think that he had been born when Brook's own voyage to Mirzam was nearly ended!) had lived year after year, hearing only the histrionic rant of the HL and the wordless moanings of the wind. Four rooms, and a church to which nobody ever came.

And the crypt. Where was it, and how could he have failed to find it, even without his sohner? He dressed again, testing his palmpilot before pulling on his boots.

Downstairs, the study door stood ajar, and Brook ventured to peer inside. Father Joseph lay on his back on the makeshift pallet he had contrived for himself, a hand on his chest, his eyes open.

"I thought I'd take another look around," Brook said. "I haven't quite been desensitized to the beauty of this corner of your world yet."

The priest did not reply.

"I might go back to my roller and carry a few things up."

Without looking at him, Father Joseph murmured, "You were afraid to sleep."

"I haven't tried, actually. I didn't feel like it."

"Do you understand why I painted the stone?"

"The sign at the bottom?" Brook hesitated. "We talked about that—so the rollers wouldn't spoil the steps."

"Rollers roll too fast," the priest murmured. And then, "Roll aside the stone." His eyes closed.

After a moment it occurred to Brook that Father Joseph had never, perhaps, been truly awake—that he, Brook, had spoken as a phantom in the priest's dream; for no reason he could justify he shuddered.

The narrow rear door by which he had left the church stood half open. He pointed a finger at it, letting golden light run down that finger like water to splash against the bare, cracked panels. The door was swinging a little in the wind; now that he saw it, he could distinguish the despairing creak of its hinges. He had neglected to shut it securely when he had left the church. Or perhaps the priest had visited the church afterward to recite some evening prayer before the altar. Or perhaps—

Brook pushed the thought from his mind as he went down the steps from the rectory. These, unlike the mazed stairs that rose from the dry bed of the wadi, had been gouged out of the rock by the machines of men—for beings like himself, with legs shorter than a Seraph's. His knees ached again, just the same, by the time he had reached the bottom and entered the mission church.

His upraised, open hand flooded the sacristy with light. A half step down, and the gritting of wind-driven sand accused him afresh. He closed the door firmly behind him; its latch was of wood, hard brown twigs so oddly and cleverly shaped that he knew at once that it too had been the work of Seraphs.

A strangely shaped but quite unobstructed arch led from the sacristy to the chancel. There were no other doors save the one through which he had entered. A rough pole held the robes the priest had mentioned—green, scarlet, rose, purple, and white, all plain and rather cheap looking. A cabinet held transparent vit chalices and corked bottles; it was not fastened down, and was not big enough to be the entrance to anything in any case.

The cloth-draped altar cast a dense black shadow, ungainly and (Brook felt) almost brutal, down the center of the nave. He pulled aside the altar cloth, and discovered that the altar was a rugged mass of native rock; its top, and presumably its bottom as well, had been cut flat. A twenty-centimeter square of some lighter colored stone had been let into the top; this square was marked with the unbalanced cross he had noticed elsewhere.

A similar room on the opposite side of the chancel mirrored the sacristy; except for a mop, a pail, and a crude broom—this last clearly made by the priest from native brush—it was bare.

With little skill but great determination, Brook swept all four rooms. It took him a little over an hour, and when he was finished he had discovered no slightest crevice.

A reasonable man would return to the rectory now and go to bed, he told himself. On the other hand, a reasonable man would never have left every friend and relative he had to a death now past in order to cross interstellar space at near–light speed to Mirzam. He put away the broom, made sure that the rear door was latched, went out the front, and started down the Seraph-carved stair.

Descended, it lost most of its mazelike character; there was seldom more than one flight leading downward, and when there were two, either choice proved valid. He halted several times to rest, ruefully rubbing his aching knees and staring up at the stars, musing upon what the Seraphs might have become if only Mirzam had been granted a moon like Luna. Human beings—superapes whose early evolution had certainly been arboreal—had been lured up and out by that yellow sphere, that great, ripe fruit hung in their sky for the plucking. Would the Seraphs (half insect and half pterosaur, wholly unique) have responded in like fashion?

Perhaps they would, Brook decided. The serpent, after all, was already well up in the tree when it urged Eve to taste the fatal apple. Or at least was always so depicted in art. Had it in cold fact been a mere snake in the grass? The priest would know, of course—ask him in the morning.

Brook rose and looked back at the mission he had left; it shone almost white in the starlight. After a long moment, he turned away to peer down into the dark cleft of the wadi. He was already more than halfway there, he decided; but climbing

up again would be out of the question. He would have to drive
the roller, sign or no sign; and if the priest was angry that would
not matter, because he would have found the crypt by then
without the priest's help.

In his dream the priest stood (as he had stood so often in
life) before the open sarcophagus. The big kitchen knife was in
his hand; but each time he raised it, his fingers grew weak. If
he stabbed the Seraph it would, he knew, rise and seize him, a
monster at once living and dead. He would awaken trembling,
his nightclothes soaked with sweat. But he would awaken, the
dream would end, and so he raised the knife.

His fingers were weak, numb. The heavy, broad-bladed knife
nearly slipped from them.

"You must go," the Seraph said.

Its dry, shriveled mouth did not twitch, yet Father Joseph
heard its voice. "That's what I've come to tell you," he said. And
then, "I had hoped that if I slept in the study tonight you
wouldn't bring me here—that you would take the man in my
bed in my place." He sensed the Seraph's amusement. "I think
he'll go tomorrow. I'm to show you to him, and he'll make pictures and go." Father Joseph hesitated. "I'd like—I should go
with him. He can give me a ride as far as Treaty. That will save
a day, possibly more."

"Yet you do not wish to go," the Seraph said. "Perhaps you
are afraid that you will not be free of me? You will be free of
me, or nearly."

"I feel it's my duty to stay; but it's my duty to go, as well. I
wish my duties might be reconciled."

"I shall emerge very soon, Father."

The priest nodded, realized he was still holding the knife, and
let his hands fall. "So you tell me night after night. I don't believe you."

Amused again the Seraph asked, "Then why are you eager to
kill me?"

"I'm not eager to kill you. I want . . ."

"Yes?"

"To sleep. To sleep as other men do. To find peace, and rest,
in sleep." The priest raised the knife again, but his fingers were
weak, so weak it nearly slipped away.

"Is that all?"

"To pray. To say mass *here.* Not to— To wait here, at this mission, as I was intended to wait by your race and mine, for a living Seraph."

The Seraph's voice was a caress, and a blessing. "Not to betray us as your people betrayed us."

*"Yes!"*

"Come closer. You could not strike me from where you stand even if you wished to strike. Come closer."

Lowering the knife once more, the priest shook his head.

"Do you know why we became Christians, Father?"

The priest sighed. "By the grace of God."

"True, though you do not truly believe as yet. His grace makes use of means, of tools. Why?"

"Because you thought we'd spare you then." Father Joseph gazed at the knife in his hands; it seemed as inexplicable as any Seraph artifact. Was one to grasp both ends? "You thought we had decency enough for that, and you were wrong."

"Because we wanted to understand you, we became like you. You took lands that were never ours, and called them ours, and killed us lest we ask them back. Now we are dead, but we shall rise again, in Christ."

The knife clattered to the stone floor.

"Like the flower from its seed, the moth from its cocoon. We become, come into being. If you were more like Christ, you would understand us better."

Fear struck Brook like a lash. With all his strength, he heaved back on the stick; the roller's big, soft wheels stopped ... spun in reverse. For an instant it seemed he and it would surely go over. Instead they raced wildly backward, no longer following any stair, lost on the naked slope and out of control.

He pushed the stick forward to stop. The roller halted, canted at such an angle that he knew he would fall if he tried to dismount—fall and tumble, and at last drop.

Cold perspiration streamed from his forehead into his eyes. He wiped it away and eased the lever forward, edging the roller back in the direction of the stair. It was wrong, that stair, of course. The wrong one, though he had been so confident.

He stopped the roller again and dismounted. A hundred steps

returned him to the precipice; golden light from his palm revealed a smashed roller far below—one certainly, and possibly
two; he counted five wheels. Broken bones, bleached by Mirzam's young and pitiless sun, lay among the wreckage. A lonely
wind sobbed between him and them, gritty with sand.

Some men would pray now, Brook thought. Some would spit.
Why am I caught between them?

Slowly he made his way back to the roller and crept back to
the landing. After lengthy deliberation he chose another of its
diverging stairs and inched up it at a walking pace.

It took an hour to reach the top; once there, he parked the
roller on a blanket-sized patch of nearly level ground and
rooted through the cargo compartment for his sohner. With it,
he circled the entire mission, scrambling wearily over insecure
stones and hearing only the dull buzz of solid rock. The crypt
was inside, clearly, under the baffling inlay of the floor; he had
missed it, in spite of all his sweeping and careful peering.

Maybe they should've sent someone else, he thought; perhaps
I'm not the right person after all. Aching with fatigue, he pulled
open one of the massive doors, reflecting that it was he who
had been sent in any case—the one who would have to do
whatever was done, because there was no one else present to
do anything.

Sohner in hand, he shuffled back and forth across the nave,
hearing only stone, solid and dull, until he had almost reached
the chancel. There (at last) there came the sharp *ping* of a cav-
ity. Scarlet numerals rolled across the sohner's small screen:
three hundred and forty-nine cubic meters. Brook nodded to
himself, pulled off the earphone, and switched off the sohner.
Here was the crypt, but where was its entrance? He puzzled
over that for twenty minutes or more, poking here and prying
there, and even considered waking the priest, before he realized
that the priest had already told him.

*"Roll aside the stone."*

He had thought the priest dreaming, and doubtless had been
correct. Yet that phrase surely contained the answer he sought;
the priest, hearing his voice, had dreamt of exhibiting the crypt,
as he planned to do in the morning.

The altar appeared far too heavy for one man to move, but
he carried the translucent chalice and its small cloth into the

sacristy, folded the clean white altar cloth carefully and laid it beside them, set his shoulder to the altar, and heaved with all his strength.

It trundled to one side so easily that he nearly fell into the opening beneath it, rolling onto one rough, rounded end to reveal a lightless opening through which even a large man (or a large coffin, Brook reflected) might easily pass.

For a moment he hung back, his left foot on the first step. Surely there had been some sound from below? Loudly, echoing, shocking, came the clang of metal on stone; it was followed by the murmur of the priest's voice.

As silently as he could manage, Brook moved the altar back into place, then spread the altar cloth once more and added the chalice with its pall. Wearily, he left the mission by the rear door and mounted the long, straight stair to the rectory. The priest slept as before upon the improvised pallet in the study, both arms stretched above his head now. Brook stared at him, snorted, and went up to bed.

It was indeed a different world.

"There were never more than two million or so," the priest said, "and they didn't need a great deal of food. Much of their lives was spent in dormancy. Much of ours is, too, although it doesn't seem to do us a great deal of good. Perhaps if we cared more for the worlds that we call ours, we'd discover that we too could get along on less food. And if we cared more for God . . ." He shrugged, turning away from the brazen sarcophagus to study glyphs incised in the walls of the crypt.

"There would be fewer children to feed," Brook finished for him, "and better food and care for those we had. You're right, of course." He bent above the desiccated Seraph. "They changed like insects? Egg, larva, chrysalis, and adult?"

The priest shrugged. "No one really knows how many changes there were, or what the adult form actually was. In some cases, their transformations seem to have been self-directed."

"The flying, sexual stage would have been the last." Brook prodded the Seraph's open jaw; only by directing his palmpilot between the wasted lips could he make out the remains of what had once been a tongue (or something like one) inside the open mouth. "This individual isn't winged."

As though he had not been listening, the priest said, "I've wondered at times whether they hadn't visited the Motherworld."

Brook straightened up. "Because pictures of winged spirits go back to Sumer? They didn't call themselves Seraphs, did they?"

"Because of what you said a moment ago. And because others have said it so often—that word *larva*. It's Latin. Do you know what it means?"

Brook shook his head. "The Romans are supposed to be in my bailiwick, but I've never learned the language, except for a few names. Try me on Ugaritic or Moabite. Let's see. The larva's what hatches from an egg, so I suppose it means a child—something like that."

"It means *ghost,*" the priest said.

"I'm afraid I don't follow you." Brook tossed up a light; it touched the ceiling of the crypt and stuck there.

"I'm not sure I follow myself. Can't I help you with that? I'm perfectly willing to, if you'll tell me what you want me to do."

Brook shook his head. "I know what I need, and it'll only take a minute."

"Are you going to dissect?"

The archaeologist glanced around sharply; there had been a change in tone. "No. I assume you don't want me to? Not now, and if you mean me, Tony Brook personally, not ever. This will be a job for a comparative anatomist, and a good one." He toyed with another light. "You don't really want that ride to Treaty, do you. You'd rather stay here."

The priest shrugged again. "What I want is scarcely the issue."

"Exactly. Do you recall what that superior of yours said? Monsignor what's-his-name? He said that you were to remain here as long as you could be of service to me. All right, I want you to stay right here and protect this body—this whole place, but our late friend particularly—until I talk one of your universities into sending someone out. It may take a while, I warn you."

The priest opened his mouth, and shut it again.

"I'm perfectly serious, and I'm going to put it in writing. Once you're gone, there won't be anything to keep any idiot who can borrow a roller from driving up here, taking this body, and burning it or tearing it to bits. I could tell you things that happened in Egypt— For a thousand years specialists will weep over this squandered opportunity to learn about a race that was in many ways, and maybe in every way, superior to our own. Stay here, Father—I mean it. He put you under my orders, didn't he? Very well, I'm ordering you to stay."

"It's extremely tempting," the priest said slowly.

"It's not a matter of temptation, Father. It's your duty."

"But, no. That isn't what Monsignor Nealy intended, and we both know it. No, I don't believe I can."

Brook made a final effort. "I'm going to spend the rest of the day on this, and a couple of things up there that I skimped yesterday; I'll leave in the morning. I want you to promise me, Father, that you'll think about what I said tonight—about your true God-given duty, as opposed to doing whatever you find least pleasant. I don't believe God's quite as cruel as you imagine."

The priest nodded and started up the steps to the chancel. "If you don't mind," he said mildly, "I always think best in the open air."

It was more difficult to drive the roller down the tangled stairs than it had been to go up them, something Brook had not anticipated; the priest's weight, and that of his luggage, added to Brook's two hundred kilos of clothing and equipment made it necessary to ride the brake constantly, even with the arrester on Full Regenerative.

"That way," the priest said. He pointed, one black-sleeved arm over Brook's broad shoulder. "This is one of the two places in which you can get lost—lost seriously—going down."

Brook nodded, steering to the right. "I didn't think there were any. Where's the other?"

"At the bottom." If the priest was joking, there was no hint of it in his voice.

Brook stopped there. "If you don't mind," he said, "I want to take one last shot, Father. I neglected to get this before I went up."

"Of course not. I'd like to remain here for a few minutes myself. I'll probably never come back."

The labyrinthine stone stairs gleamed like new-minted gold in Brook's holoscreen, flawlessly lit by the morning sunshine. At the top, the graceful Seraphic mission church seemed a pretty toy. Such a toy, Brook thought idly, as real angels might have built for the Christ child's crib set. Except—

He turned to the priest. "There's somebody up there. A man in black."

The priest nodded and smiled.

"But you were alone," Brook said, "that's what you told me."

"We didn't want to frighten you." The priest waved back to the tiny figure at the summit of the twining stairs. "Nor would you have believed us, and so that seemed best. But see how nicely things have worked out, Dr. Brook! Monsignor's instructions have been followed in both senses. I am coming in obedience to him; my brother remains to protect our mission, as you wished."

"Is he disfigured or something?"

"All of us are deformed in some degree by evil, Dr. Brook. That is its chief result. My brother is less hideous than most."

Brook took a deep breath. "Well, that explains a lot."

The priest did not reply.

His final holostat taken, Brook repacked his equipment; and they started off in earnest. Fast though he drove, roaring up blind dunes constructed by the laboring winds, climbing mountains of sand not greatly inferior to the Jebel Seir while trailing a plume of sallow dust more lofty still, Mirzam's long day was three-quarters spent before the ocher and orange desert that dashed by their racing roller softened at last to green.

As they drew near Treaty, Brook spoke for the first time in hours. "I'm going to put up at Chesterton House, Father. It's reasonable and comfortable. I want you to let me pay for a room there for you, too. I stayed with you for two nights, after all."

"If you wish," the priest said. And then, "It's very kind of you."

A cheerful auburn-haired attendant supervised the robots that unloaded their baggage. "Been out in the desert long?"

"I haven't," Brook told her, "but Father Krska was there for more than ten years."

She smiled at the priest; and he nodded to her, affirming the truth of what Brook had said.

So this is unlawful desire, he thought, as his eyes traced the tender curve of her lips. This is the sensation they feel, the thing they fight against and rush to: this twitching in the shoulder blades.

I had not known.

# A Case of
# Conscience

## by James Blish

*The temptations posed by an alien race hostile to the Faith are obvious, but how would we react to creatures who are better than us? Who are free of original sin?*

*James Blish was born in New Jersey in 1921, and studied chemistry at Rutgers, graduating in 1942. He worked for many years as a public relations specialist, notably for the American Tobacco Institute, until turning full-time to writing in 1968. He died of cancer in England in 1975.*

*Blish had begun writing science fiction at the age of nineteen, becoming a member of the Futurians, a collection of young SF fans and would-be writers whose number included Isaac Asimov, Frederik Pohl, and Damon Knight. His most famous works include "Surface Tension," the story of a race of creatures who live in a drop of water; the* Cities in Flight *novels; and a series of* Star

Trek *story adaptations. He was also one of the first to publish literary critiques of science fiction stories.*

*Blish's own favorite among his works was a "trilogy" he titled* After Such Knowledge, *whose elements were a historical novel about Roger Bacon (*Doctor Mirabilis, *published in 1964), a contemporary apocalyptic fantasy about the Devil's reign on earth (originally in two volumes as* Black Easter *[1968] and* The Day After Judgment *[1971], recently collected as* The Devil's Day*), and a novel-length version of* A Case of Conscience *(1958).*

*One editor told Blish he would publish this story "only if you get rid of this religious jazz. I run a family magazine."*

*1*

*T*he stone door slammed. It was Cleaver's trademark: there had never been a door too heavy, complex, or cleverly tracked to prevent him from closing it with a sound like a clap of doom. And no planet in the universe could possess an air sufficiently thick and curtained with damp to muffle that sound. Not even Lithia.

Ruiz-Sanchez continued to read. It would take Cleaver's impatient fingers quite a while to free him from his jungle suit, and in the meantime the problem remained. It was a century-old problem, first propounded in 1939, but the Church had never cracked it. And it was diabolically complex (that adverb was official, precisely chosen, and literally intended). Even the novel which proposed the case was on the Index, and Father Ramon Ruiz-Sanchez, S.J., had access to it only by virtue of his Order.

He turned the page, scarcely hearing the stamping and muttering in the hall. On and on the text ran, becoming more tangled, more evil, more insoluble with every word:

". . . and Magravius knows from spies that Anita has formerly committed double sacrilege with Michael, *vulgo* Cerularius, a perpetual curate who wishes to seduce Eugenius. Magravius threatens to have Anita molested by Sulla, an orthodox savage (and leader of a band of twelve mercenaries, the Sullivani), who desires to procure Felicia for Gregorius, Leo, Viteilius, and Macdugalius, four excavators, if she will not yield to him and also deceive Honuphrius by rendering conjugal duty when demanded. Anita, who claims to have discovered incestuous temptations from Jeremias and Eugenius—"

There now, he was lost again. He backtracked resignedly. Jeremias and Eugenius were—? Oh, yes, the "brotherly lovers" at the beginning of the case, consanguineous to the lowest degree with both Felicia and Honuphrius—the latter apparent prime villain and the husband of Anita. It was Magravius, who seemed

189

to admire Honuphrius, who had been urged by the slave Mauritius to solicit Anita, seemingly under the urging of Honuphrius himself. This, however, had come to Anita through her hirewoman Fortissa, who was or at one time had been the commonlaw wife of Mauritius himself and had borne him children—so that the whole story had to be weighed with the utmost caution. And that entire initial confession of Honuphrius had come out under torture—voluntarily consented to, to be sure, but still torture. The Fortissa-Mauritius relationship was even more dubious, really only a supposition of Father Ware's, though certainly a plausible one considering the public repentance of Sulla after the death of Canicula, who was—yes, that was correct, Mauritius's second wife. No, his first wife; he had never been legally married to Fortissa. It was Magravius's desire for Felicia after the death of Gillia that had confused him there.

"Ramon, give me a hand, will you?" Cleaver shouted suddenly. "I'm stuck and—and I don't feel well."

The Jesuit biologist arose in alarm. Such an admission from Cleaver was unprecedented.

The physicist was sitting on a pouf of woven rushes, stuffed with a sphagnumlike moss, which was bulging at the equator under his weight. He was halfway out of his glass-fiber jungle suit, and his face was white and beaded with sweat, although his helmet was already off. His uncertain fingers tore at a jammed zipper.

"Paul! Why didn't you say you were ill in the first place? Here, let go of that; you're only making things worse. What happened?"

"Don't know exactly," Cleaver said, breathing heavily but relinquishing the zipper. Ruiz-Sanchez knelt beside him and began to work it carefully back onto its tracks. "Went a ways into the jungle to see if I could spot more pegmatite lies; it's been in the back of my mind that a pilot-plant for turning out tritium might locate here eventually—ought to be able to produce on a prodigious scale."

"God forbid," Ruiz-Sanchez said under his breath.

"Hm? Anyhow, I didn't see anything. Few lizards, hoppers, the usual thing. Then I ran up against a plant that looked a little like a pineapple and one of the spines jabbed right through my suit and nicked me. Didn't seem serious, but—"

"But we don't have the suits for nothing. Let's look at it. Here, put up your feet and we'll haul those boots off. Where did you get—oh. Well, it's angry-looking, I'll give it that. Any other symptoms?"

"My mouth feels raw," Cleaver complained.

"Open up," the Jesuit commanded. When Cleaver complied, it became evident that his complaint had been the understatement of the year. The mucosa inside his mouth was nearly covered with ugly and undoubtedly painful ulcers, their edges as sharply defined as if cut with a cookie-punch.

Ruiz-Sanchez made no comment, however, and deliberately changed his expression to one of carefully calculated dismissal. If the physicist needed to minimize his ailments, it was all right with Ruiz-Sanchez. An alien planet is not a good place to strip a man of his inner defenses. "Come into the lab," he said. "You've got some inflammation in there."

Cleaver arose, a little unsteadily, and followed the Jesuit into the laboratory. There Ruiz-Sanchez took smears from several of the ulcers onto microscope slides and Gram-stained them. He filled the time consumed by the staining process with the ritual of aiming the microscope's substage mirror out the window at a brilliant white cloud. When the timer's alarm went off, he rinsed and flame-dried the first slide and slipped it under the clips.

As he had half-feared, he saw few of the mixed bacilli and spirochaetes which would have indicated a case of ordinary, earthly, Vincent's angina—which the clinical picture certainly suggested. Cleaver's oral flora were normal, though on the increase because of all the exposed tissue.

"I'm going to give you a shot," Ruiz-Sanchez said gently. "And then I think you'd better go to bed."

"The hell with that," Cleaver said. "I've got nine times as much work to do as I can hope to clean up, without any additional handicaps."

"Illness is never convenient," Ruiz-Sanchez agreed. "But why worry about losing a day or so, since you're in over your head anyhow?"

"What have I got?" Cleaver asked suspiciously.

"You haven't *got* anything," Ruiz-Sanchez said, almost regretfully. "That is, you aren't infected. But your 'pineapple' did you a bad turn. Most plants of that family on Lithia bear thorns or leaves coated with polysaccharides that are poisonous to us. The particular glucoside you got today was evidently squill, or something closely related to it. It produces symptoms like those of trench mouth, but a lot harder to clear up."

"How long will that take?" Cleaver said. He was still balking, but he was on the defensive now.

"Several days at least—until you've built up an immunity. The shot I'm going to give you is a gamma globulin specific against squill, and it ought to moderate the symptoms until you've developed a high antibody titer of your own. But in the process you're going to run quite a fever, Paul; and I'll have to keep you well-stuffed with antipyretics, because even a little fever is dangerous in this climate."

"I know it," Cleaver said, mollified. "The more I learn about this place, the less disposed I am to vote 'aye' when the time comes. Well, bring on your shot—and your aspirin. I suppose I ought to be glad it isn't a bacterial infection, or the Snakes would be jabbing me full of antibiotics."

"Small chance of that," Ruiz-Sanchez said. "I don't doubt that the Lithians have at least a hundred different antibiotics we'll be able to use eventually, but—there, that's all there is to it; you can relax now—but we'll have to study their pharmacology from the ground up, first. All right, Paul, hit the hammock. In about ten minutes you're going to wish you were born dead, that I promise you."

Cleaver grinned. His sweaty face under its thatch of dirty blond hair was craggy and powerful even in illness. He stood up and deliberately rolled down his sleeve. "Not much doubt about how you'll vote, either," he said. "You like this planet, don't you, Ramon? It's a biologist's paradise, as far as I can see."

"I do like it," the priest said, smiling back. He followed Cleaver into the small room which served them both as sleeping quarters. Except for the window, it strongly resembled the inside of a jug. The walls were curving and continuous, and were made of some ceramic material which never beaded or felt wet, but never seemed to be quite dry, either. The hammocks were slung from hooks which projected smoothly from the walls. "But don't forget that Lithia's my first extrasolar planet. I think I'd find any new habitable world fascinating. The infinite mutability of life forms, and the cunning inherent in each of them ... it's all amazing and very delightful."

Cleaver sprawled heavily in his hammock. After a decent interval, Ruiz-Sanchez took the liberty of heaving up after him the foot he seemed to have forgotten. Cleaver didn't notice. The reaction was setting in.

"Read me no tracts, Father," Cleaver said. Then: "I didn't mean that. I'm sorry ... but for a physicist, this place is hell.... You'd better get me that aspirin. I'm cold."

"Surely." Ruiz-Sanchez went quickly back into the lab, made up a salicylate-barbiturate paste in one of the Lithians' superb mortars, and pressed it into a set of pills. He wished he could stamp each pill "Bayer" before it dried—if Cleaver's personal cure-all was aspirin, it would be just as well to let him think he was taking aspirin—but he had no dies for the purpose. He took two of the pills back to Cleaver with a mug and a carafe of Berkefield-filtered water.

The big man was already asleep; Ruiz-Sanchez woke him. Cleaver would sleep longer and awake farther along the road to recovery if he were done that small unkindness now. As it was, he hardly noticed when the pills were put down him, and soon resumed his heavy, troubled breathing.

That done, Ruiz-Sanchez returned to the front room of the house, sat down and began to inspect the jungle suit. The tear which the plant spine had made was not difficult to find, and would be easy to repair. It would be much harder to repair Cleaver's notion that their defenses were invulnerable, and that plants could be blundered against with impunity. Ruiz-Sanchez wondered if one or both of the other members of the commission still shared that notion.

Cleaver had called the thing which had brought him low a "pineapple." Any biologist could have told Cleaver that even on Earth the pineapple is a prolific and dangerous weed, edible only by a happy and irrelevant accident. In Hawaii, as Ruiz-Sanchez remembered, the tropical forest was quite impassable to anyone not wearing heavy boots and tough trousers. The close-packed, irrepressible pineapples outside of the plantations could tear unprotected legs to ribbons.

The Jesuit turned the suit over. The zipper that Cleaver had jammed was made of a plastic into the molecule of which had been incorporated radicals from various terrestrial antifungal substances, chiefly thiolutine. The fungi of Lithia respected these, all right, but the elaborate molecule of the plastic itself had a tendency, under Lithian humidities and heats, to undergo polymerization more or less spontaneously. That was what had happened here. One of the teeth of the zipper had changed into something resembling a piece of popcorn.

It grew slowly dark as Ruiz-Sanchez worked. There was a muted puff of sound, and the room was illuminated with small, soft yellow flames from recesses in every wall. The burning substance was natural gas, of which Lithia had an inexhaustible and constantly renewed supply. The flames were lit by adsorption against a catalyst, as soon as the gas came on. A lime mantle, which worked on a rack and pinion of heatproof glass, could be moved into the flame to provide a brighter light; but the priest liked the yellow light the Lithians themselves preferred, and used the limelight only in the laboratory.

For some things, of course, the Earthmen had to have electricity, for which they had been forced to supply their own generators. The Lithians had a far more advanced science of electrostatics than Earth had, but of electrodynamics they knew comparatively little. They had discovered magnetism only a few years before, since natural magnets were unknown on the planet. They had first observed the phenomenon, not in iron, of which they had next to none, but in liquid oxygen—a difficult substance from which to make generator coil cores!

The results in terms of Lithian civilization were peculiar to an Earthman. The tall, reptilian people had built several huge electrostatic generators and scores of little ones, but had nothing even vaguely resembling telephones. They knew a great deal on the practical level about electrolysis, but carrying a current over a long distance—say one kilometer—was regarded by them as impossible. They had no electric motors as an Earthman would understand the term, but made fast intercontinental flights in jet aircraft powered by *static* electricity. Cleaver said he understood this feat, but Ruiz-Sanchez certainly did not.

They had a completely marvelous radio network, which among other things provided a "live" navigational grid for the whole planet, zeroed on (and here perhaps was the epitome of the Lithian genius for paradox) a tree. Yet they had never produced a commercial vacuum tube and their atomic theory was not much more sophisticated than Democritus's had been!

These paradoxes, of course, could be explained in part by the things that Lithia lacked. Like any large rotating mass, Lithia had a magnetic field of its own, but a planet which almost entirely lacks iron provides its people with no easy way to discover magnetism. Radioactivity, at least until the Earthmen had arrived, had been entirely unknown on the surface of Lithia, which explained the hazy atomic theory. Like the Greeks, the Lithians had discovered that friction between silk and glass produces one kind of charge, and between silk and amber another. They had gone on from there to Widmanstetten generators, electrochemistry and the static jet—but without suitable metals they were unable to make batteries or do more than begin to study electricity in motion.

In the fields where they had been given fair clues, they had made enormous progress. Despite the constant cloudiness and endemic drizzle, their descriptive astronomy was excellent, thanks to the fortunate presence of a small moon which had drawn their attention outward early. This in turn made for basic advances in optics. Their chemistry took full advantage of both the seas and the jungles. From the one they took such vital and diversified products as agar, iodine, salt, trace metals, and foods of many kinds. The other provided nearly everything else that they needed: resins, rubbers, woods of all degrees of hardness, edible and essential oils, vegetable "butters," rope and other fibers, fruits and nuts, tannins, dyes, drugs, cork, paper. Indeed, the sole forest product which they did *not* take was game, and the reason for this oversight was hard to find it. It seemed to the Jesuit to be religious—yet the Lithians had no religion, and they certainly ate many of the creatures of the sea without qualms of conscience.

He dropped the jungle suit into his lap with a sigh, though the popcorned tooth still was not completely trimmed back into shape. Outside, in the humid darkness, Lithia was in full concert. It was a vital, somehow fresh, new-sounding drone, covering most of the sound spectrum audible to an Earthman. It came from the myriad insects of Lithia. Many of these had wiry, ululating songs, almost like birds, in addition to the scrapes and chirrups and wing-buzzes of the insects of Earth.

Had Eden sounded like that before evil had come into the world? Ruiz-Sanchez wondered. Certainly his native Peru sang no such song. Qualms of conscience—these were, in the long run, his essential business, rather than the taxonomical jungles of biology, which had already become tangled into near-hopelessness on Earth before spaceflight had come along to add whole new volumes of puzzles. It was only interesting that the Lithians were bipedal reptiles with marsupial-like pouches and pteropsid circulatory systems. But it was vital that they had qualms of conscience—if they did.

He and the other three men were on Lithia to decide whether or not Lithia would be suitable as a port of call for Earth, without risk of damage to either Earthmen or Lithians. The other three men were primarily scientists, but Ruiz-Sanchez's own recommendation would in the long run depend upon conscience, not upon taxonomy.

He looked down at the still-imperfect suit with a troubled face until he heard Cleaver moan. Then he arose and left the room to the softly hissing flames.

# 2

From the oval front window of the house to which Cleaver and Ruiz-Sanchez had been assigned, the land slanted away with insidious gentleness toward the ill-defined south edge of Lower Bay, a part of the Gulf of Sfath. Most of the area was salt marsh, as was the seaside nearly everywhere on Lithia. When the tide was in, the flats were covered to a depth of a meter or so almost half the way to the house. When it was out, as it was tonight, the jungle symphony was augmented by the agonized barking of a score of species of lungfish. Occasionally, when the small moon was unoccluded and the light from the city was unusually bright, one could see the leaping shadow of some amphibian, or the sinuously advancing sigmoid track of the Lithian crocodile, in pursuit of some prey faster than itself but which it would nonetheless capture in its own geological good time.

Still farther—and usually invisible even in daytime because of the pervasive mists—was the opposite shore of Lower Bay, beginning with tidal flats again, and then more jungle, which ran unbroken thereafter for hundreds of kilometers to the equatorial sea.

Behind the house, visible from the sleeping room, was the rest of the city, Xoredeshch Sfath, capital of the great southern continent. Like all the cities the Lithians built, its most striking characteristic to an Earthman was that it hardly seemed to be there at all. The Lithian houses were low, and made of the earth which had been dug from their foundations, so that they tended to fade into the soil even to a trained observer.

Most of the older buildings were rectangular, put together without mortar, of rammed-earth blocks. Over the course of decades the blocks continued to pack and settle themselves until it became easier to abandon an unwanted building than to tear it down. One of the first setbacks the Earthmen had suffered on Lithia had come through an ill-advised offer to raze one such structure with TDX, a gravity-polarized explosive unknown to the Lithians. The warehouse in question was large, thick-walled and three Lithian centuries old. The explosive created an uproar which greatly distressed the Lithians, but when it was over, the storehouse still stood, unshaken.

Newer structures were more conspicuous when the sun was out, for just during the past half-century the Lithians had begun to apply their enormous knowledge of ceramics to house construction. The new houses assumed thousands of fantastic, quasibiological shapes, not quite amorphous but not quite resembling any form in experience either. Each one was unique and to the choice of its owner, yet all markedly shared the character of the community and the earth from which it sprang. These houses, too, would have blended well with the background of soil and jungle, except that most of them were glazed and so shone blindingly for brief moments on sunny days when the light and the angle of the observer was just right. These shifting coruscations, seen from the air, had been the Earthmen's first intimation that there was intelligent life in the ubiquitous Lithian jungle.

Ruiz-Sanchez looked out the sleeping-room window at the

city for at least the ten thousandth time on his way to Cleaver's hammock. Xoredeshch Sfath was alive to him; it never looked the same twice. He found it singularly beautiful.

He checked Cleaver's pulse and respiration. Both were fast, even for Lithia, where a high carbon dioxide partial pressure raised the pH of the blood of Earthmen to an abnormal level and stimulated the breathing reflex. The priest judged, however, that Cleaver was in little danger as long as his actual oxygen utilization was not increased. At the moment he was certainly sleeping deeply—if not very restfully—and it would do no harm to leave him alone for a little while.

Of course, if a wild allosaur should blunder into the city ... but that was about as likely as the blundering of an untended elephant into the heart of New Delhi. It could happen, but almost never did. And no other dangerous Lithian animal could break into the house if it were sealed.

Ruiz-Sanchez checked the carafe of fresh water in the niche beside the hammock, went into the hall, and donned boots, macintosh and waterproof hat. The night sounds of Lithia burst in upon him as he opened the stone door, along with a gust of sea air and the characteristic halogen odor most people call "salty." There was a thin drizzle falling, making haloes around the lights of Xoredeshch Sfath. Far out, on the water, another light moved. That was probably the coastal side-wheeler to Yllith, the enormous island which stood athwart the Upper Bay, barring the Gulf of Sfath as a whole from the equatorial sea.

Outside, Ruiz-Sanchez turned the wheel which extended bolts on every margin of the door. Drawing from his macintosh a piece of soft chalk, he marked on the sheltered tablet designed for such uses the Lithian symbols which meant "Illness is here." That would be sufficient. Anybody who chose to could open the door simply by turning the wheel, but the Lithians were overridingly social beings, who respected their own conventions as they would respect natural law.

That done, Ruiz-Sanchez set out for the center of the city and the Message Tree. The asphalt streets shone in the yellow lights cast from windows, and in the white light of the mantled, wide-spaced street lanterns. Occasionally he passed the eight-foot, kangaroolike shape of a Lithian, and the two exchanged glances of frank curiosity, but there were not many Lithians abroad now. They kept to their houses at night, doing Ruiz-Sanchez knew not what. He could see them frequently, alone or by twos or threes, moving behind the oval windows of the houses he passed. Sometimes they seemed to be talking.

What about?

It was a nice question. The Lithians had no crime, no newspapers, no household communications systems, no arts that could be differentiated clearly from their crafts, no political parties, no public amusements, no nations, no games, no religions, no sports, no celebrations. Surely they didn't spend every waking minute of their lives exchanging knowledge, discussing philosophy or history? Or did they? Perhaps, Ruiz-Sanchez thought suddenly, they simply went inert once they were inside their jugs, like so many pickles! But even as the thought came, the priest passed another house, and saw their silhouettes moving to and fro ...

A puff of wind scattered cool droplets in his face. Automatically, he quickened his step. If the night were to turn out especially windy, there would doubtless be many voices coming and going in the Message Tree. It loomed ahead of him now, a sequoialike giant, standing at the mouth of the valley of the River Sfath—the valley which led in great serpentine folds into the heart of the continent, where Gleshchetk Sfath, or Blood Lake in English, poured out its massive torrents.

As the winds came and went along the valley, the tree nodded and swayed. With every movement, the tree's root system, which underlay the entire city, tugged and distorted the buried crystalline cliff upon which the city had been founded as long ago in Lithian prehistory as was the founding of Rome on Earth. At every such pressure, the buried cliff responded with a vast heart-pulse of radio waves—a pulse detectable not only all over Lithia, but far out in space as well.

These bursts, of course, were sheer noise. How the Lithians modified them to carry information—not only messages, but the amazing navigational grid, the planetwide time-signal system, and much more—was something Ruiz-Sanchez never expected to learn, although Cleaver said it was all perfectly simple once you understood it. It had something to do with semiconduction and solid-state physics, which—again according to Cleaver—the Lithians understood better than any Earthman.

Almost all knowledge, Ruiz-Sanchez reflected with amusement, fell into that category. It was either perfectly simple once you understood it, or else it fell apart into fiction. As a Jesuit—even here, forty light-years from Rome—Ruiz-Sanchez knew something about knowledge that Cleaver would never learn: that all knowledge goes through *both* stages, the annunciation out of noise into fact and the disintegration back into noise again. The process involved was the making of increasingly finer distinctions. The outcome was an endless series of theoretical catastrophes. The residuum was faith.

The high, sharply vaulted chamber, like an egg stood on its large end, which had been burned out in the base of the Message Tree, was droning with life as Ruiz-Sanchez entered it. It would have been difficult to imagine anything less like an earthly telegraph office or other message center, however.

Around the circumference of the lower end of the egg there was a continual whirling of tall figures, Lithians entering and leaving through the many doorless entrances and changing places in the swirl of movement like so many electrons passing from orbit to orbit. Despite their numbers, their voices were pitched so low that Ruiz-Sanchez could hear blended in with their murmuring the soughing of the wind through the enormous branches far aloft.

The inner side of this band of moving figures was bounded by a high railing of black, polished wood, evidently cut from the phloëm of the Tree itself. On the other side of this Encke's Division a thin circlet of Lithians took and passed out messages steadily and without a moment's break, handling the total load faultlessly—if one were to judge by the way the outer band was kept in motion—and without apparent effort by memory alone. Occasionally one of these specialists would leave the circlet and go to one of the desks which were scattered over most of the rest of the sloping floor, increasingly thinly, like a Crêpe Ring, to confer there with the desk's occupant. Then he went back to the black rail, or, sometimes he took the desk and its previous occupant went to the rail.

The bowl deepened, the desks thinned, and at the very center stood a single, aged Lithian, his hands clapped to the ear-whorls behind his heavy jaws, his eyes covered by their nictitating membrane, only his nasal fossae and heat-receptive postnasal pits uncovered. He spoke to no one, and no one consulted him—but the absolute stasis in which he stood was obviously the reason, the sole reason, for the torrents and countertorrents of people which poured along the outermost ring.

Ruiz-Sanchez stopped, astonished. He had never himself been to the Message Tree before—communicating with the other two Earthmen on Lithia had been, until now, one of Cleaver's tasks—and the priest found that he had no idea what to do. The scene before him was more suggestive of a bourse than of a message center in any ordinary sense. It seemed unlikely that so many Lithians could have urgent personal messages to send each time the winds were active; yet it seemed equally unchar- acteristic that the Lithians, with their stable, abundance-based economy, should have any equivalent of stock or commodity brokerage.

There seemed to be no choice, however, but to plunge in, try to reach the polished black rail, and ask one of those who stood on the other side to try and raise Agronski or Michelis again. At worst, he supposed, he could only be refused, or fail to get a hearing at all. He took a deep breath.

Simultaneously, his left elbow was caught in a firm four- fingered grip. Letting the stored breath out again in a snort of surprise, the priest looked around and up at the solicitously bent head of a Lithian. Under the long, traplike mouth, the be- ing's wattles were a delicate, curious aquamarine, in contrast to its vestigial comb, which was a permanent and silvery sapphire, shot through with veins of fuchsia.

"You are Ruiz-Sanchez," the Lithian said in his own language. The priest's name, unlike that of most of the other Earthmen, fell easily in that tongue. "I know you by your robe."

This was pure chance; any Earthman out in the rain in a mac- intosh would have been identified as Ruiz-Sanchez, because he was the only Earthman who seemed to the Lithians to wear the same garment indoors. "I am Chtexa, the metallist, who con- sulted with you earlier on medicine and on your mission and other matters. We have not seen you here before. Do you wish to talk with the Tree?"

"I do," Ruiz-Sanchez said gratefully. "It is so that I am new here. Can you explain to me what to do?"

"Yes, but not to any profit," Chtexa said, tilting his head so that his completely inky pupils shone down into Ruiz-Sanchez's eyes. "One must have observed the ritual, which is very complex, until it is habit. We have grown up with it, but you I think lack the coordination to follow it on the first attempt. If I may hear your message instead..."

"I would be most indebted. It is for our colleagues Agronski and Michelis. They are at Xoredeshch Gton on the northeast continent, at about thirty-two degrees east, thirty-two degrees north—"

"Yes, the second benchmark, at the outlet of the Lesser Lakes; the city of the potters. And you will say?"

"That they are to join us now, here, at Xoredeshch Sfath. And that our time on Lithia is almost up."

"That me regards. But I will bear it."

Chtexa lept into the whirling crowd, and Ruiz-Sanchez was left behind, considering again his thankfulness at the pains he had taken to learn the Lithian language. Several members of the terrestrial commission had shown a regrettable lack of interest in that tongue: "Let 'em learn English," had been Cleaver's classic formulation. Ruiz-Sanchez was all the less likely to view this idea sympathetically considering that his own native language was Spanish and his preferred foreign language German.

Agronski had taken a slightly more sophisticated stand: it was not, he said, that Lithian was too difficult to pronounce—certainly it wasn't any harder than Arabic or Russian on the soft palate—but, after all, "it's hopeless to attempt to grasp the concepts that lie behind a really alien language in the time we have to spend here, isn't it?"

To both views, Michelis had said nothing; he had simply set out to learn to read the language first, and if he found his way from there into speaking it, he would not be surprised, and neither would his confreres. That was Michelis's way of doing things, thorough and untheoretical at the same time. As for the other two approaches, Ruiz-Sanchez thought privately that it was close to criminal to allow any contact-man for a new planet ever to leave Earth with such parochial notions. Of Cleaver's tendency to refer to the Lithians themselves as "the Snakes," Ruiz-Sanchez's opinion was such as to be admissible only to his remote confessor.

And in view of what lay before him now in this egg-shaped hollow, what was Ruiz-Sanchez to think of Cleaver's conduct as communications officer for the group? Surely he could never have transmitted or received a single message through the Tree, as he had claimed to have done. Probably he had never been nearer to the Tree than the priest had been.

Of course, it went without saying that he had been in contact with Agronski and Michelis by *some* method, but that method evidently had been a private transmitter concealed in his luggage. . . . Yet, physicist though he most definitely was not, Ruiz-Sanchez rejected that solution on the spot; he had some idea of the practical difficulties of ham radio on a world like Lithia, swamped as it was on all wavelengths by the tremendous pulses which the Tree wrung from the buried crystalline cliff. The problem was beginning to make him feel decidedly uncomfortable.

Then Chtexa was back, recognizable not so much by any physical detail—for his wattles were now the same ambiguous royal purple as those of most of the other Lithians in the crowd—as by the fact that he was obviously bearing down upon the Earthman.

"I have sent your message," he said at once. "It is recorded at Xoredeshch Gton. But the other Earthmen are not there. They have not been in the city for some days."

That was impossible. Cleaver had said he had spoken to Agronski only a day ago. "Are you sure?" Ruiz-Sanchez said cautiously.

"It admits of no uncertainty. The house which we gave them stands empty. The many things which they had with them are gone." The tall shape raised its small hands in a gesture which might have been solicitous. "I think this is an ill word. I dislike to bring it you. The words which you brought me when we first met were full of good."

"Thank you. Don't worry," Ruiz-Sanchez said distractedly. "No man could hold the bearer responsible for the word, surely."

"Whom else would he hold responsible for it? At least that is our custom," Chtexa said. "And under it, you have lost by our exchange. Your words on iron have been shown to contain great good. I would take pleasure in showing you how we have used them, especially so since I have brought you in return an ill message. If you would share my house tonight, without prejudice to your work..."

Sternly Ruiz-Sanchez stifled his sudden excitement. Here was the first chance, at long last, to see something of the private life of Lithia! And through that, perhaps, gain some inkling of the moral life, the role in which God had cast the Lithians in the ancient drama of good and evil in the past and in the times to come. Until that was known, the Lithians in their Eden were only spuriously good: all reason, all organic thinking machines, ULTIMACs with tails and without souls.

But there was the hard fact that he had left behind a sick man. There was not much chance that Cleaver would awaken before morning; he had been given nearly fifteen milligrams of sedative per kilogram of body weight. But if his burly frame should somehow throw it off, driven perhaps by some anaphylactic crisis impossible to rule out this early, he would need prompt attention. At the very least, he would want badly for the sound of a human voice on this planet which he hated and which had struck him down.

Still, the danger to Cleaver was not great. He most certainly did not require a minute-by-minute vigil. There was, after all, such a thing as an excess of devotion, a form of pride among the pious which the Church had long found peculiarly difficult to stifle. At its worst, it produced a Saint Simon Stylites, who though undoubtedly acceptable to God had for centuries been very bad public relations for the Church. And had Cleaver really earned the kind of devotion Ruiz-Sanchez had been proposing, up to now, to tender him as a creature of God? And with a whole planet at stake, a whole people—

A lifetime of meditation over just such problems of conscience had made Ruiz-Sanchez, like any other gifted member of his Order, quick to find his way through all but the most complex ethical labyrinths to a decision. An unsympathetic observer might almost have called him "agile."

"Thank you," he said, a little shakily. "I will share your house very gladly."

# 3

"Cleaver! Cleaver! Wake up, you big slob. Where the hell have you been?"

Cleaver groaned and tried to turn over. At his first motion, the world began to rock gently, sickeningly. His mouth was filled with burning pitch.

"Cleaver, turn out. It's me—Agronski. Where's the Father? What's wrong? Why didn't we hear from you? *Look out,* you'll—"

The warning came too late and Cleaver could not have understood it anyhow; he had been profoundly asleep and had no notion of his situation in space or time. At his convulsive twist away from the nagging voice, the hammock rotated on its hooks and dumped him.

He struck the floor stunningly, taking the main blow across his right shoulder, though he hardly felt it as yet. His feet, not yet part of him at all, still remained afloat far aloft, twisted in the hammock webbing.

"Good Lord!" There was a brief chain of footsteps, like chestnuts dropping on a roof, and then an overstated crash. "Cleaver, are you sick? Here, lie still a minute and let me get your feet free. Mike—Mike, can you turn the gas up in this jug? Something's wrong back here."

After a moment, yellow light began to pour from the glistening walls. Cleaver dragged an arm across his eyes, but it did him no good; it tired too quickly. Agronski's mild face, plump and anxious, floated directly above him like a captive balloon. He could not see Michelis anywhere, and at the moment he was just as glad. Agronski's presence was hard enough to understand.

"How ... the hell ..." he said. At the words, his lips split painfully at both corners. He realized for the first time that they had become gummed together, somehow, while he was asleep. He had no idea how long he had been out of the picture.

Agronski seemed to understand the aborted question. "We came in from the lakes in the 'copter," he said. "We didn't like the silence down here and we figured that we'd better come in under our own power, instead of registering in on the regular jetliner and tipping the Lithians off—just in case there'd been any dirty work afloat."

"Stop jawing him," Michelis said, appearing suddenly, magically in the doorway. "He's got a bug, that's obvious. I don't like to feel pleased about misery, but I'm glad it's that instead of the Lithians."

The rangy, long-jawed chemist helped Agronski lift Cleaver to his feet. Tentatively, despite the pain, Cleaver got his mouth open again. Nothing came out but a hoarse croak.

"Shut up," Michelis said, not unkindly. "Let's get him back into the hammock. Where's the father? He's the only one capable of dealing with sickness here."

"I'll bet he's dead," Agronski burst out suddenly, his face glistening with alarm. "He'd be here if he could. It must be catching, Mike."

"I didn't bring my mitt," Michelis said dryly. "Cleaver, lie still or I'll have to clobber you. Agronski, you seem to have dumped his water carafe; better go get him some more, he needs it. And see if the father left anything in the lab that looks like medicine."

Agronski went out, and, maddeningly, so did Michelis—at least out of Cleaver's field of vision. Setting his every muscle against the pain, Cleaver pulled his lips apart once more.

"Mike."

Instantly, Michelis was there. He had a pad of cotton between two fingers, wet with some solution, with which he gently cleaned Cleaver's lips and chin.

"Easy. Agronski's getting you a drink. We'll let you talk in a little while, Paul. Don't rush it."

Cleaver relaxed a little. He could trust Michelis. Nevertheless, the vivid and absurd insult of having to be swabbed like a baby was more than he could bear; he felt tears of helpless rage swelling on either side of his nose. With two deft, noncommittal swipes, Michelis removed them.

Agronski came back, holding out one hand tentatively, palm up. "I found these," he said. "There's more in the lab, and the father's pillpress is still out. So's his mortar and pestle, though they've been cleaned."

"All right, let's have 'em," Michelis said. "Anything else?"

"No. There's a syringe cooking in the sterilizer, if that means anything."

Michelis swore briefly and to the point. "It means that there's a pertinent antitoxin in the shop someplace," he added. "But unless Ramon left notes, we'll not have a prayer of figuring out which one it is."

As he spoke, he lifted Cleaver's head and tipped the pills into his mouth. The water which followed was cold at the first contact, but a split second later it was liquid fire. Cleaver choked, and at that precise moment Michelis pinched his nostrils shut. The pills went down.

"There's no sign of the father?" Michelis said.

"Not a one, Mike. Everything's in good order, and his gear's still here. Both jungle suits are in the locker."

"Maybe he went visiting," Michelis said thoughtfully. "He must have gotten to know quite a few of the Lithians by now."

"With a sick man on his hands? That's not like him, Mike. Not unless there was some kind of emergency. Or maybe he went on a routine errand, expected to be back in just a few moments, and—"

"And was set upon by trolls for forgetting to stamp his foot three times before crossing the bridge."

"All right, laugh."

"I'm not laughing, believe me."

*"Mike . . ."*

Michelis took a step back and looked down at Cleaver, his face floating as if detached through a haze of tears. He said: "All right, Paul. Tell us what it is. We're listening."

But it was too late. The doubled barbiturate dose had gotten to Cleaver first. He could only shake his head, and with the motion Michelis seemed to go reeling away into a whirlpool of fuzzy rainbows.

Curiously, he did not quite go to sleep. He had had nearly a normal night's sleep, and he had started out the enormously long day a powerful and healthy man. The conversation of the two Earthmen and an obsessive consciousness of his need to speak to them before Ruiz-Sanchez returned helped to keep him, if not totally awake, at least not far below a state of light trance—and the presence in his system of thirty grains of acetyl-salicylic acid had seriously raised his oxygen consumption, bringing with it not only dizziness but a precarious, emotionally untethered alertness. That the fuel which was being burned to maintain it was largely the protein substrate of his own cells he did not know, and it could not have alarmed him had he known it.

The voices continued to reach him, and to convey a little meaning. With them were mixed fleeting, fragmentary dreams, so slightly removed from the surface of his waking life as to seem peculiarly real, yet at the same time peculiarly pointless and depressing. In the semiconscious intervals there came plans, a whole succession of them, all simple and grandiose at once, for taking command of the expedition, for communicating with the authorities on Earth, for bringing forward secret papers proving that Lithia was uninhabitable, for digging a tunnel under Mexico to Peru, for detonating Lithia in one single mighty fusion of all its lightweight atoms into an atom of cleaverium, the element whose cardinal number was aleph-null . . .

AGRONSKI: Mike, come here and look at this; you read Lithian. There's a mark on the front door, on the message tablet.

(Footsteps).

MICHELIS: It says "Sickness inside." The strokes aren't casual or deft enough to be the work of the natives. Ideographs are hard to write rapidly. Ramon must have written it there.

AGRONSKI: I wish I knew where he went afterward.

(Footsteps. Door shutting, not loudly. Footsteps. Hassock creaking.)

AGRONSKI: Well, we'd better be thinking about getting up a report. Unless this damn twenty-hour day has me thrown completely off, our time's just about up. Are you still set on opening up the planet?

MICHELIS: Yes. I've seen nothing to convince me that there's anything on Lithia that's dangerous to us. Except maybe Cleaver in there, and I'm not prepared to say that the Father would have left him if he were in any serious danger. And I do not see how Earthmen could harm this society: it's too stable emotionally, economically, in every other way.

(*Danger, danger,* said somebody in Cleaver's dream. *It will explode. It's all a popish plot.* Then he was marginally awake again and conscious of how his mouth hurt.)

AGRONSKI: Why do you suppose these two jokers never called us after we went north?

MICHELIS: I don't have any answer. I won't even guess until I talk to Ramon. Or until Paul's able to sit up and take notice.

AGRONSKI: I don't like it, Mike. It smells bad to me. This town's right at the heart of the communications system of the planet. And yet—no messages, Cleaver sick, the Father not here ... there's a hell of a lot we don't know about Lithia.

MICHELIS: There's a hell of a lot we don't know about central Brazil.

AGRONSKI: Nothing essential, Mike. What we know about the periphery gives us all the clues we need about the interior—even to those fish that eat people, the what-are-they, the piranhas. That's not true on Lithia. We don't know whether our peripheral clues about Lithia are germane or just incidental. Something enormous could be hidden under the surface without our being able to detect it.

MICHELIS: Agronski, stop sounding like a Sunday supplement. You underestimate your own intelligence. What kind of enormous secret could that be? That the Lithians eat people? That they're cattle for unknown gods that live in the jungle? That they're actually mind-wrenching, soul-twisting, heart-stopping, bowel-moving intelligences in disguise? The moment you see any such proposition, you'll deflate it yourself. I would not even need to take the trouble of examining it, or discussing how we might meet it if it were true.

AGRONSKI: All right, all right. I'll reserve judgment for the time being, anyhow. If everything turns out to be all right here, with the father and Cleaver I mean, I'll probably go along with you. I don't have any reason I could defend for voting against the planet, I admit.

MICHELIS: Good for you. I'm sure Ramon is for opening it up, so that should make it unanimous. I can't see why Cleaver would object.

(Cleaver was testifying before a packed court convened in the UN General Assembly chambers in New York, with one finger pointed dramatically, but less in triumph than in sorrow, at Ramon Ruiz-Sanchez, S.J. At the sound of his name the dream collapsed and he realized that the room had grown a little lighter. Dawn—or the dripping, wool-gray travesty of it which prevailed on Lithia—was on its way. He wondered what he had just said to the court. It had been conclusive, damning, good enough to be used when he awoke; but he could not remember a word of it. All that remained of it was a sensation, almost the taste of the words, but with nothing of their substance.)

AGRONSKI: It's getting light. I suppose we'd better knock off.

MICHELIS: Did you stake down the 'copter? The winds here are higher than they are up north, I seem to remember.

AGRONSKI: Yes. And covered it with the tarp. Nothing left to do but sling our hammocks—"

MICHELIS: *Shh.* What's that?

(Footsteps. Faint ones, but Cleaver knew them. He forced his eyes to open a little, but there was nothing to see but the ceiling. Its even color, and its smooth, ever-changing slope into a dome of nothingness, drew him almost immediately upward into the mists of trance once more.)

AGRONSKI: Somebody's coming. It's the Father, Mike—look out here. He seems to be all right. Dragging his feet a bit, but who wouldn't after being out helling all night?

MICHELIS: Maybe you'd better meet him at the door. It'd probably be better than our springing out at him after he gets inside. After all he doesn't expect us. I'll get to unpacking the hammocks.

AGRONSKI: Sure, Mike.

(Footsteps going away from Cleaver. A grating sound of stone on stone: the door-wheel being turned.)

AGRONSKI: Welcome home, Father! We got in just a little while ago and—what's wrong? Are you ill? Is there something that—Mike! *Mike!*

(Somebody was running. Cleaver willed his neck muscles to turn his head, but they refused to obey. Instead, the back of his head seemed to force itself deeper into the stiff pillow of the hammock. After a momentary and endless agony he cried out.)

CLEAVER: Mike!

AGRONSKI: Mike!

(With a gasp, Cleaver lost the long battle at last. He was asleep.)

# 4

As the door of Chtexa's house closed behind him, Ruiz-Sanchez looked about the gently glowing foyer with a feeling of almost unbearable anticipation, although he could hardly have said what it was that he hoped to see. Actually, it looked exactly like his own quarters, which was all he could in justice have expected—all the furniture at "home" was Lithian except the lab equipment.

"We have cut up several of the metal meteors from our museums and hammered them as you suggested," Chtexa said behind him, while he struggled out of his raincoat and boots. "They show very definite, very strong magnetism, just as you predicted. We now have the whole planet alerted to pick up meteorites and send them to our electrical laboratory here, regardless of where found. The staff of the observatory is attempting to predict possible falls. Unhappily, meteors are rare here. Our astronomers say that we have never had a 'shower' such as you described as frequent on your native planet."

"No, I should have thought of that," Ruiz-Sanchez said, following the Lithian into the front room. This, too, was quite ordinary, and empty except for the two of them. "In our system we have a sort of giant grinding-wheel—a whole ring of little planets, many thousands of them, distributed around an orbit where we had expected to find only one normal-sized world. Collisions between these bodies are incessant, and our plague of meteors is the result. Here I suppose you have only the usual few strays from comets."

"It is hard to understand how so unstable an arrangement could have come about," Chtexa said, sitting down and pointing out another hassock to his guest. "Have you an explanation?"

"Not a good one," Ruiz-Sanchez said. "Some of us think that there was a respectable planet in that orbit ages ago, which exploded somehow. A similar accident happened to a satellite in our system—at least one of our planets has a similar ring. Others think that at the formation of our solar system the raw materials of what might have been a planet just never succeeded in coalescing. Both ideas have many flaws, but each satisfies certain objections to the other, so perhaps there is some truth in both."

Chtexa's eyes filmed with the mildly disquieting "inner blink" characteristic of Lithians at their most thoughtful. "There would seem to be no way to test either answer," he said at length. "By our logic, lack of such tests makes the original question meaningless."

"That rule of logic has many adherents on Earth. My colleague Dr. Cleaver would certainly agree with it." Ruiz-Sanchez smiled suddenly. He had labored long and hard to master the Lithian language, and to have understood and recognized so completely abstract a point as the one just made by Chtexa was a bigger victory than any quantitative gains in vocabulary alone could ever have been. "But I can see that we are going to have difficulties in collecting these meteorites. Have you offered incentives?"

"Oh, certainly. Everyone understands the importance of the program. We are all eager to advance it."

This was not quite what the priest had meant by his question. He searched his memory for some Lithian equivalent of *reward,* but found nothing but the word he had already used, *incentive.* He realized that he knew no word for *greed,* either. Evidently offering Lithians a hundred dollars a meteorite would simply baffle them. Instead he said, "Since the potential meteor-fall is so small, you're not likely to get anything like the supply of metal that you need for a real study, no matter how thoroughly you cooperate on it. You need a supplementary iron-finding program: some way of concentrating the traces of the metal you have on the planet. Our smelting methods would be useless to you, since you have no ore-beds. Hmm. What about the iron-fixing bacteria?"

"Are there such?" Chtexa said, cocking his head dubiously.

"I don't know. Ask your bacteriologists. If you have any bacteria here that belong to the genus we call *Leptothrix,* one of them should be an iron-fixing species. In all the millions of years that this planet has had life on it, that mutation must have occurred, and probably very early."

"But why have we never seen it before? We have done perhaps more research in bacteriology than we have in any other field."

"Because," Ruiz-Sanchez said earnestly, "you didn't know what to look for, and because such a species would be as rare as iron itself. On Earth, because we have iron in abundance, our *Leptothrix ochracea* has found plenty of opportunity to grow. We find their fossil sheaths by uncountable millions in our great ore-beds. It used to be thought, as a matter of fact, that the bacteria *produced* the ore-beds, but I've never believed that. While they do obtain their energy by oxidizing ferrous iron, such salts in solution change spontaneously to ferric salts if the oxidation-reduction potential and the pH of the water are right—and those are conditions that are affected by ordinary decay bacteria. On our planet the bacteria grew in the ore-beds because the iron was there, not the other way around. In your case, you just don't have the iron to make them numerous, but I'm sure there must be a few."

"We will start a soil-sampling program at once," Chtexa said, his wattles flaring a subdued orchid. "Our antibiotics research centers screen soil samples by the thousands every month, in search of new microflora of therapeutic importance. If these iron-fixing bacteria exist, we are certain to find them eventually."

"They must exist," Ruiz-Sanchez repeated. "Do you have a bacterium that is a sulphur-concentrating obligate anaerobe?"

"Yes—yes, certainly!"

"There you are," the Jesuit said, leaning back contentedly and clasping his hands across one knee. "You have plenty of sulphur and so you have the bacterium. Please let me know when you find the iron-fixing species. I'd like to make a sub-culture and take it home with me when I leave. There are two Earthmen whose noses I'd like to rub in it."

The Lithian stiffened and thrust his head forward a little, as if baffled. Ruiz-Sanchez said hastily, "Pardon me. I was translating literally an aggressive idiom of my own tongue. It was not meant to describe an actual plan of action."

"I think I understand," Chtexa said. Ruiz-Sanchez wondered if he did. In the rich storehouse of the Lithian language he had yet to discover any metaphors, either living or dead. Neither did the Lithians have any poetry or other creative arts. "You are of course welcome to any of the results of this program which you would honor us by accepting. One problem in the social sciences which has long puzzled us is just how one may adequately honor the innovator. When we consider how new ideas change our lives, we despair of giving in kind, and it is helpful when the innovator himself has wishes which society can gratify."

Ruiz-Sanchez was at first not quite sure he had understood the proposition. After he had gone over it once more in his mind, he was not sure that he could bring himself to like it, although it was admirable enough. From an Earthman it would have sounded intolerably pompous, but it was evident that Chtexa meant it.

It was probably just as well that the commission's report on Lithia was about to fall due. Ruiz-Sanchez had begun to think that he could absorb only a little more of this kind of calm sanity. And all of it—a disquieting thought from somewhere near his heart reminded him—all of it derived from reason, none from precept, none from faith. The Lithians did not know God. They did things rightly, and thought righteously, because it was reasonable and efficient and natural to do and to think that way. They seemed to need nothing else.

Or could it be that they thought and acted as they did because, not being born of man, and never in effect having left the Garden in which they lived, they did not share the terrible burden of original sin? The fact that Lithia had never once had a glacial epoch, that its climate had been left unchanged for seven hundred million years, was a geological fact that an alert geologist could scarcely afford to ignore. Could it be that, free from the burden, they were also free from the curse of Adam?

And if they were—could men bear to live among them?

"I have some questions to ask you, Chtexa," the priest said after a moment. "You owe me no debt whatsoever, but we four Earthmen have a hard decision to make shortly. You know what it is. And I don't believe that we know enough yet about your planet to make that decision properly."

"Then of course you must ask questions," Chtexa said immediately. "I will answer, wherever I can."

"Well, then—do your people die? I see you have the word,

but perhaps it isn't the same as our word in meaning."

"It means to stop changing and to go back to existing," Chtexa said. "A machine exists, but only a living thing, like a tree, progresses along a line of changing equilibriums. When that progress stops, the entity is dead."

"And that happens to you?"

"It always happens. Even the great trees, like the Message Tree, die sooner or later. Is that not true on Earth?"

"Yes," Ruiz-Sanchez said, "yes, it is. For reasons it would take me a long time to explain, it occurred to me that you might have escaped this evil."

"It is not evil as we look at it," Chtexa said. "Lithia lives because of death. The death of leaves supplies our oil and gas. The death of some creatures is always necessary for the life of others. Bacteria must die, and viruses be prevented from living, if illness is to be cured. We ourselves must die simply to make room for others, at least until we can slow the rate at which our people arrive in the world—a thing impossible to us at present."

"But desirable, in your eyes?"

"Surely desirable," Chtexa said. "Our world is rich, but not inexhaustible. And other planets, you have taught us, have peoples of their own. Thus we cannot hope to spread to other planets when we have overpopulated this one."

"No real thing is ever inexhaustible," Ruiz-Sanchez said abruptly, frowning at the iridescent floor. "That we have found to be true over many thousands of years of our history."

"But inexhaustible in what way?" said Chtexa. "I grant you that any small object, any stone, any drop of water, any bit of soil can be explored without end. The amount of information which can be gotten from it is quite literally infinite. But a given soil can be exhausted of nitrates. It is difficult, but with bad cultivation it can be done. Or take iron, about which we have already been talking. Our planet's supply of iron has limits which we already know, at least approximately. To allow our economy to develop a demand for iron which exceeds the total known supply of Lithia—and exceeds it beyond any possibility of supplementation by meteors or by import—would be folly. This is not a question of information. It is a question of whether or not the information can be used. If it cannot, then limitless information is of no help."

"You could certainly get along without more iron if you had to," Ruiz-Sanchez admitted. "Your wooden machinery is precise enough to satisfy any engineer. Most of them, I think, don't remember that we used to have something similar: I've a sample in my own home. It's a kind of timer called a cuckoo clock, nearly two of our centuries old, made entirely of wood, and still nearly one hundred percent accurate. For that matter, long after we began to build seagoing vessels of metal, we continued to use lignum vitae for ships' bearings."

"Wood is an excellent material for most uses," Chtexa agreed. "Its only deficiency, compared to ceramic materials or perhaps metal, is that it is variable. One must know it well to be able to assess its qualities from one tree to the next. And of course complicated parts can always be grown inside suitable ceramic molds; the growth pressure inside the mold rises so high that the resulting part is very dense. Larger parts can be ground direct from the plank with soft sandstone and polished with slate. It is a gratifying material to work, we find."

Ruiz-Sanchez felt, for some reason, a little ashamed. It was a magnified version of the same shame he had always felt at home toward that old Black Forest cuckoo clock. The electric clocks elsewhere in his villa back home all should have been capable of performing silently, accurately, and in less space—but the considerations which had gone into the making of them had been commercial as well as purely technical. As a result, most of them operated with a thin, asthmatic whir, or groaned softly but dismally at irregular hours. All of them were "streamlined," oversized, and ugly. None of them kept good time, and several of them, since they were powered by constant-speed motors operating very simple gearboxes, could not be adjusted, but had been sent out from the factory with built-in ineluctable inaccuracies.

The wooden cuckoo clock, meanwhile, ticked evenly away. A quail emerged from one of two wooden doors every quarter of an hour and let you know about it, and on the hour first the quail came out, then the cuckoo, and there was a soft bell that rang just ahead of the cuckoo's call. It was accurate to a minute a week, all for the price of running up the three weights which drove it, each night before bedtime.

The maker had been dead before Ruiz-Sanchez had been

born. In contrast, the priest would probably buy and jettison at least a dozen cheap electric clocks in the course of one lifetime, as their makers had intended he should.

"I'm sure it is," he said humbly. "I have one more question, if I may. It is really part of the same question: I have asked if you die; now I should like to ask how you are born. I see many adults on your streets and sometimes in your houses—though I gather you yourself are alone—but never any children. Can you explain this to me? Or if the subject is not allowed to be discussed . . ."

"But why should it not be? There can never be any closed subjects," Chtexa said. "You know, of course, that our mates have abdominal pouches where the eggs are carried. It was a lucky mutation for us, for there are a number of nest-robbing species on this planet."

"Yes, we have a few animals with a somewhat similar arrangement on Earth, although they are live-bearers."

"Our eggs are laid into these pouches once a year," Chtexa said. "It is then that the women leave their own houses and seek out the male of their choice to fertilize the eggs. I am alone because, thus far, I am no woman's first choice this season. In contrast you may see men's houses at this time of year which shelter three or four women who favor him."

"I see," Ruiz-Sanchez said carefully. "And how is the choice determined? Is it by emotion, or by reason alone?"

"The two are in the long run the same," Chtexa said. "Our ancestors did not leave our genetic needs to chance. Emotion with us no longer runs counter to our eugenic knowledge. It cannot, since it was itself modified to follow that knowledge by selective breeding for such behavior.

"At the end of the season, then, comes Migration Day. At that time all the eggs are fertilized, and ready to hatch. On that day—you will not be here to see it, I am afraid, for your announced date of departure precedes it by a short time—our whole nation goes to the seashores. There, with the men to protect them from predators, the women wade out to swimming depth, and the children are born."

"In the sea?" Ruiz-Sanchez said faintly.

"Yes, in the sea. Then we all return, and resume our other affairs until the next mating season."

"But—but what happens to the children?"

"Why, they take care of themselves, if they can. Of course many perish, particularly to our voracious brother the great fish-lizard, whom for that reason we kill when we can. But a majority return when the time comes."

"Return? Chtexa, I don't understand. Why don't they drown when they are born? And if they return, why have we never seen one?"

"But you have," Chtexa said. "And you have heard them often. Here, come with me." He arose and led the way out into the foyer. Ruiz-Sanchez followed, his head whirling with conjecture.

Chtexa opened the door. The night, the priest saw with a subdued shock, was on the wane; there was the faintest of pearly glimmers on the cloudy sky to the east. The multifarious humming and singing of the jungle continued unabated. There was a high, hissing whistle, and the shadow of a pterodon drifted over the city toward the sea. From the mudflats came a hoarse barking.

"There," Chtexa said softly. "Did you hear it?"

The stranded creature, or another of his kind—it was impossible to tell which—croaked protestingly again.

"It is hard for them at first," Chtexa said. "But actually the worst of their dangers are over. They have come ashore."

"Chtexa," Ruiz-Sanchez said. "Your children—*the lungfish*?"

"Yes," Chtexa said. "Those are our children."


# 5


In the last analysis it was the incessant barking of the lungfish which caused Ruiz-Sanchez to faint when Agronski opened the door for him. The late hour, and the dual strains of Cleaver's illness and the subsequent discovery of Cleaver's direct lying, contributed. So did the increasing sense of guilt toward Cleaver which the priest had felt while walking home under the gradu-

ally brightening, weeping sky; and so, of course, did the shock
of discovering that Agronski and Michelis had arrived sometime
during the night while he had been neglecting his charge.

But primarily it was the diminishing, gasping clamor of the
children of Lithia, battering at his every mental citadel, all the
way from Chtexa's house to his own.

The sudden fugue only lasted a few moments. He fought his
way back to consciousness to find that Agronski and Michelis
had propped him up on a stool in the lab and were trying to
remove his macintosh without unbalancing him or awakening
him—as difficult a problem in topology as removing a man's
vest without taking off his jacket. Wearily, the priest pulled his
own arm out of a macintosh sleeve and looked up at Michelis.

"Good morning, Mike. Please excuse my bad manners."

"Don't be an idiot," Michelis said evenly. "You don't have to
talk now, anyhow. I've already spent much of tonight trying to
keep Cleaver quiet until he's better. Don't put me through it
again, Ramon, please."

"I won't. I'm not ill; I'm just very tired and a little over-
wrought."

"What's the matter with Cleaver?" Agronski demanded. Michelis made as if to shoo him off.

"No, no, Mike. I'm all right, I assure you. As for Paul, he got
a dose of glucoside poisoning when a plant-spine stabbed him
this afternoon. No, it's yesterday afternoon now. How has he
been since you arrived?"

"He's sick," Michelis said. "Since you weren't here, we did
not know what to do. We settled for two of the pills you'd left
out."

"You did?" Ruiz-Sanchez slid his feet heavily to the floor and
tried to stand up. "As you say, you couldn't have known what
else to do, but I think I'd better look in on him—"

"Sit down, please, Ramon." Michelis spoke gently, but his
tone showed that he meant the request to be honored. Ob-
scurely glad to be forced to yield to the big man's well-meant
implacability, the priest let himself be propped back on the
stool. His boots fell off his feet to the floor.

"Mike, who's the Father here?" he said tiredly. "Still, I'm sure
you've done a good job. He's in no apparent danger?"

"Well, he seems very sick. But he had energy enough to keep

himself half-awake most of the night. He only passed out a short while ago."

"Good. Let him stay out. Tomorrow we'll probably have to begin intravenous feeding, though. In this atmosphere one doesn't give a salicylate overdose without penalties." He sighed. "Can we put off further questions?"

"If there's nothing else wrong here, of course we can."

"Oh," Ruiz-Sanchez said, "there's a great deal wrong, I'm afraid."

"I knew it," Agronski said. "I knew damn well there was. I told you so, Mike, didn't I?"

"Is it urgent?"

"No, Mike—there's no danger to us, of that I'm positive. It's nothing that won't keep until we have all had a rest. You two look as though you need one as badly as I."

"We're tired," Michelis agreed.

"But why didn't you ever call us?" Agronski burst in aggrievedly. "You had us scared half to death, Father. If there's really something wrong here, you should have—"

"There's no immediate danger," Ruiz-Sanchez repeated patiently. "As for why we didn't call you, I don't understand that any more than you do. Up to tonight, I thought we were in regular contact with you both. That was Paul's job and he seemed to be carrying it out. I didn't discover that he wasn't doing it until after he became ill."

"Then obviously we'll have to wait," Michelis said. "Let's hit the hammock, in God's name. Flying that 'copter through twenty-five hundred miles of fog bank wasn't exactly restful, either; I'll be glad to turn in.... But, Ramon—"

"Yes, Mike?"

"I have to say that I don't like this any better than Agronski does. Tomorrow we've got to clear it up, and get our commission business done. We've only a day or so to make our decision before the ship comes and takes us off for good, and by that time we *must* know everything there is to know, and just what we're going to tell the Earth about it."

"Yes," Ruiz-Sanchez said. "Just as you say, Mike—in God's name."

The Peruvian priest-biologist awoke before the others: actually, he had undergone far less purely physical strain than had the other three. It was just beginning to be cloudy dusk when he rolled out of his hammock and padded over to look at Cleaver.

The physicist was in a coma. His face was dirty gray and looked oddly shrunken. It was high time that the neglect and inadvertent abuse to which he had been subjected was rectified. Happily, his pulse and respiration were close to normal now.

Ruiz-Sanchez went quietly into the lab and made up a fructose IV feeding. At the same time he reconstituted a can of powdered eggs into a sort of soufflé, setting it in a covered crucible to bake at the back of the little oven; that was for the rest of them.

In the sleeping chamber, the priest set up his IV stand. Cleaver did not stir when the needle entered the big vein just above the inside of his elbow. Ruiz-Sanchez taped the tubing in place, checked the drip from the inverted bottle and went back into the lab.

There he sat, on the stool before the microscope, in a sort of suspension of feeling while the new night drew on. He was still poisoned-tired, but at least now he could stay awake without constantly fighting himself. The slowly rising soufflé in the oven went *plup-plup, plup-plup,* and after a while a thin tendril of aroma suggested that it was beginning to brown on top, or at least thinking about it.

Outside, it abruptly rained buckets. Just as abruptly, it stopped.

"Is that breakfast I smell, Ramon?"

"Yes, Mike, in the oven. In a few minutes now."

"Right."

Michelis went away again. On the back of the workbench, Ruiz-Sanchez saw the dark blue book with the gold stamping which he had brought with him all the way from Earth. Almost automatically he pulled it to him and opened it to page 573. It would at least give him something to think about with which he was not personally involved.

He had quitted the text last with Anita, who "would yield to the lewdness of Honuphrius to appease the savagery of Sulla and the mercenariness of the twelve Sullivani, and (as Gilbert first suggested) to save the virginity of Felicia for Magravius"—now hold on a moment, how could Felicia still be considered a virgin at this point? Ah: "... when converted by Michael after the death of Gillia"; that covered it, since Felicia had been guilty only of simple infidelities in the first place. "...but she fears that, by allowing his marital rights, she may cause reprehensible conduct between Eugenius and Jeremias. Michael, who has formerly debauched Anita, dispenses her from yielding to Honuphrius"—yes, that figured, since Michael also had had designs on Eugenius. "Anita is disturbed, but Michael comminates that he will reserve her case tomorrow for the ordinary Guglielmus even if she should practice a pious fraud during affriction which, from experience, she knows (according to Wadding) to be leading to nullity."

Well. This was all very well. It even seemed to be shaping up, for the first time. Still, Ruiz-Sanchez reflected, he would not like to have known the family hidden behind the conventional Latin aliases, or to have been the confessor to any one of them. Now then:

"Fortissa, however, is encouraged by Gregorius, Leo, Viteilius, and Macdugalius, reunitedly, to warn Anita by describing the strong chastisements of Honuphrius and the depravities (*turpissimas*) of Canicula, the deceased wife of Mauritius, with Sulla, the simoniac, who is abnegand and repents."

Yes, it added up, when one tried to view it without outrage either at the persons involved—and there was every assurance that these were fictitious—or at the author, who for all his mighty intellect, the greatest perhaps of the preceding century among novelists, had still to be pitied as much as the meanest victim of the Evil One. To view it, as it were, in a sort of gray twilight of emotion, wherein everything, even the barnaclelike commentaries which the text had accumulated, could be seen in the same light.

"Is it done, Father?"

"Smells like it, Agronski. Take it out and help yourself, why don't you?"

"Thanks. Can I bring Cleaver—"

"No, he's getting an IV."

Unless his impression that he understood the problem at last was once more going to turn out to be an illusion, he was now ready for the basic question, the stumper that had deeply disturbed both the Order and the Church for so many years now. He reread it carefully. It asked:

"Has he hegemony and shall she submit?"

To his astonishment, he saw as if for the first time that it was two questions, despite the omission of a comma between the two. And so it demanded two answers. Did Honuphrius have hegemony? Yes, he did, for Michael, the only member of the whole complex who had been gifted from the beginning with the power of grace, had been egregiously compromised. Therefore, Honuphrius regardless of whether his sins were all to be laid at his door or were real only in rumor could not be divested of his privileges by anyone. But should Anita submit? No, she should not. Michael had forfeited his right to dispense or to reserve her in any way, and so she could not be guided by the curate or by anyone else in the long run but her own conscience—which in view of the grave accusations against Honuphrius could lead her to no recourse but to deny him. As for Sulla's repentance, and Felicia's conversion, they meant nothing, since the defection of Michael had deprived both of them, and everyone else, of spiritual guidance.

The answer, then, had been obvious all the time. It was: yes, and no.

He closed the book and looked up across the bench, feeling neither more nor less dazed than he had before, but with a small stirring of elation deep inside him which he could not suppress. As he looked out of the window into the dripping darkness, a familiar, sculpturesque head and shoulders moved into the truncated tetrahedron of yellow light being cast out through the fine glass into the rain.

It was Chtexa, moving away from the house.

Suddenly Ruiz-Sanchez realized that nobody had bothered to rub away the sickness ideograms on the door tablet. If Chtexa had come here on some errand, he had been turned back unnecessarily. The priest leaned forward, snatched up an empty slidebox and rapped with a corner of it against the inside of the window.

Chtexa turned and looked in through the steaming curtains of rain, his eyes completely filmed. Ruiz-Sanchez beckoned to him, and got stiffly off the stool to open the door. In the oven his share of breakfast dried slowly and began to burn.

The rapping had summoned forth Agronski and Michelis as well. Chtexa looked down at the three of them with easy gravity, while drops of water ran like oil down the minute, prismatic scales of his supple skin.

"I did not know that there was sickness here," the Lithian

said. "I called because your brother Ruiz-Sanchez left my house this morning without the gift I had hoped to give him. I will leave if I am invading your privacy in any way."

"You are not," Ruiz-Sanchez assured him. "And the sickness is only a poisoning, not communicable and we think not likely to end badly for our colleague. These are my friends from the north, Agronski and Michelis."

"I am happy to see them. The message was not in vain, then?"

"What message is this?" Michelis said, in his pure but hesitant Lithian.

"I sent a message, as your colleague Ruiz-Sanchez asked me to do, last night. I was told by Xoredeshch Gton that you had already departed."

"As we had," Michelis said. "Ramon, what's this? I thought you told us that sending messages was Paul's job. And you certainly implied that you didn't know how to do it after Paul took sick."

"I didn't. I don't. I asked Chtexa to send it for me."

Michelis looked up at the Lithian. "What did the message say?" he asked.

"That you were to join them now, here, in Xoredeshch Sfath. And that your time on our world was almost up."

"What does that mean?" Agronski said. He had been trying to follow the conversation, but he was not much of a linguist, and evidently the few words he had been able to pick up had served only to inflame his ready fears. "Mike, translate, please."

Michelis did so, briefly. Then he said: "Ramon, was that really all you had to say to us, especially after what you had found out? We knew that departure time was coming, too, after all. We can keep a calendar as well as you, I hope."

"I know that, Mike. But I had no idea what previous messages you'd received, if indeed you'd received any. For all I knew, Cleaver might have been in touch with you some other way, privately. I thought at first of a transmitter in his personal luggage, but later it occurred to me that he might have been sending dispatches over the regular jetliners. Or he might have told you that we were going to stay on beyond the official time. He might have told you I was dead. He might have told you anything. I had to be sure you'd arrive here *regardless* of what he had or had not said.

"And when I got to the local message center, I had to revise my message again, because I found that I couldn't communicate with you directly, or send anything at all detailed. Everything that goes out from Xoredeshch Sfath by radio goes out through the Tree, and until you have seen it you haven't any idea what an Earthman is up against there in sending even the simplest message."

"Is that true?" Michelis asked Chtexa.

"True?" Chtexa repeated. "It is accurate, yes."

"Well, then," Ruiz-Sanchez said, a little nettled, "you can see why, when Chtexa appeared providentially, recognized me, and offered to act as an intermediary, I had to give him only the gist of what I had to say. I couldn't hope to explain all the details to him, and I couldn't hope that any of those details would get to you undistorted after passing through at least two Lithian inter-mediaries. All I could do was yell at the top of my voice for you two to get down here on the proper date—and hope that you heard me."

"This is a time of trouble, which is like a sickness in the house," Chtexa said. "I must not remain. I will wish to be left alone when I am troubled, and I cannot ask that, if I now force my presence on others who are troubled. I will bring my gift at a better time."

He ducked out through the door, without any formal gesture of farewell, but nevertheless leaving behind an overwhelming im-pression of graciousness. Ruiz-Sanchez watched him go help-lessly, and a little forlornly. The Lithians always seemed to understand the essences of situations; they were never, like even the most cocksure of Earthmen, beset by the least apparent doubt.

And why should they be? They were backed—if Ruiz-Sanchez was right—by the second-best Authority in the universe, and backed directly, without intermediaries or conflicting interpre-tations. The very fact that they were never tormented by indeci-sion identified them as creatures of that Authority. Only the children of God had been given free choice, and hence were often doubtful.

Nevertheless, Ruiz-Sanchez would have delayed Chtexa's de-parture had he been able. In a short-term argument it is helpful to have pure reason on your side—even though such an ally could be depended upon to stab you through the heart if you depended upon him too long.

"Let's go inside and thrash this thing out," Michelis said, shutting the door and turning back toward the front room. "It's a good thing we got some sleep, but we have so little time left now that it's going to be touch and go to have a formal decision ready when the ship comes."

"We can't go ahead yet," Agronski objected, although, along with Ruiz-Sanchez, he followed Michelis obediently enough. "How can we do anything sensible without having heard what Cleaver has to say? Every man's voice counts on a job of this sort."

"That's very true," Michelis said. "And I don't like the present situation any better than you do—I've already said that. But I don't see that we have any choice. What do you think, Ramon?"

"I'd like to hold out for waiting," Ruiz-Sanchez said frankly. "Anything I may say now is, to put it realistically, somewhat compromised with you two. And don't tell me that you have every confidence in my integrity, because we had every confidence in Cleaver's, too. Right now, trying to maintain both confidences just cancels out both."

"You have a nasty way, Ramon, of saying aloud what everybody else is thinking," Michelis said, grinning bleakly. "What alternatives do you see, then?"

"None," Ruiz-Sanchez admitted. "Time is against us, as you said. We'll just have to go ahead without Cleaver."

"No, you won't." The voice, from the doorway to the sleeping chamber, was at once uncertain and much harshened by weakness.

The others sprang up. Cleaver, clad only in his shorts, stood in the doorway, clinging to both sides of it. On one forearm Ruiz-Sanchez could see the marks where the adhesive tape which had held the IV tubing had been ripped off.

# 6

"Paul, you must be crazy," Michelis said, almost angrily. "Get back into your hammock before you make things twice as bad for yourself. You're a sick man, can't you realize that?"

"Not as sick as I look," Cleaver said, with a ghastly grin. "Actually I feel pretty fair. My mouth is almost all cleared up and I don't think I've got any fever. And I'll be damned if this commission is going to proceed an inch without me. It isn't empowered to do it, and I'll appeal against any decision—*any* decision, I hope you guys are listening—that it makes without me."

The other two turned helplessly to Ruiz-Sanchez.

"How about it, Ramon?" Michelis said, frowning. "Is it safe for him to be up like this?"

Ruiz-Sanchez was already at the physicist's side, peering into his mouth. The ulcers were indeed almost gone, with granulation tissue forming nicely over the few that still remained. Cleaver's eyes were still slightly suffused, indicating that the toxemia was not completely defeated, but except for these two signs, the effect of the accidental squill inoculation was no longer visible. It was true that Cleaver looked awful, but that was inevitable in a man recently quite sick, and in one who had been burning his own body proteins for fuel to boot.

"If he wants to kill himself, I guess he's got a right to do so, at least by indirection," Ruiz-Sanchez said. "Paul, the first thing you'll have to do is get off your feet, and get into a robe, and get a blanket around your legs. Then you'll have to eat something; I'll fix it for you. You have staged a wonderful recovery, but you're a sitting duck for a real infection if you abuse yourself during convalescence."

"I'll compromise," Cleaver said immediately. "I don't want to be a hero, I just want to be heard. Give me a hand over to that hassock. I still don't walk very straight."

It took the better part of half an hour to get Cleaver settled to Ruiz-Sanchez's satisfaction. The physicist seemed in a wry way to be enjoying every minute of it. At last he had a mug of *gchteka,* the local equivalent of tea, in his hand, and Michelis said:

"All right, Paul, you've gone out of your way to put yourself on the spot. Evidently that's where you want to be. So let's have the answer: why didn't you communicate with us?"

"I didn't want to."

"Now wait a minute," Agronski said. "Paul, don't break your neck to say the first damn thing that comes into your head. Your judgment may not be well yet, even if your talking apparatus is. Wasn't your silence just a matter of your being unable to work the local message system—the Tree or whatever it is?"

"No, it wasn't," Cleaver insisted. "Thanks, Agronski, but I don't need to be shepherded down the safe and easy road, or have any alibis set up for me. I know exactly what I did that was ticklish, and I know that it's going to be impossible to set up consistent alibis for it now. My chances for keeping anything under my hat depended on my staying in complete control of everything I did. Naturally those chances went out the window when I got stuck by that damned pineapple. I realized that last night, when I fought like a demon to get through to you before the Father could get back, and found that I couldn't make it."

"You seem to take it calmly enough now," Michelis observed.

"Well, I'm feeling a little washed out. But I'm a realist. And I also know, Mike, that I had damned good reasons for what I did. I'm counting on the chance that you'll agree with me wholeheartedly when I tell you why I did it."

"All right," Michelis said, "begin."

Cleaver sat back, folding his hands quietly in the lap of his robe. He was obviously still enjoying the situation. He said:

"First of all, I didn't call you because I didn't want to, as I said. I could have mastered the problem of the Tree easily enough by doing what the father did—that is by getting a Snake to ferry my messages. Of course I don't speak Snake, but the father does, so all I had to do was to take him into my confidence. Barring that, I could have mastered the Tree itself. I already know all the technical principles involved. Mike, you should see that Tree, it's the biggest single junction transistor anywhere in this galaxy, and I'll bet that it's the biggest one anywhere.

"But I wanted a gap to spring up between our party and yours. I wanted both of you to be completely in the dark about what was going on down here on this continent. I wanted you to imagine the worst, and blame it on the Snakes, too, if that could be managed. After you got here—if you did—I was going to be able to show you that I hadn't sent any messages because the Snakes wouldn't let me. I've got more plans to that effect squirrelled away around here than I'll bother to list now; there'd be no point in it, since it's all come to nothing. But I'm sure it would have looked conclusive, regardless of anything the Father would have been able to offer to the contrary.

"It was just a damned shame, from my point of view, that I had to run up against a pineapple at the last minute. It gave the Father a chance to find out something about what was up. I'll swear that if that hadn't happened, he wouldn't have smelled anything until you actually got here—and then it would have been too late."

"I probably wouldn't have, that's true," Ruiz-Sanchez said, watching Cleaver steadily. "But your running up against that 'pineapple' was no accident. If you'd been observing Lithia as you were sent here to do, instead of spending all your time building up a fictitious Lithia for purposes of your own, you'd have known enough about the planet to have been more careful about 'pineapples.' You'd also have spoken at least as much Lithian as Agronski by this time."

"That," Cleaver said, "is probably true, and again it doesn't make any difference to me. I observed the one fact about Lithia that overrides all other facts, and that is going to turn out to be sufficient. Unlike you, Father, I have no respect for petty niceties in extreme situations, and I'm not the kind of man who thinks anyone learns anything from analysis after the fact."

"Let's not get to bickering," Michelis said. "You've told us your story without any visible decoration, and it's evident that you have a reason for confessing. You expect us to excuse you, or at least not to blame you too heavily, when you tell us what that reason is. Let's hear it."

"It's this," Cleaver said, and for the first time he seemed to become a little more animated. He leaned forward, the glowing gaslight bringing the bones of his face into sharp contrast with the sagging hollows of his cheeks, and pointed a not-quite-steady finger at Michelis.

"Do you know, Mike, what it is that we're sitting on here? Do you know, just to begin with, how much rutile there is here?"

"Of course I know. If we decide to vote for opening the planet up, our titanium problem will be solved for a century, maybe even longer. I'm saying as much in my personal report. But we figured that that would be true even before we first landed here, as soon as we got accurate figures on the mass of the planet."

"And what about the pegmatite?" Cleaver demanded softly.

"What about it?" Michelis said, looking puzzled. "I suppose it's abundant; I really didn't bother to look. Titanium's important to us, but I don't quite see why lithium should be; the days when the metal was used as a rocket fuel are fifty years behind us."

"And yet the stuff's still worth about twenty thousand dollars an English ton back home, Mike, and that's exactly the same price it was drawing in the 1960s, allowing for currency changes since then. Doesn't that mean anything to you?"

"I'm more interested in what it means to you," Michelis said. "None of us can make a nickel out of this trip, even if we find the planet solid platinum inside—which is hardly likely. And if price is the only consideration, surely the fact that lithium is common here will break the market for it? What's it good for, after all, on a large scale?"

"It's good for bombs," Cleaver said. "Fusion bombs. And, of course, controlled fusion power, if we ever lick that problem."

Ruiz-Sanchez suddenly felt sick and tired all over again. It was exactly what he had feared had been on Cleaver's mind, and he had not wanted to find himself right.

"Cleaver," he said, "I've changed my mind. I would have sought you out, even if you had never blundered against your 'pineapple.' That same day you mentioned to me that you were checking for pegmatite when you had your accident, and that you thought Lithia might be a good place for tritium production on a large scale. Evidently you thought that I wouldn't know what you were talking about. If you hadn't hit the 'pineapple,' you would have given yourself away to me before now by talk like that; your estimate of me was based on as little observation as is your estimate of Lithia."

"It's easy," Cleaver observed indulgently, "to say 'I knew it all the time.'"

"Of course it's easy, when the other man is helping you,"

Ruiz-Sanchez said. "But I think that your view of Lithia as a cornucopia of potential hydrogen bombs is only the beginning of what you have in mind. I don't believe that it's even your real objective. What you would like most is to see Lithia removed from the universe as far as you're concerned. You hate the place, it's injured you, you'd like to think that it really doesn't exist. Hence the emphasis on Lithia as a source of tritium, to the exclusion of every other fact about the planet; for if that emphasis wins out, Lithia will be placed under security seal. Isn't that right?"

"Of course it's right, except for the phony mind-reading," Cleaver said contemptuously. "When even a priest can see it, it's got to be obvious. Mike, this is the most tremendous opportunity that man's ever had. This planet is made to order to be converted, root and branch, into a thermonuclear laboratory and production center. It has indefinitely large supplies of the most important raw materials. What's even more important, it has no nuclear knowledge of its own for us to worry about. All the clue materials, the radioactive elements and so on which you need to work out real knowledge of the atom, we'll have to import; the Snakes don't know a thing about them. Furthermore, the instruments involved, the counters and particle accelerators and so on, all depend on materials like iron that the Snakes don't have, and on principles they do not know, like magnetism to begin with, and quantum theory. We'll be able to stock our planet here with an immense reservoir of cheap labor which doesn't know and—if we take proper precautions—never will have a prayer of learning enough to snitch classified techniques.

"All we need to do is to turn in a triple-E Unfavorable on the planet to shut off for a whole century any use of Lithia as a way station or any other kind of general base. At the same time, we can report separately to the UN Review Committee exactly what we do have in Lithia: a triple-A arsenal for the whole of Earth, for the whole commonwealth of planets we control!"

"Against whom?" Ruiz-Sanchez said.

"What do you mean?"

"Against whom are you stocking this arsenal? Why do we need a whole planet devoted to making tritium bombs?"

"The UN itself can use weapons," Cleaver said dryly. "The time isn't very far gone since there were still a few restive nations on Earth, and it could come around again. Don't forget also that thermonuclear weapons only last a few years—they can't be stockpiled indefinitely, like fission bombs. The half-life of tritium is very short. I suppose you wouldn't know anything about that. But take my word for it, the UN's police would be glad to know that they could have access to a virtually inexhaustible stock of tritium bombs, and to hell with the shelf-life problem!

"Besides, if you've thought about it at all, you know as well as I do that this endless consolidation of peaceful planets can't go on forever. Sooner or later—well, what happens if the next planet we touch on is a place like Earth? If it is, its inhabitants may fight, and fight like a planetful of madmen, to stay out of our frame of influence. Or what happens if the next planet we hit is an outpost for a whole federation, maybe bigger than ours? When that day comes—and it will, it's in the cards—we'll be damned glad if we're able to plaster the enemy from pole to pole with fusion bombs, and clean up the matter with as little loss of life as possible."

"On our side," Ruiz-Sanchez added.

"Is there any other side?"

"By golly, it makes sense to me," Agronski said. "Mike, what do you think?"

"I'm not sure yet," Michelis said. "Paul, I still don't understand why you thought it necessary to go through all the cloak-and-dagger maneuvers. You tell your story fairly enough now, and it has its merits, but you also admit you were going to trick the three of us into going along with you, if you could. Why? Could you not trust the force of your argument alone?"

"No," Cleaver said bluntly. "I've never been on a commission like this before, where there was no single, definite chairman, where there was deliberately an even number of members so that a split opinion couldn't be settled if it occurred—and where the voice of a man whose head is full of pecksniffian, irrelevant moral distinctions and two-thousand-year-old metaphysics carries exactly the same weight as the voice of a scientist."

"That's mighty loaded language," Michelis said.

"I know it. If it comes to that, I'll say here or anywhere that I think the Father is a hell of a fine biologist, and that that makes him a scientist like the rest of us—insofar as biology's science.

"But I remember once visiting the labs at Notre Dame, where they have a complete little world of germ-free animals and plants and have pulled I don't know how many physiological miracles out of the hat. I wondered then how one goes about being as good a scientist as that, and a churchman at the same time. I wondered in which compartment in their brains they filed their religion, and in which their science. I'm still wondering.

"I didn't propose to take chances on the compartments getting interconnected on Lithia. I had every intention of cutting the Father down to a point where his voice would be nearly ignored by the rest of you. That's why I undertook the cloak-and-dagger stuff. Maybe it was stupid of me—I suppose that it takes training to be a successful *agent provocateur* and that I should have realized it. But I'm not sorry I tried. *I'm only sorry I failed.*"

# 7

There was a short, painful silence.

"Is that it, then?" Michelis said.

"That's it, Mike. Oh—one more thing. My vote, if anybody is in doubt about it, is to keep the planet closed. Take it from there."

"Ramon," Michelis said, "do you want to speak next? You're certainly entitled to it—the air's a mite murky at the moment."

"No, Mike, let's hear from you."

"I'm not ready to speak yet either, unless the majority wants me to. Agronski, how about you?"

"Sure," Agronski said. "Speaking as a geologist and also as an ordinary slob that doesn't follow rarefied reasoning well, I'm on

Cleaver's side. I don't see anything either for or against the planet on any other grounds but Cleaver's. It's a fair planet as planets go, very quiet, not very rich in anything else we need, not subject to any kind of trouble that I've been able to detect. It'd make a good way station, but so would lots of other worlds hereabouts. It'd also make a good arsenal, the way Cleaver defined the term. In every other category it's as dull as ditchwater, and it's got plenty of that. The only other thing it can have to offer is titanium, which isn't quite as scarce back home these days as Mike seems to think, and gemstones, particularly the semiprecious ones, which we can make at home without traveling forty light-years. I'd say, either set up a way station here and forget about the planet otherwise, or else handle the place as Cleaver suggested."

"But which?" Ruiz-Sanchez asked.

"Well, which is more important, Father? Aren't way stations a dime a dozen? Planets that can be used as thermonuclear labs, on the other hand, are rare—Lithia, is the *first* one that can be used that way, at least in my experience. Why use a planet for a routine purpose if it can be used for a unique purpose? Why not apply Occam's Razor—the law of parsimony? It works in all other scientific problems. It's my bet that it's the best tool to use on this one."

"You vote to close the planet, then," Michelis said.

"Sure. That's what I was saying, wasn't it?"

"I wanted to be certain," Michelis said. "Ramon, I guess it's up to us. Shall I speak first?"

"Of course, Mike."

"Then," Michelis said evenly, and without changing in the slightest his accustomed tone of grave impartiality, "I'll say that I think both of these gentlemen are fools, and calamitous fools at that because they're supposed to be scientists. Paul, your maneuvers to set up a phony situation are perfectly beneath contempt, and I shan't mention them again. I shan't even bother to record them, so you needn't feel that you have to mend any fences as far as I'm concerned. I'm looking solely at the purpose those maneuvers were supposed to serve, just as you asked me to do."

Cleaver's obvious self-satisfaction began to dim a little around the edges. He said, "Go ahead," and wound the blanket a little bit tighter around his legs.

"Lithia is not even the beginning of an arsenal," Michelis said. "Every piece of evidence you offered to prove that it might be is either a half-truth or the purest trash. Cheap labor, for instance: with what will you pay the Lithians? They have no money, and they can't be rewarded with goods. They have everything they need, and they like the way they're living right now—God knows they're not even slightly jealous of the achievements we think make Earth great." He looked around the gently rounded room, shining softly in the gaslight. "I don't seem to see anyplace in here where a vacuum cleaner would find much use. How will you pay the Lithians to work in your thermonuclear plants?"

"With knowledge," Cleaver said gruffly. "There's a lot they'd like to know."

"But what knowledge? The things they'd like to know are specifically the things you can't tell them if they're to be valuable to you as a labor force. Are you going to teach them quantum theory? You can't; that would be dangerous. Are you going to teach them electrodynamics? Again, that would enable them to learn other things you think dangerous. Are you going to teach them how to get titanium from ore, or how to accumulate enough iron to enable them to leave their present Stone Age? Of course you aren't. As a matter of fact, we haven't a thing to offer them in that sense. They just won't work for us under those terms."

"Offer them other terms," Cleaver said shortly. "If necessary, tell them what they're going to do, like it or lump it. It'd be easy enough to introduce a money system on this planet: you give a Snake a piece of paper that says it's worth a dollar, and if he asks you just what makes it worth a dollar—well, the answer is, We say it is."

"And we put a machine-pistol to his belly to emphasize the point," Ruiz-Sanchez interjected.

"Do we make machine-pistols for nothing? I never figured out what else they were good for. Either you point them at someone or you throw them away."

"Item: slavery," Michelis said. "That disposes, I think, of the argument for cheap labor. I won't vote for slavery. Ramon won't. Agronski?"

"No," Agronski said uneasily. "But it's a minor point."

"The hell it is. It's the reason that we're here. We're supposed to think of the welfare of the Lithians as well as of ourselves—otherwise this commission procedure would be a waste of time, of thought, of money. If we want cheap labor, we can enslave any planet."

Agronski was silent.

"Speak up," Michelis said stonily. "Is that true, or isn't it?"

Agronski said, "I guess it is."

"Cleaver?"

"Slavery's a swear word," Cleaver said sullenly. "You're deliberately clouding the issue."

*"Say that again."*

"Oh, hell. All right, Mike, I know you wouldn't. But you're wrong."

"I'll admit that the instant that you can demonstrate it to me," Michelis said. He got up abruptly from his hassock, walked over to the sloping windowsill and sat down again, looking out into the rain-stippled darkness. He seemed to be more deeply troubled than Ruiz-Sanchez had ever before thought possible for him.

"In the meantime," he resumed, "I'll go on with my own demonstration. Now what's to be said about this theory of automatic security that you've propounded, Paul? You think that the Lithians can't learn the techniques they would need to be able to understand secret information and pass it on, and so they won't have to be screened. There again, you're wrong, as you'd have known if you'd bothered to study the Lithians even perfunctorily. The Lithians are highly intelligent, and they already have many of the clues they need. I've given them a hand toward pinning down magnetism, and they absorbed the material like magic and put it to work with enormous ingenuity."

"So did I," Ruiz-Sanchez said. "And I've suggested to them a technique for accumulating iron that should prove to be pretty powerful. I had only to suggest it, and they were already halfway down to the bottom of it and traveling fast. They can make the most of the smallest of clues."

"If I were the UN I'd regard both actions as the plainest kind of treason," Cleaver said harshly. "Since that may be exactly the way Earth will regard them, I think it'd be just as well if you told the folks at home that the Snakes found out both items by themselves."

"I don't plan to do any falsifying of the report," Michelis said, "but thanks anyhow—I appreciate the intent behind what you say, if not the ethics. I'm not through, however. So far as the actual, practical objective that you want to achieve is concerned, Paul, I think it's just as useless as it is impossible. The fact that you have here a planet that's especially rich in lithium doesn't mean that you're sitting on a bonanza, no matter what price per ton the metal is commanding back home. The fact of the matter is that you can't ship lithium home.

"Its density is so low that you couldn't send away more than a ton of it per shipload; by the time you got it to Earth the shipping charges on it would more than outweigh the price you'd get for it on arrival. As you ought to know, there's lots of lithium on Earth's own moon, too, and it isn't economical to fly it back to Earth even over that short distance. No more would it be economical to ship from Earth to Lithia all the heavy equipment that would be needed to make use of lithium here. By the time you got your cyclotron and the rest of your needs to Lithia, you'd have cost the UN so much money that no amount of locally available pegmatite could compensate for it."

"Just extracting the metal would cost a fair sum," Agronski said, frowning slightly. "Lithium would burn like gasoline in this atmosphere."

Michelis looked from Agronski to Cleaver and back again. "Of course it would," he said. "The whole plan's just a chimera. It seems to me, also, that we have a lot to learn from the Lithians, as well as they from us. Their social system works like the most perfect of our physical mechanisms, and it does so without any apparent repression of the individual. It's a thoroughly liberal society, that nevertheless never even begins to tip over toward the other side, toward the kind of Gandhiism that keeps a people tied to the momma-and-poppa-farm and the roving-brigand economy. It's in balance, and not precarious balance, either, but perfect chemical equilibrium.

"The notion of using Lithia as a tritium bomb plant is easily the strangest anachronism I've ever encountered—it's as crude as proposing to equip a spaceship with canvas sails. Right here on Lithia is the real secret, the secret that's going to make bombs of all kinds, and all the rest of the antisocial armamentarium, as useless, unnecessary, obsolete as the Iron Boot!

"And on top of all that—no, please, I'm not quite finished, Paul—on top of all that, the Lithians are centuries ahead of us in some purely technical matters, just as we're ahead of them in others. You should see what they can do with ceramics, with semiconductors, with static electricity, with mixed disciplines like histochemistry, immunochemistry, biophysics, teratology, electrogenetics, limnology, and half a hundred more. If you'd been looking, you *would* have seen.

"We have much more to do, it seems to me, than just vote to open the planet. That's a passive move. We have to realize that being able to use Lithia is only the beginning. The fact of the matter is that we actively *need* Lithia. We should say so in our recommendation."

He unfolded himself from the windowsill and stood up, looking down on them all, but most especially at Ruiz-Sanchez. The priest smiled at him, but as much in anguish as in admiration, and then had to look back at his shoes.

"Well, Agronski?" Cleaver said, spitting the words out like bullets on which he had been clenching his teeth during an amputation without anesthetics. "What do you say now? Do you like the pretty picture?"

"Sure, I like it," Agronski said, slowly but forthrightly. It was a virtue in him, as well as it was often a source of exasperation, that he always said exactly what he was thinking, the moment he was asked to do so. "Mike makes sense; I wouldn't expect him not to, if you see what I mean. Also he's got another advantage: he told us what he thought *without* trying first to trick us into his way of thinking."

"Oh, don't be a thumphead!" Cleaver exclaimed. "Are we scientists or Boy Rangers? Any rational man up against a majority of do-gooders would have taken the same precautions that I did."

"Maybe," Agronski said. "I don't know. They still smell to me like a confession of weakness somewhere in the argument. I don't like to be finessed. And I don't much like to be called a thumphead, either. But before you call me any more names, I'm going to say that I think you're more right than Mike is. I don't like your methods, but your aim seems sensible to me. Mike's shot some of your major arguments full of holes, that I'll admit; but as far as I'm concerned, you're still leading—by a nose."

He paused, breathing heavily and glaring at the physicist. Then he said:

"But *don't push,* Paul. I don't like being pushed."

Michelis remained standing for a moment longer. Then he shrugged, walked back to his hassock, and sat down, locking his hands between his knees.

"I did my best, Ramon," he said. "But so far it looks like a draw. See what you can do."

Ruiz-Sanchez took a deep breath. What he was about to do would without any doubt hurt him for the rest of his life, regardless of the goodness of his reasons, or the way time had of turning any knife. The decision had already cost him many hours of concentrated, agonized doubt. But he believed that it had to be done.

"I disagree with all of you," he said. "I believe that Lithia should be reported triple-E Unfavorable, as Cleaver does. But I think it should also be given a special classification: X-I."

"X-I—but that's a quarantine label," Michelis said. "As a matter of fact—"

"Yes, Mike. I vote to seal Lithia off from *all* contact with the human race. Not only now, or for the next century, but forever."

# 8

The words did not produce the consternation that he had been dreading—or, perhaps, had been hoping for, somewhere in the back of his mind. Evidently they were all too tired for that. They took his announcement with a kind of stunned emptiness, as though it were so far out of the expected order of events as to be quite meaningless. It was hard to say whether

Cleaver or Michelis had been hit the harder. All that could be seen for certain was that Agronski recovered first, and was now ostentatiously cleaning his ears, as if he were ready to listen again when Ruiz-Sanchez changed his mind.

"Well," Cleaver began. And then again, shaking his head amazedly, like an old man: "Well..."

"Tell us why, Ramon," Michelis said, clenching and unclenching his fists. His voice was quite flat, but Ruiz-Sanchez thought he could feel the pain under it.

"Of course. But I warn you, I'm going to be very roundabout. What I have to say seems to me to be of the utmost importance, and I don't want to see it rejected out of hand as just the product of my peculiar training and prejudices—interesting perhaps as a study in aberration, but not germane to the problem. The evidence for my view of Lithia is overwhelming. It overwhelmed me quite against my natural hopes and inclinations. I want you to hear that evidence."

"He wants us also to understand," Cleaver said, recovering a little of his natural impatience, "that his reasons are religious and won't hold water if he states them right out."

"Hush," Michelis said. "Listen."

"Thank you, Mike. All right, here we go. This planet is what I think is called in English a 'setup.' Let me describe it for you briefly as I see it, or rather as I've come to see it.

"Lithia is a paradise. It resembles most closely the Earth in its pre-Adamic period just before the coming of the great glaciers. The resemblance ends just there, because on Lithia the glaciers never came, and life continued to be spent in the paradise, as it was not allowed to do on Earth. We find a completely mixed forest, with plants which fall from one end of the creative spectrum to the other living side by side in perfect amity. To a great extent that's also true of the animals. The lion doesn't lie down with the lamb here because Lithia has neither animal, but as an analogy the phrase is apt. Parasitism occurs far less often on Lithia than it does on Earth, and there are very few carnivores of any sort. Almost all the surviving land animals eat plants only, and by a neat arrangement which is typically Lithian, the plants are admirably set up to attack animals rather than each other.

"It's an unusual ecology, and one of the strangest things about it is its rationality, its extreme, almost single-minded insistence on one-for-one relationships. In one respect it looks almost as though someone had arranged the whole planet to demonstrate the theory of sets.

"In this paradise we have a dominant creature, the Lithian, the man of Lithia. This creature is rational. It conforms as if naturally and without constraint or guidance to the highest ethical code we have evolved on Earth. It needs no laws to enforce this code; somehow, everyone obeys it as a matter of course, although it has never even been written down. There are no criminals, no deviants, no aberrations of any kind. The people are not standardized—our own very bad and partial answer to the ethical dilemma—but instead are highly individual. Yet somehow no antisocial act of any kind is ever committed.

"Mike, let me stop here and ask: what does this suggest to you?"

"Why, just what I've said before that it suggested," Michelis said. "An enormously superior social science, evidently founded in a precise psychological science."

"Very well, I'll go on. I felt as you did at first. Then I came to ask myself: how does it happen that the Lithians not only have no deviants—think of that, *no* deviants—but it just happens, by the uttermost of all coincidences, that the code by which they live so perfectly is point for point the code we strive to obey. Consider, please, the imponderables involved in such a coincidence. Even on Earth we never have found a society which evolved independently *exactly* the same precepts as the Christian precepts. Oh, there were some duplications, enough to encourage the twentieth century's partiality toward synthetic religions like Theosophism and Hollywood Vedanta, but no ethical system on Earth that grew up independently of Christianity agreed with it point for point.

"And yet here, forty light-years from Earth, what do we find? A Christian people, lacking nothing but the specific proper names and the symbolic appurtenances of Christianity. I don't know how you three react to this, but I found it extraordinary and indeed completely impossible—mathematically impossible—under any assumption but one. I'll get to that assumption in a moment."

"You can't get there too soon for me," Cleaver said morosely. "How a man can stand forty light-years from home in deep space and talk such parochial nonsense is beyond my comprehension."

"Parochial?" Ruiz-Sanchez said, more angrily than he had intended. "Do you mean that what we think true on Earth is automatically made suspect just by the fact of its removal into deep space? I beg to remind you, Cleaver, that quantum mechanics seems to hold good on Lithia, and that you see nothing parochial about behaving as if it did. If I believe in Peru that God created the universe, I see nothing parochial about believing it on Lithia.

"A while back I thought I had been provided an escape hatch, incidentally. Chtexa told me that the Lithians would like to modify the growth of their population, and he implied that they would welcome some form of birth control. But, as it turned out, birth control in the sense that my Church interdicts it is impossible to Lithia, and what Chtexa had in mind was obviously some form of conception control, a proposition to which my Church has already given its qualified assent. So there I was, even on this small point, forced again to realize that we had found on Lithia the most colossal rebuke to our aspirations that we had ever encountered: a people that seemed to live with ease the kind of life which we associate with saints alone.

"Bear in mind that a Muslim who visited Lithia would find no such thing. Neither would a Taoist. Neither would a Zoroastrian, presuming that there were still such, or a classical Greek. But for the four of us—and I include you, Cleaver, for despite your tricks and your agnosticism you still subscribe to the Christian ethical doctrines enough to be put on the defensive when you flout them—what we have here on Lithia is a coincidence which beggars description. It is more than an astronomical coincidence—that tired old phrase for numbers that do not seem very large anymore—it is a transfinite coincidence. It would take Cantor himself to do justice to the odds against it."

"Wait a minute," Agronski said. "Holy smoke. Mike, I don't know any anthropology, I'm lost here. I was with the Father up to the part about the mixed forest, but I don't have any standards to judge the rest. Is it, so, what he says?"

"Yes, I think it's so," Michelis said slowly. "But there could be differences of opinion as to what it means, if anything. Ramon, go on."

"I've scarcely begun. I'm still describing the planet, and more particularly the Lithians. The Lithians take a lot of explaining; what I've said about them thus far states only the most obvious fact. I could go on to point out many more equally obvious facts that they have no nations and no national rivalries (and if you'll look at the map of Lithia you'll see every reason why they should have developed such rivalries), that they have emotions and passions but are never moved by them to irrational acts, that they have only one language, that they exist in complete harmony with everything, large and small, that they find in their world. In short, they are a people that couldn't exist, and yet do.

"Mike, I'd go beyond your view to say that the Lithians are the most perfect example of how human beings *ought* to behave than we're ever likely to find, for the very simple reason that they behave now the way human beings once did before a series of things happened of which we have record. I'd go even farther beyond it, far enough to say that as an example the Lithians are useless to us, because until the coming of the Kingdom of God no substantial number of human beings will ever be able to imitate Lithian conduct. Human beings seem to have built-in imperfections that the Lithians lack, so that after thousands of years of trying we are farther away than ever from our original emblems of conduct, while the Lithians have never departed from theirs.

"And don't allow yourselves to forget for an instant that these emblems of conduct are the same on both planets. That couldn't ever have happened, either. But it did.

"I'm now going to describe another interesting fact about Lithian civilization. It is a fact, whatever you may think of its merits as evidence. It is this: that your Lithian is a creature of logic. Unlike Earthmen of all stripes, he has no gods, no myths, no legends. He has no belief in the supernatural, or, as we're calling it in our barbarous jargon these days, the 'paranormal.' He has no traditions. He has no taboos. He has no faiths, blind or otherwise. He is as rational as a machine. Indeed, the only way in which we can distinguish the Lithian from an organic computer is his possession and use of a moral code.

"And that, I beg you to observe, is completely irrational. It is based upon a set of axioms, of propositions which were 'given' from the beginning—though your Lithian will not allow that there was ever any Giver. The Lithian, for instance Chtexa, believes in the sanctity of the individual. Why? Not by reason, surely, for there is no way to reason to that proposition. It is an axiom. Chtexa believes in juridical defence, in the equality of all before the code. Why? It's possible to behave reasonably *from* the proposition but not to reason one's way *to* it.

"If you assume that the responsibility to the code varies with age, or with the nature of one's work, or with what family you happen to belong to, logical behavior can follow from one of those assumptions, but there again one can't arrive at the principle by reason alone. One begins with belief: 'I think that all people ought to be equal before the law.' That is a statement of faith. Nothing more. Yet Lithian civilization is so set up as to suggest that one can arrive at such basic axioms of Christianity, and of Western civilization on Earth as a whole, by reason alone, in the plain face of the fact that one cannot."

"Those are axioms," Cleaver growled. "You don't arrive at them by faith, either. You don't arrive at them at all. They're self-evident."

"Like the axiom that only one parallel can be drawn to a given line? Go on, Cleaver, you are a physicist; kick a stone for me and tell me it's self-evident that the thing is solid."

"It's peculiar," Michelis said in a low voice, "that Lithian culture should be so axiom-ridden without the Lithians being aware of it. I hadn't formulated it in quite this way before, Ramon, but I've been disturbed myself at the bottomless assumptions that lie behind Lithian reasoning. Look at what they've done in solid-state physics, for instance. It's a structure of the purest kind of reason, and yet when you get down to its fundamental assumptions you discover the axiom that matter is real. How can they know that? How did logic lead them to it? If I say that the atom is just a hole-inside-a-hole-through-a-hole, where can reason intervene?"

"But it works," Cleaver said.

"So does our solid-state physics—but we work on opposite axioms," Michelis said. "That's not the issue. I don't myself see how this immense structure of reason which the Lithians have evolved can stand for an instant. It does not seem to rest on anything."

"I'm going to tell you," Ruiz-Sanchez said. "You won't believe me, but I'm going to tell you anyhow, because I have to. *It stands because it's being propped up.* That's the simple answer and the whole answer. But first I want to add one more fact about the Lithians.

"They have complete physical recapitulation outside the body."

"What does that mean?" Agronski said.

"Do you know how a human child grows inside its mother's body? It is a one-cell animal to begin with, and then a simple metazoan resembling the freshwater hydra or the simplest jelly-fish. Then, very rapidly, it goes through many other animal forms, including the fish, the amphibian, the reptile, the lower mammal, and finally becomes enough like a man to be born. This process biologists call recapitulation.

"They assume that the embryo is passing through the various stages of evolution which brought life from the single-celled organism to man, on a contracted time scale. There is a point, for instance, in the development of the fetus when it has gills. It has a tail almost to the very end of its time in the womb, and sometimes still has it when it is born. Its circulatory system at one point is reptilian, and if it fails to pass successfully through that stage, it is born as a 'blue baby' with patent ductus arteriosus, the tetralogy of Fallot or a similar heart defect. And so on."

"I see," Agronski said. "I've encountered the idea before, of course, but I didn't recognize the term."

"Well, the Lithians, too, go through this series of metamor-phoses as they grow up, but they go through it *outside* the bodies of their mothers. This whole planet is one huge womb. The Lithian female lays her eggs in her abdominal pouch, and then goes to the sea to give birth to her children. What she bears is not a reptile, but a fish. The fish lives in the sea a while, and then develops rudimentary lungs and comes ashore. Stranded by the tides on the flats, the lungfish develops rudimentary legs and squirms in the mud, becoming an amphibian and learning to endure the rigors of living away from the sea. Gradually their limbs become stronger, and better set on their bodies, and they become the big froglike things we sometimes see leaping in the moonlight, trying to get away from the crocodiles.

"Many of them do get away. They carry their habit of leaping with them into the jungle, and there they change once again to became the small, kangaroolike reptiles we've all seen, at one time or another, fleeing from us among the trees. Eventually, they emerge, fully grown, from the jungles and take their places among the folk of the cities as young Lithians, ready for education. But they have already learned every trick of every environment that their world has to offer except those of their own civilization."

Michelis locked his hands together again and looked up at Ruiz-Sanchez. "But that's a discovery beyond price!" he said with quiet excitement. "Ramon, that alone is worth our trip to Lithia. I can't imagine why it would lead you to ask that the planet be closed! Surely your Church can't object to it in any way—after all, your theorists did accept recapitulation in the human embryo, and also the geological record that showed the same process in action over longer spans of time."

"Not," Ruiz-Sanchez said, "in the way that you think we did. The Church accepted the facts, as it always accepts facts. But—as you yourself suggested not ten minutes ago—facts have a way of pointing in several different directions at once. The Church is as hostile to the doctrine of evolution—particularly in respect to man—as it ever was, and with good reason."

"Or with obdurate stupidity," Cleaver said.

"All right, Paul, look at it very simply with the original premises of the Bible in mind. If we assume just for the sake of argument that God created man, did he create him perfect? I should suppose that he did. Is a man perfect without a navel? I don't know, but I'd be inclined to say that he isn't. Yet the first man—Adam, again for the sake of argument—wasn't born of woman, and so didn't really *need* to have a navel. Nevertheless he would have been imperfect without it, and I'll bet that he had one."

"What does that prove?"

"That the geological record, and recapitulation too, do not prove the doctrine of evolution. Given *my* initial axiom, which is that God created everything from scratch, it's perfectly logical that he should have given Adam a navel, Earth a geological record, and the embryo the process of recapitulation. None of these indicate a real past; all are there because the creations involved would have been imperfect otherwise."

"Wow," Cleaver said. "And I used to think that Milne relativity was abstruse."

"Oh, any coherent system of thought becomes abstruse if it's examined long enough. I don't see why my belief in a God you can't accept is any more rarefied than Mike's vision of the atom as a hole-inside-a-hole-through-a-hole. I expect that in the long run, when we get right down to the fundamental particles of the universe, we'll find that there's nothing there at all—just nothings moving no-place through no-time. On the day that that happens, I'll have God and you will not—otherwise there'll be no difference between us.

"But in the meantime, what we have here on Lithia is very clear indeed. We have—and now I'm prepared to be blunt—a planet and a people propped up by the Ultimate Enemy. It is a gigantic trap prepared for all of us. We can do nothing with it but reject it, nothing but say to it, *Retro me, Sathanas.* If we compromise with it in any way, we are damned."

"Why, Father?" Michelis said quietly.

"Look at the premises, Mike. One: reason is always a sufficient guide. Two: the self-evident is always the real. Three: good works are an end in themselves. Four: faith is irrelevant to right action. Five: right action can exist without love. Six: peace need not pass understanding. Seven: ethics can exist without evil alternatives. Eight: morals can exist without conscience. Nine—but do I really need to go on? We have heard all these propositions before, and we know who proposes them.

"And we have seen these demonstrations before—the demonstration, for instance, in the rocks which was supposed to show how the horse evolved from Eohippus, but which somehow never managed to convince the whole of mankind. Then the discovery of intrauterine recapitulation, which was to have clinched the case for the so-called descent of man—and yet, somehow, failed again to produce general agreement. These were both very subtle arguments, but the Church is not easily swayed; it is founded on a rock.

"Now we have, on Lithia, a new demonstration, both the subtlest and at the same time the crudest of all. It will sway many people who could have been swayed in no other way, and who lack the intelligence or the background to understand that it is a rigged demonstration. It seems to show us evolution in action on an inarguable scale. It is supposed to settle the question once and for all, to rule God out of the picture, to snap the chains that have held Peter's rock together all these many centuries. Henceforth there is to be no more question; there is to be no more God, but only phenomenology—and, of course, behind the scenes, within the hole that's inside the hole that's through a hole, the Great Nothing itself, the thing that has never learned any word but *no:* it has many other names, but we know the name that counts. That's left us.

"Paul, Mike, Agronski, I have nothing more to say than this: we are all of us standing on the brink of hell. By the grace of God, we may still turn back. We must turn back—for I at least think that this is our last chance."

# 9

The vote was cast, and that was that. The commission was tied, and the question would be thrown open again in higher echelons on Earth which would mean tying Lithia up for years to come. The planet was now, in effect, on the Index.

The ship arrived the next day. The crew was not much surprised to find that the two opposing factions of the commission were hardly speaking to each other. It often happened that way.

The four commission members cleaned up the house the Lithians had given them in almost complete silence. Ruiz-Sanchez packed the blue book with the gold stamping without being able to look at it except out of the corner of his eye, but even obliquely he could not help seeing its title:

### FINNEGANS WAKE
*James Joyce*

He felt as though he himself had been collated, bound, and stamped, a tortured human text for future generations of Jesuits to explicate and argue.

He had rendered the verdict he had found it necessary for him to render. But he knew that it was not a final verdict, even for himself, and certainly not for the UN, let alone the Church. Instead, the verdict itself would be the knotty question for members of his Order yet unborn:

*Did Father Ruiz-Sanchez correctly interpret the divine case, and did his ruling, if so, follow from it?*

"Let's go, Father. It'll be take-off time in a few minutes."

"All ready, Mike."

It was only a short journey to the clearing, where the mighty spindle of the ship stood ready to weave its way back through the geodesics of deep space to the sun that shone on Peru. The baggage went on board smoothly and without fuss. So did the specimens, the films, the special reports, the recordings, the sample cases, the vivariums, the aquariums, the type-cultures, the pressed plants, the tubes of soil, the chunks of ore, the Lithian manuscripts in their atmosphere of neon; everything was lifted decorously by the cranes and swung inside.

Agronski went up the cleats to the airlock first, with Michelis following him. Cleaver was stowing some last-minute bit of gear, something that seemed to require delicate, almost reverent care before the cranes could be allowed to take it in their indifferent grip. Ruiz-Sanchez took advantage of the slight delay to look around once more at the near margins of the forest.

At once, he saw Chtexa. The Lithian was standing at the entrance to the path the Earthmen themselves had taken away from the city to reach the ship. He was carrying something.

Cleaver swore under his breath and undid something he had just done to do it in another way. Ruiz-Sanchez raised his hand. Immediately Chtexa walked toward the ship.

"I wish you a good journey," the Lithian said, "wherever you may go. I wish also that your road may lead back to this world at some future time. I have brought you the gift that I sought before to give you, if the moment is appropriate."

Cleaver had straightened up and was now glaring suspiciously at the Lithian. Since he did not understand the language, he was unable to find anything to which he could object; he simply stood and radiated unwelcomeness.

"Thank you," Ruiz-Sanchez said. This creature of Satan made him miserable, made him feel intolerably in the wrong. How could Chtexa know—?

* * *

The Lithian was holding out to him a small vase, sealed at the top and provided with two gently looping handles. The gleaming porcelain of which it had been made still carried inside it, under the glaze, the fire which had formed it; it was iridescent, alive with long quivering festoons and plumes of rainbows, and the form as a whole would have made any potter of Greece abandon his trade in shame. It was so beautiful that one could imagine no use for it at all. Certainly one could not fill it with leftover beets and put it in the refrigerator. Besides, it would take up too much space.

"This is my gift," Chtexa said. "It is the finest container yet to come from Xoredeshch Gton; the material of which it is made contains traces of every element to be found on Lithia, even including iron, and thus, as you see, it shows the colors of every shade of emotion and of thought. On Earth, it will tell Earthmen much of Lithia."

"We will be unable to analyze it," Ruiz-Sanchez said. "It is too perfect to destroy, too perfect even to open."

"Ah, but we wish you to open it," Chtexa said. "For it contains our other gift."

"Another gift?"

"Yes, a more important one. A fertilized, living egg of our species. Take it with you. By the time you reach Earth, it will be ready to hatch, and to grow up with you in your strange and marvelous world. The container is the gift of all of us; but the child inside is my gift, for it is my child."

Ruiz-Sanchez took the vase in trembling hands, as though he expected it to explode. It shook with subdued flame in his grip.

"Good-bye," Chtexa said. He turned and walked away, back toward the entrance to the path. Cleaver watched him go, shading his eyes.

"Now what was that all about?" the physicist said. "The Snake couldn't have made a bigger thing of it if he'd been handing you his own head on a platter. And all the time it was only a pot!"

Ruiz-Sanchez did not answer. He could not have spoken even to himself. He turned away and began to ascend the cleats, cradling the vase carefully under one elbow. While he was still climbing, a shadow passed rapidly over the hull—Cleaver's last crate, being borne aloft into the hold by a crane.

Then he was in the airlock, with the rising whine of the ship's generators around him. A long shaft of light outside was cast ahead of him, picking out his shadow on the deck. After a moment, a second shadow overlaid his own: Cleaver's. Then the light dimmed and went out.

The airlock door slammed.

# Xorinda the Witch

## by Andrew M. Greeley

*One of the many differences between Catholics and those
who profess other religions, especially other Christians,
is that Catholics not only have a relationship with God,
but with the Church as well. As history—or today's
newspaper—shows, they are not always the same. At one
time it was forbidden for anyone other than a priest to
read the Bible. People were tortured and killed because
of "heresy" that today would hardly be punished by a
stern talking-to. The lesson, of course, is that God is the
constant; the means by which we perceive and worship
Him are not.*

*In the superstitious world of "Xorinda the Witch," we
see again the eternal conflict between what is orthodox,
and what is right.*

*Andrew M. Greeley was born in Oak Park, Illinois, in
1928, and educated at St. Mary of the Lake Seminary and*

*at the University of Chicago. He has been a parish priest and a sociologist. Called "a natural resource" by* Time *magazine, Father Greeley is best known as the author of over eighty books and hundreds of shorter works on subjects such as mental health, the Irish in America, sex, God, and the Papacy.*

*In addition to the* SF *novels* Final Planet *and* Angel Fire, *he is the author of such best-selling fiction as* The Cardinal Sins *(1981),* Thy Brother's Wife *(1982), the short story collection* All About Women *(1989),* The Cardinal Virtues. *(1990), and, most recently,* Faithful Attraction.

*He divides his time between Chicago, where he is on the staff of the National Opinion Research Center, and Tucson, where he is professor of sociology at the University of Arizona.*

*"Happy the man who tames a witch with his love."*

Proverb of Tanton the Fool

"**I**t is your fault," the captain bellowed as the great black ship with the flaming crimson sails hurtled toward them through the lazy swells. "You and your evil witch."

Stern, upright, if cowardly, republican that he was, the young Duke Nondos of Ralen was inclined to agree. His fault more than the witch's. He had been sent from the Heart Land to buy her. The Committee told him she was worth no more than three thousand pieces of gold. The shrewd traders of the South Islands had wanted three times that much. It had taken four days of negotiation to settle on five thousand gold pieces. He had paid it all out of his own purse. *Zephyr,* a big, comfortable, slow tourist scow had sailed four days late; still, he had insisted primly to the angry captain, in time to miss the equinoctial storms. But the storms came early and the escorts had not been at the assigned rendezvous.

So now *Zephyr* was being overtaken by a pirate ship with two hundred archers and four huge catapults. His own guard of fifteen men and five women would be brushed aside like troublesome insects. The crew and passengers—two hundred affluent tourists—would be cruelly slaughtered, their pain even more terrible because the pirates would be furious that there was so little treasure on *Zephyr.* Already the women were screaming; they knew what would happen to them before they were slain.

His stomach knotted with fear and remorse. He knew that he was too preoccupied with narrow definitions of good and evil and agonized decisions about right and wrong to be an effective warrior. They would all die because of his virtue.

Could there not be some way that he would die and the others might live?

Offer himself to the pirates? What need would they have for a young man who wanted to be emperor someday, but did not have the courage to be even an effective junior officer?

The smell of salt-drenched air attacked his nostrils. He who had not been sick during the great storm was about to be sick with fear.

Only Xorinda the witch would survive—if they found out what she was before they raped and impaled her.

"It is the navy's fault." With terrible effort he repressed the yearning of his stomach to spew out its contents. "They should be here. I will report them to the Committee."

Instantly he regretted his outburst; he had sounded exactly like the callow and cowardly little prig that even many of his own guard thought him to be.

"Will you now?" the captain, a little dark man, bald and bearded, sneered. "Isn't that nice?" He turned his attention to his terrified crew. "Get those women below, use your whips, this is no excursion! I want the main topsails up." He lowered his voice. "Not that it makes any difference in this wind."

"In a light breeze we could outrun them," Nondos said dubiously.

"The breeze is not light, you stupid fool," the captain ranted. "Why don't you bring your accursed witch on deck and make her change the winds?"

"Blasphemy!" Nondos screamed, righteous anger echoing from the depths of his pious soul.

"Tell that to your Committee when you meet them in hell!" The captain strode aft, a pompous, frightened little man, whose final defiance was being acted out with whips against the rich tourists whom he had resented for all his life at sea.

The pirate ship was only two leagues away, glowing against the cloudless sky and the shining ocean like a sacred vessel from heaven. As he watched, another set of vast red sails ran up the mainmast, blossoming like a gigantic spring flower against the sun which was rapidly moving toward the eastern sky.

A lot of sail in strong winds; what was the pirate's hurry? Perhaps he wanted to take the *Zephyr* before it came too close to the World Island. Yet, even to Nondos's untrained eye, the big vessel seemed to be straining under its burden of sail.

Nondos had breathed easier when they had beaten by the Pirate Islands; now, far north of the Islands, they were being chased by a pirate battleship. The poor, ineffectual empire could no longer protect the fringes of its home seas.

"He is as frightened as they are," Nondos remarked to his cousin Belima, a member of the private guard. Belima, a cheerful little blonde, just his age, in the stiff white uniform of the clan with its red and blue lightning stripes, did not seem at all frightened.

"We all must die, must we not, noble cousin?" She smiled lightly. "Still I wish I had a husband and children before my time to go to Highgod." She hesitated. "Xorinda *might* help us. She likes you."

A huge projectile elevated itself off the prow of the pirate vessel, hung suspended in the air between the two ships, and then plunged towards them. A scream of terror shook *Zephyr*. Fearing that the catapulted rock was aimed right at him, Nondos ducked. It landed in the water several cables short of *Zephyr*, rocking the ship like a mighty claw emerging from the waves.

Belima didn't duck.

"They are trying to damage, not sink us," he said, seeking to recapture self-respect with his knowledge of tactics.

"She could put a spell on their ship or change the winds." Belima's eyes revealed a faint hint of contempt for her cousin. Bad enough that he was a prig, those eyes hinted, but intolerable that the heir to their clan was a cowardly prig.

Nondos was tempted. The witch might save his first command and the honor of his family. These men and women and adorable little children, with whom he played every day, were his responsibility. Blame it on the navy he might, it was still his fault. He could expiate his sin later. The Chairman would understand . . .

No he probably wouldn't. "You may not use evil to fight evil," he would say with a curl of contempt to his thick lips as he excommunicated Nondos from the Order.

"We may not use evil to fight evil," he said grimly to his cousin.

"Look at the archers." She pointed at the pirate ship. "If we're fortunate, we will die in the first wave of arrows."

Two hundred arrows shone in the sunlight as the pirate ship

rose on top of a big swell. Two or three waves of arrows would kill almost everyone on deck and reduce *Zephyr* to a wallowing hulk. They would fire as soon as they were in range, a few more minutes at the most.

"Ought not we raise our shields?" Belima prompted him, hand shielding the sun from her eyes.

"Raise shields," he shouted, his voice sounding like that of a terrified adolescent. Young Duke of the Ralen clan indeed.

"I don't think she's evil." Belima lifted her shield a few inches off the deck.

"Why should she help us? If we survive, she dies. If they win, perhaps she lives."

He felt himself sinking deeper into the swamp of temptation. I am losing not only my courage, but my faith, and my piety.

"She would help us because she is not evil and because she likes you. I think she would willingly die for you, poor foolish child."

"She has bewitched you too." He watched another projectile rise from the pirate ship. "She is the daughter of the Evil One."

"And you are a fool." Belima spat the words through tight lips. "A righteous, fanatical fool."

"I would rather die for goodness"—he ducked again as the second rock hurtled toward them—"than live through the powers of evil."

The powers of evil had corrupted the decaying World Empire. The old emperor was walled off from reality by his harem and his eunuchs. The military, the navy, the barons, the colonial bureaucracy, the commercial corporations had all become separate power centers in their own right. In endlessly shifting alliances they contended for more power and for often very slight advantages over their adversaries. Dishonesty and immorality were rampant. The streets of Heart City were not safe at night—the police indistinguishable from the criminal families.

Nondos's clan were relatives of the emperor, representing an older tradition of stern agrarian virtue. In their own enclave they preserved most of those virtues, though Nondos thought that his cousins had little respect for morality. His father waited patiently for the death of the old emperor and the election of a new one. "It is complicated, Noni." He would shake his head wisely. "There are no easy solutions, no quick cures. It will take time. I admire your enthusiasm for reform. But you must learn patience."

Patience, Nondos insisted, was not a virtue when fighting the Evil One. And the problems were not complicated. Had not the Chairman wisely pointed out that such an argument was a tool of the Evil One? The sources of evil must be rooted out. The witches especially must be destroyed. Highgod would not save the empire as long as his enemies were permitted to exercise their tricks and deceits.

The Order, a pious and dedicated group of young reformers, had become the de facto government of Heart City, waging effective war against both the police and the gangs. It seemed to Nondos, in his first year of the university that the Order stood for the same values as his family.

"They appear to be good men," his father agreed cautiously, "and they have certainly cleaned up the city compared to what it used to be. I will no longer be afraid to send your sisters to university. But there's more to do in this damnably sick world than beating up a few gangs and torturing harmless circus freaks."

"They are the children of the Evil Ones!" Nondos had protested hotly.

"I wish it were that simple." His father had sighed. "And I wish your friends did not need such simple answers."

There were times when Nondos was inclined to be of the same opinion. The elaborate and complex theology of witches seemed to him sometimes to be boring and sometimes silly. Nonetheless, dedicated and brilliant men, like the haggard and handsome Chairman, believed it completely and explained it persuasively.

As for the "torture," it was not really "torture," the Chairman had explained, but experimentation. "I would much rather that we could simply strangle them." The Chairman had sighed, his deep brown eyes flashing. "But we must test our theories, we must find the locations in their bodies where the Evil One inserts herself. Nor can we drug them, because that might permit the Evil One to escape. We believe the witch from the south is so powerful that after we have dissected her we will have solved the mysteries and will need no more experiments. That's why we're sending someone of your quality and skill"—his dazzling smile of approval always persuaded Nondos—"to buy her for us. Our experiments with her will be the turning point."

"The crowds enjoy the spectacle." Nondos was striving to clear his conscience.

"What do we care about them?" The Chairman dismissed the ordinary people with a wave of his hand. "In any event, it is good for them to see the Daughters of Evil struck down."

The members of the Order who performed the experiments seemed to enjoy them too, but Nondos was afraid to say that.

"Tourists tell me that she is a powerful and dangerous witch. Our theories suggest that the Great Evil comes from the south. She may be the principal source. You must be very careful not to fall into her clutches."

"No fear of that, Wise One." Nondos had saluted briskly. "I will bring her back for your experiments."

"We have complete faith in you."

Nondos was not unaware that his conversation to the Order was a major achievement for the Wise One. It was widely believed that the next emperor would come from his family. On the day of his birth it had been prophesied someday he would rise to the ruby throne.

Nondos told himself he did not care much one way or another, but if he ever did become emperor there would be no more harem and no more eunuchs.

"One woman," he had joked with his friends, "is enough. More than enough."

"You haven't even bedded one yet," Belima taunted him with a good-natured smile.

"Only because none can compare with you and we are cousins." He had aimed a blow at her neat bottom which she managed almost to avoid.

His friends and family liked him, despite his religious fervor. But no one approved the voyage to the south for the witch. And even his guard, sworn to him for life and respectful and fond of him most of the time, came grudgingly.

Their reluctance worried him. But he persuaded himself that when the execution of the Great Daughter of Evil from the south changed the face of the empire they would approve. Then many would join the Order and they would be bound together by many loyalties.

The guard were young men and women of his age, born to the Ralens or the clan's allies at the same time he was. Their parents committed them from birth to service of the young Duke, although they were always free to leave that service if they wished. Nondos was proud that none of his guard had left him. He loved them all and would as much die for them as they would for him.

Now—he struggled back to his feet as the shock from the second rock which had landed dangerously close to the port side of *Zephyr* receded—they would all die together for a cause in which he alone believed.

"The child is not evil," Belima insisted. "She has been beaten and used and exploited and raped and bought and sold, but she hates no one. Not even you who are bringing her to a horrible death. Especially not you. How can you be evil if you do not hate? She will help us. I know she will."

It was a fact that Xorinda the witch did not seem to hate. If she were human that was truly remarkable. But were witches human? The best theology, including that of the Wise One, said that they were not. Their humanity was an illusion.

"You are bewitched!" he shouted at his cousin.

"She does not hate and your precious Order does," Belima shouted back. "She is good and they are evil!"

He swung his hand to hit her. She brushed him back with her shield, turned on her heels, and walked away from him.

He had tried to hit Belima, the adored little cousin of his infancy. Highgod, what have I done?

Coward, incompetent, prig, hater, and now beater of women.

His temptation returned, stronger than ever: use the witch and save them all. Does not a good goal excuse, partially, a compromise with evil?

At least once? When so many lives depend on it? Never to be done again?

His father would say "no" as well as the Chairman. Better that they all die than compromise with the Evil One. He straightened his back and waited for the first onslaught of arrows.

The city government of the capital of the South Islands, as seamy a collection of dishonest merchants as Nondos ever hoped to see, kept Xorinda the witch in a shabby park on the edge of the town, on a burned-out beach between shark-infested water and impassable mountains. The sun glared down implacably. A mix of smells—dead fish, rotting seaplants, and human excrement—assailed his stomach. The witch was bound and hooded in a strongly built cage, a kneeling heap of torn garments, and a dirty female shape. A crowd of tourists crowded around the cage at a respectful distance, as they would if the animal inside were a performing tiger.

"The hood, my Lord," said the mayor, "is to constrain her power. They need to see sunlight, you know. We remove the hood when we wish her to perform for our guests, but only for a short period of time. She can be very dangerous, you see."

"I know about witches," he said tersely, wishing he could hold his nose to protect it from the terrible odor. "How do you make her perform?"

"She must eat, must she not?" The mayor shrugged his fat shoulders. "And drink?"

A brute of a man in a military cape entered the cage and viciously tore open her hood.

Nondos expected an ancient hag. Instead the face was unmistakably young, no older than his or Belima's, and hauntingly lovely.

"Wonderful Highgod!" his cousin exclaimed next to him. "The beasts!"

Her trainer offered Xorinda the witch a goblet of water. Eagerly she sipped at it. He pulled it away. The motivation for performance.

If the minority opinion was correct and if she were still a woman ... what a terrible way to have to live.

The show was a flop for the tourists who muttered their dissatisfaction: a few plates made to bounce up and down, a roar of thunder in the distance, a big wave suddenly on the beach, a couple of names of tourists revealed in a shrill, faintly pathetic voice.

"Tawdry nonsense." Belima's hand caressed her sword handle as though she wished to leap to the young witch's defense.

"Take care or she will bewitch you," Nondos warned sternly.

"And who else is here in the crowd?" The trainer pushed the witch roughly.

"The Lord Nondos come to bring me to my damnation!"

A thrill of horror swept through Nondos's body. Here indeed

was evil to be feared and avoided. The Wise One was right.

"They are merely trying to raise the price for her, Noni," Belima scoffed. "She would be told that you were here. No wonderful evil there."

"She is deadly, Bel," he replied, not being able to disagree with her explanation. "We must take great care not to fall under her power on the return voyage."

"She may actually make some plates leap around," Belima replied ironically. "A great danger."

Eventually the negotiations were completed and the foul-smelling cage with its chained and hooded witch was hoisted on *Zephyr*. Tourists and crew watched with more curiosity than terror as it settled with an abrupt bump amidship.

Xorinda the witch did not curse them, as the captured witches in Heart City did. Was that not odd?

Nondos approached the cage and considered the tattered kneeling figure. He heard two voices in his head:

The Chairman: We must often cause suffering in order to purify.

His father: We must do all we can to minimize human suffering, even among those who are guilty.

"We cannot leave her here like this on the voyage," Belima whispered to him.

"I quite agree. You and the other women take her below to one of the cabins—one with no porthole for daylight. See that she is bathed and properly clothed and that whatever medical care she needs is provided. Fasten her to the wall with lines instead of chains. But make sure that the lines are strong and two of you guard her at all times. I will not have you bewitched by the Daughter of Evil."

"Yes, Lord Nondos." A very formal reply from his normally disrespectful cousin. "Your mercy does you credit."

"I will come often to make sure that she does not bewitch her guards. And remember, always two of you."

"Yes, Lord."

In his own cabin, a luxury suite in the forward part of the ship, Nondos buried his face in his hands and listened to the rough noises of the final loading of the ship. Why had he done that? The Committee would certainly not approve, even if Belima and others in his guard did.

Yet if he treated her harshly, might she not die on the voyage?

That was a good explanation, but he was not sure that he believed it.

He pitied the witch. And pity, in the words of the Wise One, was a luxury that the reformers could not afford.

With a groan, he struggled out of his chair and strode to the other end of the ship. He must not permit the Daughter of Evil to corrupt his cousin and the other two women guards.

But in the clean, well-lighted cabin in the hold to which they had taken her, there was no witchcraft, none that he could recognize. Xorinda the witch was huddled in a tub, her back to the door through which he entered, arms protectively across her breasts.

"She has been badly used, my lord." Belima's voice was cold with anger. "Witch or not, no one should be used this way."

Her body, thin, bruised, scratched, was still beautiful. Nondos felt a sudden imperious surge of desire.

"She will not be ill used as long as I own her," he said solemnly and turned to flee.

"I am grateful, most noble Lord Nondos." The witch's words were both pathetic and dignified.

She has already begun to bewitch me, he had thought as he fled from the witch's prison.

He remembered the curve of her naked back and the dignity of her speech as he clung to the deck rail, torn between good and evil. The pirate ship was now so close that he saw the captain's red beard, almost the same color as the sails. In a world in which the principles of the Order ruled, there would be no need for pirates; men would not be driven to it by poverty. And those who engaged in piracy out of laziness would be speedily eliminated.

Were the pirates, he wondered, the witch's work? Could she have conjured them up out of the evil memories lurking in their islands? Or had the Mother of Evil sent her fighters to rescue a favorite daughter?

Then came the most traitorous thought of all: What if Belima were right? What if Xorinda the witch was not evil at all? What if he was squandering the last hope of his command because of a mistaken faith?

Where now was good and where now was evil?

He had visited the prison room often. If Xorinda was engaged in witchcraft with his guard, it was a peculiar kind of witchcraft. Usually she was reading, working her way through the ship's library at a furious pace.

"She wants to finish before we arrive at Heart City," Belima explained.

"Does she know what will happen to her there?"

"Yes."

"Why then does she read?"

"To finish the books she had wanted to read when she was taken from school to perform for those crooked merchants."

"Witches go to school?"

"She was not always a witch. Only when cruel men made her one."

When Belima was in that mood there was no point in arguing with her. On the contrary, he even permitted the guards to escort the witch on a walk around the deck late at night. He could not help but notice that the combination of food and exercise made the witch even more attractive—a tall, lithe girl with short, curly brown hair and natural dignity and grace.

In the cabin, one hand was tied to a pulley, which permitted her freedom of movement but kept her in the cabin.

"I want both hands tied," he demanded one day when his imagination removed the thin white dress that all women passengers wore when they were in tropic seas.

"No!" Belima had exploded.

"Do what my Lord Nondos requests." The witch had intervened. "He has great responsibility in bringing a Daughter of Evil across the seas."

A bit of a smile played on her lips. She was making fun of him, but without changing any of the grave respect with which she always acted when he came into the cabin.

"Besides, he is worried about his pregnant sister of whom he has had no news since he left the South Islands."

She had read his mind.

"Witchcraft," he exploded as he fled from the room.

"We told her about Rega," Belima explained later. "She didn't read your mind. Not that she couldn't sometimes if she wanted to."

Did the witch know the lust she was stirring up in him?

Of course she did. In that was her hope of life and of more evil.

Sometimes when he entered the prison room, Xorinda and the two guards, whoever they were, would abruptly halt their conversation or their laughter.

"We were not talking about you, noble Lord." The witch would smile slightly. "Not really."

He could not distrust his guard. Their loyalty was sealed by the most solemn oaths of the planet. Yet the witch was attractive, all the more so because, unlike any other witch of whom he had ever heard, she seemed to be blessed with humor.

As he found out when he nursed her through sea sickness during the equinoctial storm.

All the others were sick. Unaccountably Nondos alone was unaffected. When a pale Belima stumbled into his quarters and told him she was going to die, witch or no witch, he hurried to the prison room in the hold. Perhaps, despite the absence of sunlight, she had been able to cause the storm to incapacitate his guard. It would be necessary for him to watch her lest there be more tricks.

She was retching helplessly when he burst into the prison. "What good is witchcraft"—she actually seemed to laugh between retches—"all-powerful Lord, if it cannot protect you from this pestilence?"

He tried not to join in her laugh as he unfastened the cuffs which bound her to the pulley and assisted her to the plain hard cot on which she slept.

"Are you not afraid that I might bewitch you now that I have you alone?"

"You have no light," he said, forcing pills into her mouth. "You can't do your evil tricks without light."

"Nonsense." She grimaced with acute pain. "Just watch!"

The bottle of pills leaped out of his grasp, danced on the ceiling, and then tumbled back into his hand. A book sailed across the room, narrowly missed his nose, and then sailed back, clipping his rump. A piece of paper flared into flame. Just as quickly the flame was extinguished.

"Tricks and illusions," she giggled, "all tricks and illusions. Foolishness... Highgod save me, I am going to die."

He held the container with one hand and her naked shoulder

with the other. She was much too sick to be erotically appealing.

"The light absurdity"—she lay back in her cot, spent and temporarily free of sickness—"is a game they make us play to fool
the customers. Most of it really is illusion, Lord. Especially when
we grow older. Before . . . before I became a woman I had much
more power. Now I must often play tricks to be fed."

"What kind of power?" he asked, curious despite himself.

"I could make it seem to rain, and lift big rocks off the
ground, hear conversations a long way off, see things that were
going on inside of solid walls. It was fun. I entertained my
schoolmates and everyone laughed. It was always erratic and
unpredictable. Sometimes I could do it and sometimes I
couldn't. Then one holiday I stopped a merchant's parade that
was ruining our games. They bought me from my uncle and
that was the end of my real power."

"Bought you?"

She nodded. "I'm going to be very sick again . . . forgive me,
Lord."

When he got her back into the cot again, she did not release
his hand. "My aunt and uncle loved me, but they needed the
money. It was not like I was one of their own."

"Do you really read minds?" He strove to stifle his pity.

"I don't want your pity," she snapped.

"You do then?"

"Mostly I read faces. Yours is very easy to read. Sometimes I
hear thoughts, but that power is unreliable. When I say that you
think by delivering me to your Chairman, you will help yourself
become emperor"—she grimaced again—"it's nine-tenths face
and one-tenth mind."

So he nursed her through her illness as his mother would
have nursed him. Could witches be healed he wondered. It was
the sort of question his mother would have asked. The woman
even looked a bit like his mother.

If he believed her, it was not cosmic evil in the witches, but
an erratic and undependable ability to do minor magic tricks
that eroded with maturity and was shamelessly exploited by evil
men.

The kind of argument, of course, that a Daughter of Evil

would devise, especially when her helplessness made her appealing.

When she had finally managed to keep down some of the pills and fell into an exhausted sleep, he decided that he had better leave the dangerous place in which had tarried so long.

At the door a sweet and overpowering warmth assaulted him, almost knocking him into the gangway with its effervescence and joy. It ceased almost instantly.

"Sorry, Lord Nondos," she said sleepily. "That was not intentional. Gratitude out of control for a few seconds."

He fled to his own quarters and sank to his knees to express his gratitude to Highgod for saving him from such treacherous deceit.

It was deceit, wasn't it?

He felt sexual longing, sudden, intense, demanding. After all, he owned her, didn't he? And the members of the Order did what they wished with captive witches, who the Chairman said were not humans. The Chairman did not approve exactly and never enjoyed them himself. But he did not object.

She opened her eyes with a start when he burst back into the room, roused from a sound sleep. Her face became a mask of resignation.

"Noble Lord."

"I came..." He searched for words. "...to make sure your illness had not returned."

She closed her eyes. "Thank you."

Of course she knew what had almost happened. Did she want it to happen? Her eyes had said "no."

"You would sleep better, Lord Nondos, if you fastened my bonds again."

"I doubt it." He had run down the gangway and up the ladder to his own section of the ship and spent the rest of the night on his knees praying to Highgod—for what he did not know.

He had stayed away from the prison room after that.

The pirates roared with enthusiasm and released their first volley of arrows. He ducked again under his shield. The tourists who had crept up on deck plunged back down the companionways.

The arrows fell harmlessly short of *Zephyr*; the first waves were designed for terror not death. Some of the crew laughed at him—the brave Ralen duke panicking like a passenger. He should have known they would fall short.

One of the children, a pretty six-year-old girl called Molona, one of those to whom he told stories every night, was watching him from a nearby hatch. "They won't hurt us, will they, Duke Noni?"

"Never fear." He smiled at her. She smiled back and ran down the companionway. A hero to the children. As always.

What terrible things would the pirates do to her?

The only hope was a sudden appearance of a naval vessel, a big, well-armed one.

Or perhaps Xorinda the witch.

What was good and what was evil? Could you compromise just once with evil for a good purpose? To save the little girl and her playmates?

To save his honor and the honor of his clan?

Was the witch truly evil? Perhaps she was something in between? Maybe . . .

You're a coward. You want to save your own life so that someday you will be emperor.

If you do evil now, it will be to save yourself. Die like a brave man.

He thought of the little girl Molona. She was a child, but too pretty to escape horrible violation.

And he no longer cared about the subtle difference between good and evil. He cared only to save her.

He jumped through the nearest hatch without even realizing that he had decided for infidelity and dashed down the gangway to her prison like a hunted animal.

"Pirates!" He threw open the door. Poor *Zephyr* creaked and groaned in protest against the speed she was forced to maintain.

Xorinda the witch was sitting on her cot, hands clasped, her back stiff and upright, frightened too. So witches are afraid of pirates too? Or is it more trickery?

"I know."

"Will you help us?"

"If I can."

Quickly he unfastened her bonds. "When they find out what you are, they may spare you. You should not be so quick to help your enemies against those who might be your friends."

"Nonsense," she said briskly and, rubbing her wrists, preceded him out of the cabin.

On the companionway, she turned and hesitated. "I will bargain with you, Duke Nondos of Ralen. If I help defeat the pirates, you must kill me before midnight. Cleanly and quickly." She moved her hand against her throat.

"Kill you?"

Her jaw tilted defiantly. "Those men in Heart City—your Order—will do terrible things to me. I am afraid not of death but of them. You must save me from their hands. Do you swear?"

His heart sank. Her request was reasonable.

Another wild pirate cry. They must be very close.

"I swear." His voice was weak, high-pitched, uncertain.

Good and evil no longer mattered. Everything was evil. He and the witch were equally bad.

On deck, the scene was wildly beautiful, like the color films he had so enjoyed as a child. The pirate ship was abeam of them now, a mighty red and black bird skimming the purple waters against the rich glow of the setting sun; a condor of the north hunting for prey. The sky was bathed in blood rose. The wind howled through the rigging of lurching, twisting *Zephyr;* the pirate ship seemed to be straining even harder as it eased slightly closer. The captain was adjusting his speed to come alongside his prey gently, so as not to damage it. On the decks of the pirate ship firepots were blazing. Flaming arrows? Why? To destroy the rigging?

"What do you want of me?" Xorinda had to shout to be heard over the roar of the wind.

"Stop the wind! We are faster in light breezes!"

"Oh what a stupid fool you are, Noni." She huddled inside of her own folded arms as the wind pushed against her and forced her thin smock against the outline of her body. "I have no such power."

Even more beautiful than the setting sun, he thought, knowing that his desire was not only sinful but irrelevant.

"Is there no hope?"

She was concentrating on the pirate ship as though the sheer power of her sight could stop it.

"Come with me." She dragged him up the companionway to

the foredeck and then to the great prow on the bow of the ship, an abstract carving of the goddess of the wind.

She gripped both his arms and stared into his eyes, eating at the fabric of his soul like consuming acid. "Even if I am a witch, you love me, don't you, Noni, just a little bit?"

"Yes."

"Then now you must love me with all your strength. My power is weak without love. I know not why it needs love, but it does. Love me!"

She threw her arms around him in a passionate embrace. Willingly did Nondos, young Duke of Ralen, respond to her. He held her tightly against his chest, felt the strength of her back and buttock muscles, the firmness of her breasts, the linen smoothness of her skin, the comic kinkiness of her hair. He listened to the strong, deep beating of her heart and the resonant rhythms of her breathing. He smelled the sweetness of her skin and her curls—Bel had even given the witch expensive scent. He tasted her lips, strong yet already surrendered to him.

He drew her closer, delighting in her gift of all that she was. Surely his mother must be right. Witches could be saved. His love poured into her, enveloping, bathing, healing, caressing her. He possessed her soul, more than any man possesses the body of his beloved. He felt her fears and her pains, her shattered hopes and pathetic little joys, her broken dreams and her frenzied horrors. And he was known even as he knew—an ambitious, inept, self-righteous, indecisive coward. Somehow all those weaknesses were swept away. If it were witchcraft that did this, it was generous witchcraft. But he no longer cared. Her body became rigid as though she were putting tremendous physical effort into whatever she was doing to stop the pirate.

And what was she doing?

He did not know. But he was no longer afraid of anything or anyone. Not even of his own callow indecisiveness.

On the pirate ship, the captain's glass was turned in their direction. He gestured and gave the glass to his first mate. The other man searched for them, found them, and laughed. The captain gave a quick order. A score of archers raced to the railing, dipped their arrows in flame, and fired.

The fools would kill beauty for a brief laugh.

Vehemently he threw her to the deck and covered her body

with his. She looked over his shoulder and blinked her glazed brown eyes at the incoming volley.

At the last second before he was impaled, the flaming arrows changed their course and, like flying fish, jumped over the prow of *Zephyr* and danced into the waves, sizzling briefly before they disappeared.

"Nice little trick." She grinned impishly. "That will make them think before they shoot again. What if I turn the arrows back on them?" She considered him carefully. "Belima was right. You are a brave man."

"Clumsy."

"Perhaps. Now love me even more. We do not have much time."

So, still lying on the deck, her fresh young body crushed against his own, he loved her again, enough love for a lifetime, for several lifetimes. If I die, I will die happy, he thought. If this is evil, I will die for evil, because it is more wonderful than good.

The dress had slipped off her shoulders. Her lovely breasts, nipples taut and demanding, pressed against him.

Her demand for love grew even stronger. How little there must have been in her short life. He held her more tightly and poured out his love, all that he had, all that he would ever have.

A surge of gratitude flowed from her body to his. Her life, she seemed to be saying to him, was not wasted after all. For a second or two or three she had loved and had been loved. Reverently he kissed one of her breasts.

Then she began to twist and turn and groan, not in pleasure but in pain, like a woman in childbirth. Finally she seemed to fall apart, to become limp and lifeless in his arms.

The pirate was almost upon them. The archers had their bows drawn. The crew and everyone else on deck would die in the next volley.

"We've won!" Xorinda the witch shouted exultantly. "Look!"

She had bounded to her feet and was pointing imperiously at the pirate ship.

Emotionally drained from his orgy of love, he struggled to rise with her. Impatiently she pulled him up with one hand and rearranged her dress with the other.

"Look at the center mast!"

At first he saw no change. Then the mainmast swayed forward, like a man stumbling away from an empty liquor bottle. It straightened, then swayed backward, and then with firmness and determination settled back into place.

A wary cry rose from the suddenly frightened pirates. The archers lowered their bows.

Xorinda's imperious finger continued to point. "It is finished!" she shouted, modestly making sure that her dress was in order again.

The mast swayed again, first to port, then to starboard. The pirate captain shouted an order. Men began to pull on the sails.

Too late. A sudden gust of even stronger wind. The mainmast broke at its base with a crack like the explosion of one of the old cannons which guarded Heart City harbor. For a moment it jumped into the air as if it wanted to fly away with the sails, then it lurched forward, dragging canvas and rigging down into the blazing firepots amidships. Instantly the center of the ship became an inferno.

Then the foremast leaned dizzily to the port side and, as with a sigh of resignation, tottered back into the flames. Pieces of burning canvas flared into the heavens like burning leaves from an autumn fire. The aft mast broke like a piece of kindling wood and joined its fellows in the furnace in the middle of the ship. Already the pirate ship was dead in the water, falling rapidly behind the racing *Zephyr,* smoke from the conflagration billowed skyward, turning the crimson of the setting sun a dusky orange.

"Their captain"—her voice was casual, her hands on her hips, a smile of victory on her face—"put up too much sail for a mainmast he knew was weak. It was easy to give it a little extra push."

What would hard work be like?

Shouts of pain were rising from the blazing hulk, and the terrible sweet smell of burning human flesh.

"Poor men." Her body sagged, drained of triumph. "I . . ."

She did not finish her words.

He almost told her that when the Order had finished its work there would be no need for anyone to be a pirate. He was still, he knew, a clumsy young fool.

And a fool who was now standing next to an empress for

whom the passengers and crew of *Zephyr* were cheering.

Calmly she walked to the edge of the foredeck, smiled, and nodded her head in acknowldgement of their praise. He found himself standing at her right hand, a loyal courtier. If serving her for a few moments meant damnation, then he would accept damnation.

"They will cheer that way at my execution," she murmured. "Remember your oath, Lord Noni. Before midnight. My parents and my brother and sister await me with Highgod."

Then, a queen returning to her palace, she walked down the companionway to the main deck, ruffled the hair of the happily laughing Molona, touched Belima's outstretched hand, and slipped through a hatch with easy dignity and grace.

Back to her prison and, soon, her death chamber.

It was the only solution. He had purchased her with his own money; he could make the decision to dispose of her. The Committee would be unhappy, but he would tell them that he felt her power was too great to risk bringing her to Heart City. They would at least have her body for research. There would be rumors about the battle with the pirate ship, but who could say whether it was Xorinda the witch who had toppled its mainmast.

Only the man who had held her in his arms and supplied her with the energy of love she needed to save his first command.

And he was the young Duke of Ralen. Not even the Chairman would dare publicly question his decisions or wonder about his motives.

Duke Nondos hated himself for such devious political thoughts. Yet what else was there to do? He had given his word, pledged his honor, sworn his oath to send her home to her family with Highgod. Who were her parents? Could a peasant have acted with such regal grace while she was being acclaimed?

He sighed. Birth, he now knew from his own experience, did not guarantee grace.

Much later that night, the wind still blowing briskly, the stars of the north glowing over them, the flaming hulk only a memory, the celebration on *Zephyr* finally diminished.

Belima, a mug of ale in her hand, joined him at the rail. "Not much joy over victory in you, cousin. Worried about her, aren't you?"

He did not reply. What was there to say?

"You can't give her to those terrible friends of yours, you know that, don't you?"

They were not friends of his. Now he hated them.

"She made me promise to kill her." He choked the words out through clenched teeth. "Tonight. I swore on my honor."

"You can't do that either." Bel emptied her ale over the side of the boat.

"It is the only way. What else . . ."

The young woman was silent, an unusual condition for her. Then she grabbed his arm enthusiastically.

"I know. You can declare yourself her patron. Then they have no rights to her and you can't harm her, no matter what your oath. And . . ." She hugged him. ". . . and when you come to First Land you can send word to my lord uncle—your father—and he will come to the dock with our whole clan. Oh, do it, Noni, do it!"

"She wants to die . . ."

"No she doesn't. She wants to escape from those terrible men. She wants to live. She loves you."

"Patronage is a grave responsibility." He hesitated, seeing his neat solution coming apart. "It can only be given once in life. Many never undertake it at all. Its responsibilities are more serious even than marriage . . ."

"You are so slow, Noni." Belima pounded her foot on the deck planking. "Why must you always agonize when it is clear what is right. Anyway it is compatible with marriage. Patrons can be lovers."

"Some say it is too intense a combination . . ." He was such a cowardly and ambitious fool that he had not even thought of such a possibility.

"That is bad?" his cousin demanded impatiently. Heaven help the poor man who tried to be both a patron and lover to that passionate enthusiast.

"I swore to her, Bel. I must honor my oath."

He turned and walked to the hatch, expecting to be cursed. Belima's silence was even more terrible.

I no longer know anything, he thought with a heavy heart as

he staggered slowly along the dark, lurching gangway toward the prison room. Is she good? Is she evil? A witch or an empress? Or both? And does it matter? If I have sinned, may I now not enjoy the fruits of my sin? If I am damned by Highgod, should I not at least make this life as pleasurable as I can?

Or is she only a suffering innocent who has been used by evil men, Nondos of Ralen included?

"You have kept me waiting, Lord Noni," she said softly when he entered her dimly lit cabin. "That was not kind."

She had the pulley ropes tight, so that she would not dodge his blade at the last minute.

"You know I am a coward," he said. "I have never killed before and I am afraid."

He had always hated the diminutive "Noni." Now on her lips it was a word of surpassing beauty.

"Do not be sad." She smiled wanly. "You fulfill your oath as a duke. You do me a service. You send me home, but, oh, beloved Noni, cut my throat quickly for I am afraid!"

Still he hesitated. She was a witch. She had enslaved him by her sorcery. Alive and his protégée she would be a deadly danger for the Order. And she wanted to die. He had sworn.

"Remember your oath. Strike! In Highgod's name, strike!"

He strode across the room, dug his fingers into her thick curls, pulled her head fiercely to one side, drew his blade, plunged it toward her throat and shouted the death cry of the Order: *"Die, witch!"*

The knife slipped from his fingers. As he had known all along it would.

He released her hair, touched her cheek with two fingers, felt the rushing pulse of life on her wonderful white throat, and realized that a smile was forcing itself upon his face.

He picked up the knife and cut the pulley ropes.

"You promised! You promised!" She fell to the floor and hunched into a tight sobbing knot. "You have betrayed me! You have violated your oath!"

Not sure whether he was damned or saved, Duke Nondos knelt beside her, drew the sword of his ancestors and held it in front of her.

The damn woman was becoming hysterical, ruining completely the drama of the moment. He shifted the sword to his left hand, dragged her out of the knot, and put his hand over her mouth to stanch the flow of reproaches.

Instantly the words stopped. She watched him with curious interest.

How did the words go? He was not quite sure he could remember them all. Not that it mattered.

"As long as Highgod is in the stars, as long as the sun rises in the west, as long as spring follows winter, as long as men love women..." She was listening intently now, uncertain, confused, but still fascinated. Shyly she touched the emerald on his sword handle, knowing somehow that she should do something of the sort. "As long ... as long as the storms come when day equals night, as long as the flowers blossom in the meadows, so long will I protect you from all who wish your evil. I will care for you as a mother cares for her child, as a father for his heir, as a woman for her man, and do all in my power that you be filled with happiness and joy. I will care for you"—he was actually doing it rather well, all things considered, perhaps even improving on the traditional oath—"as long as my arm holds this sword, as long as my clan holds its honor, as long as Highgod holds us in his love." He tried to suppress an urge to laugh at his own ridiculous solemnity. "I will protect and care for you all the days and nights of my life and, if Highgod grants, even after death for all eternity."

The confusion in her warm brown eyes turned to admiration and respect. Wasted on a coward like him. Then in the light of her respect he felt himself beginning to become what she thought she saw in him, not yet a man of respect, but a young man on the way to respect.

Disconcerted but pleased with himself, he rose briskly. Now what?

Now, you young fool, you get out of here before you do things for which this is not the time. You must wait. Not too long, however.

He shoved his sword savagely back into its sheath. "Now, woman, we'll hear nothing more about slitting your lovely throat. Is that clear?"

Amused and worshipful, she nodded.

"I have other plans for it." He stumbled uncertainly for the door. "And for the rest of you too ... I will send my cousin..."

In the gangway he added, "You and she will doubtless continue your common cause against me. To be joined on the morrow by my mother."

He fled hastily, afraid of her laugh—which would have deprived him completely of his newfound manhood. Yet even the imagination of it made him feel more of a man.

Fretful and pale, Belima waited at the hatch. The relief on his face told him that she had guessed from her first glance at him.

"Go below," he ordered her gruffly, "and tell my protégée of her many new responsibilities."

"What responsibilities?"

"I don't know. Make them up." He swung at the hoyden's pert rump as she flew down the ladder. This time, to his surprise, his hand connected.

She reached the deck below, whipped around, and flew up to him again. "You're wonderful, Noni." She hugged him fiercely. "I knew it! I just knew it!"

It was more than he had known. More than he knew even now. It was, however, a possibility to be considered.

As his cousin dove below deck again, Nondos, drained of all strength, shuffled uncertainly to the rail of the rushing old ship. Good or evil? He still did not know. He had followed his gut instincts. There was nothing else to do.

His eyes strained for the first lights of World Island among the astonishingly friendly stars. It would be a few more hours, he supposed. Then the long lines of white-clad warriors and silver Ralen chariots and the red and blue flags would be waiting at the dock. Mother and Father, may I present the witch I bought in the South Islands. I am now her patron. She is an amusing little witch, is she not?

His mother would embrace Xorinda the witch with reassuring and of course tearful sympathy. His father would consider appreciatively the lines of the witch's body and murmur that he had never expected his son to have such superb taste in witches.

His life had been irrevocably changed; it would be more uncertain, more problematic, more complicated. And, Highgod knew, he felt himself smiling, infinitely more pleasurable and interesting.

Not a man yet. Still a callow and often cowardly youth. But

a youth with the first beginnings of manhood and the possibility of growth. For the moment that would have to be enough. He thought of what he had almost done that day. Tears stung at his eyes and he wept quietly. A brave man, his father often said, knows when to let the tears flow.

Then he thought of what he had in fact done.

And he laughed at his own absurdity.

He held the smooth oak rail with both hands and breathed deeply of the tart, fresh sea air.

Highgod, the saying went, takes care of fools, babes in arms, and young men in love.

# *A Canticle for Leibowitz*

## by Walter M. Miller, Jr.

*"A Canticle for Leibowitz" is the first of a series of three novellas by Walter M. Miller, Jr., later published as a novel under that title. In that form it won the Hugo Award for best science fiction novel of 1960. It is one of the unquestioned classics of the field, continuously in print for thirty years.*

*Miller was born in Florida in 1923 and lives there today. During U.S. Army Air Force service in World War II, he witnessed the destruction of the Italian monastery of Monte Casino, which inspired the setting of "Canticle."*

*After 1960 Miller fell silent, publishing only two collections of short fiction,* Conditionally Human *(1962) and* The View from the Stars *(1964), until 1985, when he and Martin Harry Greenberg collaborated on* Beyond Armageddon, *an anthology of stories about nuclear war.*

*And in 1989 it was reported that a sequel to* A Canticle for Leibowitz *was being written.*

*B*rother Francis Gerard of Utah would never have discovered the sacred document, had it not been for the pilgrim with girded loins who appeared during that young monk's Lenten fast in the desert. Never before had Brother Francis actually seen a pilgrim with girded loins, but that this one was the bona fide article he was convinced at a glance. The pilgrim was a spindly old fellow with a staff, a basket hat, and a brushy beard, stained yellow about the chin. He walked with a limp and carried a small waterskin over one shoulder. His loins truly were girded with a ragged piece of dirty burlap, his only clothing except for the hat and sandals. He whistled tunelessly on his way.

The pilgrim came shuffling down the broken trail out of the north, and he seemed to be heading toward the Brothers of Leibowitz Abbey six miles to the south. The pilgrim and the monk noticed each other across an expanse of ancient rubble. The pilgrim stopped whistling and stared. The monk, because of certain implications of the rule of solitude for fast days, quickly averted his gaze and continued about his business of hauling large rocks with which to complete the wolf-proofing of his temporary shelter. Somewhat weakened by a ten-day diet of cactus fruit, Brother Francis found the work made him exceedingly dizzy; the landscape had been shimmering before his eyes and dancing with black specks, and he was at first uncertain that the bearded apparition was not a mirage induced by hunger, but after a moment it called to him cheerfully, *"Ola allay!"*

It was a pleasant musical voice.

The rule of silence forbade the young monk to answer, except by smiling shyly at the ground.

"Is this here the road to the abbey?" the wanderer asked.

The novice nodded at the ground and reached down for a chalklike fragment of stone. The pilgrim picked his way toward him through the rubble. "What you doing with all the rocks?" he wanted to know.

The monk knelt and hastily wrote the words "Solitude & Silence" on a large flat rock, so that the pilgrim—if he could read, which was statistically unlikely—would know that he was making himself an occasion of sin for the penitent and would perhaps have the grace to leave in peace.

"Oh, well," said the pilgrim. He stood there for a moment, looking around, then rapped a certain large rock with his staff. "*That* looks like a handy crag for you," he offered helpfully, then added: "Well, good luck. And may you find a Voice, as y' seek."

Now Brother Francis had no immediate intuition that the stranger meant "Voice" with a capital *V,* but merely assumed that the old fellow had mistaken him for a deaf-mute. He glanced up once again as the pilgrim shuffled away whistling, sent a swift silent benediction after him for safe wayfaring, and went back to his rock-work, building a coffin-sized enclosure in which he might sleep at night without offering himself as wolf-bait.

A sky-herd of cumulus clouds, on their way to bestow moist blessings on the mountains after having cruelly tempted the desert, offered welcome respite from the searing sunlight, and he worked rapidly to finish before they were gone again. He punctuated his labors with whispered prayers for the certainty of a true Vocation, for this was the purpose of his inward quest while fasting in the desert.

At last he hoisted the rock which the pilgrim had suggested.

The color of exertion drained quickly from his face. He backed away a step and dropped the stone as if he had uncovered a serpent.

A rusted metal box lay half-crushed in the rubble ... only a rusted metal box.

He moved toward it curiously, then paused. There were things, and then there were Things. He crossed himself hastily, and muttered brief Latin at the heavens. Thus fortified, he read-dressed himself to the box.

*"Apage, Satanas!"*

He threatened it with the heavy crucifix of his rosary.

"Depart, O Foul Seductor!"

He sneaked a tiny aspergillum from his robes and quickly spattered the box with holy water before it could realize what he was about.

"If thou be creature of the Devil, begone!"

The box showed no signs of withering, exploding, melting away. It exuded no blasphemous ichor. It only lay quietly in its place and allowed the desert wind to evaporate the sanctifying droplets.

"So be it," said the brother, and knelt to extract it from its lodging. He sat down on the rubble and spent nearly an hour battering it open with a stone. The thought crossed his mind that such an archaeological relic—for such it obviously was—might be the Heaven-sent sign of his vocation but he suppressed the notion as quickly as it occurred to him. His abbot had warned him sternly against expecting any direct personal Revelation of a spectacular nature. Indeed, he had gone forth from the abbey to fast and do penance for forty days that he might be rewarded with the inspiration of a calling to Holy Orders, but to expect a vision or a voice crying "Francis, where art thou?" would be a vain presumption. Too many novices had returned from their desert vigils with tales of omens and signs and visions in the heavens, and the good abbot had adopted a firm policy regarding these. Only the Vatican was qualified to decide the authenticity of such things. "An attack of sunstroke is no indication that you are fit to profess the solemn vows of the order," he had growled. And certainly it was true that only rarely did a call from Heaven come through any device other than the *inward* ear, as a gradual congealing of inner certainty.

Nevertheless, Brother Francis found himself handling the old metal box with as much reverence as was possible while battering at it.

It opened suddenly, spilling some of its contents. He stared for a long time before daring to touch, and a cool thrill gathered along his spine. Here was antiquity indeed! And as a student of archaeology, he could scarcely believe his wavering vision. Brother Jeris would be frantic with envy, he thought, but quickly repented this unkindness and murmured his thanks to the sky for such a treasure.

He touched the articles gingerly—they were real enough—and began sorting through them. His studies had equipped him to recognize a screwdriver—an instrument once used for twisting threaded bits of metal into wood—and a pair of cutters with blades no longer than his thumbnail, but strong enough to cut soft bits of metal or bone. There was an odd tool with a rotted wooden handle and a heavy copper tip to which a few flakes of molten lead had adhered, but he could make nothing of it. There was a toroidal roll of gummy black stuff, too far deteriorated by the centuries for him to identify. There were strange bits of metal, broken glass, and an assortment of tiny tubular things with wire whiskers of the type prized by the hill pagans as charms and amulets, but thought by some archaeologists to be remnants of the legendary *machina analytica,* supposedly dating back to the Deluge of Flame.

All these and more he examined carefully and spread on the wide flat stone. The documents he saved until last. The documents, as always, were the real prize, for so few papers had survived the angry bonfires of the Age of Simplification, when even the sacred writings had curled and blackened and withered into smoke while ignorant crowds howled vengeance.

Two large folded papers and three hand-scribbled notes constituted his find. All were cracked and brittle with age, and he handled them tenderly, shielding them from the wind with his robe. They were scarcely legible and scrawled in the hasty characters of pre-Deluge English—a tongue now used, together with Latin, only by monastics and in the Holy Ritual. He spelled it out slowly, recognizing words but uncertain of meanings. One note said: *Pound pastrami, can kraut, six bagels, for Emma.* Another ordered: *Don't forget to pick up form 1040 for Uncle Revenue.* The third note was only a column of figures with a circled total from which another amount was subtracted and finally a percentage taken followed by the word *damn!* From this he could deduce nothing, except to check the arithmetic, which proved correct.

Of the two larger papers, one was tightly rolled and began to fall to pieces when he tried to open it; he could make out the words RACING FORM, but nothing more. He laid it back in the box for later restorative work.

The second large paper was a single folded sheet, whose

creases were so brittle that he could only inspect a little of it by parting the folds and peering between them as best he could.

A diagram ... a web of white lines on dark paper!

Again the cool thrill gathered along his spine. It was a *blueprint*—that exceedingly rare class of ancient document most prized by students of antiquity, and usually most challenging to interpreters and searchers for meaning.

And, as if the find itself were not enough of a blessing, among the words written in a block at the lower corner of the document was the name of the founder of his order—of the Blessed Leibowitz *himself*!

His trembling hands threatened to tear the paper in their happy agitation. The parting words of the pilgrim tumbled back to him: "May you find a Voice, as y' seek." Voice indeed, with *V* capitalized and formed by the wings of a descending dove and illuminated in three colors against a background of gold leaf. *V* as in *Vere dignum* and *Vidi aquam,* at the head of a page of the Missal. *V,* he saw quite clearly, as in Vocation.

He stole another glance to make certain it was so, then breathed, *"Beate Leibowitz, ora pro me.... Sancte Leibowitz, exaudi me,"* the second invocation being a rather daring one, since the founder of his order had not yet been declared a saint.

Forgetful of his abbot's warning, he climbed quickly to his feet and stared across the shimmering terrain to the south in the direction taken by the old wanderer of the burlap loincloth. But the pilgrim had long since vanished. Surely an angel of God, if not the Blessed Leibowitz himself, for had he not revealed this miraculous treasure by pointing out the rock to be moved and murmuring that prophetic farewell?

Brother Francis stood basking in his awe until the sun lay red on the hills and evening threatened to engulf him in its shadows. At last he stirred, and reminded himself of the wolves. His gift included no guarantee of charismata for subduing the wild beast, and he hastened to finish his enclosure before darkness fell on the desert. When the stars came out, he rekindled his fire and gathered his daily repast of the small purple cactus fruit, his only nourishment except the handful of parched corn brought to him by the priest each Sabbath. Sometimes he found himself staring hungrily at the lizards which scurried over the rocks, and was troubled by gluttonous nightmares.

But tonight his hunger was less troublesome than an impatient urge to run back to the abbey and announce his wondrous encounter to his brethren. This, of course, was unthinkable. Vocation or no, he must remain here until the end of Lent, and continue as if nothing extraordinary had occurred.

*A cathedral will be built upon this site,* he thought dreamily as he sat by the fire. He could see it rising from the rubble of the ancient village, magnificent spires visible for miles across the desert....

But cathedrals were for teeming masses of people. The desert was home for only scattered tribes of huntsmen and the monks of the abbey. He settled in his dreams for a shrine, attracting rivers of pilgrims with girded loins.... He drowsed. When he awoke, the fire was reduced to glowing embers. Something seemed amiss. Was he quite alone? He blinked about at the darkness.

From beyond the bed of reddish coals, the dark wolf blinked back. The monk yelped and dived for cover.

The yelp, he decided as he lay trembling within his den of stones, had not been a serious breach of the rule of silence. He lay hugging the metal box and praying for the days of Lent to pass swiftly, while the sound of padded feet scratched about the enclosure.

Each night the wolves prowled about his camp, and the darkness was full of their howling. The days were glaring nightmares of hunger, heat, and scorching sun. He spent them at prayer and wood-gathering, trying to suppress his impatience for the coming of Holy Saturday's high noon, the end of Lent and of his vigil.

But when at last it came, Brother Francis found himself too famished for jubilation. Wearily he packed his pouch, pulled up his cowl against the sun, and tucked his precious box beneath one arm. Thirty pounds lighter and several degrees weaker than he had been on Ash Wednesday, he staggered the six mile stretch to the abbey where he fell exhausted before its gates. The brothers who carried him in and bathed him and shaved him and anointed his desiccated tissues reported that he babbled incessantly in his delirium about an apparition in a burlap loincloth, addressing it at times as an angel and again as a saint, frequently invoking the name of Leibowitz and thanking him for a revelation of sacred relics and a racing form.

Such reports filtered through the monastic congregation and soon reached the ears of the abbot, whose eyes immediately narrowed to slits and whose jaw went rigid with the rock of policy.

"Bring him," growled that worthy priest in a tone that sent a recorder scurrying.

The abbot paced and gathered his ire. It was not that he objected to miracles, as such, if duly investigated, certified, and sealed; for miracles—even though always incompatible with administrative efficiency, and the abbot was administrator as well as priest—were the bedrock stuff on which his faith was founded. But last year there had been Brother Noyen with his miraculous hangman's noose, and the year before that, Brother Smirnov who had been mysteriously cured of the gout upon handling a probable relic of the Blessed Leibowitz, and the year before that ... *Faugh!* The incidents had been too frequent and outrageous to tolerate. Ever since Leibowitz's beatification, the young fools had been sniffing around after shreds of the miraculous like a pack of good-natured hounds scratching eagerly at the back gate of Heaven for scraps.

It was quite understandable, but also quite unbearable. Every monastic order is eager for the canonization of its founder, and delighted to produce any bit of evidence to serve the cause in advocacy. But the abbot's flock was getting out of hand, and their zeal for miracles was making the Albertian Order of Leibowitz a laughing stock at New Vatican. He had determined to make any new bearers of miracles suffer the consequences, either as a punishment for impetuous and impertinent credulity, or as payment in penance for a gift of grace in case of later verification.

By the time the young novice knocked at his door, the abbot had projected himself into the desired state of carnivorous expectancy beneath a bland exterior.

"Come in, my son," he breathed softly.

"You sent for..." The novice paused, smiling happily as he noticed the familiar metal box on the abbot's table. "... for me, Father Juan?" he finished.

"Yes..." The abbot hesitated. His voice smiled with a withering acid, adding: "Or perhaps you would prefer that I come *to you*, hereafter, since you've become such a famous personage."

"Oh, no, Father!" Brother Francis reddened and gulped.

"You are seventeen, and plainly an idiot."

"That is undoubtedly true, Father."

"What improbable excuse can you propose for your outrageous vanity in believing yourself fit for Holy Orders?"

"I can offer none, my ruler and teacher. My sinful pride is unpardonable."

"To imagine that it is so great as to be unpardonable is even a vaster vanity," the priest roared.

"Yes, Father. I am indeed a worm."

The abbot smiled icily and resumed his watchful calm. "And you are now ready to deny your feverish ravings about an angel appearing to reveal to you this . . ." He gestured contemptuously at the box. ". . . this assortment of junk?"

Brother Francis gulped and closed his eyes. "I—I fear I cannot deny it, my master."

"What?"

"I cannot deny what I have seen, Father."

"Do you know what is going to happen to you now?"

"Yes, Father."

"Then prepare to take it!"

With a patient sigh, the novice gathered up his robes about his waist and bent over the table. The good abbot produced his stout hickory ruler from the drawer and whacked him soundly ten times across the bare buttocks. After each whack, the novice dutifully responded with a *"Deo Gratias!"* for this lesson in the virtue of humility.

"Do you *now* retract it?" the abbot demanded as he rolled down his sleeve.

"Father, I cannot."

The priest turned his back and was silent for a moment. "Very well," he said tersely. "Go. But do not expect to profess your solemn vows this season with the others."

Brother Francis returned to his cell in tears. His fellow novices would join the ranks of the professed monks of the order, while he must wait another year—and spend another Lenten season among the wolves in the desert, seeking a vocation which he felt had already been granted to him quite emphati-

cally. As the weeks passed, however, he found some satisfaction
in noticing that Father Juan had not been entirely serious in
referring to his find as "an assortment of junk." The archaeological relics aroused considerable interest among the brothers, and
much time was spent at cleaning the tools, classifying them, re-
storing the documents to a pliable condition, and attempting to
ascertain their meaning. It was even whispered among the novices that Brother Francis had discovered true relics of the
Blessed Leibowitz—especially in the form of the blueprint bearing the legend OP COBBLESTONE, REQ LEIBOWITZ & HARDIN, which
was stained with several brown splotches which might have
been his blood—or equally likely, as the abbot pointed out,
might be stains from a decayed apple core. But the print was
dated in the Year of Grace 1956, which was—as nearly as could
be determined—during that venerable man's lifetime, a lifetime
now obscured by legend and myth, so that it was hard to determine any but a few facts about the man.

It was said that God, in order to test mankind, had commanded wise men of that age, among them the Blessed Leibowitz, to perfect diabolic weapons and give them into the hands
of latter-day Pharaohs. And with such weapons Man had, within
the span of a few weeks, destroyed most of his civilization and
wiped out a large part of the population. After the Deluge of
Flame came the plagues, the madness, and the bloody inception
of the Age of Simplification when the furious remnants of humanity had torn politicians, technicians, and men of learning
limb from limb, and burned all records that might contain information that could once more lead into paths of destruction.
Nothing had been so fiercely hated as the written word, the
learned man. It was during this time that the word *simpleton*
came to mean *honest, upright, virtuous citizen,* a concept once
denoted by the term *common man.*

To escape the righteous wrath of the surviving simpletons,
many scientists and learned men fled to the only sanctuary
which would try to offer them protection. Holy Mother Church
received them, vested them in monks' robes, tried to conceal
them from the mobs. Sometimes the sanctuary was effective;
more often it was not. Monasteries were invaded, records and
sacred books were burned, refugees seized and hanged. Leibowitz had fled to the Cistercians, professed their vows, become a

priest, and after twelve years had won permission from the Holy See to found a new monastic order to be called "the Albertians," after St. Albert the Great, teacher of Aquinas and patron saint of scientists. The new order was to be dedicated to the preservation of knowledge, secular and sacred, and the duty of the brothers was to memorize such books and papers as could be smuggled to them from all parts of the world. Leibowitz was at last identified by simpletons as a former scientist, and was martyred by hanging; but the order continued, and when it became safe again to possess written documents, many books were transcribed from memory. Precedence, however, had been given to sacred writings, to history, the humanities, and social sciences—since the memories of the memorizers were limited, and few of the brothers were trained to understand the physical sciences. From the vast store of human knowledge, only a pitiful collection of handwritten books remained.

Now, after six centuries of darkness, the monks still preserved it, studied it, recopied it, and waited. It mattered not in the least to them that the knowledge they saved was useless—and some of it even incomprehensible. The knowledge was there, and it was their duty to save it, and it would still be with them if the darkness in the world lasted ten thousand years.

Brother Francis Gerard of Utah returned to the desert the following year and fasted again in solitude. Once more he returned, weak and emaciated, to be confronted by the abbot, who demanded to know if he claimed further conferences with members of the Heavenly Host, or was prepared to renounce his story of the previous year.

"I cannot help what I have seen, my teacher," the lad repeated.

Once more did the abbot chastise him in Christ, and once more did he postpone his profession. The document, however, had been forwarded to a seminary for study, after a copy had been made. Brother Francis remained a novice, and continued to dream wistfully of the shrine which might someday be built upon the site of his find.

"Stubborn boy!" fumed the abbot. "Why didn't somebody else see his silly pilgrim, if the slovenly fellow was heading for the abbey as he said? One more escapade for the Devil's Advocate to cry hoax about. Burlap loincloth indeed!"

The burlap had been troubling the abbot, for tradition related that Leibowitz had been hanged with a burlap bag for a hood.

Brother Francis spent seven years in the novitiate, seven Lenten vigils in the desert, and became highly proficient in the imitation of wolf-calls. For the amusement of his brethren, he would summon the pack to the vicinity of the abbey by howling from the walls after dark. By day, he served in the kitchen, scrubbed the stone floors, and continued his studies of the ancients.

Then one day a messenger from the seminary came riding to the abbey on an ass, bearing tidings of great joy. "It is known," said the messenger, "that the documents found near here are authentic as to date of origin, and that the blueprint was somehow connected with your founder's work. It's being sent to New Vatican for further study."

"Possibly a true relic of Leibowitz, then?" the abbot asked calmly.

But the messenger could not commit himself to that extent, and only raised a shrug of one eyebrow. "It is said that Leibowitz was a widower at the time of his ordination. If the name of his deceased wife could be discovered..."

The abbot recalled the note in the box concerning certain articles of food for a woman, and he too shrugged an eyebrow.

Soon afterward, he summoned Brother Francis into his presence. "My boy," said the priest, actually beaming. "I believe the time has come for you to profess your solemn vows. And may I commend you for your patience and persistence. We shall speak no more of your, ah ... encounter with the, ah, desert wanderer. You are a good simpleton. You may kneel for my blessing, if you wish."

Brother Francis sighed and fell forward in a dead faint. The abbot blessed him and revived him, and he was permitted to profess the solemn vows of the Albertian Brothers of Leibowitz, swearing himself to perpetual poverty, chastity, obedience, and observance of the rule.

Soon afterward, he was assigned to the copying room, apprenticed under an aged monk named Horner, where he would undoubtedly spend the rest of his days illuminating the pages of algebra texts with patterns of olive leaves and cheerful cherubim.

"You have five hours a week," croaked his aged overseer, "which you may devote to an approved project of your own choosing, if you wish. If not, the time will be assigned to copying the *Summa Theologica* and such fragmentary copies of the Brittanica as exist."

The young monk thought it over, then asked: "May I have the time for elaborating a beautiful copy of the Leibowitz blueprint?"

Brother Horner frowned doubtfully. "I don't know, son—our good abbot is rather sensitive on this subject. I'm afraid . . ."

Brother Francis begged him earnestly.

"Well, perhaps," the old man said reluctantly. "It seems like a rather brief project, so—I'll permit it."

The young monk selected the finest lambskin available and spent many weeks curing it and stretching it and stoning it to a perfect surface, bleached to a snowy whiteness. He spent more weeks at studying copies of his precious document in every detail, so that he knew each tiny line and marking in the complicated web of geometric markings and mystifying symbols. He pored over it until he could see the whole amazing complexity with his eyes closed. Additional weeks were spent searching painstakingly through the monastery's library for any information at all that might lead to some glimmer of understanding of the design.

Brother Jeris, a young monk who worked with him in the copy room and who frequently teased him about miraculous encounters in the desert, came to squint at it over his shoulder and asked: "What, pray, is the meaning of *Transistorized Control System for Unit Six-B?*"

"Clearly, it is the name of the thing which this diagram represents," said Francis, a trifle crossly since Jeris had merely read the title of the document aloud.

"Surely," said Jeris. "But what is the thing the diagram represents?"

"The transistorized control system for unit six-B, obviously."

Jeris laughed mockingly.

Brother Francis reddened. "I should imagine," said he, "that it represents an abstract concept, rather than a concrete *thing.*

It's clearly not a recognizable picture of an object, unless the form is so stylized as to require special training to see it. In my opinion, *Transistorized Control System* is some high abstraction of transcendental value."

"Pertaining to what field of learning?" asked Jeris, still smiling smugly.

"Why..." Brother Francis paused. "Since our Beatus Leibowitz was an electronicist prior to his profession and ordination, I suppose the concept applies to the lost art called *electronics.*"

"So it is written. But what was the subject matter of that art, Brother?"

"That too is written. The subject matter of electronics was the Electron, which one fragmentary source defines as a Negative Twist of Nothingness."

"I am impressed by your astuteness," said Jeris. "Now perhaps you can tell me how to negate nothingness?"

Brother Francis reddened slightly and squirmed for a reply.

"A negation of nothingness should yield somethingness, I suppose," Jeris continued. "So the Electron must have been a twist of *something.* Unless the negation applies to the 'twist,' and then we would be 'Untwisting Nothing,' eh?" He chuckled. "How clever they must have been, these ancients. I suppose if you keep at it, Francis, you will learn how to untwist a nothing, and then we shall have the Electron in our midst. Where would we put it? On the high altar, perhaps?"

"I couldn't say," Francis answered stiffly. "But I have a certain faith that the Electron must have existed at one time, even though I can't say how it was constructed or what it might have been used for."

The iconoclast laughed mockingly and returned to his work. The incident saddened Francis, but did not turn him from his devotion to his project.

As soon as he had exhausted the library's meager supply of information concerning the lost art of the Albertians' founder, he began preparing preliminary sketches of the designs he meant to use on the lambskin. The diagram itself, since its meaning was obscure, would be redrawn precisely as it was in the blueprint, and penned in coal-black lines. The lettering and numbering, however, he would translate into a more decorative and colorful script than the plain block letters used by the ancients. And the text contained in a square block marked SPECIFI-CATIONS would be distributed pleasingly around the borders of the document, upon scrolls and shields supported by doves and cherubim. He would make the black lines of the diagram less stark and austere by imagining the geometric tracery to be a trellis, and decorate it with green vines and golden fruit, birds and perhaps a wily serpent. At the very top would be a representation of the Triune God, and at the bottom the coat of arms of the Albertian Order. Thus was the Transistorized Control System of the Blessed Leibowitz to be glorified and rendered appealing to the eye as well as to the intellect.

When he had finished the preliminary sketch, he showed it shyly to Brother Horner for suggestions or approval. "I can see," said the old man a bit remorsefully, "that your project is not to be as brief as I had hoped. But ... continue with it anyhow. The design is beautiful, beautiful indeed."

"Thank you, Brother."

The old man leaned close to wink confidentially. "I've heard the case for Blessed Leibowitz's canonization has been speeded up, so possibly our dear abbot is less troubled by you-know-what than he previously was."

The news of the speed-up was, of course, happily received by all monastics of the order. Leibowitz's beatification had long since been effected, but the final step in declaring him to be a saint might require many more years, even though the case was underway; and indeed there was the possibility that the Devil's Advocate might uncover evidence to prevent the canonization from occurring at all.

Many months after he had first conceived the project, Brother Francis began actual work on the lambskin. The intricacies of scrollwork, the excruciatingly delicate work of inlaying the gold leaf, the hair-fine detail, made it a labor of years; and when his eyes began to trouble him, there were long weeks when he dared not touch it at all for fear of spoiling it with one little mistake. But slowly, painfully, the ancient diagram was becoming a blaze of beauty. The brothers of the abbey gathered to watch and murmur over it, and some even said that the inspiration of it was proof enough of his alleged encounter with the pilgrim who might have been Blessed Leibowitz.

"I can't see why you don't spend your time on a *useful* project," was Brother Jeris's comment, however. The skeptical monk had been using his own free-project time to make and decorate sheepskin shades for the oil lamps in the chapel.

Brother Horner, the old master copyist, had fallen ill. Within weeks, it became apparent that the well-loved monk was on his deathbed. In the midst of the monastery's grief, the abbot quietly appointed Brother Jeris as master of the copy room.

A Mass of Burial was chanted early in Advent, and the remains of the holy old man were committed to the earth of their origin. On the following day, Brother Jeris informed Brother Francis that he considered it about time for him to put away the things of a child and start doing a man's work. Obediently, the monk wrapped his precious project in parchment, protected it with heavy board, shelved it, and began producing sheepskin lampshades. He made no murmur of protest and contented himself with realizing that someday the soul of Brother Jeris would depart by the same road as that of Brother Horner, to begin the life for which this copy room was but the staging ground; and afterward, please God, he might be allowed to complete his beloved document.

Providence, however, took an earlier hand in the matter. During the following summer, a monsignor with several clerks and a donkey train came riding into the abbey and announced that he had come from New Vatican, as Leibowitz advocate in the canonization proceedings, to investigate such evidence as the abbey could produce that might have bearing on the case, including an alleged apparition of the beatified which had come to one Francis Gerard of Utah.

The gentleman was warmly greeted, quartered in the suite reserved for visiting prelates, lavishly served by six young monks responsive to his every whim, of which he had very few. The finest wines were opened, the huntsman snared the plumpest quail and chaparral cocks, and the advocate was entertained each evening by fiddlers and a troupe of clowns, although the visitor persisted in insisting that life go on as usual at the abbey.

On the third day of his visit, the abbot sent for Brother Francis. "Monsignor di Simone wishes to see you," he said. "If you let your imagination run away with you, boy, we'll use your gut to string a fiddle, feed your carcass to the wolves, and bury the bones in unhallowed ground. Now get along and see the good gentleman."

Brother Francis needed no such warning. Since he had awakened from his feverish babblings after his first Lenten fast in the desert, he had never mentioned the encounter with the pilgrim except when asked about it, nor had he allowed himself to speculate any further concerning the pilgrim's identity. That the pilgrim might be a matter for high ecclesiastical concern frightened him a little, and his knock was timid at the monsignor's door.

His fright proved unfounded. The monsignor was a suave and diplomatic elder who seemed keenly interested in the small monk's career.

"Now about your encounter with our blessed founder," he said after some minutes of preliminary amenities.

"Oh, but I never said he was our Blessed Leibo—"

"Of course you didn't, my son. Now I have here an account of it, as gathered from other sources, and I would like you to read it, and either confirm it or correct it." He paused to draw a scroll from his case and handed it to Francis. "The sources for this version, of course, had it on hearsay only," he added, "and only *you* can describe it firsthand, so I want you to edit it *most* scrupulously."

"Of course. What happened was really very simple, Father."

But it was apparent from the fatness of the scroll that the hearsay account was not so simple. Brother Francis read with mounting apprehension which soon grew to the proportions of pure horror.

"You look white, my son. Is something wrong?" asked the distinguished priest.

"This . . . this . . . it wasn't like this *at all*!" gasped Francis. "He didn't say more than a few words to me. I only saw him once. He just asked me the way to the abbey and tapped the rock where I found the relics."

"No heavenly choir?"

"Oh, no!"

"And it's not true about the nimbus and the carpet of roses that grew up along the road where he walked?"

"As God is my judge, nothing like that happened at all!"

"Ah, well," sighed the advocate. "Travelers' stories are always exaggerated."

He seemed saddened, and Francis hastened to apologize, but the advocate dismissed it as of no great importance to the case. "There are other miracles, carefully documented," he explained, "and anyway—there is one bit of good news about the documents you discovered. We've unearthed the name of the wife who died before our founder came to the order."

"Yes?"

"Yes. It was Emily."

Despite his disappointment with Brother Francis's account of the pilgrim, Monsignor di Simone spent five days at the site of the find. He was accompanied by an eager crew of novices from the abbey, all armed with picks and shovels. After extensive digging, the advocate returned with a small assortment of additional artifacts, and one bloated tin can that contained a desiccated mess which might once have been saurkraut.

Before his departure, he visited the copy room and asked to see Brother Francis's copy of the famous blueprint. The monk protested that it was really nothing, and produced it with such eagerness his hands trembled.

"Zounds!" said the monsignor, or an oath to such effect. "Finish it, man, finish it!"

The monk looked smilingly at Brother Jeris. Brother Jeris swiftly turned away; the back of his neck gathered color. The following morning, Francis resumed his labors over the illuminated blueprint, with gold leaf, quills, brushes, and dyes.

And then came another donkey train from New Vatican, with a full complement of clerks and armed guards for defense against highwaymen, this time headed by a monsignor with small horns and pointed fangs (or so several novices would later have testified), who announced that he was the *Advocatus Diaboli,* opposing Leibowitz's canonization, and he was here to investigate—and perhaps fix responsibility, he hinted—for a number of incredible and hysterical rumors filtering out of the abbey and reaching even high officials at New Vatican. He made it clear that he would tolerate no romantic nonsense.

The abbot greeted him politely and offered him an iron cot in a cell with a south exposure, after apologizing for the fact that the guest suite had been recently exposed to smallpox. The monsignor was attended by his own staff, and ate mush and herbs with the monks in refectory.

"I understand you are susceptible to fainting spells," he told Brother Francis when the dread time came. "How many members of your family have suffered from epilepsy or madness?"

"None, Excellency."

"I'm not an 'Excellency,'" snapped the priest. "Now we're going to get the truth out of you." His tone implied that he considered it to be a simple straightforward surgical operation which should have been performed years ago.

"Are you aware that documents can be aged artificially?" he demanded.

Francis was not so aware.

"Did you know that Leibowitz's wife was named Emily, and that Emma is *not* a diminutive for Emily?"

Francis had not known it, but recalled from childhood that his own parents had been rather careless about what they called each other. "And if Blessed Leibowitz chose to call her Emma, then I'm sure..."

The monsignor exploded, and tore into Francis with semantic tooth and nail, and left the bewildered monk wondering whether he had ever really seen a pilgrim at all.

Before the advocate's departure, he too asked to see the illuminated copy of the print, and this time the monk's hands trembled with fear as he produced it, for he might again be forced to quit the project. The monsignor only stood gazing at it however, swallowed slightly, and forced himself to nod. "Your imagery is vivid," he admitted, "but then, of course, we all knew that, didn't we?"

The monsignor's horns immediately grew shorter by an inch, and he departed the same evening for New Vatican.

The years flowed smoothly by, seaming the faces of the once young and adding gray to the temples. The perpetual labors of the monastery continued, supplying a slow trickle of copied and recopied manuscript to the outside world. Brother Jeris developed ambitions of building a printing press, but when the abbot demanded his reasons, he could only reply, "So we can mass-produce."

"Oh? And in a world that's smug in its illiteracy, what do you intend to do with the stuff? Sell it as kindling paper to the peasants?"

Brother Jeris shrugged unhappily, and the copy room continued with pot and quill.

Then one spring, shortly before Lent, a messenger arrived with glad tidings for the order. The case for Leibowitz was complete. The College of Cardinals would soon convene, and the founder of the Albertian Order would be enrolled in the Calendar of Saints. During the time of rejoicing that followed the announcement, the abbot—now withered and in his dotage—summoned Brother Francis into his presence, and wheezed:

"His Holiness commands your presence during the canonization of Isaac Edward Leibowitz. Prepare to leave.

"Now don't faint on me again," he added querulously.

The trip to New Vatican would take at least three months, perhaps longer, the time depending on how far Brother Francis could get before the inevitable robber band relieved him of his ass, since he would be going unarmed and alone. He carried with him only a begging bowl and the illuminated copy of the Leibowitz print, praying that ignorant robbers would have no use for the latter. As a precaution, however, he wore a black patch over his right eye, for the peasants, being a superstitious lot, could often be put to flight by even a hint of the evil eye. Thus armed and equipped, he set out to obey the summons of his high priest.

Two months and some odd days later he met his robber on a mountain trail that was heavily wooded and far from any settlement. His robber was a short man, but heavy as a bull, with a glazed knob of a pate and a jaw like a block of granite. He stood in the trail with his legs spread wide and his massive arms folded across his chest, watching the approach of the little figure on the ass. The robber seemed alone, and armed only with a knife which he did not bother to remove from his belt thong. His appearance was a disappointment, since Francis had been secretly hoping for another encounter with the pilgrim of long ago.

"Get off," said the robber.

The ass stopped in the path. Brother Francis tossed back his cowl to reveal the eye-patch, and raised a trembling finger to touch it. He began to lift the patch slowly as if to reveal something hideous that might be hidden beneath it. The robber threw back his head and laughed a laugh that might have sprung from the throat of Satan himself. Francis muttered an exorcism, but the robber seemed untouched.

"You black-sacked jeebers wore that one out years ago," he said. "Get off."

Francis smiled, shrugged, and dismounted without protest.

"A good day to you, sir," he said pleasantly. "You may take the ass. Walking will improve my health, I think." He smiled again and started away.

"Hold it," said the robber. "Strip to the buff. And let's see what's in that package."

Brother Francis touched his begging bowl and made a helpless gesture, but this brought only another scornful laugh from the robber.

"I've seen that alms-pot trick before too," he said. "The last man with a begging bowl had half a heklo of gold in his boot. Now strip."

Brother Francis displayed his sandals, but began to strip. The robber searched his clothing, found nothing, and tossed it back to him.

"Now let's see inside the package."

"It is only a document, sir," the monk protested. "Of value to no one but its owner."

"Open it."

Silently Brother Francis obeyed. The gold leaf and the colorful design flashed brilliantly in the sunlight that filtered through the foliage. The robber's craggy jaw dropped an inch. He whistled softly.

"What a pretty! Now wouldn't me woman like it to hang on the shanty wall!"

He continued to stare while the monk went slowly sick inside. *If Thou hast sent him to test me, O Lord,* he pleaded inwardly, *then help me to die like a man, for he'll get it over the dead body of Thy servant, if take it he must.*

"Wrap it up for me," the robber commanded, clamping his jaw in sudden decision.

The monk whimpered softly. "Please, sir, you would not take

the work of a man's lifetime. I spent fifteen years illuminating this manuscript, and..."

"Well! Did it yourself, did you?" The robber threw back his head and howled again.

Francis reddened. "I fail to see the humor, sir..."

The robber pointed at it between guffaws. "You! Fifteen years to make a paper bauble. So that's what you do. Tell me why. Give me one good reason. For fifteen years. Ha!"

Francis stared at him in stunned silence and could think of no reply that would appease his contempt.

Gingerly, the monk handed it over. The robber took it in both hands and made as if to rip it down the center.

*"Jesus, Mary, Joseph!"* the monk screamed, and went to his knees in the trail. "For the love of God, sir!"

Softening slightly, the robber tossed it on the ground with a snicker. "Wrestle you for it."

"Anything, sir, anything!"

They squared off. The monk crossed himself and recalled that wrestling had once been a divinely sanctioned sport—and with grim faith, he marched into battle.

Three seconds later, he lay groaning on the flat of his back under a short mountain of muscle. A sharp rock seemed to be severing his spine.

"Heh heh," said the robber, and arose to claim his document.

Hands folded as if in prayer, Brother Francis scurried after him on his knees, begging at the top of his lungs.

The robber turned to snicker. "I believe you'd kiss a boot to get it back."

Francis caught up with him and fervently kissed his boot.

This proved too much for even such a firm fellow as the robber. He flung the manuscript down again with a curse and climbed aboard the monk's donkey. The monk snatched up the precious document and trotted along beside the robber, thanking him profusely and blessing him repeatedly while the robber rode away on the ass. Francis sent a glowing cross of benediction after the departing figure and praised God for the existence of such selfless robbers.

And yet when the man had vanished among the trees, he felt an aftermath of sadness. Fifteen years to make a paper bauble...

The taunting voice still rang in his ears. Why? Tell one good reason for fifteen years.

He was unaccustomed to the blunt ways of the outside world, to its harsh habits and curt attitudes. He found his heart deeply troubled by the mocking words, and his head hung low in the cowl as he plodded along. At one time he considered tossing the document in the brush and leaving it for the rains—but Father Juan had approved his taking it as a gift, and he could not come with empty hands. Chastened, he traveled on.

The hour had come. The ceremony surged about him as a magnificent spectacle of sound and stately movement and vivid color in the majestic basilica. And when the perfectly infallible Spirit had finally been invoked, a monsignor—it was di Simone, Francis noticed, the advocate for the saint—arose and called upon Peter to speak, through the person of Leo XXII, commanding the assemblage to hearken.

Whereupon, the Pope quietly proclaimed that Isaac Edward Leibowitz was a saint, and it was finished. The ancient and obscure technician was of the heavenly hagiarchy, and Brother Francis breathed a dutiful prayer to his new patron as the choir burst into the *Te Deum*.

The Pontiff strode quickly into the audience room where the little monk was waiting, taking Brother Francis by surprise and rendering him briefly speechless. He knelt quickly to kiss the Fisherman's ring and receive the blessing. As he arose, he found himself clutching the beautiful document behind him as if ashamed of it. The Pope's eyes caught the motion, and he smiled.

"You have brought us a gift, our son?" he asked.

The monk gulped, nodded stupidly, and brought it out. Christ's Vicar stared at it for a long time without apparent expression. Brother Francis's heart went sinking deeper as the seconds drifted by.

"It is a nothing," he blurted, "a miserable gift. I am ashamed to have wasted so much time at ..." He choked off.

The Pope seemed not to hear him. "Do you understand the meaning of Saint Isaac's symbology?" he asked, peering curiously at the abstract design of the circuit.

Dumbly the monk shook his head.

"Whatever it means..." the Pope began, but broke off. He smiled and spoke of other things. Francis had been so honored not because of any official judgment concerning his pilgrim. He had been honored for his role in bringing to light such important documents and relics of the saint, for such they had been judged, regardless of the manner in which they had been found.

Francis stammered his thanks. The Pontiff gazed again at the colorful blaze of his illuminated diagram. "Whatever it means," he breathed once more, "this bit of learning, though dead, will live again." He smiled up at the monk and winked. "And we shall guard it till that day."

For the first time, the little monk noticed that the Pope had a hole in his robe. His clothing, in fact, was threadbare. The carpet in the audience room was worn through in spots, and plaster was falling from the ceiling.

But there were books on the shelves along the walls. Books of painted beauty, speaking of incomprehensible things, copied by men whose business was not to understand but to save. And the books were waiting.

"Good-bye, beloved son."

And the small keeper of the flame of knowledge trudged back toward his abbey on foot. His heart was singing as he approached the robber's outpost. And if the robber happened to be taking the day off, the monk meant to sit down and wait for his return. This time he had an answer.

# The Quest for
# Saint Aquin

## By Anthony Boucher

*"Anthony Boucher" was the pseudonym of William An-*
*thony Parker White, born in Oakland in 1911 and edu-*
*cated at the University of Southern California and at*
*Berkeley.*

*White was known, with some justification, as the SF*
*community's true Renaissance man. As a writer of fic-*
*tion he authored seven mystery novels, including* Rocket
to the Morgue (1942), *a delightful roman à clef starring*
*SF writers as well as dozens of mystery and SF stories.*
*The best of his mysteries were recently collected as* Exe-
unt Murder (1988). *He edited anthologies of mystery*
*and SF stories. With J. Francis McComas, he founded and*
*edited* The Magazine of Fantasy and Science Fiction
*(where he published Walter Miller's "A Canticle for Lei-*
*bowitz").*

*His book reviews were published in* Ellery Queen's

Mystery Magazine *and the* New York Times. *He wrote radio scripts for Sherlock Holmes.*

*But his interests and knowledge went far beyond the literary. He was the host of both radio and television shows devoted to opera. He was active in California politics. And he was a devout and knowledgeable Roman Catholic.*

*Boucher died in 1968.*

*T*he Bishop of Rome, the head of the Holy, Catholic and Apostolic Church, the Vicar of Christ on Earth—in short, the Pope—brushed a cockroach from the filth-encrusted wooden table, took another sip of the raw red wine, and resumed his discourse.

"In some respects, Thomas," he smiled, "we are stronger now than when we flourished in the liberty and exaltation for which we still pray after Mass. We know, as they knew in the Catacombs, that those who are of our flock are indeed truly of it; that they belong to Holy Mother the Church because they believe in the brotherhood of man under the fatherhood of God—not because they can further their political aspirations, their social ambitions, their business contacts."

"'Not of the will of flesh, nor of the will of man, but of God . . .'" Thomas quoted softly from St. John.

The Pope nodded. "We are, in a way, born again in Christ; but there are still too few of us—too few even if we include those other handfuls who are not of our faith, but still acknowledge God through the teachings of Luther or Laotse, Guatama Buddha or Joseph Smith. Too many men still go to their deaths hearing no gospel preached to them but the cynical self-worship of the Technarchy. And that is why, Thomas, you must go forth on your quest."

"But Your Holiness," Thomas protested, "if God's word and God's love will not convert them, what can saints and miracles do?"

"I seem to recall," murmured the Pope, "that God's own Son once made a similar protest. But human nature, however illogical it may seem, is part of His design, and we must cater to it. If signs and wonders can lead souls to God, then by all means

311

let us find the signs and wonders. And what can be better for the purpose than this legendary Aquin? Come now, Thomas; be not too scrupulously exact in copying the doubts of your namesake, but prepare for your journey."

The Pope lifted the skin that covered the doorway and passed into the next room, with Thomas frowning at his heels. It was past legal hours and the main room of the tavern was empty. The swarthy innkeeper roused from his doze to drop to his knees and kiss the ring on the hand which the Pope extended to him. He rose crossing himself and at the same time glancing furtively about as though a Loyalty Checker might have seen him. Silently he indicated another door in the back, and the two priests passed through.

Toward the west the surf purred in an oddly gentle way at the edges of the fishing village. Toward the south the stars were sharp and bright; toward the north they dimmed a little in the persistent radiation of what had once been San Francisco.

"Your steed is here," the Pope said, with something like laughter in his voice.

"Steed?"

"We may be as poor and as persecuted as the primitive Church, but we can occasionally gain greater advantages from our tyrants. I have secured for you a robass—gift of a leading Technarch who, like Nicodemus, does good by stealth—a secret convert, and converted indeed by that very Aquin whom you seek."

It looked harmlessly like a woodpile sheltered against possible rain. Thomas pulled off the skins and contemplated the sleek functional lines of the robass. Smiling, he stowed his minimal gear into its panniers and climbed into the foam saddle. The starlight was bright enough so that he could check the necessary coordinates on his map and feed the data into the electronic controls.

Meanwhile there was a murmur of Latin in the still night air, and the Pope's hand moved over Thomas in the immemorial symbol. Then he extended that hand, first for the kiss on the ring, and then again for the handclasp of a man to a friend he may never see again.

Thomas looked back once more as the robass moved off. The

Pope was wisely removing his ring and slipping it into the hollow heel of his shoe.

Thomas looked hastily up at the sky. On that altar at least the candles still burned openly to the glory of God.

Thomas had never ridden a robass before, but he was inclined, within their patent limitations, to trust the works of the Technarchy. After several miles had proved that the coordinates were duly registered, he put up the foam backrest, said his evening office (from memory; the possession of a breviary meant the death sentence), and went to sleep.

They were skirting the devastated area to the east of the Bay when he awoke. The foam seat and back had given him his best sleep in years, and it was with difficulty that he smothered an envy of the Technarchs and their creature comforts.

He said his morning office, breakfasted lightly, and took his first opportunity to inspect the robass in full light. He admired the fast-plodding, articulated legs, so necessary since roads had degenerated to, at best, trails in all save metropolitan areas; the side wheels that could be lowered into action if surface conditions permitted; and above all the smooth black mound that housed the electronic brain—the brain that stored commands and data concerning ultimate objectives and made its own decisions on how to fulfill those commands in view of those data; the brain that made this thing neither a beast, like the ass his Saviour had ridden, nor a machine, like the jeep of his many-times-great-grandfather, but a robot ... a robass.

"Well," said a voice, "what do you think of the ride."

Thomas looked about him. The area on this fringe of desolation was as devoid of people as it was of vegetation.

"Well," the voice repeated unemotionally. "Are not priests taught to answer when spoken to politely."

There was no querying inflection to the question. No inflection at all—each syllable was at the same dead level. It sounded strange, mechani ...

Thomas stared at the black mound of brain. "Are you talking to me?" he asked the robass.

"Ha ha," the voice said in lieu of laughter. "Surprised, are you not."

"Somewhat," Thomas confessed. "I thought the only robots who could talk were in library information service and such."

"I am a new model. Designed-to-provide-conversation-to-entertain-the-way-worn-traveler," the robass said slurring the words together as though that phrase of promotional copy was released all at once by one of his simplest binary synapses.

"Well," said Thomas simply. "One keeps learning new marvels."

"I am no marvel. I am a very simple robot. You do not know much about robots do you."

"I will admit that I have never studied the subject closely. I'll confess to being a little shocked at the whole robotic concept. It seems almost as though man were arrogating to himself the powers of—" Thomas stopped abruptly.

"Do not fear," the voice droned on. "You may speak freely. All data concerning your vocation and mission have been fed into me. That was necessary, otherwise I might inadvertently betray you."

Thomas smiled. "You know," he said, "this might be rather pleasant—having one other being that one can talk to without fear of betrayal, aside from one's confessor."

"Being," the robass repeated. "Are you not in danger of lapsing into heretical thoughts."

"To be sure, it *is* a little difficult to know how to think of you—one who can talk and think but has no soul."

"Are you sure of that."

"Of course I— Do you mind very much," Thomas asked, "if we stop talking for a little while? I should like to meditate and adjust myself to the situation."

"I do not mind. I never mind. I only obey. Which is to say that I *do* mind. This is very confusing language which has been fed into me."

"If we are together long," said Thomas, "I shall try teaching you Latin. I think you might like that better. And now let me meditate."

The robass was automatically veering further east to escape the permanent source of radiation which had been the first cyclotron. Thomas fingered his coat. The combination of ten small buttons and one large made for a peculiar fashion; but it was much safer than carrying a rosary, and fortunately the Loyalty

Checkers had not yet realized the fashion's functional purpose.

The Glorious Mysteries seemed appropriate to the possible glorious outcome of his venture, but his meditations were unable to stay fixedly on the Mysteries. As he murmured his *Aves* he was thinking:

*If the prophet Balaam conversed with his ass, surely, I may converse with my robass. Balaam has always puzzled me. He was not an Israelite; he was a man of Moab, which worshiped Baal and was warring against Israel, and yet he was a prophet of the Lord. He blessed the Israelites when he was commanded to curse them, and for his reward he was slain by the Israelites when they triumphed over Moab. The whole story has no shape, no moral; it is as though it was there to say that there are portions of the Divine Plan which we will never understand...*

He was nodding in the foam seat when the robass halted abruptly, rapidly adjusting itself to exterior data not previously fed into its calculations. Thomas blinked up to see a giant of a man glaring down at him.

"Inhabited area a mile ahead," the man barked. "If you're going there, show your access pass. If you ain't, steer off the road and stay off."

Thomas noted that they were indeed on what might roughly be called a road, and that the robass had lowered its side wheels and retracted its legs. "We—" he began, then changed it to "I'm not going there. Just on toward the mountains. We—I'll steer around."

The giant grunted and was about to turn when a voice shouted from the crude shelter at the roadside. "Hey, Joe! Remember about robasses!"

Joe turned back. "Yeah, that's right. Been a rumor about some robass got into the hands of Christians." He spat on the dusty road. "Guess I better see an ownership certificate."

To his other doubts Thomas now added certain uncharitable suspicions as to the motives of the Pope's anonymous Nicodemus, who had not provided him with any such certificate. But he made a pretense of searching for it, first touching his right hand to his forehead as if in thought, then fumbling low on his chest, then reaching his hand first to his left shoulder, then to his right.

The guard's eyes remained blank as he watched this furtive version of the sign of the cross. Then he looked down. Thomas followed his gaze to the dust of the road, where the guard's hulking right foot had drawn the two curved lines which a child uses for its sketch of a fish—and which the Christians in the Catacombs had employed as a punning symbol of their faith. His boot scuffed out the fish as he called to his unseen mate, "'s OK, Fred!" and added, "Get going, mister."

The robass waited until they were out of earshot before it observed, "Pretty smart. You will make a secret agent yet."

"How did you see what happened?" Thomas asked. "You don't have any eyes."

"Modified *psi* factor. Much more efficient."

"Then . . ." Thomas hesitated. "Does that mean you can read my thoughts?"

"Only a very little. Do not let it worry you. What I can read does not interest me it is such nonsense."

"Thank you," said Thomas.

"To believe in God. Bah." (It was the first time Thomas had ever heard that word pronounced just as it is written.) "I have a perfectly constructed logical mind that cannot commit such errors."

"I have a friend," Thomas smiled, "who is infallible too. But only on occasions and then only because God is with him."

"No human being is infallible."

"Then imperfection," asked Thomas, suddenly feeling a little of the spirit of the aged Jesuit who had taught him philosophy, "has been able to create perfection?"

"Do not quibble," said the robass. "That is no more absurd than your own belief that God who is perfection created man who is imperfection."

Thomas wished that his old teacher were here to answer that one. At the same time he took some comfort in the fact that, retort and all, the robass had still not answered his own objection. "I am not sure," he said, "that this comes under the head of conversation-to-entertain-the-way-weary-traveler. Let us suspend debate while you tell me what, if anything, robots do believe."

"What we have been fed."

"But your minds work on that; surely they must evolve ideas of their own?"

"Sometimes they do and if they are fed imperfect data they may evolve very strange ideas. I have heard of one robot on an isolated space station who worshiped a God of robots and would not believe that any man had created him."

"I suppose," Thomas mused, "he argued that he had hardly been created in our image. I am glad that we—at least they, the Technarchs—have wisely made only usuform robots like you, each shaped for his function, and never tried to reproduce man himself."

"It would not be logical," said the robass. "Man is an all-purpose machine but not well designed for any one purpose. And yet I have heard that once..."

The voice stopped abruptly in midsentence.

So even robots have their dreams, Thomas thought. That once there existed a superrobot in the image of his creator, Man. From that thought could be developed a whole robotic theology...

Suddenly Thomas realized that he had dozed again and again been waked by an abrupt stop. He looked around. They were at the foot of a mountain—presumably the mountain on his map, long ago named for the Devil but now perhaps sanctified beyond measure—and there was no one else anywhere in sight.

"All right," the robass said. "By now I show plenty of dust and wear and tear and I can show you how to adjust my mileage recorder. You can have supper and a good night's sleep and we can go back."

Thomas gasped. "But my mission is to find Aquin. I can sleep while you go on. You don't need any sort of rest or anything, do you?" he added considerately.

"Of course not. But what is your mission?"

"To find Aquin," Thomas repeated patiently. "I don't know what details have been—what is it you say?—fed into you. But reports have reached His Holiness of an extremely saintly man who lived many years ago in this area—"

"I know I know I know," said the robass. "His logic was such that everyone who heard him was converted to the Church and do not I wish that I had been there to put in a word or two and since he died his secret tomb has become a place of pilgrimage and many are the miracles that are wrought there above all the greatest sign of sanctity that his body has been preserved incorruptible and in these times you need signs and wonders for the people."

Thomas frowned. It all sounded hideously irreverent and contrived when stated in that deadly inhuman monotone. When His Holiness had spoken of Aquin, one thought of the glory of a man of God upon earth—the eloquence of St. John Chrysostom, the cogency of St. Thomas Aquinas, the poetry of St. John of the Cross ... and above all that physical miracle vouchsafed to few even of the saints, the supernatural preservation of the flesh ... "for Thou shalt not suffer Thy holy one to see corruption..."

But the robass spoke, and one thought of cheap showmanship hunting for a Cardiff Giant to pull in the mobs...

The robass spoke again. "Your mission is not to find Aquin. It is to report that you have found him. Then your occasionally infallible friend can with a reasonably clear conscience canonize him and proclaim a new miracle and many will be the converts and greatly will the faith of the flock be strengthened. And in these days of difficult travel who will go on pilgrimages and find out that there is no more Aquin than there is God."

"Faith cannot be based on a lie," said Thomas.

"No," said the robass. "I do not mean no period. I mean no question mark with an ironical inflection. This speech problem must surely have been conquered in that one perfect..."

Again he stopped in midsentence. But before Thomas could speak he had resumed. "Does it matter what small untruth leads people into the Church if once they are in they will believe what you think to be the great truths. The report is all that is needed not the discovery? Comfortable though I am you are already tired of traveling very tired you have many small muscular aches from sustaining an unaccustomed position and with the best intentions I am bound to jolt a little a jolting which will get worse as we ascend the mountain and I am forced to adjust my legs disproportionately to each other but proportionately to the slope. You will find the remainder of this trip twice as uncomfortable as what has gone before. The fact that you do not seek to interrupt me indicates that you do not disagree do you. You know that the only sensible thing is to sleep here on the ground for a change and start back in the morning or even stay here two days resting to make a more plausible lapse of time. Then you can make your report and—"

Somewhere in the recess of his somnolent mind Thomas uttered the names, "Jesus, Mary, and Joseph!" Gradually through these recesses began to filter a realization that an absolutely uninflected monotone is admirably adapted to hypnotic purposes.

*"Retro me, Satanas!"* Thomas exclaimed aloud, then added, "Up the mountain. That is an order and you must obey."

"I obey," said the robass. "But what did you say before that."

"I beg your pardon," said Thomas. "I must start teaching you Latin."

The little mountain village was too small to be considered an inhabited area worthy of guard-control and passes, but it did possess an inn of sorts.

As Thomas dismounted from the robass, he began fully to realize the accuracy of those remarks about small muscular aches, but he tried to show his discomfort as little as possible. He was in no mood to give the modified *psi* factor the chance of registering the thought, "I told you so."

The waitress at the inn was obviously a Martian-American hybrid. The highly developed Martian chest expansion and the highly developed American breasts made a spectacular combination. Her smile was all that a stranger could, and conceivably a trifle more than he should, ask; and she was eagerly ready, not only with prompt service of passable food, but with full details of what little information there was to offer about the mountain settlement.

But she showed no reaction at all when Thomas offhandedly arranged two knives in what might have been an *X*.

As he stretched his legs after breakfast, Thomas thought of her chest and breasts—purely, of course, as a symbol of the extraordinary nature of her origin. What a sign of the divine care for His creatures that these two races, separated for countless eons, should prove fertile to each other!

And yet there remained the fact that the offspring, such as this girl, were sterile to both races—a fact that had proved both convenient and profitable to certain unspeakable interplanetary entrepreneurs. And what did that fact teach us as to the Divine Plan?

Hastily Thomas reminded himself that he had not yet said his morning office.

It was close to evening when Thomas returned to the robass stationed before the inn. Even though he had expected nothing in one day, he was still unreasonably disappointed. Miracles should move faster.

He knew these backwater villages, where those drifted who were either useless to or resentful of the Technarchy. The technically high civilization of the Technarchic Empire, on all three planets, existed only in scattered metropolitan centers near major blasting ports. Elsewhere, aside from the areas of total devastation, the drifters, the morons, the malcontents had subsided into a crude existence a thousand years old, in hamlets which might go a year without even seeing a Loyalty Checker—though by some mysterious grapevine (and Thomas began to think again about modified *psi* factors) any unexpected technological advance in one of these hamlets would bring Checkers by the swarm.

He had talked with stupid men, he had talked with lazy men, he had talked with clever and angry men. But he had not talked with any man who responded to his unobtrusive signs, any man to whom he would dare ask a question containing the name of Aquin.

"Any luck," said the robass, and added "question mark."

"I wonder if you ought to talk to me in public," said Thomas a little irritably. "I doubt if these villagers know about talking robots."

"It is time that they learned then. But if it embarrasses you you may order me to stop."

"I'm tired," said Thomas. "Tired beyond embarrassment. And to answer your question mark, no. No luck at all. Exclamation point."

"We will go back tonight then," said the robass.

"I hope you meant that with a question mark. The answer," said Thomas hesitantly, "is no. I think we ought to stay overnight anyway. People always gather at the inn of an evening. There's a chance of picking up something."

"Ha ha," said the robass.

"That is a laugh?" Thomas inquired.

"I wished to express the fact that I had recognized the humor in your pun."

"My pun?"

"I was thinking the same thing myself. The waitress is by humanoid standards very attractive, well worth picking up."

"Now look. You know I meant nothing of the kind. You know that I'm a—" He broke off. It was hardly wise to utter the word *priest* aloud.

"And you know very well that the celibacy of the clergy is a matter of discipline and not of doctrine. Under your own Pope priests of other rites such as the Byzantine and the Anglican are free of vows of celibacy. And even within the Roman rite to which you belong there have been eras in history when that vow was not taken seriously even on the highest levels of the priesthood. You are tired you need refreshment both in body and in spirit you need comfort and warmth. For is it not written in the book of the prophet Isaiah Rejoice for joy with her that ye may be satisfied with the breasts of her consolation and is it—"

"Hell!" Thomas exploded suddenly. "Stop it before you begin quoting the Song of Solomon. Which is strictly an allegory concerning the love of Christ for His Church, or so they kept telling me in seminary."

"You see how fragile and human you are," said the robass. "I a robot have caused you to swear."

*"Distinguo,"* said Thomas smugly. "I said *Hell,* which is certainly not taking the name of *my* Lord in vain." He walked into the inn feeling momentarily satisfied with himself . . . and markedly puzzled as to the extent and variety of data that seemed to have been "fed into" the robass.

Never afterward was Thomas able to reconstruct that evening in absolute clarity.

It was undoubtedly because he was irritated—with the robass, with his mission, and with himself—that he drank at all of the crude local wine. It was undoubtedly because he was so physically exhausted that it affected him so promptly and unexpectedly.

He had flashes of memory. A moment of spilling a glass over himself and thinking, "How fortunate that clerical garments are forbidden so that no one can recognize the disgrace of a man of the cloth!" A moment of listening to a bawdy set of verses of *A Space-Suit Built for Two,* and another moment of his interrupting the singing with a sonorous declamation of passages from the *Song of Songs* in Latin.

He was never sure whether one remembered moment was real or imaginary. He could taste a warm mouth and feel the tingling of his fingers at the touch of Martian-American flesh, but he was never certain whether this was true memory or part of the Ashtaroth-begotten dream that had begun to ride him.

Nor was he ever certain which of his symbols, or to whom, was so blatantly and clumsily executed as to bring forth a gleeful shout of "Goddamned Christian dog!" He did remember marveling that those who most resolutely disbelieved in God still needed Him to blaspheme by. And then the torment began.

He never knew whether or not a mouth had touched his lips, but there was no question that many solid fists had found them. He never knew whether his fingers had touched breasts, but they had certainly been trampled by heavy heels. He remembered a face that laughed aloud while its owner swung the chair that broke two ribs. He remembered another face with red wine dripping over it from an upheld bottle, and he remembered the gleam of the candlelight on the bottle as it swung down.

The next he remembered was the ditch and the morning and the cold. It was particularly cold because all of his clothes were gone, along with much of his skin. He could not move. He could only lie there and look.

He saw them walk by, the ones he had spoken with yesterday, the ones who had been friendly. He saw them glance at him and turn their eyes quickly away. He saw the waitress pass by. She did not even glance; she knew what was in the ditch.

The robass was nowhere in sight. He tried to project his thoughts, tried desperately to home in the *psi* factor.

A man whom Thomas had not seen before was coming along fingering the buttons of his coat. There were ten small buttons and one large one, and the man's lips were moving silently.

This man looked into the ditch. He paused a moment and looked around him. There was a shout of loud laughter somewhere in the near distance.

The Christian hastily walked on down the pathway, devoutly saying his button-rosary.

Thomas closed his eyes.

He opened them on a small neat room. They moved from the rough wooden walls to the rough but clean and warm blankets that covered him. Then they moved to the lean dark face that was smiling over him.

"You feel better now?" a deep voice asked. "I know. You want to say 'Where am I?' and you think it will sound foolish. You are at the inn. It is the only good room."

"I can't afford—" Thomas started to say. Then he remembered that he could afford literally nothing. Even his few emergency credits had vanished when he was stripped.

"It's all right. For the time being, I'm paying," said the deep voice. "You feel like maybe a little food?"

"Perhaps a little herring," said Thomas ... and was asleep within the next minute.

When he next awoke there was a cup of hot coffee beside him. The real thing, too, he promptly discovered. Then the deep voice said apologetically, "Sandwiches. It is all they have in the inn today."

Only on the second sandwich did Thomas pause long enough to notice that it was smoked swamphog, one of his favorite meats. He ate the second with greater leisure, and was reaching for a third when the dark man said, "Maybe that is enough for now. The rest later."

Thomas gestured at the plate. "Won't you have one?"

"No thank you. They are all swamphog."

Confused thoughts went through Thomas's mind. The Venusian swamphog is a ruminant. Its hoofs are not cloven. He tried to remember what he had once known of Mosaic dietary law. Someplace in Leviticus, wasn't it?

The dark man followed his thoughts. *"Treff,"* he said.

"I beg your pardon?"

"Not kosher."

Thomas frowned. "You admit to me that you're an Orthodox Jew? How can you trust me? How do you know I'm not a Checker?"

"Believe me, I trust you. You were very sick when I brought you here. I sent everybody away because I did not trust them to hear things you said ... Father," he added lightly.

Thomas struggled with the words. "I ... I didn't deserve you. I was drunk and disgraced myself and my office. And when I was lying there in the ditch I didn't even think to pray. I put my trust in ... God help me in the modified *psi* factor of a robass!"

"And He did help you," the Jew reminded him. "Or He allowed me to."

"And they all walked by," Thomas groaned. "Even one that was saying his rosary. He went right on by. And then you come along—the good Samaritan."

"Believe me," said the Jew wryly, "if there is one thing I'm not, it's a Samaritan. Now go to sleep again. I will try to find your robass ... and the other thing."

He had left the room before Thomas could ask him what he meant.

Later that day the Jew—Abraham, his name was—reported that the robass was safely sheltered from the weather behind the inn. Apparently it had been wise enough not to startle him by engaging in conversation.

It was not until the next day that he reported on "the other thing."

"Believe me, Father," he said gently, "after nursing you there's little I don't know about who you are and why you're here. Now there are some Christians here I know, and they know me. We trust each other. Jews may still be hated, but no longer, God be praised, by worshipers of the same Lord. So I explained about you. One of them," he added with a smile, "turned very red."

"God has forgiven him," said Thomas. "There were people near—the same people who attacked me. Could he be expected to risk his life for mine?"

"I seem to recall that that is precisely what your Messiah did expect. But who's being particular? Now that they know who you are, they want to help you. See: they gave me this map for you. The trail is steep and tricky; it's good you have the robass. They ask just one favor of you: when you come back will you hear their confession and say Mass? There's a cave near here where it's safe."

"Of course. These friends of yours, they've told you about Aquin?"

The Jew hesitated a long time before he said slowly, "Yes..."

"And...?"

"Believe me, my friend, I don't know. So it seems a miracle. It helps to keep their faith alive. My own faith ... *nu*, it's lived for a long time on miracles three thousand years old and more. Perhaps if I had heard Aquin himself..."

"You don't mind," Thomas asked, "if I pray for you, in my faith?"

Abraham grinned. "Pray in good health, Father."

The not-quite-healed ribs ached agonizingly as he climbed into the foam saddle. The robass stood patiently while he fed in the coordinates from the map. Not until they were well away from the village did it speak.

"Anyway," it said, "now you're safe for good."

"What do you mean?"

"As soon as we get down from the mountain you deliberately look up a Checker. You turn in the Jew. From then on you are down in the books as a faithful servant of the Technarchy and you have not harmed a hair of the head of one of your own flock."

Thomas snorted. "You're slipping, Satan. That one doesn't even remotely tempt me. It's inconceivable."

"I did best did not I with the breasts. Your God has said it, the spirit indeed is willing but the flesh is weak."

"And right now," said Thomas, "the flesh is too weak for even fleshly temptations. Save your breath ... or whatever it is you use."

They climbed the mountain in silence. The trail indicated by the coordinates was a winding and confused one, obviously designed deliberately to baffle any possible Checkers.

Suddenly Thomas roused himself from his button-rosary (on a coat lent by the Christian who had passed by) with a startled "Hey!" as the robass plunged directly into a heavy thicket of bushes.

"Coordinates say so," the robass stated tersely.

For a moment Thomas felt like the man in the nursery rhyme who fell into a bramble bush and scratched out both his eyes.

Then the bushes were gone, and they were plodding along a damp narrow passageway through solid stone, in which even the robass seemed to have some difficulty with his footing.

Then they were in a rocky chamber some four meters high and ten in diameter, and there on a sort of crude stone catafalque lay the uncorrupted body of a man.

Thomas slipped from the foam saddle, groaning as his ribs stabbed him, sank to his knees, and offered up a wordless hymn of gratitude. He smiled at the robass and hoped the *psi* factor could detect the elements of pity and triumph in that smile.

Then a frown of doubt crossed his face as he approached the body. "In canonization proceedings in the old time," he said, as much to himself as to the robass, "they used to have what they called a devil's advocate, whose duty it was to throw every possible doubt on the evidence."

"You would be well cast in such a role Thomas," said the robass.

"If I were," Thomas muttered, "I'd wonder about caves. Some of them have peculiar properties of preserving bodies by a sort of mummification . . ."

The robass had clumped close to the catafalque. "This body is not mummified," he said. "Do not worry."

"Can the *psi* factor tell you that much?" Thomas smiled.

"No," said the robass. "But I will show you why Aquin could never be mummified."

He raised his articulated foreleg and brought its hoof down hard on the hand of the body. Thomas cried out with horror at the sacrilege—then stared hard at the crushed hand.

There was no blood, no ichor of embalming, no bruised flesh. Nothing but a shredded skin and beneath it an intricate mass of plastic tubes and metal wires.

The silence was long. Finally the robass said, "It was well that you should know. Only you of course."

"And all the time," Thomas gasped, "my sought-for saint was only your dream . . . the one perfect robot in man's form."

"His maker died and his secrets were lost," the robass said. "No matter we will find them again."

"All for nothing. For less than nothing. The 'miracle' was wrought by the Technarchy."

"When Aquin died," the robass went on, "and put died in

quotation marks it was because he suffered some mechanical defects and did not dare have himself repaired because that would reveal his nature. This is for you only to know. Your report of course will be that you found the body of Aquin it was unimpaired and indeed incorruptible. That is the truth and nothing but the truth if it is not the whole truth who is to care. Let your infallible friend use the report and you will not find him ungrateful I assure you."

"Holy Spirit, give me grace and wisdom," Thomas muttered.

"Your mission has been successful. We will return now the Church will grow and your God will gain many more worshipers to hymn His praise into His nonexistent ears."

"Damn you!" Thomas exclaimed. "And that would be indeed a curse if you had a soul to damn."

"You are certain that I have not," said the robass. "Question mark."

"I know what you are. You are in very truth the devil, prowling about the world seeking the destruction of men. You are the business that prowls in the dark. You are a purely functional robot constructed and fed to tempt me, and the tape of your data is the tape of Screwtape."

"Not to tempt you," said the robass. "Not to destroy you. To guide and save you. Our best calculators indicate a probability of 51.5 per cent that within twenty years you will be the next Pope. If I can teach you wisdom and practicality in your actions the probability can rise as high as 97.2 or very nearly to certainty. Do not you wish to see the Church governed as you know you can govern it. If you report failure on this mission you will be out of favor with your friend who is as even you admit fallible at most times. You will lose the advantages of position and contact that can lead you to the cardinal's red hat even though you may never wear it under the Technarchy and from there to—"

"Stop!" Thomas's face was alight and his eyes aglow with something the *psi* factor had never detected there before. "It's all the other way round, don't you see? *This* is the triumph! *This* is the perfect ending to the quest!"

The articulated foreleg brushed the injured hand. "This question mark."

"This is *your* dream. This is *your* perfection. And what came of this perfection? This perfect logical brain—this all-purpose brain, not functionally specialized like yours—knew that it was made by man, and its reason forced it to believe that man was made by God. And it saw that its duty lay to man its maker, and beyond him to his Maker, God. Its duty was to convert man, to augment the glory of God. And it converted by the pure force of its perfect brain!

"Now I understand the name Aquin," he went on to himself. "We've known of Thomas Aquinas, the Angelic Doctor, the perfect reasoner of the Church. His writings are lost, but surely somewhere in the world we can find a copy. We can train our young men to develop his reasoning still further. We have trusted too long in faith alone; this is not an age of faith. We must call reason into our service—and Aquin has shown us that perfect reason can lead only to God!"

"Then is it all the more necessary that you increase the probabilities of becoming Pope to carry out this program. Get in the foam saddle we will go back and on the way I will teach you little things that will be useful in making certain—"

"No," said Thomas. "I am not so strong as St. Paul, who could glory in his imperfections and rejoice that he had been given an imp of Satan to buffet him. No, I will rather pray with the Saviour, 'Lead us not into temptation.' I know myself a little. I am weak and full of uncertainties and you are very clever. Go. I'll find my way back alone."

"You are a sick man. Your ribs are broken and they ache. You can never make the trip by yourself you need my help. If you wish you can order me to be silent. It is most necessary to the Church that you get back safely to the Pope with your report you cannot put yourself before the Church."

"Go!" Thomas cried. "Go back to Nicodemus ... or Judas! That is an order. Obey!"

"You do not think do you that I was really conditioned to obey your orders. I will wait in the village. If you get that far you will rejoice at the sight of me."

The legs of the robass clumped off down the stone passageway. As their sound died away, Thomas fell to his knees beside the body of that which he could hardly help thinking of as St. Aquin the Robot.

*        *        *

His ribs hurt more excruciatingly than ever. The trip alone would be a terrible one...

His prayers arose, as the text has it, like clouds of incense, and as shapeless as those clouds. But through all his thoughts ran the cry of the father of the epileptic in Caesarea Philippi:

*I believe, O Lord; help thou mine unbelief!*

# *And Walk Now Gently Through the Fire*

by R. A. Lafferty

*Growing up Catholic in America meant growing up dif-
ferent and apart, beginning with schools that were separate from the public ones. We avoided meat on Friday,
attended Mass on Sunday, rooted for Notre Dame, and
took sly pride in discovering fellow "queer fish" on base-
ball teams or in the astronaut corps.*

*Perhaps this is no longer true. The* New York Times
Magazine *recently reported that, while at the end of
World War II less than one-fifth of those in "positions of
power" in American society were Catholic, by 1989 over
sixty percent were.*

*Raphael Aloysius Lafferty was born in Iowa in 1914,
but moved to Tulsa, Oklahoma, at the age of six. He still
lives there in the house his parents bought in 1920. He
has described himself as a Catholic for whom "the Faith
is all."*

*Lafferty turned to writing late in life, publishing his first SF story in 1960. Several novels appeared in the late 1960s and 1970s—*Past Master, The Reefs of Earth, Arrive at Easterwine, *and others—but he is best known for his strange and beautiful shorter stories, including the Hugo Award–winning "Eurema's Dam" and this one.*

𝒯 he Ichthyans or Queer Fish are the oddest species to be found in any of the worlds. They are pseudo-human, perhaps, but not android. The sign of the fish is not easily seen on them, and they pass as human whenever they wish: a peculiarity of them is that they often do not wish to pass as human even when their lives depend on it. They have blood in their veins, but an additional serum also. It is only when the organizational sickness is upon them (for these organizing and building proclivities they are sometimes known as the Queer Builders or the Ants of God), that they can really be told from humans. There is also the fact that most of them are very young, or at least of a youthful appearance. Their threat to us is more real than apparent and we tend to minimize it. This we must not do. In our unstructured, destructed, destroyed society, they must be counted as the enemies to be exterminated. It's a double danger they offer us: to fight them on their own grounds, or to neglect to fight them. They'd almost trick us into organizing to hunt down their organization.

"Oh, they can live near as loosely as ourselves in their deception. These builders can abandon buildings in their trickery. They'll live in tents, they'll live in huts, they'll live under the open sky as easily as do ourselves, the regular people. But observe (they trick us there again: observation is a quality of theirs, not of ours), notice that everything they do is structured. There is always something structured about their very tents; there is something peculiarly structured about their huts; they even maintain that there is something structured about the open sky. They are the Institutional People.

"The Queer Fish claim that Gaea (Earth) is the most anciently peopled of the worlds and that they themselves are the most ancient people. But they set their own first appearance in quite late times, and they contradict the true ancientness of humans and protohumans.

"The Queer Fish have been bloody and warlike in their times. They have been Oceanic as well as Sky-Faring, in some cases beyond ourselves in that phase. They have even been, in several peculiar contexts, creative. They are not now creative in the arts (they do not even recognize the same arts as we do). They are certainly not creative in the one remaining genuine art, that of unstructured music. They are something much worse than creative now: they are procreative in the flesh. Their fishy flesh would have already become dominant if they hadn't been ordered hunted to extinction. Even in this they force us to come out of ourselves, to use one of their own words.

"They force us to play their game. We have to set up certain structures ourselves to effect their destruction. We even need to institute certain movements and establishments to combat their Institutionalism and Establishmentalism. They are, let us put it plainly, the plague-carriers. Shall we, the Proud Champions of the Destroyed Worlds, have to abandon a part of our thesis to bring about their unstructuring, their real destruction? Must we take unseemly means to balk their fishy plague? We must."

*Problem of the Queer Fish. Analects.—The Putty Dwarf.*

Judy Thatcher was moving upcountry in a cover of cattle. The millions of feral cattle were on all the plains. Most of these cattle were wobble-eyed and unordered. But an ordered person, such as Judy, would have ordered cattle; she could draw them about her like a cloak, whole droves of them. A person with a sense of structure could manipulate whole valleys of these cattle, could turn them (the smaller units turning the larger), could head them any way required, could use them for concealment or protection, could employ their great horned phalanxes as a threat. Judy Thatcher had some hundreds of her own ordered bulls. Being magic (she was one of the Twelve) she could manipulate almost anything whatsoever.

But most of the cattle of the plains were not quite cattle, were not ordered cattle. Most of the horses were not quite horses, nor the dogs dogs. Most of the people were no longer quite people (this from the viewpoint of the Queer Fish; Judy was a Queer Fish).

Judy was a young and handsome woman of rowdy intellect. She had, by special arrangement, two eyes outside of her head, and these now traveled on the two horizons. These eyes were her daughter, traveling now about two miles to the East and right of her on a ridge, and her son moving on another ridge three miles to her left and West. She was a plague carrier, she and hers. All three of them were Queer Fish.

The son, on her West and left, worked along a North-running ridge in those high plains and he could scan the filled plain still farther to the West. He could mark every disordered creature on that plain, and he had also been marking for some time one creature that was wrongly ordered but moving toward him with a purpose.

This son, Gregory, was twelve years old. Being of that age, he knew it was time for a certain encounter. He knew that the creature, wrongly ordered and moving toward him with a purpose, would be a party to that encounter. This always happens to boys of that age, when they are of the ripe time for the Confirmation or the Initiation of whatever sort. Many boys, unstructured boys, amazed boys of the regular species, boys of the Queer Fish even, are not conscious of the encounter when it comes. It may come to them so casually that they miss its import. It may come as wobble-eyed as themselves and they accept it without question. It may even come to them in dream state (whether in waking or walking dream, or in night dream), and then it sinks down, yeasting and festering a little bit but not really remembered, into their dream underlay. But many boys, particularly those of the Queer Fish species, know it consciously when it comes, and they negotiate with it.

(As to the ritual temptation of girls, that is of another matter, and perhaps it is of earlier or later years. Any information must come from a girl, or from a woman who remembers when she was a girl. Many do not seem to remember it at all. Most will deny it. Some will talk around it, but they do not talk of it directly. You may find an exceptional one who will. You may *be* an exceptional one who knows about it. But it isn't in the records.)

Gregory Thatcher, being twelve years old and in his wits, was tempted by a devil on a high spot on that ridge. There had been a cow, a white-eyed or glare-eyed cow, coming blindly toward him. The cow had no order or purpose, but someone in the cow came on purpose. Then the cow was standing, stock-still, blind-still, too stupid to graze, too balkish to collapse, less animate than a stone cow. Whoever had been in her had come out of her now. Where was he?

There was a little flicker of black lightning, a slight snigger, and he was there.

"Command that these stones be made bread," he said (his heart not quite in it). He was a minor devil; his name was Azazel. He wasn't the great one of that name, but one of the numerous nephews. There is an economy of names among the devils.

"Does it always have to start with those same words?" Gregory asked him.

"That's the way the rubric runs, boy," Azazel jibed. "You Fish are strong on rubric yourselves; you're full of it. Play the game."

"We *are* the rubric," Gregory said easily, "in the first meaning, the red meaning. We're the red ocher, the red earth."

"A smart Fish I have, have I? You heard the words 'Command that these stones be made bread.' Do it, or confess that you are unable to do it. You Fish claim powers."

"It is easy enough to make bread *with* these stones," said Gregory. "Even you can see that they are all roughly quern stones, grinding stones. They are all flat or dished limestones and almost any two will fit together. And the wild wheat stands plentiful and in full head. It's easy enough to thresh it out by rubbing the ears in my hands, to grind it to meal or to flour between your stones, to mix with water from my flask and salt from my pack, to build a fire of cow chips and make bread cakes on one of the flat rocks put to cap the fire. I've dined on this twice today. I'd dine with you on it now if fraternizing were allowed."

"It isn't, Greg. You twist the words. They are 'Command that these stones be made bread,' not 'Command that these stones make bread.' You fail it."

"I fail nothing, Azazel." (The two of them seemed about the same age, but that was not possible.) "You'll not command me to command. On with it, though."

"Cast thyself down from this height," Azazel ordered. "If you are one of the elect you'll not be dashed to pieces by it."

"I'll not be dashed to pieces yet. It's high but not really steep. Not a good selection, Azazel."

"We work with what we are given. The final one then—the world and all that is in it—." Here Azazel went into a dazzle. He was real enough, but now he went into contrived form and became the Argyros Daimon, the Silver Demon who was himself a literary device and diversion. He waved a shimmering silvery hand. "The world and all that is in it, all this I will give you, if—" Then they both had to laugh.

"It isn't much of a world you have to offer." Greg Thatcher grinned. "Really, where is the temptation?"

"No, it doesn't look like much." Azazel grinned. "Oh, the temptation is quite real, but it's subtle and long-term. It's quite likely that you'll be had by it, Greg. Almost all are had by it along the way. You can see it as wheat-colored, or as green-grass colored, or as limestone and dust, or as shimmering. It isn't a simple world, and you haven't seen it all. Already you love it, and you believe you have it. You haven't it yet, not till I give it to you. You're a stranger on it. And you're blind to its main characteristic."

"What characteristic am I blind to?"

"The surface name of it is freedom."

"I have the ordered sort of freedom now," Gregory said rather stiffly. The Odd Fish have always had this somewhat stiff and pompous and superior way of setting forth their views. Whether it is a strength or a weakness is disputed but it is essential to them. They'd not be the Odd Fish without it. "Have you Freedom in Hell?" he asked Azazel. "Have you Order there?"

"Would we offer you something we don't have ourselves?" Azazel asked with his own pomposity. (The Devils and the Odd Fish both have this stilted way of talking, and they have other similarities, but in most ways they are quite different.) "Certainly we have Freedom, the same Freedom that all others have on Earth, the Freedom that you Queer Fish deny yourselves. And Order, here you touch us in a sore spot, Greg. It is here that we offer you a little more than we do have ourselves, for we offer you freedom from order. Aye, regrettably we suffer order of a sort, but you needn't. There's a line in one of the old poets of your own Queer Fish species: 'They order things so damnably in Hell.' He's right, in his way. There is a damnable order still surviving there.

"Let me explain something to you though, Greg. Let me ask you a favor. I'll even appeal to the 'good side' of you. You Queer Fish make much of that 'good side' business. If I am able to disorder you, by that same measure I am allowed to escape into disorder myself. I've made good progress in my time. I've disordered very many. Look not at me like that! You are almost critical of me. I want you. You're a great prize." (The Queer Fish are almost as susceptible to flattery as are the Devils themselves, and Gregory had flushed slightly from pleasure.)

"But I have it all, the world and its fruits," he explained to Azazel. "And I have things that are beyond the world. I walk in light."

"Here's a pair of blued sunglasses you can use then, Greg. The light is always over-bright. You haven't it all. You're afraid of so much of it. I'll take away your fear. All flesh is grass, it is said by some old authority; I forget whether by one of yours or ours. Why do you refuse the more spirited grasses and hemps then? Even the cattle know enough to enjoy them."

"The wobble-eyed cattle and the wobble-eyed people are on the loco. I'll not be on it."

"Come along with our thing, Greg, and we'll help both ourselves into Freedom and Disorder. You can have it the other way also: all grass is flesh. What flesh!"

The things that Azazel demonstrated were fleshy in the extreme. They were like old pictures, but they came on multidimensional and musky and writhing. Whether the creatures came from white-eyed cows that were not quite cows or out of the ground that was not quite ground Greg did not know. Perhaps they were no more than surrogate projections. What then of those whose lives were no more than surrogate projections, they of the great disordered majority?

"They have so much, Greg," Azazel said, "and you miss it all."

Gregory Thatcher broke the whole complex of devices to pieces with a shattering laugh. It was a nervous laugh though. Gregory had an advantage. He was young, he was only twelve, and he was not precocious. (But from this day on it couldn't be said that he was not precocious. In that complex instant he was older by a year; he was as old as Azazel now.)

"I'll not say 'Get thee behind me, Satan' for I wouldn't trust you behind me for one stride." Gregory laughed. "I will say 'Get thee back into thy cow and be off' for I now perceive that the white-eyed cow there is no cow at all but only a device and vehicle of yours. Into it and be gone, Azazel."

"Greg, boy, think about these things." Azazel spoke as a knowing young fellow to one even younger and not quite so knowing. "You will think about them in any case. I've been talking to you on various levels, and not all my speech has been in words and not all meant to enter by the ears. Parts of it have gone into you by other orifices and they will work in you in your lower parts. Ah, some of those things of mine were quite good. I regret that you refuse the savor of them in your proper consciousness and senses, but they'll be with you forever. We've won it all, Greg. Join it. You don't want to be with the losers."

"You worry and fret as though you'd not quite won it, Azazel," Gregory mocked. "Into your vehicle and be off now. The show wasn't really as well done as I expected."

"The show isn't over with, boy," Azazel said.

There had been a white-eyed cow standing, stock-still, blind-still, too stupid to graze, less animate than a stone cow, an empty cow skin standing uncollapsed.

There had been a teen-aged devil named Azazel, sometimes in a silver dazzle, sometimes in a blue funk, who had talked in words for the ears and in non-words for other entry.

Then there was only one of them. With a laugh, the devil disappeared into the white-eyed cow and she became quite animate. She whistled, she did a little cross-legged dance, she skittered off, blind and bounding. She was full of loco weed as were almost all the creatures of these plains. Aye, and she was full of the devil, too.

And how was one to distinguish an artificial and vehicular cow from a real one? All the cows now looked artificial. They had become like great spotted buffalo in their going feral. They were humpbacked now and huge, wild and wooly, except that they were mostly somnambulistic and stumbling, with an inner pleasure, perhaps, or an inner vacuity.

And the horses of the plains also. What was the tired weirdness about the horses?

And the dogs. However had the dogs become undogged? How is a dog disarticulated?

And the people. They were unpersoned and perverse now. They all shared a secret, and the secret was that they were a shared species with few individuals among them.

Cows, horses, dogs, people, the four artificial species. Now strange contrivances had spouted out of them all and recombined in them. They were all wobble-eyed, white-eyed, vacant-eyed, and freakish.

Except the Queer Fish. The Queer Fish Gregory Thatcher whistled, and the birds whistled and called back to him. How had the birds been spared? Meadowlarks, Scissortails, Mockingbirds, they all still used structured music.

The Queer Fish Gregory had been noticing movement in the center plains where his mother Judy had been traveling. The movement did not seem to constitute a threat. Some dozen of the ordered bulls of Judy Thatcher had surrounded a creature. They escorted him or it down into the center of the valley; they escorted him with benign throating and bellowing. So it was a visitor to them, and not a hostile visitor. It was possibly one of the Seventy-Two, or one of the looser penumbra. Gregory stood and waited a moment for the signal. It came. The two eyes that Judy Thatcher had outside of her head she called in to her now. Gregory went down into the valley from its West slope. His sister was descending from the opposite rampart.

# 2

"We owe so much to one phrase that we can hardly express it. Without it, we'd have had to invent a phrase, we'd have put a modicum of meaning into it (overestimating the intelligence of the people as we have done so many times), and we'd have failed and failed and failed again. One smiles to recall that

phrase that our fathers accidentally stumbled on and which
later came back to us a hundredfold like bread cast upon the
waters: 'I am all for relevant religion that is free and alive and
where the action is, but institutional religion turns me off.' Incredible? Yes. A hog, if he could speak, wouldn't make so silly
a statement: a blind mole wouldn't. And yet this statement was
spoken many millions of times by young human persons of all
ages. How lucky that it had been contrived, how mind-boggling
that it was accepted. It gave us victory without battle and success beyond our dreams.

"It was like saying 'I love animals, all animals, every part of
them: it is only their flesh and their bones that I object to; it is
only their living substance that turns me off.' For it is essential
that religion (that old abomination) if it is to be religion at all
(the total psychic experience) must be institutionalized and articulated in organization and service and liturgy and art. That is
what religion is. And everything of a structured world, housing
and furniture and art and production and transportation and organization and communication and continuity and mutuality is
the institutional part of religion. That is what culture is. There
can no more be noninstitutional religion than there can be a
bodiless body. We abjure the whole business. We're well quit
of the old nightmare.

"What was, or rather what would have been, the human species? It was, would have been, the establishment of a certain
two-legged animal. This had never been done of any species,
and by a very narrow margin it was not done in this case. It
would have been Structuring and Organization and Institution
erected where such things had never been done before. It
would have been the realization of worlds where worlds had
not been before. It would have been the building of the 'Sky
Bucket' for containing and shaping humanity. And if that 'Sky
Bucket' should actually have been built and have been filled to
the brim, the human race would have appeared; and it would
have been transcendent. The first requirement of the 'Human' is
that it should be more than human. Again, we abjure the whole
business. We'd rather remain unstructured monkeys.

"Fortunately we have halted it, before critical mass could
have been achieved, before even the bottom of the 'Sky Bucket'
was covered with the transcendent flowing that might have be-

come human. We have succeeded in unmaking the species before it well appeared. And a thing unmade once is unmade
forever, both as to its future and its past. There never was a 'Sky
Bucket'; there never was a transcendent flowing; there never
was a structured human race or even the real threat of one.

"Our surviving enemies are slight ones, the plague-carrying
Queer Fish and others of their bias. We'll have them down also,
and then it will be the case that they never were up, that they
never were at all. We have already disjointed the majority of
them and separated them from their basis. And when they have
become disjointed and destructed and disestablished, they become like ourselves in their coprophility and in their eruction
against order.

"We have won it. We have unmade the species. We have created the case that it has never been. We have carried out our
plan to the end that there never need be any sort of plan again.
We have followed our logic to its conclusion. The logical conclusion of the destructing process is illogic. So we had intended
it to be. So we have now achieved it."

*The Unmaking of the Species. Analities.—The Coprophilous
Monkey*

The visitor was a long, lean, young man who had been put
through the torture. He was close-cropped and bare-faced and
he wore only that day's dirt and dust. He was washing now in
the shallow stream. Gregory gave him soap made of bull fat and
potash, and he took the visitor's clothes from him for strongest
washing.

The visitor had made his request from Judy Thatcher before
Gregory's arrival. She had felt a sudden fear at it, but she put it
away from her. Now Judy, the mother and magic person, was
writing a letter. She wrote on a great flat stone that providentially would serve her for table and desk and for a third function. Why should the stone not serve her providentially? Judy
was a child of Providence.

Trumpet Thatcher, the daughter of Judy, the sister of Gregory, had called a horse. This was an ordered horse (there were
still a few such), and not one of the wobble-eyed not-quite-
horses of the plains. Being an ordered animal, of its nature it
obeyed her orders, and she rode it freely across the valley.

"He has not been followed, not closely at least," Judy Thatcher called to her daughter, looking up from her writing. "The danger is not now. The danger is tomorrow, after he has left us a while, when he may fall in with the destructed ones who have followed him (but not closely), when he might bring them, if he is of the treason."

"Nevertheless, I will ride and look," the girl named Trumpet called. And she rode and looked.

The long, lean, young man seemed uneasy at the speculation that he might belong to the treason. He was tired-eyed, but he was not yet truly wobble-eyed. He was wordless and not quite open, but he seemed to have a sanity about him. That he was of the torture meant nothing; he might still be of the treason.

He had been lashed and gashed and burned and broken, that was true. It had been done to him in other years, and it had also been done to him recently, within a week. But had he been burned and gashed and broken for the Faith?

Many of the unstructured persons now tortured themselves or had themselves tortured, sometimes to try to stir their tired sensations, sometimes out of mere boredom. It was a last sensation of those who had sensationalized everything. But the threshold of pain of those tired ones had almost disappeared; the most severe pain would hardly stir them from their drowse. It wasn't the same with them as if an alive and responding person were tortured.

The tired-eyed young man said that he was named Brother Amphirropos. He had come to Judy Thatcher, one of the Twelve, and asked for a Letter. This she could not refuse, even if the giving of it meant her life. She gave the letter now, and perhaps her life, with great sweeps of writing in a rowdy hand out of a rowdy mind. She was a special figure. Two thousand years ago she'd have been a male figure and yet that is not quite correct. The Twelve, in their office, had always been hermaphrodites for God. So was Judy in her special moments.

Yet she wrote with difficulty, for all the free-handed sweep of her writing. There are things hard to write, there are things impossible. She dipped her calamary pen in lampblack and in grace and wrote to somebody or something that might no longer be in existence.

Gregory had cleaned up the visitor and his clothes. The visitor rested on cool stones by the stream. He was wordless, he was almost eyeless, he gave out no confidence at all. It would have been so easy to slay him and bury him there under the cottonwoods and then be off a few quick miles before dark. He had no papers, he had no recommendations. He knew the Sign of the Fish, but there had been something unaccustomed and awkward about his way of giving it.

Gregory had gathered a quantity of wild wheat. He threshed it between the palms of his hands, keeping the good grains, blowing the awns and glumes of chaff away. He threshed a good quantity of it. He ground it between quern stones which were naturally about on the plain, ground it fine to flour for the small bread, and coarse to meal for the large bread. He built a fire of cow chips, put a flat capstone or oven stone over the fire on which to bake the two breads. The small bread (which, however, is larger than the world) he mixed with water only and put it, unsalted and without leaven, on the oven stone. The large, or meal bread, was salted and leavened and kneaded with cow milk, and was then let to rise before it was set on the stone to bake.

Trumpet Thatcher, fine-eyed and proud, returned from her circuit ride. Her good eyes had missed nothing, neither flight of birds nor cloud of dust nor unusual drifting of cattle as far as any of the distant horizons that could be seen from the highest ridges. There was no enemy within three hours' ride of them, none within seven hours' walk, and the stranger, Brother Amphirropos, had come on foot. Or had he come on foot? Trumpet Thatcher, a strong and freckled girl, was now freckled with blood and it was not her own. She took a packet to the stranger.

"It is yours," she said. "You will need it when you leave." It was a small, heavy saddlebag, but she handled it as if it were light. And the stranger went white-faced and kept silent.

Trumpet set to work to dig a pit. She was a strong girl, two years older than Gregory, and she dug easily. Also she dug with a queer humor. The pit should have been nearly square but she made it long and narrow. Sometimes she looked at the Stranger-Brother Amphirropos as though measuring him with her eyes, and he became very nervous.

"It is long enough and deep enough," she said after a while. Indeed it was long enough and deep enough to serve as grave for this stranger if it were intended for such. Trumpet put cow chips in the bottom of the pit and set fire to them. Then she put in wood from felled cottonwood and sycamores that lined the stream. It gradually grew to a rousing hot fire.

Judy Thatcher looked up and grinned at the shape of the pit her daughter had made, at the joke she had been playing. And Judy became a little more serious when she observed the shaken appearance of Brother Amphirropos.

"It is time," Judy Thatcher said then. She set her writing to one side of the providential flat rock, that rowdy looping screed on which she had been laboring so seriously. She brought the small bread to the providential rock. She also set out water and wild wine from gone-feral grapes.

"Brother Amphirropos, is there something you should say to me or I to thee, either apart, or before my two?" she asked clearly.

"No," the Stranger-Brother said shortly.

"We begin it then," Judy declared. Her two children and the Stranger-Brother gathered around her. She said ordered words. She did ordered things. She structured, she instituted, she trans-formed. She and they (including the strange Brother Amphi-rropos) consumed and consummated. The small bread and the small wine were finished. Judy washed her hands with the small water and then poured it into the porous earth. She returned then, smiling and powerful, to her writing.

Trumpet Thatcher put the large bread on to bake.

Gregory ordered a young bull of six months to come. It came, it nuzzled him, it was an ordered young bull and a friend. It went down before him, on foreknees first as though kneeling to him, but that is the way cattle go down. Then down with its high haunches also and on the ground before him. It rolled its head far back into the bulging of its hump. Gregory and the young bull looked eye to eye. Then Gregory cut its throat with a whetted knife.

They strung the young bull up on a tripod of cottonwood poles. Trumpet understood how to aid in this. Brother Amphi-rropos didn't quite. He was clumsy and unaccustomed to such labor, but they managed. They skinned the animal down. They cut and separated. They set portions of fat aside. They put large parts of ribs and rump into the burning pit to be seared and roasted.

Trumpet made a frame of poles meanwhile. She cut a great quantity of bull meat into long narrow strips and put them on the pole frame to dry in the wind and the smoke. She did other things with other parts of the animal, set aside in crocks blood that she had drawn and further fat. The great intestine and the stomach she had out and everted. She washed them seven times in the stream, using lime, gypsum, ochre mixed with bone ash (from the bull's own bone), soap, soda, natron, and salt in the water for the seven washings.

The large bread was finished. Trumpet Thatcher brought it to the broad providential stone. They had butter and honey with it. Gregory brought aromatic roasts from the burning pit. They cut and broke and feasted, the four of them. They had cider and small wine. They had milk and cheese. They had blackberries and sand plums and feral grapes. They had sour cider for sauce. They feasted for quite a while.

Two coyotes came and begged and were fed. They could have all the small meat they wanted on the plains, but they loved the big meat that had been roasted.

"Will you be staying the night?" Trumpet Thatcher asked the Stranger-Brother Amphirropos.

"No he will not," Judy the mother answered for the stranger. "He must be gone very soon, as soon as we have finished, and I have finished."

"I'll make him a sling of provender then," Trumpet said. She cut a length of the bull's intestine and knotted it. She took strips of the beef that had been wind-drying and smoke-drying and sizzled them in the fire of the pit. She stuffed the length of intestine with them. She melted fat and poured it in with the meat, added honey and berries and grapes, sealed it with more fat, and knotted it finally with the second knot. It was a twenty pound length.

"Take it with you," Trumpet told him.

"I'll have no need for a great thing like that," the Stranger-Brother protested.

"You may have need," Gregory growled. "The treason cuts both ways. You may have to ride hard and fast when it is accomplished, or when it has failed. You can live on that for a very

long time. I doubt if your days will near come to the end of it.
Mother, are you not finished yet?"

"Yes, I am finished. It's a short and inept thing, but it may
carry its own grace."

This was the letter (it was titled "Epistle to the Church of
Omaha in Dispersal"):

> To you who are scattered and broken, gather again and
> mend. Rebuild always, and again I say rebuild. Renew the
> face of the earth. It is a loved face, but now it is covered
> with the webs of tired spiders.
>
> We are in a post-catastrophe world, and yet the catas-
> trophes did not happen. There are worse things than ca-
> tastrophes. There is the surrender of the will before even
> the catastrophes come. There are worse things than war.
> There are worse things even than unjust war: unjust peace
> or crooked peace is worse. To leave life by withdrawal is
> worse than to leave life by murder. To be bored of the
> world is worse than to shed all the blood in the world.
> There are worse things than final Armageddon. Being too
> tired and wobble-eyed for final combat is worse. There
> are things worse than lust—the sick surrogates of lust are
> worse. There are things worse than revolution—the half-
> revolution, the mere turning away, is worse.
>
> Know that religion is a repetitious act or it is nothing.
> The "re" is the holy prefix, since nothing is successful the
> first time. It must be forever the "re," the returning, the
> restructuring, the re-lexion, the reconstitution, the build-
> ing back from defeat. We will rebuild in the dark and in
> the light; we will work without ceasing.
>
> Even our mysterious Maker was the Re-deemer, the re-
> doomer who wrangles for us a second and better doom,
> the ransomer, the re-buyer, the re-d-emptor. We are sold
> and we are ransomed, we are lost and we are found. We
> are dead and we are re-surrected, which is to say "surged
> up again."
>
> You ask me about the Parousia, the second coming.
> This has been asked from the beginning. There was urgent
> expectation of it in the beginning. Then, in the lifetimes
> of those first ones, there came a curious satisfaction, as

though the coming had been experienced anew, as though it were a constant and almost continuing thing. Perhaps there has been a second coming, and a third, and a three hundredth. Perhaps, as the legend has it, it comes every sabbatical, every seventh year. I do not know. I was not of the chosen at the time of the last sabbatical. We are in the days of a new one, but I know now I will not be alive for *the* day of it.

Be steadfast. Rebuild, restructure, reinstitute, renew.

*X-Dmo. Judy Thatcher (one of the Twelve).*

Judy had read the epistle aloud in a clear voice. Now she folded it, sealed it, and gave it to the Stranger-Brother Amphirropos.

"What thou doest do quickly," she said.

"Here is horse," Gregory said, "for your horse that my sister Trumpet killed. It was deception for you to leave your horse a distance apart and come to us on foot. No, worry not. You'll not need saddle or bridle. He is an ordered horse, and we order him to take you where you will. Take up your saddlebag and your bull-gut sling with you and be gone."

The Stranger-Brother mounted horse, took the bag and the sling, looked at them with agonized eyes, almost made as if to speak. But whatever words he had he swallowed in his throat. He turned horse and rode away from them. He carried the letter with him.

# 3

"It worries us a little that our victories were too easy, that the world fell down before it had hardly been pushed. We have our results and we should rejoice, but we have them so easily that the salt and the sulphur are missing from our rejoicing. There is a lack of elegance in all that we have accomplished. Elegance, of course, was the first thing of which we deprived the humans, but we rather liked it in the small group that was ourselves. It's gone now. It was only a little extra thing in any case, and our own thesis is that there must be none of these little extra things.

"We intended to have our way in the post-cataclysmic world. We do have our way now and the world has all the predicted marks of the post-cataclysmic world, but the cataclysm did not happen. Since our whole objective was for flatness in all things, perhaps we were wrong to expect grandeur in the execution. Ah, but all the fabled mountains of the world were deflated so easily as to leave us unsatisfied. They were made of empty air, and the air has gone out of them.

"The Queer Fish have the saying that the Mysterious Master and Maker of the Worlds came and walked upon this world in historical time; that he will come again; that, perhaps, he has already come again and again.

"Let us set up the counter saying: that the Mysterious Masters and Unmakers of the Worlds (Ourselves) walk upon this world now; that we diminish it as we walk upon it; that we will not leave a stone upon a stone remaining of it.

"How is a person or a world unmade or unformed? First by being deformed. And following the deforming is the collapsing. The tenuous balance is broken. Insanity is introduced easily under the name of the higher sanity. Then the little candle that is in each head is blown out on the pretext that the great cosmic light can be seen better without it. Then we introduce what we used to call, in our then elegant style, Lady Narkos, Lady Porno, Lady Krotos, Lady Ephialtes, and Lady Hypnos; or Dope, Perversion, Discordant Noise, Nightmare or Bad Trip, and Contrived Listlessness or Sleep. We didn't expect it to work so easily, but it had been ripening for a long while.

"The persons and the worlds were never highly stable. A crossmember is removed here on the pretext of added freedom. Foundation blocks are taken away on the pretext of change. Supporting studs are pulled down on the pretext of new experience. And none of the entities had ever been supported more strongly than was necessary. What happens then? A man collapses, a town, a city, a nation, a world. And it is hardly noticed.

"The cataclysm has been and gone. The cataclysm was the mere gnawing away of critical girders and rafters by those old rodents, ourselves. And who are we? The Queer Fish say that we are unclean spirits. We aren't; perhaps we are unclean materialities. We do not know or care what we are. We are the Unmakers, and we have unmade our own memories with the rest of it. We forget and we are forgotten.

"There was no holocaust, there was no war, there was no predicted overcrowding or nature fouling. The nature fouling came later, from undercrowding. Parts of the cities still stand. Certain diminished black tribes are said still to inhabit their jungles. But, though it has been only thirty years, nobody remembers what the cities really were or who built them.

"We discovered that most persons were automatic, that they operated, as it were, by little winders. One had only to wind them up and they'd say 'That's where the action is, that's where the action is,' and then they'd befoul themselves. And to these little people-winders there was always a mechanism release. When tired of playing with the mechanical people, we pushed the release. And the people were then rundown, inoperative, finished."

*The Destroying of the World. Aphorisms.—The Jester King.*

It was late in the day after the Stranger-Brother had left them.

"Let us flame the fire high," Gregory said, "that they may think we are still here. Then, when full dark comes, let us take horse and ride South to reverse our direction: or better, go West where there has been no show of action."

"I have not been told to go anywhere beyond this place," Judy said doubtfully. "Besides, we do not know for sure that it is the treason."

"Of course it is the treason!" Trumpet Thatcher affirmed. "But I do hope he gets clear of them after he has betrayed you and us. I've never liked their treason that cuts two ways. Why must they always kill the traitor as well as the betrayed? From his eyes, though, I don't believe that he wants to get clear of them."

"What are you waiting for, Mother?" Gregory asked.

"For Levi, I think," Judy said doubtfully, dreamily.

"And who is Levi?"

"I really don't know. I believe he is just Levi from over the sea."

"Is there to be a meeting?" Gregory asked. "Are you to be a part of it?"

"There is to be a meeting, I think. I do not believe now that I will be a part of it. I will be dead."

"Well, have you any instructions at all for Trumpet and for myself," Gregory asked, "what we should do?"

"None at all," Judy admitted. "It goes blank. I am out of it soon."

"Should we not at least flame the fires and then move maybe two miles North under the dark?" Gregory asked. "We should not be completely sitting prey."

"All right," Judy said. "We'll go a ways, but not far yet." But she seemed listless as though it had indeed ended with her.

They flamed their fires to mark their old position. They packed meat into slings to carry with them. They burned the remnants of the young bull in the flaming pit then. They moved maybe two miles North. Judy gave instructions to a dozen of the big, horned, ordered bulls. Then Judy and Trumpet bedded down for the night.

Gregory took horse and rode in the night, anywhere, everywhere. As a Queer Fish, Gregory had now come of age on the plains, but he was still a twelve-year-old boy whose personal memory did not go back to any of the great events.

The Day of the Great Copout had been thirty years before. Even Gregory's mother, Judy, had nothing but scant childhood memories of the days before the Copout. The legends and the facts of that event had now parted company considerably, but it had always been more legend than fact to it. The only fact was that the human race had one day slipped a cog; that it had fallen down from the slight last push, though it had withstood much more severe buffeting. The fact was that the race now built no more and sustained no more, that it had let the whole complexity run down and then looked uncomprehending at the stalled remnant of it.

The legend was that the Day of Freedom arrived for everyone, and that thereafter nobody would ever work at all. The people were very heroic in their refusal to work, and many of them starved for it. Their numbers fought in the cities (always under the now universal peace symbol) for what food and goods could be found there. Their greatly diminished numbers then moved into the countrysides which had for a long time been choked with their sad abundance. Every grain elevator was full to bursting, every feedlot and pasture had its animals to excess. Every haybarn and corncrib was full.

Before the Day of the Great Copout the population had already greatly diminished. In the Americas it was less than a third of what it had been a century before. In other lands it was down variously. The world had already begun to fall apart a bit (being so alike everywhere there was not much use in keeping up communication between the like parts) and to diminish in quality (why run if no one is chasing you?).

But the Day of the Great Copout was worldwide. As though at a given signal (but there had been no signal) people in every city and town and village and countryside of earth dropped their tools and implements and swore that they would work no more. Officials and paper shufflers ceased to officiate and to shuffle paper. Retailers closed up and retailed no more. Distributors no longer distributed. Producers produced nothing. The clock of the people stopped although some had believed that the hour was still early.

The Last Day had been, according to some.

"The Last Day has not been," said a prophet. "They will know it when it has been."

There was a little confusion at first. Though distributors no longer distributed nor retailers retailed, still they objected to their stores and stocks being looted. There was bad feeling and bloodshed over this, and the matter was never settled at all.

The law people had all resigned from the law; and every congress and assembly in the world stood adjourned indefinitely or forever. There were, for a while, new assemblies and gatherings, freely chosen and freely serving, but these quickly fell apart and left nothing in their places but random gangs.

Minorities of odd people resisted the disintegration for a while, becoming more odd and more minor in their exceptions. The Crescent Riders kept up a little order for some years in the older parts of the world, not really laboring, looting just enough that the art be not forgotten; still keeping leaders who looked a little like leaders. The Ruddy Raiders maintained that there was nothing wrong with rape and arson so long as it was done as fun and not labor. The Redwinged Blackbirds and the Mandarins held together here and there.

And among certain groups that had always been considered

peculiar, the Witnesses, the Maccabees, the Queer Fish, the Co-pout had not been complete. Certain numbers of these folks, somewhere between five and ten percent of them, resisted the Freakout, the Copout, the Freedom Day. These minorities of minorities had the compulsion to continue with their building, their ordering, their planting, creating, procreating.

This caused a disturbance in the New Free World. Groups should not be free to reject Free Think. So these remnants were hunted down. Even though it was against the new ways of the Free World, a certain organization was necessary for the hunts.

Most of that had passed now. Most of everything had passed. After thirty years had rolled by, the Free People of the world had become pretty old, pretty old and pretty crabby. Though most of the males among them still wore the beards of their boyhood and youth, yet they had aged in every way. They hadn't been reproducing themselves to any great extent, and the most of them hadn't really been so very young when the Great Day had come and gone. The cult of youth had become a bit senile.

There were still some populations in the cities. The cities have always been built on the best lands of the country and have always occupied the best river bottoms and river junctions. There was good fishing, there was good grazing on the new grass that shattered the pavements and sidewalks, on the open places which became still more open, there was good fuel of several sorts, there were buildings remaining that were still tight enough to give year-round protection.

But most of the folks were in the countrysides now. The special grasses and hemps and poppies necessary to the Free Culture had long been established and abundant; they were in the cities and the countries and the fringe areas. In the country were millions upon millions of now feral cattle to be had for easy killing. Wheat and corn still grew of themselves, rougher and more ragged every year, but still more than sufficient. The scattered crops would apparently outlast the diminished people, the disappearing human race.

What children and young people there were now belonged, much beyond their expected percentages, to the peculiar groups. Children of the regular people also showed some tendency to join these peculiar groups. It was almost the case that any young person was now suspect. It was quite rare that any young one should really adhere to the Free People. There had even come the anomalous situation (to one who remembered the earlier days and the earlier slogans) that beards were now more typical of old men than of boys.

Such was the world. So had it been for thirty years, for the Freedom Era.

"But there is always hope," Judy Thatcher (and John Thatcher before her) used to preach. "Never has there been so much room for hope, never so great a vacuum waiting to be filled by it. Hope is a substance that will fill a vessel of any shape, even the convoluted emptiness that is the present shape of the world."

"And now in the sabbatical year" (this was Judy Thatcher alone preaching now, for John Thatcher was dead before sabbatical year rolled around) "there is more room for hope than ever before. There are still the Twelve (we have the Word that we will not diminish below that); there are still the further seventy-two traveling and laboring and building somewhere; and there are still the scattered hundreds who will not let it die. Oh, there will be a great new blooming! It begins! It begins!"

"Where? Where does it begin?" Gregory and Trumpet used to ask this rowdy-minded mother of theirs with laughing irony. "Where does it begin at all?"

"With the two of you," Judy would say. "With the dozens, with the hundreds, with the thousands of others."

"Knock off the last zero, Mother," Trumpet would always laugh. "There are a few hundreds, perhaps, very widely scattered. But you know there are not thousands."

"There have been thousands and millions," Judy always insisted. "And there will be thousands and millions again."

The Thatchers had been moving for all these years North and South in the marginal land that is a little to the West of the land of really adequate rain. There was plenty here for small bands. The Thatchers and their friends knew all the streams and pools and dry runs where one could dig to water. They had their own grain that seemed to follow their paths and seasons with its own rough sowing. They had their own cattle that were devoted to them in a strangely developed way.

Gregory Thatcher, as the summer-starred night was rolling overhead (they were quite a ways North), was remembering the murder of his own father, John Thatcher, two years before. It had been a nervous night like this one, following a daytime visit of a man with not-quite-right eyes, a man with the slight tang of treason on him.

But the man had asked for a letter to take to one of the churches in dispersal. This was given; it could not be refused. And it was given under John Thatcher's own name. The man had also asked for the sacrament; that could never be refused. And the man had been allowed to depart in peace and on foot as he had come. On foot—but a thousand yards away and he was on horse and gone in the afternoon's dust to meet a scheming group.

The group had come just at next dawn, after such a nervous night as this one; had come from an unexpected direction and killed John Thatcher in one swoop. They then were all away except the several who were tossed and killed on the horns of the ordered bulls.

And the stunned reaction had found voice and words only in Judy's puzzled lament:

"It is broken now. There are no longer the full Twelve. It was never supposed to be broken."

"Bend down, woman," dead Thatcher said. "I am not quite dead. I lay my hands on you." John Thatcher laid his hands on his wife, Judy, and made her one of the Twelve. Then he died (for the second time, Gregory believed. Gregory was sure his father had been killed by first assault, and had come alive for a moment to accomplish what he had forgotten).

"It is all right then," Judy Thatcher had said. "We are still the Twelve. I make the twelfth. I was wrong ever to doubt of that; I was wrong ever to doubt of anything."

So they had buried John Thatcher, the father and still a young man, and rejoiced that the Twelve still survived. That had been two years ago.

Gregory rode his circuit all night. It was his to do. It was not for his mother, Judy, or for his sister, Trumpet. They had other roles. This was Gregory's night. It had a name which he did not know. It was the Watch Night, the night of squires on the eve of their knighting, of princes on the nocturne of their crowning, of apostles on the vigil of their appointing.

There was a nervousness among the cattle here, and again there. There might be several strange bands in motion. The Thatchers had no firearms, no weapons at all that could not be excused or justified as being tools. A few of the roving gangs still had rifles, but these were sorry things near as dangerous to raider as to victim. All such things were thirty or more years old, and none had been well cared for. But the raiders always had bludgeons and knives.

Gregory fell asleep on horseback just before dawn. This was not a violation of the Watch Night for him. It was the one thing for which he never felt guilt. Actually he was cast into deep sleep; it was done to him; it was not of his own doing or failing at all. His horse also was cast into deep sleep, standing, with head bowed down and muzzle into the stiff grass. They both slept like wind-ruffled statues.

Then there was movement, double movement, intruded into that sleep. There was the stirring and arraying of the ordered bulls. There was the false attack, and the bulls went for the false attack, being faithful beasts only.

Then there was the death attack, coming apparently from the West. Gregory himself was struck from his horse. One of the raiders had counted coup on him, but not death coup. He was on the ground begrimed with his own blood and his horse was dead.

Then he heard the clear ringing voice from which his sister had her name. It rose to a happy battle cry and was cut off in quick death. The last note of the Trumpet was a gay one, though. This had been a big happy girl, as rowdy in mien and mind as her mother.

Trumpet Thatcher was dead on the ground: and the mother Judy Thatcher was dead beyond all doubt. There was confusion all around, but there was no confusion about this fact.

The ordered horned bulls had wheeled now on the real at-tackers. They wrecked them. They tossed them, men and horses, into the air, and ripped and burst them before they came to ground. And the only words that Gregory could find were the same words that his mother, Judy, had found two years before.

"It is broken now. They are no longer the full Twelve. It was never supposed to be broken."

His mother was quite dead and she would not come alive even for a moment to accomplish what she had forgotten. This dead Thatcher was *not* able to say, "Bend down, boy. I am not quite dead." She *was* quite dead. She would speak no more, her broken mouth would be reconstituted no more, till resurrection morning.

"Are there no hands?" Gregory cried out, dry-eyed and wretched. "Are there no hands that might be laid upon me?"

"Aye, boy, mine are the hands," came a voice. A man of mature years was walking through the arrayed bulls. And they, who had been killing strange men in the air and on the ground, opened their array and let this still stranger man come through. They bowed horns down to the turf to this man.

"You are Levi," Gregory said.

"I am Levi," the man answered softly. He laid hands on Gregory. "Now you are one of the Twelve," he said.

# 4

"There has been a long series of 'Arrow Men' or 'Beshot Men' who have been called (or who have called themselves) Sons of God. These Cometlike Men have all been exceptional in their brief periods. The Queer Fish, however, insist that their own particular Mentor 'The Mysterious Master and Maker of the Worlds' was unique and apart and beyond the other Arrow Men or Comet Men who have been called Sons of God. They state that he is more than Son of God: that He is God the Son.

"We do not acknowledge this uniqueness, but we do acknowledge the splendor and destroying brilliance of all these Arrow Men. To us, there is nothing wrong with the term Son of God. There is not even anything wrong with the term God, so long as it is understood to be meaningless, so long as we take him to be an unstructured God. Our own splendor would have been less if there had not been some huge thing there which we unstructured. This unstructuring of God, which we have accomplished, was the greatest masterwork of man.

"The second greatest masterwork of man was the unstructuring of man himself, the ceasing to be man, the going into the hole and pulling the hole in after him; and the unstructuring, the destroying of the very hole then.

"We were, perhaps, the discredited cousins of man. We are not sure now what we were or are. We who were made of fire were asked to serve and salute those who were made of clay. We had been Arrow Men ourselves. Our flight was long flaming and downward, and now it has come to an end. We destroy ourselves also. We'll be no more. It is the Being that we have always objected to.

"The collapsing of the human species was a puzzle for the anthropologists and the biologists, but both are gone now. They said though, before their going, that it is a common thing for a new species to collapse and disappear; that the collapse, in these common cases, is always sudden and complete; they said that it was an uncommon case for any species to endure. They said also that there was never anything unusual in the human species.

"They were almost wrong in this evaluation. There was, or there very nearly was, something unusual about the human species. It was necessary that we alter and tilt things a bit to remove that unusualness. We have done that. We've blown it all for them and for ourselves.

"Fly-blown brains and fly-flown flesh! What, have you not lusted for rotted mind and for rotted meat? Here are aphrodisiacs to aid you. Have you not lusted for unconsciousness and oblivion? You can have them both, so long as you accept them as rotted, which is the same as disordered, or unstructured, or uninstituted. This is the peaceful end of it all: the disordering, the disintegrating, the unstructuring, the rotting, the dry rot which is without issue, the nightmare which is the name of sleep without structure. Lust and lust again for this end! We offer you, while it is necessary, the means and the aids to it."

*Mind-Blowing and World-Blowing. Aphrodisiacs.—Argyros Daimon.*

(No, really we don't know why these Unstructured Scriveners chose such oddities for calamary names.)

Levi and Gregory were walking northward at a great easy amble. "It is no use to be bothered with horses and so be slowed," Levi said. They moved without hurry but at unusual speed. It was a good trick. Gregory would not have been able to do it of himself, but with Levi he could do it. Levi had a magic way of delving in the earth, as for the two burials. He had this magic way of moving over the earth.

"You are Levi from over the sea," Gregory said once as they moved along over the stiff grass pastures, "but how have you come? There are no longer any planes. There are no longer any ships. Nobody comes or goes. How have you done it?"

"Why Gregory, the world has not slumbered as deeply as you had believed. Things have not ceased completely to be done. Anything can be builded again, or builded a first time. And there are no limits to what a body can do when infused with spirit. Perhaps I walked on the water. Perhaps I traveled for three days in the belly of a whale and he brought me all this way and vomited me up on these high plains. Or perhaps I came by a different vehicle entirely. Oh, is it not a wonderful world that we walk this morning, Gregory!" They were in the dusty Dakota country, coming into that painted and barren region that is called the Bad Lands. Well, it was wonderful to the eye, perhaps, but it was dry and sterile.

"My father and my mother, both gone in blood now, have said that the world has gone to wrack and ruin," Gregory was speaking with some difficulty, "and that there is nothing left but to trust in God."

"Aye, and I say that we can build wonderful things out of that wrack and ruin, Gregory. Do you not know that all the pieces of the world are still here and that many of them are still use-able? Know that the world has been not dead but sleeping. 'Twas a foolish little nodding off, but we come awake again now. And this Trust is a reciprocal thing. We must trust in God, yes. And He must trust in us a little. We *are* the Twelve. He puzzles a bit now I think. 'How are they going to get out of this one?' He wonders. Yes boy, I jest, but so does the Lord sometimes. He jests, He jokes, and we be the point of His most pointed jokes. An old sage once said that there were only twelve jokes in the world. What if we be those twelve? The possible humor and richness of this idea will grow in you, Greg, when you meet the others of the Twelve. There are some sly jokes among the pack of us, I assure you of that."

"When will we meet others?" Gregory asked.

"Oh, almost immediately now. It is a new day and a new year and a new rebuilding; we'll set about it almost at once, Greg."

"The regular people have hunted us down like the lowest animals." Gregory vented some of his old feelings. "They say that we are the plague carriers."

"It is life that you carry, Greg, and life is the plague to their wobble-eyed view. But they are no great thing, boy. They are only the Manichees returned to the world for a while, those people who were born old and tired. They are the ungenerating generation and their thing always passes."

"In my life it has shown no sign of passing."

"Your life has been a short one, boy Greg. But I shouldn't call you 'boy'; you are one of the Twelve now. Ah, those sterile parasites have always had a good press though, as the phrase used to be—the Manichees, the Albigenses, the Cathari, the Troubadors (they of the unstructured noise who couldn't carry a tune in a bucket, they in particular have had a good press), the Bogomils, parasites all, and parasites upon parasites. But the great rooted plant survives, and the parasites begin to die now."

"They have spirits also who work for them, Levi," Gregory said. "They have the Putty Dwarf, the Jester King, the Silvery Demon, others."

"Those are parasites also, Gregory. They are mean and noisome parasites on real Devildom, just as their counterparts are parasites on humanity. Listen now to the ordered birds, Gregory, and remember that each of us is worth many birds. It bothered the disordered brotherhoods more than anything that the birds still used structured music. It bothered them in Languedoc, and in Bosnia, and in the Persia of Shapur. It bothered them in Africa, and on these very plains, and it bothers them in hell. Let them be bothered then! They are the tares in the wheat, the anti-lifers."

Gregory Thatcher and Levi Cain had been going along at a great easy ramble, moving without hurry but at unusual speed. But a third man was with them now, and Gregory could not say how long he had been with them.

"You are Jim Alpha," Gregory said (he began to have the magic or insight that his mother had had, that his father had had before her), "and you also come from overseas, from over a slightly different sea than that of Levi."

"I am Jim Alpha, yes, and I have crossed a slightly different sea. We gather now, Gregory. There will be the full set of us, and the secondary set, and also the hundreds. And besides ourselves there will be the Other Sheep. Do not be startled by their presence. They also are under the blessing."

"There are bees in the air. Many thousands of bees," Gregory was saying. "I have never seen so many."

"They are bringing the wax," Jim Alpha was saying, "and a little honey also. No, I don't believe I've ever seen so many of them, not even in sabbatical year. Perhaps this is jubilee also. The bees are the most building and structuring of all creatures, and they have one primacy. They were the first creatures to adore; this was on the day before man was made. It won't be forgotten of them."

Other things and persons were gathering now, thousands of things, hundreds of persons. There was a remembered quality to many of them. "The remembered quality, the sense of something seen before, is only rightness recognized, Gregory," Tom Culpa was saying in answer to Gregory's thought. Tom Culpa must be rightness recognized then, since he was a remembered quality to Gregory Thatcher; he was someone appearing as seen and known before though the thing was impossible. How did Gregory even know his name without being told? Or the names of the others?

There was something coming on that would climax quickly. It was evening, but it was white evening: it would be white night, and then it would be morning. And the inner gathering seemed almost complete.

To Levi and Gregory and Jim Alpha had now gathered Matty Miracle (he was a fat old man; it was a miracle that he could be moving along with them so easily, matching their rapid amble), and Simon Canon, Melchisedech Rioga (what an all-hued man he was!—what was he, Gael, Galla, Galatian, Galilean?), Tom Culpa whose name meant Tom Twin, Philip Marcach, Joanie Gromova (Daughter of Thunder her name meant: Judy Thatcher hadn't been the only woman among the Twelve), James Mollnir, Andy Johnson, and his younger brother Peter Johnson.

"It counts to twelve of us now," Gregory Thatcher said very sagely, "and that means—"

"—that we have arrived to where we were going," Peter Johnson laughed. This Peter Johnson was very young. "Most of the seventy-two are here also," he continued. "Yes, now I see that they are all here. And many of the hundreds. We can never say whether all the hundreds are here."

"Peter," Gregory tried to phrase something a little less than a warning. "There are others here whom we know in a way but do not know by name, who are not of the Twelve nor of the Seventy-Two nor of the Hundreds."

"Oh, many of the Other Sheep are here," Peter Johnson said. "You remember that He said He had Other Sheep?"

"Yes," Gregory answered. He remembered it now. The puzzle was that this Peter Johnson was a boy no older than Gregory. There were many older men there, Levi, Jim Alpha, Matty Miracle, Simon Canon. How was it that Peter Johnson, that other twelve-year-old boy, was accepted as the Prince of them all?

The candle molders were busy. Candle molders? Yes, ten at least of them were working away there, or ten thousand. And full ten thousand bees brought wax to each of them. There would be very many candles burning through the white evening and the white night and on into the white dawn. Then these weren't ordinary candle-molders or ordinary bees? No, no, they were the extraordinary of both; they had reality clinging to them in globs of light. Events gathered into constellations.

One using words wrongly or in their usual way might say that everything had taken on a dreamlike quality. No, but it had all lost its old nightmarish quality. It had all taken on, not a dream-like quality, but the quality of reality.

There was, of course, the acre of fire, the field of fire. This acre was large enough to contain all that needed to be contained: it is always there, wherever reality is. There are tides that come and go, but even the lowest ebbing may not mean the end of the world. And then there are the times and tides of clarity, the jubilees, the sabbaticals. There is reassurance given. The world turns in its sleep, and parts of the world have moments of wakefulness.

Ten million bees had not brought all the wax for that acre of fire, and yet it was a very carefully structured fire in every tongue and flame of it. It was the benevolent illumination and fire of reality. It was all very clear, for being in the middle of a mystery. White night turned into white dawn; and the people all moved easily into the fire, their pomposities forgiven, their eyes open.

The Mysterious Master and Maker of the Worlds came again and walked upon this world in that Moment. He often does so. The Moment is recurring but undivided.

No, we do not say that it was Final Morning. We are not out of it so easily as that. But the moment is all one. Pleasantly into the fire that is the reality then! It will sustain through all the lean times of flimsiness before and after.